If Only You Fell

IF ONLY SERIES BOOK TWO

STEFANIE CASTRO

To those who are searching for ways to build the foundation of a new normal. You are seen and you are loved. ❤

Spotify Playlist

THE MAN • ALOE BLACC
LOOK I LIKE • ALANA SPRINGSTEEN
DIE A HAPPY MAN • THOMAS RHETT
HEAVEN • KANE BROWN
TEQUILA • DAN + SHAY
CALL IT A NIGHT • MURPHY ELMORE
LIFE WITH YOU • KELSEY HART
RIDE • CHASE RICE, MACY MALOY

Spotify Playlist

UNDER MY SKIN • NATE SMITH
I'M GONNA LOVE YOU • MURPHY ELMORE
SUN AIN'T KISSED • RYAN ROBINETTE, TANA MATZ
LIKE YOU NEVER HAD IT • FLORIDA GEORGIA LINE
ON MY WAY TO YOU • CODY JOHNSON
DANCE WITH YOU • BRETT YOUNG
SPEECHLESS • DAN + SHAY
SPIN YOU AROUND (1/24) • MORGAN WALLEN

Spotify Playlist

MISTAKE • CHRIS LANE
WEIGHT OF YOUR WORLD • CHRIS STAPLETON
WRECKAGE • NATE SMITH
CRAVING YOU • THOMAS RHETT, MAREN MORRIS
ALL TO MYSELF • DAN + SHAY
THE GOOD ONES • GABBY BARRETT
AS YOU LEAVE • CANAAN COX
ALREADY DRANK THAT BEER • ASHLEY COOKE

Spotify Playlist

BLESS THE BROKEN ROAD • RASCAL FLATTS
TALK YOU OUT OF IT • FLORIDA GEORGIA LINE
SUNRISE • MORGAN WALLEN
MEANT TO BE (FEAT. FLORIDA GEORGE LINE) • BEBE REXHA
FOLLOW ME • UNCLE KRACKER
YOURS • RUSSELL DICKERSON
I DON'T KNOW ABOUT YOU • CHRIS LANE
NO CALLER ID • MEGAN MORONEY

Spotify Playlist

TUCSON TOO LATE • JORDAN DAVIS
YOUR PLACE • ASHLEY COOKE
RAIN IN THE REARVIEW • ANNE WILSON
I WILL (WHEN YOU DO) • AVERY ANNA, DYLAN MARLOWE
EYES ON YOU • CHASE RICE
GOOD GIRL • DUSTIN LYNCH
HOMESICK • KANE BROWN
LOVE YOU AGAIN • CHASE MATTHEW

Note to Readers

To My Amazing Readers,

Elody's story was always going to be emotional for me, but as I added layers, the more my heart poured out in a way I wasn't expecting. As you move forward and read, please know there are some content warnings I want to be transparent about. If you'd like to know what's coming, please visit my website for content warnings. If you do not want to have any spoilers, please continue forward without interruption.

Also, if you haven't read book 1, *If Only You Knew*, I highly encourage you to do so as this book will have spoilers regarding what happens to the characters, Becca and Shane, in that storyline. This is an interconnected series. That being said, each book can be read as a standalone, but I suggest you to read them in order to minimize spoilers and enhance your reading experience.

Enjoy Elody and Wyatt's journey to finding love with one another. Their story is one that really spoke to me the more I wrote it. I hope you fall in love with them as much as I did; especially Wyatt and his dirty mouth.

Happy Reading!
Stefanie ♥

Prologue

ELODY

Five Years Ago

I hold his hand in mine. I can't help but notice how frail it looks. What was once my big, handsome, fit husband is now a delicate form of himself. I can hear the cries of my children downstairs. I know this will sit heaviest on the shoulders of my oldest and will hurt differently due to all his experiences with his father up to this point. I know he'll feel those memories latch to the deepest part of his mind and continue with him in a way that won't with his younger siblings.

I don't know what's worse, seeing the only man you've ever loved dying in front of you or knowing the pain will continue after he takes his last breath. I'm a shell of the person I was before. I think Beau's death is going to take a part of me with him. I think losing his warmth, his touch, his love will be one of the biggest losses my heart will ever endure. And I know that I will have to mourn silently because we have three children who need a mother—a mother who is whole, not one who is lost.

I met Beau when we were in kindergarten. He was taller

than all the other boys, even at such a young age, and he always had a beautiful smile. He has these irresistible dimples that I never could keep from looking at when he gave that megawatt smile to anyone around. But when that smile started to be directed at me in high school, my heart was his. He may not have known it, but I think I was always his. From high school until right now, Beau has been my rock. If I'm being honest, he has been my heart and soul. But most of all, he has been my best friend. He has held me when I've cried, he's laughed with me as we've gone through all our biggest moments, and he has even let me mourn the what-ifs this life will bring once he's no longer here with us anymore.

About eight months ago, Beau went to the doctor after experiencing gallstones for over a year. What was thought to be an easy fix, a simple surgery to remove these pain-invoking stones, turned out to bring the realization that Beau was dying. He was discovered to have gallbladder cancer, something we were never prepared to hear. Beau is young, only thirty-seven. We had just completed our family with our youngest child just turning a year old. Now, here we are, me asking God to give me more time because our story cannot be this close to the end. But, like most things in life, this is out of my control.

Beau opted out of chemotherapy once he realized the cancer had metastasized into his lungs. He wanted to enjoy his time with me and the kids. It was a source of a lot of fights in the beginning, but soon, I realized we were spending more time arguing than enjoying the time we had together. We set out on travels to see our best friend Becca and her kids in New York. We also went to Florida for Beau to dip his feet in the ocean one last time. Each moment together, I was there, snapping pictures when and where I could.

With each snapshot, I saw pieces of my husband wither away. Beau was athletic growing up. He was a star playing basketball, and Beau even coached our eldest when he was playing until his diagnosis. He was always running, lifting weights, and hiking when possible. He has been a firefighter since we graduated from college and the epitome of strength when I looked at him. He found a love in that profession, and until he was unable to continue due to his sickness, he ran toward his firehouse as if his life depended on it.

He was active and healthy, and now, I'm here, preparing to say goodbye to my high school sweetheart. This summer will mark nineteen years we've been married. But I don't see that celebration being the two of us this time. We are close to the end. His breaths are getting shallow, and he's so incredibly weak. The hospice nurse is here; however, Becca, a physician and my closest girlfriend, asked that Lily leave Beau and me alone for a minute so we could have some time together. Becca is in the hall, and I can hear her faint sobs. I know she can sense we are close to permanently saying goodbye—to her, the best friend who has been there for her in so many ways, and to me, my husband, who is my entire world.

"Ellie, love, is that you?" Beau speaks. It's more of a whisper, as he barely has the energy to open his eyes. I have his hand against my cheek, wishing the fingers that now touch my skin held the warmth they once did.

Upon hearing his voice, I muster whatever strength I have and bring my gaze up to meet his beautiful brown eyes. With whatever energy he can pull, he squeezes my hand, and I squeeze back, careful not to hurt him. In the past, if I were to squeeze his hand, I'd try to make it the strongest grip possible, and he always responded with a little tease in the interaction, acting as if I had broken his with how much strength I possess.

Today is no different, although I don't squeeze anywhere near the way I used to in fear of actually hurting him. Another part of my heart breaks knowing that the love of my life is so close to gone from this earth that I won't have our common little moments together as we grow older.

"That's all you've got," he responds to my hand strength,

and a faint smile glides across his features while a tear falls down mine.

I can't muster much else in return. I can't hide my sadness anymore. I've tried for so long as I knew this day was coming, but with each sunrise came another day with Beau. But I know today the sun will set, and so will his time on this earth.

"Ellie, I'm so sorry I have to leave you but know that I have loved you from the bottom of my heart for most of my life."

He swipes his thumb back and forth on my hand, that simple gesture reminding me how much I need him in my physical world more than he will ever know.

"Did you ever know I had a crush on you in middle school?"

I shake my head, unable to form words, as my emotions are taking over right now.

He continues, "You were so pretty, with that blond hair and those big, beautiful blue eyes. And your smile, Ellie. You took my breath away. I was smitten, even as a young teen. The day you started dating me, I think my life really began." He starts to cough, and I look at him with worry etched across my face.

Once his coughing spell subsides, he looks at me. So much sadness in his expression that my heart aches beyond what I thought possible. I'm so angry that this is the end for us. I am usually a happy, optimistic person, so these negative feelings are new to me.

Until the moment I learned of Beau's diagnosis, I was never one to carry anger within me. But since that dreadful day when the doctor threw the life we had built upside down, I have felt anything but positive. But I try to carry on for Beau's sake, showing him my strength versus the weakness I feel to my core, knowing my world is about to collapse. I hope to find some lesson in this because I'm failing to see how losing Beau will bring anything bright to my future. I am already lost, and he's still physically by my side.

I run my hands through his hair, his skin damp to the touch.

"I have loved you far more than I haven't, Beau Lorrent." I kiss his forehead, and I see him closing his eyes, savoring my touch.

"I don't want to leave you, but I don't think I have much of a choice anymore, my love. I hope you know how much beauty you've brought to my life. Being my wife, then making me a father, has made me the luckiest man on the planet. Thank you for being my light, my beautiful Elody. Hold my heart as you move forward, but don't let anger seep in. You've always been my happy girl. Don't forget that as you navigate life without me. I'll always be with you. Each time you talk to me and a breeze passes, know that I am with you. And whenever you speak toward the sky, know that I'm listening and wishing I could hold you and kiss you."

It takes him time to get all the words out, but I sit there, absorbing what he's just said. He sighs, closes his eyes and little do I know that it's the last time I'll hear my husband speak to me.

I know this is his hard part; saying goodbye to us, knowing that we will have to carry on without him, hurts him in ways I will never comprehend. But the hard part is just beginning for us as a family. I have been in pain watching the man I love deteriorate into a shell of himself. But trying to comprehend what comes after his physical presence isn't here with us any longer? That's something I haven't figured out how to navigate.

The hours pass, the sun is setting, and soon, his breathing becomes more rapid and shallow. I know that the worst moment of our lives together is fast approaching, and the lump that has been lodged in my throat feels like it might suffocate me. I keep telling Beau that I love him and that my heart will always be his. I move my fingers through his thinning hair, which was once thick and full. He opens his eyes one last time, as if he's taking my features in for the last time.

Finally, he closes his eyes, shielding me from the beautiful browns from ever looking at me again. I try to memorize everything about him in these last few seconds, still seeing my Beau from before the illness in his current sunken features. I kiss him on the cheek and one last kiss on the lips. That's when I hear him take a deep breath and exhale for the last time.

The tears are constant now, as if a dam has broken and all the pent-up sadness I had held in from my husband and children has just let go. It feels as if the hole Beau has left in my heart is permanent. My husband has passed away, and I'm a widower with three young children. I don't know what the rest of my story will be, but one thing is for certain: my husband is gone, and so is my heart.

Chapter One

WYATT

Present Day

"What in the actual fuck are these guys doing?" I say under my breath, my words only loud enough that those next to me can hear.

The players are running drills, and the amount of times I've blown my whistle has been exorbitant. Is this their first time defending the puck? This is a nightmare if I've ever seen one. Phil Cummings, my offensive coordinator, stands by me, looking at the playbook and wondering how we can improve as a whole. I'm watching my team with so much frustration that I could pick up the Zamboni and throw it across the ice.

My gaze goes back to Cummings' as his pensive brows knit together, and I wonder if that's how my expression looks all the time. I've been told, mostly by my sister, that I am a broody guy, on and off the ice. When I look out onto the group of players we have to mold, I can't help but think what a mistake it is for me to be leading this team.

I'm a fucking hockey player, not a coach, but here I am. I

was one of the greats, right there with Gretsky and Orr. But now I feel like a rookie all over again, except this time, I don't have years of training under my belt like I did as a player coming into the league. I run my hands through my hair, wishing I was on the ice, able to distract myself with a puck and a stick. That's the only place I've felt calm, with the exception of my number one girl by my side.

We run a few more drills, and I call it when I see that pushing the guys on the ice will only lead to injury instead of success. I round up the players and think of what to say as they all look at me with bewilderment. Most of these guys were playing in the AHL prior to being recruited. We have only a few veteran NHL guys, but most are greener than the fucking bag of spinach sitting in my fridge. I try to tamper down the frustration as I begin talking to them.

I have to remember that I was hired to mold them into great players, and that type of outcome will not come from a coach that acts like a dick toward his players. I was led by some of the best men I've gotten the privilege to call coach, and now I must keep my temper aside and bring out the best in these guys, even if I'm realizing this hill I thought I was climbing is more like a mountain.

"The most important thing a team holds is trust. I know we are all still getting used to one another as we move around the ice. But for us to win a championship, you have to know who will have your back out there. The connection each of you has with one another, it goes beyond the puck and that hockey stick. It is about knowing each other's movements. It's about feeling that when you're driving yourself closer to that goal, your teammate is there to defend you when you move.

"You guys do not lack talent, but right now, we are lacking camaraderie. Our goal is to get our hands on the cup, but first, we need to make ourselves a team, a family, a brotherhood. Take some time to hang out together. No funny business. Yes, puck bunnies are enticing, but remember, we need heads in the game. You need to understand one and than just on the ice. Now, hit the showers. I'll see rested, and laced up tomorrow."

"Yes, coach!" The guys begin to skate off the ice and move toward the locker room.

I decide to say one last thing, "Oh, and gentlemen. Don't fucking take this shot for granted."

I give them my normal scowl, and I can see my words are sinking in as they answer with a nod and continue toward the showers. Their asses are on the line, and they need to get their shit together, or we won't make it past the regular season. I have no problem making them run drills until they're puking in the penalty box. But they also need to understand the gift they have been given to play in the NHL.

The players have disappeared to clean themselves up and ice their bodies while I stand there, looking around the arena, reminding myself why I'm here in a different capacity than I was a few years back as a player in this league. I look over at Cummings and try to dispel the tension I feel surrounding my muscles. I hit the gym before everyone arrived this morning, but I can already sense some time on the ice might be what's needed to hopefully get my mind focused to spend the rest of my afternoon with my favorite person.

"Listen, we need to get these guys on the same page. I have some ideas if you've got a moment to discuss the plays I have in mind," Cummings states. He's always been a planner, and I would expect nothing less from him.

Phil Cummings and I went to university together; however, he always aspired for a coaching position, whereas I had my sights set on playing professionally. He and his wife were looking for a change when I was approached about coaching, and I explained that I would not coach a team without Phil by my side. So here we are; I'm in a position I

...ever fathomed would be mine, while Cummings radiates joy at the opportunity. As much as these players are looking to me for guidance, I'm learning as much as I can from Cummings whenever and wherever I can.

The New York Brawlers were once considered one of the best teams in the professional sport; however, through bad ownership, winning a championship has been more of a thing of the past versus something that has occurred recently. A new owner for the team came on after the last one disgracefully found himself surrounded by bad press. Once the new owner took over, he restructured the entire team. He and the general manager had a vision, and apparently, I was at the center of that plan. It took quite some convincing, as I had left the sport a little over a year prior to be with the only girl I love.

I look down at my phone and don't see any notifications from my sister. I expected some updates from her on how Tessa is doing, but nothing yet. I nod my head for Cummings and me to take our meeting in my office. We spend an hour going back and forth on plays to see how this might work best for the players we have on the ice.

By the time we finish looking them over, I'm exhausted and can't look at another screen or discuss another play. Cummings must sense my need to leave my office and decides to head home to his wife and son. He's well aware I'm still finding my bearings in this coaching position. I was never structured enough to sit behind a desk, but I find that this lifestyle works best for Tessa and me in the long run.

I quickly change into some gear and lace up. Just sitting on the bench as I lace up my skates gives me the adrenaline rush I need. I spend the next hour moving along the ice, running drills of my own. I was born to be on the ice since the first set of skates were placed on my feet at five years old. When I step on it, all my worries seem to disappear. I just see me, the puck, and an opponent to beat. Even though I am going through the motions solo, my mind is now rewired to think about my players. Some of the plays Phil and I discussed begin to come up, and I start to envision how certain players will respond on the ice. Maybe I'm more cut out for this job than I realized.

Once I feel like I've gotten my time in and let go of some of the frustration I was holding onto, I leave the rink and begin to make my way toward the showers. The water hitting my aching muscles feels good. I still haven't stopped my training from when I was still a player a year and a half ago. I feel like the routine of my workouts helps my mind stay focused, and it's a type of therapy I have found works best for me, hence the gym I put into my penthouse in one of the fanciest sky-rises I've ever lived in. I am a creature of habit, and I like order in my life. My mother says I'm a control freak, but life doesn't give me much room not to be this way. I need order and structure, not just for my sake, but for the livelihood of those around me.

I wrap the towel around my waist, letting the beads of water drip down from my hair. I reach my bag, and the moment I do, I hear the ping from my phone. All anxiety returns to my body as I rummage through my bag to grab my cell. When I unlock the screen, I see multiple texts waiting for me from my sister. Once I click into the app, I let go of a breath I hadn't realized I was holding. All is well, and they're headed toward the arena now, a little earlier than planned. My emotions are constantly heightened, and I can never seem to let go of thinking the worst when it comes to my pride and joy.

I carved out some uninterrupted time this afternoon with the one person who has become my world, and I can't help the smile that spreads across my face. I might scowl at all things in life except her. She's the only one that can get me to soften along the edges. The only opinion that matters to me is my little blond beauty, whose eyes sparkle with so much love for life, even though life hasn't been as fair to her as she deserves.

I finish getting ready, pull the door open, and walk into

the hallway. I am looking down at my phone, preparing a text to Juliette, when I hear a squeal coming down the hall, making me pause and look to my left. That's when I see the most beautiful girl to grace this earth that I have the honor of calling my daughter.

A little blond ball of hair, curls bouncing as her body vibrates with energy, comes barreling my way, giggling as she moves through the halls. I drop my bag onto the ground, opening my arms to the only person who holds my heart.

"Daddy! Daddy! Daddy!" My five-year-old princess screams as I pull her up into my arms and swing her in the air.

Her laughter is constant at this rate, and all I wish is to bottle her laughter and save it for days when my soul needs resuscitation. I move us in a circle, twirling her while placing kisses on her cheeks. When I come to a stop, she's got the biggest smile spread across her face, her eyes twinkling as they usually are because she is the happiest person I have ever known.

Beside me, I feel my sister's fingers tickling my daughter's side, causing Tessa to laugh even harder while squirming in my grasp. I release this ball of energy, and she begins running around the halls while Juliette hands me the backpack I have no doubt my daughter begged her to carry.

If anyone saw us standing together, they'd never guess we're related. My sister is my complete opposite. I am six-six, muscles taking over most of my frame, with dirty blond hair that is long enough I can pull it back with a hair tie. I have stubble across my jaw and tattoos that cover my arms, along with one hand covered with ink as well. The work of art shows that I've used my skin as a canvas, much like my scars from all the fights I've been in throughout my hockey career have marked a story of my time on the ice.

My sister, however, is short, around five-one, with dark brown hair and dark eyes to my icy blue. She has no ink on her skin and is so fair she burns just thinking of going out to the beach on a summer day. And as people say, I am much like Grumpy from Snow White, and my sister would be considered Snow White herself, physically and emotionally.

"She had a great first day of school," Juliette says, watching her niece move around the halls with a spirit I have grown to envy.

The smile across my sister's face is genuine; my little girl is the apple of her eye, and she shows it with all the time she's willing to spend with her without me even prompting. The tension I was holding in my shoulders due to the first day of school jitters for Tessa finally releases, and I feel myself let go of a deep breath. This year will be challenging for us, as I know Tessa's new lifestyle will come with its own ups and downs. On top of that, I have never left Tessa under anyone's care aside from my parents and sister.

Giving my sister my full attention while I know Juliette is watching Tessa run her energy off, I ask, "How was the teacher? Did she seem attentive to Tessa's needs? Did she pull Tessa aside and ask her all the questions I printed out?"

Although I haven't met Tessa's kindergarten teacher, I had definitely made it known that Tessa's health is a priority, and she needs supervision and monitoring throughout the day. I had made a list, which I laminated to ensure nothing happened to it, and asked Juliette to present it to the teacher this morning. I will be missing a lot of events as the school year commences this fall, and I need to make sure everything goes smoothly.

Roughly eighteen months ago, our lives were turned upside down when my sweet girl started feeling ill. I was on the road with my Nashville team, while Tessa stayed with my sister and parents. Away games were always so hard on my daughter, so when she first started complaining about being tired, we all assumed it was simply from sleeping poorly while missing me as I was out on a long stretch of away games.

However, she only felt worse as the days dragged on, her

lack of appetite and lethargy worsening, pushing my folks to take Tessa to her pediatrician. I got a frantic call from Juliette shortly after the appointment, saying Tessa had to be rushed to the hospital. I have never left a game so quickly. I flew back in time to find out she was diagnosed with type 1 diabetes mellitus, something I would later learn as insulin-dependent diabetes. It's commonly developed during childhood, but the reasoning is still unclear.

The moment I realized how life-changing this was going to be for all of us, I finished out the season and announced my retirement. The twelve months that followed were incredibly difficult. Trying to ensure a child keeps their blood sugars in check while I, as the parent, learn about the illness and how to care for her was a huge shift for me. And since then, I've only trusted my parents and sister to look after her if I can't. It has been all hands on deck for us to figure out how to make Tessa's life as "normal" as possible.

Through all this, the feelings of being a single parent intensified. Tessa's mother signed away her rights when Tessa was only a few days old. Sabrina was not someone I saw forever with, but I was willing to try for the sake of our child. When she told me she was pregnant after we had only been together casually a handful of times, I was shocked but quickly started to redirect my thoughts toward how I could make our lives work together.

Unfortunately, Sabrina had other plans as her delivery date grew nearer. I might be a grumpy prick, but Sabrina is fucking Satan. Her true colors came out when Tessa was just a few hours old. While the nurses were still cleaning our daughter off after birth, Sabrina decided to drop the bomb on me that she couldn't be in our child's life, much less raise another human being. And, of course, she wanted money so she could start again, stating that she needed to start over and get her body back.

None of this behavior showed up when she was pregnant; however, now that I think about it, she was always pretty indifferent about us making plans for the future with our baby. Because I hadn't had much time with Sabrina prior her pregnancy with Tessa, and I was busy being a professional hockey player, I didn't put much weight on her behavior being abnormal. My sister and parents kept warning me, but I wanted to believe in something better. I think, all I really wanted, was the life I saw my parents build and my vision was tainted in many ways.

It was the first and last time I gave my heart to someone else, aside from my daughter and family. I wanted the love I saw growing up between my own parents, so I will be the first to admit I was heartbroken Sabrina didn't want more with me, but I was also livid that she wanted nothing with a child we created together.

Sabrina ended up leaving me behind with a new child and a new life, all while she moved on and never looked back. I have gotten updates on Tessa's mother from my agent and some of my old teammates who might run into her. Once she recovered from giving birth, Sabrina wasted no time getting back out on the scene, partying like she hadn't just added to the human population. Apparently, she is currently shacked up with some Hollywood hotshot and doesn't seem to remember that time in life when she gave birth to an amazing baby girl.

But truth be told, having Sabrina walk away was probably for the best, as Tessa was truly a ray of light versus her mother's dark cloud. We didn't need that, but it doesn't mean the idea of what she did doesn't leave a bitter taste in my mouth, even as my daughter thrives right in front of me.

The more I hear about how Sabrina is doing now, the more confident I am that her leaving was the ultimate gift. Although I do think my daughter would thrive even more with a mother around, she is loved by those surrounding her. So, I look at my sister and parents as my saviors because, without them, I wouldn't have felt comfortable playing my favorite sport for those last few years prior to my retirement. I relocated my entire family to New York when I got this job, and it seems we are all adjusting easier than expected.

My parents were still in Oklahoma, my hometown, when I got drafted to the NHL. After Tessa was born, they visited us in Nashville far more often than being in our small town, so moving wasn't such a tough decision for them when I took this coaching position. At the time of Tessa's diagnosis, I was playing for the Nashville Hawks and won three championships with them during my time there.

At the time this job offer came to me, Juliette was staying with me in Nashville after her difficult break-up with her girlfriend. When Tessa fell ill, my sister didn't hesitate to offer her help, sitting with me on late nights, researching all we could on diabetes and how this would impact not just Tessa's life, but all of our futures.

She's an editor for a big publishing house, but her job is done remotely, and that gives her the flexibility to help with Tessa now that I need the extra assistance. To say my sister welcomed this change to a big city is an understatement and she's thriving as we figure out our surroundings here.

I hadn't planned on returning to work in any capacity, as playing professionally came with a lot of perks, especially financially. I didn't need to work for financial gain after my retirement; however, my mother and sister pretty much shoved me toward this job when it was offered. They said I was becoming obsessive over Tessa's care and that the poor girl needed to live a little—their words, not mine. She's five, almost six, so I have no idea how a child needs to live it up, but I did as they asked, and it seems that my need to keep myself occupied with something besides Tessa's blood sugars seems to have worked for balancing my attitudes with everyone; aside from me fuming at the way my players are working out on the ice.

"Xander, you laminated a dang list!" My sister pulls me from my thoughts, calling me by my nickname, which is what everyone in my profession took on as my given name in the hockey world. The only people who call me by my birth name are my parents.

My sister continues, "The teacher did the best she could, but she did say that there are twenty-four kids in the class. It's not something she can do on the hour, every hour. I told you to just let it be. The school and her teacher know how to handle diabetic children. Plus, the nurse got your thesis-long instruction booklet regarding her medical history and necessities. Tessa isn't the first child with this diagnosis at this school. And I promise you, her teacher is attentive to all the kids. She is really incredible. She's got the patience of a saint."

My sister huffs at the end, and if I'm really nitpicking here, I would say she's insinuating that I am not a patient person.

"Maybe she isn't the first kid with diabetes, but she's my only child, who happens to be diabetic. I will not pay tuition to a private school, which, let me remind you, costs more than some people's entire college education, for my simple demands to be ignored."

I cross my arms across my chest, really letting my sister see I am as intimidating as people think. Unfortunately, my attempt falls short, and all I get in response to my imposing frame is my sister laughing at me.

"Oh, please. Don't cross your arms and act all macho," she mimics my stance, rolling her eyes as she does so.

"I get it. Tessa is your world. She's the center of all our lives. I'm not arguing that fact. She needs care. But you're failing to see she's getting it. And you want her to feel like she fits in, don't you? You don't want Tessa to feel ostracized because she has a chronic illness, right?

"Well, I think the teacher knows what she's doing. Mrs.

Lorrent is amazing with the kids. And the woman has eyes, Xan. She can see how the kids are doing, and if Tessa seems lethargic, she can tell. She knows the signs. I mean, you made a wallet-sized list with signs and symptoms of low blood sugar. You're a bit ridiculous, bro," my sister shoves me with her elbow.

I look over and call out to my girl, who has started a conversation with other staff roaming the halls. She makes friends everywhere she goes, and with how she's become a part of the Brawlers family this summer, she's got everyone wrapped around her little finger. I put my hand out for her to grab when she gets by my side. Tessa's little hand gets swallowed by my own, and she swings my arm forward and back, still smiling as if today is the best so far. Knowing her positive outlook on life, today *is* her favorite.

"So, munchkin, how was your first day of school? Do you like your teacher?"

I look down and give her a genuine smile, as I save all of those for her. She looks up at me, and her big doe eyes stare back. I don't know what happened, but her mother and I made the most beautiful creation. Tessa has my exact hair, even with the soft curls, as I had as a child. My hair got a little darker as I got older, but it was this exact same shade of blond when I was growing up. But her eyes are what really make Tessa stand out the most for me. Even now, after five years with this beautiful soul in my life, her eyes take my breath away. Somehow, Sabrina and I contributed blue to her, but the way the light reflects off her irises, they seem almost violet. It's a different blue from what her mother and I have, and they are absolutely breathtaking.

"Oh yes, Daddy. It was the best day ever. So far, my favoritest day of all my days."

Even when Tessa was in a hospital room, she always had this positive outlook on her life. Endless poking and prodding was done when she was in that large hospital bed, but she always had a great attitude about it. She started each day with a smile, even if the day prior had pushed her limits on all she had to endure. It seems that all my concerns about how this disease would consume her life hasn't affected her demeanor. She has continued to be positive, even when I felt like my world was falling apart.

Tessa continues, "Mrs. Lorrent is the best teacher I've ever had."

"She's the only teacher you've ever had—Ouch! What the heck, Juliette?" I turn my gaze toward my sister.

"What was that for?" I rub my side, where my sister has just elbowed me with all her might. She might look tiny, but her pointy bones really do a number on me.

With a fake smile where she's clenching her teeth, my sister looks at me, "Oh, I'm sorry, it just seemed like you were giving attitude regarding the teacher comment. At least act like you don't have a stick up your B-U-T-T."

She accomplishes saying all this without moving her mouth and her face displaying a permanent smile so it won't give off negative vibes toward the five-year-old who is holding my hand tightly on the other side of me.

"Auntie Julie said BUTT!" Tessa says and giggles afterward. "Mrs. Lorrent said I'm a great speller."

I stare at my sister and squint my eyes, telling her with my gaze that she better watch her mouth. My daughter is smarter than the average five-year-old and can already spell words. Found this out the hard way when I was spelling something out that wasn't the nicest a few months back regarding Tessa's mother, and my daughter caught on. Luckily, she didn't know who I was talking about and disregarded the reason behind my rudeness.

Looking back at Tess, I tell her, "You are a good speller. Too bad Auntie Julie has a potty mouth."

Tessa looks ahead as we walk through the hall toward the elevator.

"Ew, Auntie puts her mouth on the potty?" Tessa scrunches her nose and makes a disgusted look with her features. I can't help but laugh, while my sister now points a scowl my way.

"No, sweetheart. No mouth of mine is going near a potty. It's just an expression," my sister responds before sticking her tongue at me like we are back to our elementary school days and maturity is out the door.

Luckily, Tessa doesn't catch it because I wouldn't see the end of that gesture from my daughter if she learned this from her aunt.

We leave the arena and walk toward my car. Once I get everything inside, I tell them to wait one moment, as I forgot something in my office. I set the temperature to something comfortable for them to wait inside. The car plays movies, and Tessa is so distracted, trying to figure out what to stream, she probably doesn't even hear me speaking. Juliette takes a moment to look at me, wondering what I'm up to. I try to keep from having eye contact with her, as she's some sort of witch and can figure things out without me saying a word. I don't need her bothering me about what I'm about to do.

I close the driver's door and begin walking back toward the arena, seething now that Juliette and Tessa aren't in my company. How dare that teacher think she can just ignore my request to do the hourly check-ins with my daughter when I explicitly asked her to? This is ridiculous. I will give her a piece of my mind through an email. Does she even know who I am?

With my long legs, my strides get me to my office quicker than I expected. I walk in, slamming the door behind me. I access my email from my desk, knowing I need my keyboard and computer to compose this email to avoid typos from my large fingers if I were to use my phone. I'll get my thoughts written out for the teacher and hopefully get my point across about how important my instructions are for the well-being of my child before meeting back up with Juliette and Tessa to start our drive home. I will not let this ruin my little date with my daughter this afternoon, but I will definitely give this teacher a piece of my mind.

Chapter Two

ELODY

I say goodbye to my last student, waving at him and his mom as they walk away toward the front of the school. I make my way through my little classroom, taking a moment to myself at the front of the room.

The first day of school is always daunting. The lead-up causes me to lose sleep as I'm always too excited to meet my little kindergarten students to start off the year. But once the first day is over, I feel like all that excitement has morphed into pure exhaustion.

Thank goodness the first day of school for these little ones is on a Friday each year. The school starts on a staggered schedule, the older grades starting on Monday, and each grade trickles from there. Kinder is the youngest grade at this school, and they always start them on a Friday. Unlike many other schools, our kindergarten students have a full day, so it's a lot for them to adjust to all at once. Having the weekend to absorb the newness of their first day helps the kids prepare for a full week next week. I let my head fall back, and I close my eyes. I know the moment I leave this classroom, my next job starts.

My own children, at least the two younger ones, will be

coming in here any minute with excitement that they can sleep in tomorrow. I promised Becca I'd keep her twins with me tonight as she has a shift at the hospital, and her ex, Hudson, is preparing for a big court case that starts next week. Luckily, my oldest, Tyler, will walk home with Becca's kids now that they are all at the same school, so that's one less pick up I have to do before getting home. The high school is closer to our brownstone than this school, so I know they'll be home before us this afternoon.

I have a few more minutes before I have to put my mask on. I'm usually a very happy person. Let me rephrase: I used to be an overall happy person. My energy, even at forty-three, is quite high, but since losing Beau, I've felt a large part of my light died with him. So I put on a mask now when I'm around everyone, showing myself to be the put-together woman everyone knows me to be.

As someone who felt like she had it all, burying Beau taught me that no matter what, life can throw a curveball. But the way I think of it, if I fake it enough, maybe I will start to be that old version of myself that everyone seems to love. It's been five years of donning a mask to hide the ache I feel deep down, but I do find joy in seeing my kids thriving, even after moving to an entirely new state after their father's passing.

In all honesty, I didn't let myself mope for too long after Beau passed. I had three small children to care for, and after losing one parent, I didn't want them to think they lost another. I had to put on a brave exterior and face the life we had to now get used to without the one person who gave me light, much like I gave him the same.

My natural disposition is to be happy. I have so much love to give, and it all goes to my village—my kids, sister, parents, and my best friend Becca and her family. But on days like today, where I sit here in my classroom and reminisce, I can't help but wish I had my Beau to greet me when I walked through the door later today.

He used to love hearing about my first day of school. We'd put the kids down, and he'd grab a bottle of wine; we'd sit on our favorite rocking chairs on our wrap-around porch, and he'd listen while I told him all about the newest personalities in my classroom. We lived in a beautiful home down the street from where we grew up in Saddle Ridge, Nebraska. We had everything we ever dreamed of. We had built the life we had always talked about. But I didn't account for the things we hadn't planned for, like cancer and saying goodbye to the love of my life at the age of thirty-eight.

As I sit here in my quiet classroom, I keep my eyes closed and imagine myself on that porch, my sweet husband by my side, asking me about my day. I can imagine him reaching for my hand and rubbing his thumb across it; that simple touch soothing me in ways I never thought I'd miss so early on in my life. I feel the tear fall down my left cheek as I reminisce about my love, unable to control the emotion seeping from my eyes.

I allow myself this moment to just absorb the pain because letting my kids see me hurting is not what I want for them. Tyler, my oldest, already holds so much weight on his shoulders because he feels it's necessary for the sake of his siblings and myself. My sweet boy, who I see so much of his father in his features, is a worrier, and if I can do anything to ease that burden off of him, I will. So I'll give myself this moment but leave it here when I walk out of my classroom this afternoon.

I hear their feet long before my two younger kids, Hannah and Mia, come sauntering in. Hannah is my little twin, and at only age nine, she already has that ray of sunshine personality I had. She sees the world with so much positivity, and since Beau's passing, I envy her ability to love this life so fiercely, even after losing a parent. Mia is a perfect mix of Beau and me; she's my little cuddle buddy. She is always by my side and always helping me where possible around the house.

She was only two when Beau passed away, and from how she remembers him, her recollection is choppy at best. She's always known life as just the four of us, not remembering much about a life with a father figure. I think she senses I live this life much like I'm missing a limb, so she works to be my little caretaker. I wouldn't be surprised if she entered the medical field years from now. She seems to be genuinely interested in her Aunt Becca's medical practice and always asks for crazy stories from Becca's time at the hospital. Mia is a nurturer, and she is always there to help, even if she doesn't realize how much she contributes to being a part of my strength on a daily basis.

"Hi, Mom!" Hannah comes in, smiling as if the entire day wasn't a huge adjustment after an entire summer off.

I look over and smile at her, feeling like I'm looking in a mirror of myself years prior.

"Mom, I stopped by to see Miss Thomas at the nurse's office, and she said a kid threw up all over the floor," Mia tells me with a gleam in her eyes, like she's telling me about her first day of residency instead of her first day of second grade.

I can't help making a face of disgust, and both my daughters can't help but chuckle. They both know I am a wuss when it comes to cleaning up vomit. But hearing them laugh is a balm to my broken heart, and I'll take it as a way to start my night.

"That sounds disgusting, Mia, but I appreciate you telling me this story now versus at the dinner table. I doubt anyone wants to be thinking of that while they're eating my lasagna tonight."

I stand up at my desk and begin putting things in order. We have the nighttime staff that vacuums and cleans up the room, but I always try to keep my room tidy where possible. Plus, kindergarteners are notorious for leaving things behind, as most are not accustomed to the school schedule and being accountable for their things after a full day of interacting with peers.

I find a scrunchie on the ground, purple with white polka-dots, and try to recall who wore this at the start of the day. Little Tessa Christianson pops in my head with her adorable smile and beautiful blond hair.

The moment that child walked into my room, I felt a pull toward her. Her violet eyes were mesmerizing, but her demeanor was even more incredible. From what her aunt and the school nurse have told me, she's had her fair share of difficulties adjusting to her new lifestyle as a type 1 diabetic. But from what I gathered from our day together, nothing got her down. She was responsive to anything I said to the class, along with being one of my social butterflies among her classmates. She seemed to take in the environment of the classroom but also adapted to the structure quite quickly.

Her wonderful personality wasn't the only memorable thing about this child. I have only met her aunt so far in our interactions; Tessa's father is some hotshot retired hockey player turned coach now, so I have not had the privilege to interact with him. Well, aside from interacting via laminated demands he had made for me regarding Tessa's care.

Juliette, Tessa's aunt, came up to me at drop-off and seemed quite embarrassed when she handed the list of demands her brother had concocted. I don't blame her. He seems like a pretentious asshole with the way he listed things off to me, as if I was some idiot when it came to watching out for my students. But what he failed to realize is that no student is above another. If I got a laminated list of demands from every adult that dropped off their child, I'd need twenty-three other teachers in this room with me so each child got the one-to-one attention their parents expected.

I smiled and chuckled at Juliette when she handed me the list, along with a mini-version that listed the immediate needs Tessa might require if her blood sugar dropped below a certain number. I let Juliette know that Tessa was in good hands and that I had diabetic children in my class previously, although this year, Tessa was my only one.

Juliette seemed far more relaxed than what I imagine her brother to be like, and she smiled and simply let it go after that. It's hard for me to really take this father seriously if he can't even come here himself to ensure I get the list and understand his demands. I placed the laminated list in my desk drawer and left it at that. I had already been told by the nurse about Tessa's needs, and I also remember the signs of low blood sugar from previous students of mine.

Our school has many children with needs that go beyond my abilities in the classroom. I am not a doctor nor a nurse; however, I am trained in basic CPR, along with comprehending signs and symptoms related to illnesses I may encounter in my young students. On top of that, Tessa is put on a different schedule than her classmates, having to visit the nurse a defined number of times to get her sugars checked and regulated. Medicine has come a long way since I was in elementary school. Back in the eighties, if one was a type 1 diabetic, there were numerous hospitalizations and so many inaccurate blood sugar readings and insulin dosing, it was overwhelming.

There was only one little boy in my childhood school who had type 1 diabetes. He was a year younger than me, and he was constantly missing school. But medicine today is a whole new ballgame. Tessa has a blood sugar device attached to her upper arm. It is replaced every couple of days, in addition to making blood sugar monitoring much simpler. There is an app associated with the device, and you simply move the phone over it, and it will give the person's blood sugars. It is quite interesting, and I have had to use it in my previous classrooms to monitor a child's blood sugar if they seemed to be lethargic and unable to walk safely to the nurse.

That being said, I kept open communication with Miss Thomas to make sure the plan of care was seamless between the two of us. Prior to today's start, I already had Tessa's app downloaded and synced to my phone.

I put the scrunchie in my desk drawer, grabbing the laminated list of demands before locking my desk up. I grab the laptop I use for my lessons and pack it in my laptop bag, also making sure I have stowed my phone alongside my other belongings and put the bag on my shoulder.

I already know I have work to do before Monday's class, as I'm hoping to get some outdoor activities lined up for next week before our weather turns to the blistering cold I know is right around the corner.

"Mom, when we get home, can we make some cupcakes?" Hannah asks as she pulls the straps of her backpack onto her shoulders and looks up at me with pleading eyes. My little baker with her culinary dreams. It's hard to say no to her, especially if I get to be the taste tester.

"Sure, sweetie. I won't be helping aside from the transfer into and outside of the oven. I want you to take the lead on this one, and I'll be at the kitchen table to help if you need it. Sound like a plan?"

Hannah is nodding her head, smiling from ear to ear. I look back at Mia, who is walking much slower than us, and that's when I realize her nose is in a book. I move my head to the side to see what the title of her book is, and it's a book on the human body that Becca had gifted her last week. How is a seven-year-old so much into science and biology already?

If Mia isn't grilling Becca about her profession, she's got her nose in a book. I love to read, but I'll admit it didn't start until after I had kids. I needed an escape from the day-to-day parenting I was taking on, and a good thriller or romance story was my escape, especially after Beau passed away.

Mia finally catches up to us while I'm holding the door open for her before she walks through, and I turn off the lights and close my classroom door. I take a big inhale and close my eyes for a moment. I have to find the energy deep down to entertain my household until bedtime.

I say a little prayer to my husband up above, asking for the strength to get through tonight as I'm emotionally and physically drained, in addition to wishing I had a partner by my side as I tackle parenting this evening. Even though I'm inside the hall, I feel a whoosh of air across my face, and it feels like a million little kisses from my Beau, telling me I'm going to be okay.

* * *

Hannah's cupcakes are a success, and everyone is nearly licking the crumbs off their plates by the end of the evening. Luckily, I planned ahead with a lasagna that was simply put into the oven and ready quickly after everyone got home this afternoon.

Becca's kids are easily mixed in with the dynamic of my household, that I barely notice the difference of having two more mouths to feed. Each one has a task after dinner, knowing they have to either clean up the kitchen table, wash dishes, put away leftovers, or dry the clean dishes.

I leave them to do their chores, Becca's twins included, and walk into my office. This brownstone was the first big purchase I made after Beau's passing. I had sold our home in Nebraska within months of Beau's death. I had heard from others that rash decisions should not be made after the passing of a loved one, but I couldn't stand being in that home without Beau. I tried, I truly did, but I failed miserably to move forward. Once the mourners left and I was stuck in that home with memories seeping into all the walls, I could feel my lungs collapsing. Taking a breath became a struggle.

I called Becca in a panic, feeling as if I owed it to my kids and Beau's memory to try and stick it out in Saddle Ridge. But after days of talking it through with my best friend, she and I came up with a plan. She was in the middle of getting a divorce from Hudson, and she already knew she'd be staying in her home. She saw the "for sale" sign on this brownstone a few days after I initially told her my feelings about leaving Saddle Ridge, and she said our chats had manifested this into the universe, and I needed to move closer to her.

I used the money from our Nebraska home as a down payment on this one and started a new life. Tyler must have felt similar to me because when I mentioned selling the only house he and his siblings ever called home, he was ecstatic. I think we all felt a piece of us no longer resided in our home state, and leaving felt like the right move.

I grab my laptop case, pull out my Mac, and boot it up. My background photo that greets me is the last photo I have of Beau before he became ill. Mia is so tiny, looking up at her father, while the rest of us are looking directly at the camera. The smiles we hold have so much hope in them. I still remember the feelings behind this photo shoot.

My eyes are drawn to Beau, even all these years later, when all I have left are these memories to look back on. He was my favorite person besides my children and Becca. I feel the tug in my heart as I touch the screen with my fingertips, hoping I'll feel the warmth of his skin instead of the cold plastic that lies over his features now.

I take a deep breath and preclude myself from revealing the emotion pouring from my eyes. The tears are always something I feel myself fighting. No matter how much I may cry, it won't bring back my Beau. So, I feel like it's useless at this point to focus on the things I can't change. Life's too short; that's what his illness left me realizing. I will put my best foot forward to ensure our kids have magnificent futures.

I move the mouse over the mail icon and open up my email. I try to keep my email clean to make sure if the school or any parents try to get a hold of me, I don't miss any correspondence. The most recent email I see is from my mother-in-law, Beau's mother, and I can already feel my heart rate accelerate. I can't avoid it, or the next way she'll reach out is by phone, and I don't need her in my ear, finding ways to make me feel guilty for moving her only grandchildren away.

Even all these years later, she finds ways to make jabs at me, and I don't need that added stress in my life. Our door is always open for her to visit; however, she misses no opportunity to let guilt be her method of attack when it comes to interactions with me.

Her email is quite short and straight to the point, thank goodness. She is asking about FaceTiming in October, hoping to see the kids dressed up for Halloween. The kids have gone back to Saddle Ridge throughout the years since we moved, but for me, it still harbors too much pain, and our visits are short when we go back. My own parents remain in my hometown, and seeing them is always a much-needed reunion. However, my parents are traveling more often, and they tend to plan a stop in New York each time they go anywhere, so I haven't taken the kids back to Nebraska in some time.

I need to do better for Beau's family, as they don't have any other children or grandchildren to dote on. My parents have both their daughters in one city, and they seem to be enjoying retirement to the fullest. Plus, my mother and Becca's mom have a girls' trip annually, where my dad and Rick have gotten to bond as well when their wives are traveling around the states.

My mom and Becca's mother, Grace, bonded immediately when Becca and I became friends, and they have a very similar relationship to mine with Becca. However, Becca lives only a few doors down, so I guess we've got them there. Grace and Rick live in upstate New York and seem to love that life. It's a little less hectic than the city, and they've done well in the quiet their small town brings them.

I go through a few more emails, mostly junk, before I reach one with a name I recognize. WXChristianson@brawlers.org is the email address, and I already know this is Tessa's father. I wonder if he's emailing to thank me for a good first day for his daughter. I open it up, prepared to read something positive and light. Unfortunately, it's anything but.

Mrs. Lorrent,

This is Xander Christianson, Tessa's father. I have not had a chance to meet you in person; however, you have met my sister, Tessa's aunt, Juliette. I believe my sister dropped off a few fact sheets to you regarding Tessa's medical condition and how she must be monitored. I inquired about Tessa's first day when she came home from school, and I'm shocked to hear you did not do anything I asked. I was clear she needed hourly checks by you as her teacher, along with the blood sugar checks with the school nurse. I know her blood sugar was checked by the nurse because I get updates on the app, but not checking in with a child while they're in your classroom throughout the day seems reckless and irresponsible. Not to mention the fact that I pay you to do exactly that —keep my kid safe.

Do better, Mrs. Lorrent. My child deserves the best care.

-Xander Christianson

I can't help my mouth hanging open as I finish reading this email. Were those cupcakes laced because I must be hallucinating. I have never, in all my years as a teacher, received such a note from a parent before. I have always been known as a patient, kind, welcoming, attentive, and overall good teacher. I love my career in education, and this guy is treating me like I don't know my nose from my ass. What is his problem?

I spoke to Juliette before she picked up Tessa and explained the day went smoothly and that Tessa was a dream of a student, especially as a child who has never gone to school in this capacity before. Juliette did not seem angry in any way, nor was she disappointed, when I told her I did not pull Tessa aside the countless number of times the laminated instructions asked me to do so.

However, I felt it best I observe her and not let her feel like she was being treated differently than her peers. I can read my students well, and I know when someone is feeling off, even if they don't suffer from a chronic illness. She never made it seem like my care was reckless. And let me just say, it's the first day of kindergarten, not the first day at NASA.

I read the email three more times because I really am having a hard time wrapping my head around his words. But sure enough, nothing changes in what is written, and the only thing this email is doing is making my blood boil.

I slam my computer shut and push back from my desk. I feel tears prickling at the corners of my eyes. Right now, my heart hurts because I miss Beau a little extra. What I wouldn't give to feel his strong arms around me, letting me cry out my emotions.

I feel lonely in so many ways, and this email is simply heightening that feeling. I take in my office, the soothing neutral tones something I chose to keep me calm as I worked on my lesson plans. Too bad the colors are doing nothing to pull me out of this dumpster fire I'm in right now.

This feeling is foreign to me. I get along with everyone, and I've simply never had to deal with this type of behavior before. Plus, I'm stuck with this jackass of a father the entire year. Tessa must get her sweetness from everyone else in her life because that is not a trait I see coming from her hockey-playing father.

I'll have to compose a response, but I have no idea what I will say at this point. My parents always taught me to keep myself from reacting when I'm upset. Their philosophy has always been threefold: Would I want my response reciprocated back to me? How would my response be received? Most importantly, is it kind? Right now, I know none of my responses to these questions would fall in the appropriate category, and I will take some time to figure out what a proper response would be.

I stand up and take a deep inhale and exhale, hoping I can let go of the tension I feel in my shoulders. My sister teaches yoga for a living, and I'm hoping some of her mantras from the classes I've taken from her will seep in because I will need them. I already know this will be a trying year, and it all has to do with one person: Xander Christianson.

Chapter Three

WYATT

I wake up before the sun after another restless night. I am staring at the shadows on my ceiling, trying to rid my mind of all the thoughts passing through. I look on my nightstand and see it's four-thirty in the morning. I try to hide my irritation because my body is not resting the way it needs. I am usually well-conditioned to sleep at an exact time and get enough sleep each night. However, since I sent that email to Tessa's teacher, I can't shake how I'm feeling about my behavior.

After I drafted the email to Mrs. Lorrent and sent it, I joined Tessa and Juliette to drive home. Juliette lives in my building, a few floors down. I bought my sister her apartment because I felt guilty asking her to change her entire life around to accommodate my new schedule. Giving her a residence to call home was the least I could do. Plus, if I had an emergency or a string of away games now that I'm coaching, Tessa is just an elevator ride up from her room and toys whenever she needs them.

After saying goodbye to Juliette, Tessa and I went on our little date last night. I took her out to a movie, followed by dinner and ice cream. The weather is still warm enough, and I can pull off a few more outings where we finish off a meal with something cold. The only problem was, all through our night out, I was constantly checking her blood sugars and making sure she didn't have huge fluctuations.

Some days, blood sugar monitoring feels like a full-time job in and of itself, and last night, it dawned on me I may have been quite harsh on Tessa's new teacher. She had a room full of students, and here I was, being a prick. Tessa is my world, but the way I went about addressing Mrs. Lorrent was low, even for a grumpy asshole like me.

After running my words from my email through my head again, failing to let it go and falling back asleep, I throw my covers off and walk toward my en suite bathroom. If I'm not going to get more sleep, I may as well start my day early. Tessa will most likely sleep in a bit after being exhausted after her first day yesterday. I should have about two hours to fit a workout in before I have to start my day with my daughter.

There's a late practice scheduled for this afternoon, even though it's a Saturday. The guys need to get into a rhythm to hopefully flow with one another before the season begins. Every second counts, and hopefully, with time, the guys will find their flow, on and off the ice. The trust these guys need to gain for one another will make all the difference, and I hope what I said resonates with them as we move forward to preseason games.

I'm brushing my teeth when I hear the ping from my phone, indicating a new email has come through. Most of my old teammates span across the globe, with the majority in retirement, so it shouldn't surprise me that someone is emailing me at this early hour.

I finish getting ready in the restroom and walk back to my nightstand to unplug my charged phone. I open the email app and immediately see a response from Tessa's teacher. I feel the acceleration of my pulse and find myself hesitating to open the reply.

I roll my eyes to myself. When have I ever been scared of

someone talking back to me? I've never backed down from a fight, and throwing verbal punches, and literal ones, at another individual wasn't something I ever felt nervous about when I got on that ice. Why was I letting this make me feel so out of control?

I click on the email and read what she has to say back:

Mr. Christianson,

Thank you for your email. Having Tessa in my class is an absolute joy. Although it was only one day so far, I can see her heart is made of gold and will bring a brightness to my year. It was wonderful meeting Tessa's aunt, Juliette, as well.

Regarding your instructions, I appreciate you giving that as a reference. I wanted you to know that I've had students with type 1 diabetes in my class before and am well-versed in how to care for children who are insulin-dependent. That being said, I know that this is not only new to Tessa but also for you. It can be overwhelming to send your child to school, but I want you to know that she is in good, capable hands. If I feel an issue arises, I will not hesitate to reach out. Our school nurse is also great with the students and has a strict schedule that she keeps me informed about so that we do not delay in nurse visits throughout the day. I know how time-sensitive diabetic regimens are for those with insulin-dependent diabetes.

Please reach out with any other concerns.

Have a lovely weekend,
    Mrs. Elody Lorrent

I read the email one more time, feeling my nostrils flare. Why am I annoyed? Did I expect a fight back? Did it disappoint me that she didn't throw some shade my way because I was such an ass to her, to begin with? I guess I wanted her to be rude back instead of being so kind with her response. I wanted her to have some fight in her to warrant my previous behavior. But instead, she's killing me with kindness? We are definitely different personalities because I feel like I'm always on guard when it comes to confrontations. But in this case, I deserved her wrath. I was an absolute dick to her in that first email, and I was expecting some choice words from her. Now I feel even more guilty.

Her email does not justify a response, so I let it be and change into some workout clothes. I head to the kitchen to get my ready-made pre-workout shake from the fridge. Once I've consumed said shake, I walk by my daughter's room, deciding to quietly walk in and place my phone near her blood sugar device. Luckily, the left arm it is currently on is the exposed arm, so I can easily see how her sugars are doing. Fortunately, she doesn't need an intervention at this time, and I feel myself letting go of the breath I am constantly holding when it comes to Tessa and her chronic illness.

I converted one of the spare rooms into a gym, so I walk out of Tessa's room as quietly as I walked in and navigate down the hall toward the room with all my fitness equipment. I realize my behavior toward Tessa, her health, and her care are all to the extreme. I began seeing a therapist regularly when Tessa was born. I've taken a lot of time to discuss my feelings, and I've gotten a lot out of having someone listen to me and help me decipher them.

When I really pull back and inspect my relationship with my child, it's hard to let go of the fact that Tessa's had it unfair much of her life. Her mother discarded that chance to be with her in order to live as someone who is only after the next best thing. It's hard to explain to a little girl why her mother doesn't call or visit. It's hard to make sense of something in the mind of a child when it barely makes sense to an adult in their forties, like me.

When Tessa was diagnosed with diabetes, it felt like life wasn't cutting her a break. The fact this is something that she will have to live with forever is hard for me to wrap my head around. All the success I've had regarding my professional hockey career, along with all the money I can throw at this illness, will not make her immune to the turmoil this disease brings along with it. I know that when I was growing up, the advances in medicine still had not occurred, so many people with diabetes had several other health problems stemming from their condition.

I'm grateful medicine has advanced in the way it has, but the difficulties of this chronic illness lie front and center of her daily lifestyle, and it's hard for me to come to terms with that on most days. As someone who loves to have control, not having it in this sense nearly brings me to my knees. It's something I am still learning to maneuver, but it's obvious everyone else is handling it better than me, even the five-year-old sleeping in her bed right now.

I've had time to adjust to her diagnosis; however, I have held on to how hard this will be for her instead of realizing how amazing she's coping since her diagnosis. I live for Tessa, and if anything were to happen to her, I don't know what my life would be anymore. She is my everything, and keeping her safe and healthy is my number one priority.

I begin my cardio workout, and once I'm done, I move on to my weights. Before I realize it, the sun has fully risen, and I can feel my muscles letting go of the anger and frustration. It's amazing how much my body needs movement in this way. It brings me peace in a way that it's hard to explain. I keep at it for another thirty minutes until I see my little one at the opening of the doorway, rubbing her eyes.

Her hair is wild, much like it is every morning. She is a restless sleeper, and I have learned from first-hand experience that my daughter is a fighter in her dreams. She kicks and swings her arms around. When I've shared a bed with her in the past, I used to fear rolling over on her. I should have feared getting a black eye instead. She is not someone to mess with while in a deep slumber. She sleeps in every single position—diagonal, perpendicular, feet at the top of the bed, etcetera. If there's a way to sleep on a bed, she's tried it.

Her beautiful eyes look up at me, and she smiles. I can't help but smile back because she is my reason for breathing now. She is my everything. I will move mountains if I must in order to keep her happy and healthy.

"Hey, Pumpkin. Want some breakfast?"

She is still half asleep and simply nods her head. She knows the drill. We walk over to the kitchen, and I lift her up onto the barstool. I grab my phone and open the blood sugar app, swiping it across the device to see where her sugars are in order to calculate her insulin dose before eating breakfast.

I get her medicated, and we decide pancakes are a good breakfast choice. Tessa loves to start the day with fruit, so she grabs some washed blueberries from the fridge and gets them divvied up into little containers to enjoy with the pancakes while I gather everything I need to mix the batter. She asks Alexa to play some music, and we are both dancing, Tessa wiggling in her helper stool, and I'm moving around the kitchen to the beat of the music as I mix the batter.

Once the food is ready, we both sit together at the island, and I ask her what she's planning on doing with her grandparents this afternoon. My parents take her every Saturday when I am working, and it's a relief she will be able to do something fun around the city while I'm at the arena.

We eat as if we haven't seen food in days, and once done, we begin clearing our plates. We are a good team; she dries the dishes as I wash them. She has her stool by my side, so we are working together to get everything in order before my parents arrive to whisk her away.

Once done and we have her snacks and medication for her to take along for her Saturday adventures, I pull out my phone and make sure my parents haven't messaged me with any changes in their plans. Luckily, all seems to be set for their time together, so Tessa and I decide to get ready for the day ahead. Maybe a stroll through Central Park will be a nice way to finish out our morning before I head to work.

* * *

Two and a Half Months Later

Thanksgiving is upon us, and life is moving along faster than I know what to do with it. We are well into the NHL season, and my team is improving with each game they play. I work them hard at practice because I see their potential as individual players and as a team. I know it's premature, but I really feel we could make it to the playoffs. But we have to pull more wins than losses at this rate, and there is no time to snooze when everyone else has their eyes on the same prize.

We are on the road in my old hometown of Nashville, and these fans are relentless. They don't seem to hold their love for me the same way they did when I played for their home team, but I can't focus on that right now. My heart will always hold a special place for Tennessee, but I have other places my heart belongs to now.

I miss my little girl so much. The FaceTime calls are not easing my heart the way I wanted them to. The team has been playing away games for over a week, and I can't help myself from looking at the game clock, not only to countdown this game and hopefully another win for us, but to see how much longer I have until I'm on the plane and back to the city. I love this game, but since Tessa was born, a part of my heart stays behind whenever I'm away.

I yell at my guys to pick up the pace. We're up by one goal, and there's no room for error right now. I want this win, and I want the team to feel this victory to their core. The clock is winding down, and it seems defense has nothing on my men, moving that puck around like it was the easiest thing.

Once the buzzer goes off, you would think the Brawlers just won the cup the way we are celebrating, but, no matter what, it is a huge win for us as we head into Thanksgiving week. We have home games coming up, and I know the guys are ready to get home and enjoy a much-needed break from traveling.

I know I am looking forward to it. I look over at Cummings, and the smile he has across his face says it all. He's excited about the prospects this win brings us. We are a step closer to our goal, and what an accomplishment it would be to coach a team that hasn't seen a playoff run in over a decade.

Once I speak to my team in the locker room, I make my way into my temporary office to grab some of my stuff to head to the airport. Cummings is standing at the doorway when I turn around.

"You're welcome to come over for Thanksgiving if you'd like. I know you've probably got plans, but it might be good for Tessa to see some more kiddos and play in the yard." Cummings has a home outside the city, with a stretch of land that provides the freedom to run around, much like Tessa had when I lived here in Nashville.

I smile at the kindness my friend is providing. He's always thoughtful about Tessa's needs, and I feel comfortable being completely honest with him regarding the difficulties that have arisen with her diagnosis.

"I'll check with my family to see if that would work for them. You're okay having five extra mouths to feed?"

I already know his answer, but I always like to point out that we are a unit, and I can't make plans like this without including my sister and parents. We hadn't planned much for Thanksgiving as we have a game the night before, and my mind has been solely focused on Tessa's adjustment to school and coaching this team.

Luckily, things have been quiet regarding Tessa's teacher, and any other issues I may have wanted to bring up seemed to have died down after my last interaction with Mrs. Lorrent. Unfortunately, I still haven't met said teacher in person due to scheduling issues on my end, so my sister continues to be the primary contact for all school activities.

Juliette has even attended back-to-school night and the first parent-teacher conference. I felt awful not being there, but I had responsibilities to attend to, so I couldn't really focus on anything else. This is the commitment I signed up for, and I haven't gotten much pushback from Tessa's teacher or from the school itself.

"We'd love to host your entire family, Xander. I know everything has been a huge adjustment these last few months. Allowing Tessa to be cared for beyond your family in order to attend school hasn't been easy on you. Let her come over and play with my kids while you take a moment to relax as well." Cummings says.

"I am relaxed!" I say, a bit more irritated in my tone than I was hoping to excuse.

"Oh, I know," Cummings says as if to say he thinks the complete opposite.

I can see the small smirk he's holding back, and I can see that my answer alone shows how much tension I'm holding onto in my life.

He continues, "Just check with your family and let me know soon so we can prepare enough food for all of us. My sisters and brother will be there, along with their families and my parents."

Cummings' entire family lives on the East Coast, so they alternate which holiday they will be hosting. It all depends on the hockey season and when and where our games will be held during the holidays. This year, out of convenience, Cummings is taking on the responsibility.

"I'll send a text to my family and ask if they already made plans. I know Tessa would love to hang out with the kids. She's making friends at school, but I haven't felt comfortable with too many play dates yet, as I have yet to meet these kids and their families. Juliette offered to go with Tessa, but I feel like she's done enough for me. I need to find some time to interact with these families myself. Hopefully, over her winter break, I can do just that," I say as we make our way toward the team bus.

We get on the bus and find our seats. I am minutes away from boarding that plane and seeing my Tessa again. My heart feels like it's been pulling toward her, and I can't wait to see her beaming smile.

* * *

We land in the city later than expected as the flight got delayed due to weather. The city is colder now than when I left, the winter fighting the bits of fall that are trying to hold on. I know this cold front is here to stay and most likely worsen, so I shouldn't let this uncontrollable weather upset me, but it has left me in a sour mood. I'm much more inclined to enjoy the warmer months, maybe because I'm in a cold arena most of the day.

Luckily the drive from the airport to my building didn't take too long, now that traffic has died down. I look down at my watch as I ride the elevator, realizing with more certainty that Tessa is most likely sleeping now that I'm arriving this late.

The elevator doors open, and my apartment door is already open, my sister standing there to greet me. I try to leave my piss-poor mood behind, but it's following me. My sister is smiling, but there's something about her demeanor that is a bit reserved. Something happened, and she's holding it in to keep me from imploding. I can tell by her expression.

"Hey, Juliette. What's up?" I can't help my sharp tone, but I know my shitty attitude will get a lot worse from whatever Juliette is about to say.

Juliette closes the door behind me as I set my bags down. She looks up at me, straightening her spine, as if preparing for battle. If she doesn't come out with it soon, she might have me spitting fire, so she better get to it.

"Tessa had a tough day at school."

She's looking anywhere but at me now because she knows when it comes to Tessa, I will burn down anything in my path to see that my daughter's needs are met.

Juliette continues, "She's fine. It was more just little kids being mean to her. But it turns out that she spilled something on her sweater, and when she removed it, some kid started pointing at her glucose monitor and began making fun of her. They said her arm looked robotic and that she was weird."

Now my sister is wringing her fingers together because she knows I'm going to lose my shit with this information.

"Xander, I took care of it. I spoke to Mrs. Lorrent, and I was assured the child was spoken to and it won't happen again. Tessa was quite upset over this, but after school, I took her to her favorite bookstore and got a new book and a treat for her to eat. She seemed to have completely forgotten about it by the time we had dinner with Mom and Dad."

I walk past my sister, going straight to Tessa's room, wanting to see her myself. I know she's sleeping, but I need to see her face after being away for so long. I'm holding in my anger, breathing through my nose. I know I'm about to blow a gasket, but before I ask any questions and possibly breathe fire toward my sister after what she just told me, I just want to see my reason for living before tackling this situation.

I slowly open Tessa's door and see her sound asleep. She's clutching a stuffed platypus that she's had since she was a baby.

It used to be bright white, but now it looks more gray. Even after washing it, it still looks the same, as if the gray is now its new permanent color. Little does she know I have three more of these stuffed animals in the hallway closet in case something happens to "Ducky" and I need a spare.

I close her door, walking away as quietly as I can manage, and meet my sister back in the kitchen. It's spotless, but my sister is wiping the countertops down with a cloth. It's her nervous habit, and she's trying to keep herself occupied, knowing I'm going to lose it and she's going to be a witness to my bad temper.

"So, is the kid expelled?"

My sister stops her circles on the counter with the cloth, dropping her head down. It's only then I realize she's taking a deep breath, her shoulders moving up and down, seeming to try to control herself now with my question. She looks over at me, bewilderment in her gaze.

"For making fun of a kid's glucose monitor? No, Xander, the kid wasn't expelled or suspended. They're five and six-year-old kids in kindergarten. I think this is more a lesson, not an instance where the kid needs to be reprimanded to the fullest extent. Kids are cruel, but it's moments like these that are teachable. I know it's hard for you to wrap your head around it, but kids need to be taught how to treat others, and some need a little more lessons in the matter. Mrs. Lorrent took care of it, and she was completely transparent about what actions were taken when she was made aware of the incident."

I feel my shoulders tense with the mention of her name. Mrs. Lorrent is still a sensitive subject for me. I have felt guilty about my last interaction with her via email, but apparently, all that guilt is put aside right now. My only concern is that Tessa is in a kind environment. I'm pissed, and I itch to let this teacher have a piece of my mind once again.

I'm containing the urge to write an email to her right this instant, but after speaking to my therapist in the last few weeks, she gave me some exercises to try when I feel my not-so-pleasant mood is rising. Instead of reacting immediately, I should let myself calm down. So I'm doing everything I can to do exactly that.

With another deep breath, I ask, "So what were the consequences for the child?"

Juliette has returned to wiping down the already pristine counter, her gaze away from me. I already know I'm not going to like the response.

"The child was spoken to, and that's that. We will see if he messes with Tessa again or if he learned how to be a kind individual."

"That's it?" I ask, my volume rising as I try to keep my daughter from waking up but still exuding the frustration I feel inside.

My sister throws the cloth on the counter and turns toward me.

"You know what, Xander, I think you're forgetting how people can be. Not everything can be controlled, and this isn't just a lesson for the child who was rude to Tessa. This is also a dose of reality for Tessa, too. She needs to see how the world works and how to navigate it. She's got a chronic condition, and not every situation is going to cater to her. I am not trying to be cruel, but I want her to learn how to handle all situations in life.

"I am not going to baby her and not let her experience things in life. If we, as her family, can make sure she knows how to handle these interactions properly, she will navigate them well. She won't crumble when someone says something rude. She will stand taller and excel because she has to figure these things out. We can't expect expulsion or suspension because that's not how life works."

My sister is now the one trying to keep calm as she is exacerbated by this conversation.

"She's six now, Juliette. She's not a teenager who's trying

to avoid being bullied. She's a tiny child who needs protection."

I walk toward the fridge, looking for a drink. I'd love to have some alcohol, but I don't want to feel like shit tomorrow. The joys of aging.

"You know what, Wyatt, you need to pull back a bit and realize that life happens."

The fact my sister is using my first name shows how angry she is. She never addresses me formally unless I'm being an ass, which I clearly am, as I seem to be insinuating blame on the wrong people.

Juliette continues, "And Tessa is protected. You have some nerve to assume that the school doesn't care for her. You don't see the people that surround her and try to do their best to keep Tessa and her classmates happy in an educational environment. It beats the schooling we got, where teachers were high and mighty. This is such a different scenario. And Mrs. Lorrent assured me she would have her eye on this child."

I'm sipping my water as I watch my sister head for the door.

"Look, Jules, I'm sorry." My apology causes my sister's death glare to soften a bit, so I decide to continue. "You know how I get when it comes to Tessa. I will always try to make life easier for her. She's gotten dealt the shitty end of the stick when it comes to her mother and now her health."

"I know, but you are not really putting in the effort to look beyond those two things. You're focusing on the negative that she's had to deal with, but try to take some time to look at the positive. She's such a good kid, and her life is far easier than others. She has an amazing father and an extended family that will bend over backward to see that she is cared for properly. If I felt there was more you could do, I would have called you before you came home. But there's nothing that Mrs. Lorrent hasn't already handled herself. Put some trust in others,

Xander. We are on the same team. It's not about us against them."

She's opening the door, and I stop her with my hand on her shoulder.

"You're right, Jules. I'm sorry for my reaction. I'll take a look at my schedule and see if I can find some time to meet Mrs. Lorrent in person after Thanksgiving."

This seems to appease my sister. She's been on my ass about putting some time into going down to the school and meeting the educator that seems to adore my daughter. I have not had time, but I'll admit that things were working so well recently that I didn't put much energy toward messing with it.

"Okay, Xander, I appreciate you putting in the effort. I don't want you to think I'm upset with caring for Tessa the way I have. But you seem so upset when I make updates like these that I think it would only serve as a positive to meet Mrs. Lorrent yourself. She really is incredible. Her heart is made for this job, and it shows."

She then brings herself up on her tippy toes and kisses my cheek. "Thank you, big bro. I know you're a softie at heart," she laughs as she walks away toward the elevator.

"I have an early meeting tomorrow with the GM, so I'll see you bright and early, right?" I ask my sister as she presses the button for her floor.

"Of course. Tell Tessa I will take her for a cake pop at Starbucks before school."

She laughs as I roll my eyes. My sister is a Starbucks fanatic, and she's making my daughter equally obsessed. But the way my sister loves my daughter, I wouldn't trade it for anything in this world. I'm very lucky to have the family I do. The way they've put their needs aside to help me with Tessa is something I could never repay them for.

I move along in my apartment and get the house in order for me to go to bed. I do one last check on Tessa and head to my room. My mind is going in so many directions, and I know that as a parent, I'm not alone in that feeling. Parenthood is tough, and the more I go through it, especially on my own, without her mother, the tougher it seems to be. The moment I feel like I am grasping something, the route changes, and I have to figure out something new.

The worst part is going through these motions alone. I know my family is here to support me, but I always wonder what it would feel like to have a partner in this with me, bouncing ideas off of to see if this is the right way to handle a situation versus another. I long for that type of companionship.

Before I had Tessa, I was known as a playboy in the NHL world. Dating was something I did when I wasn't on the ice, and I had a hook-up in each city we played in. Now that I have a daughter of my own, it's hard not to cringe at those memories. I had so much pent-up energy after a game, especially a win, that I had to find myself balls-deep in a woman by the end of the night.

However, that all changed when Sabrina told me she was pregnant. I wanted to do what was best for my child, even if the baby wasn't born yet. I knew I had to pull my head out of my ass and be an adult for the sake of this new little baby that would be entering my life.

I thought I was taking those steps with someone who wanted the same thing. Turns out I was fooling myself because the moment I heard my daughter cry, I was the only one captured by her. I felt my world shift, and she was the only reason for my existence from that point on. Add in the fact that I was holding this newborn and walking toward fatherhood completely alone, I had to step it up even more than I realized. I don't regret any decisions I made for Tessa's sake. She needed and still needs a responsible parent to turn to, and I will provide that for her. I will always show up for my girl, no matter what.

I've calmed down a bit and decide to send a quick email to

Tessa's teacher. I need to get a meeting set up to ensure this person knows how serious I am about Tessa's care and how she is treated. It's been a long time coming, and I should have done this before school even started. But the way they hold on to the school assignments until the Friday before school begins, it left me with little time to schedule something before Tessa's first day. Since then, I've been so busy acclimating as a coach with my first team in this position.

Once I get the email sent off, I finish getting ready for bed and lie down. As a joke, I purchased an Alaskan King-sized bed after a dare with an old teammate. I lost the bet, and I had to purchase it a few years back, and this thing is gigantic. It's larger than I ever dreamed, but on nights like this, I feel more alone than I realized.

Seeing the movers try to fit it in this room after getting it transported up to my penthouse apartment in this building was something out of a *Friends* episode. The episode where Ross yells, "PIVOT," is all I thought about when I saw the movers struggling. I smile at the memory, my previous bad mood dissipating a bit.

Hopefully, Tessa can have a good day tomorrow to make up for today's crappy one. It's a half-day on Fridays, and Juliette will pick her up. My day is packed tomorrow, starting early on, so I won't see much of Tessa aside from when she wakes up in the morning. Luckily with her Thanksgiving break, we can have some dedicated time together in the days to come.

Chapter Four

ELODY

I wake up, ready to tackle the last day of school before Thanksgiving break. This year has gone swimmingly, aside from yesterday's issue with Caleb and Tessa. I saw Tessa trying to hold back tears when Caleb decided to be mean toward her. Those two got along great since school started. I don't know what happened to cause him to switch gears and poke fun at Tessa's glucose monitor.

I think the issue was handled well, and Caleb apologized, but the damage was done, and I could see Tessa covering the device as the day carried on. She felt uncomfortable, and that broke my heart.

I expected an email from "Mr. Grumpy" as the day went on, but by the time I went to bed, I still had nothing waiting for me from Xander Christianson. I know he'll have some choice words to give, I can feel it to my core, but somehow, he has kept it to himself.

Maybe he's starting to realize that life is full of unexpected turns. He has to know that I would never put Tessa in a situation that would be cruel or hurtful to her on purpose. Caleb was being a kid, and it's moments like those that make the kids grow in ways that are astonishing.

I still need to get to the bottom of why Caleb's mood toward Tessa has shifted, but for now, I feel like I should praise the fact my ass didn't get chewed out by Tessa's grumpy father. I hate having this outlook on the famous hockey player, but he really hasn't put an effort to see him differently since his choice words a few months back.

I get my day started earlier than anyone else in my house, as I know once all my kids are up, it's a bit chaotic, to say the least. I get myself ready, makeup all set, and my hair up to get through the busy day I have planned for my little kindergarteners.

I have a turkey project they're making for them to use as a centerpiece at their family dinner this coming week, and I'm so excited to do this with them. I have no planned curriculum for the day as there isn't much time on short days like today. It's nice to have an early out on Fridays, but when it's a craft, I wish I had more time to get the art projects done.

I make my way downstairs and begin to get lunches ready to go for my own children. Everything is in order, and I have a few extra minutes to check my email before waking my kids. As I'm walking to retrieve my phone, my sister, Laney, walks into the kitchen. She moved in with me when I relocated to the city, and it's been nice to have her around. She's been through so much, and I don't take a minute for granted after nearly losing her in my past.

"Morning, Laney. Want some coffee?"

My sister grimaces as if the coffee is poison I'm offering her. I hope she isn't coming down with something. She went to bed earlier than all of us last night, skipping dinner, saying she wasn't able to hold anything down.

I grab my phone and realize there's something wrong with my sign-in for my work email, and I was logged out. No wonder I didn't hear a ping early this morning as I got ready for work. The phone must have updated overnight and somehow logged me out. I will never understand technology.

With a sigh, I re-sign in and realize my jubilant demeanor was short-lived. Mr. Christianson *has* reached out. I open the email, nervous about how he's going to respond to me.

Dear Mrs. Lorrent,

I have been away with my team for some games and just returned to find out that Tessa had a tough day. I'm upset about the way she was treated, and I hope this will be rectified before this other child escalates in his poor behavior. To say I'm disappointed is an understatement.

I have some time the week after the Thanksgiving break to meet. Are you around that Tuesday, by any chance? I can do 4 o'clock that afternoon. Please let me know by end of day today so I can ensure I block that time out. I would like to use the time to discuss how Tessa is doing in class and also discuss the matter with this other child in more detail.

Again, I hope there won't be any other issues throughout the day regarding this child and my daughter. I expect you are going to keep an eye out.

Thanks,
    Xander Christianson

I can't help but be annoyed by his email. He sounds condescending, and I just hate how he acts like I'm the shit under his shoe because I'm his daughter's teacher. Maybe it's me, and I'm taking it the wrong way, but he's not really asking me to keep an eye out. He's insinuating that I wasn't doing just that, resulting in this incident yesterday. I must have a strange expression because Laney pipes up as I'm looking at my phone.

"You okay, Ells? You look like you might throw that phone

across the room," she says as she sips on some tea I didn't even see her make.

I look from her down to my phone. I'm still uncertain how I feel about this email. I decide to quickly respond to his email and then address my sister's question.

Mr. Christianson,

Yes, I can meet that day. I will be in my classroom, 103B. If you check in at the front, they will show you where my classroom is situated down the hall. Have a lovely Thanksgiving break.

Sincerely,
    Mrs. Lorrent

There. I was cordial. That's all I can hope for when I interact with parents. It's a little ridiculous that it's been months since school started, and I'm only now going to meet this parent. He is definitely a dick, but let's see if he's as pompous in person as he is behind a screen.

Looking up to meet my sister's gaze, I soften. She looks a little better than last night, so hopefully, whatever it was, it has passed. The Thanksgiving holiday is my favorite, and we always combine our family with Becca's. I love preparing the food and making new memories with everyone. The kids are growing far too fast, and I need to cherish these moments while we are all under one roof.

"Yes, I'm fine. I just had to handle that jackass parent that finds a way to put a damper on my day. I woke up excited about today's craft with my class, but he's a grumpy cloud that sits above my head now. So annoying."

I move around the kitchen, and an idea pops into my head. I turn toward Laney again, seemingly catching her off-guard with my sudden excitement.

I bring my hands up, "I know what we need!" I'm bouncing up and down, my anger simmering by the second. "We need to go have a girls' night. Let's go out to a bar or something tonight. I need to get out of my routine, and I need to let go of this parent that has been the bane of my existence this year."

My sister seems less than enthused, so I pull out all my begging tools I keep in my back pocket. Jutting my bottom lip out, I pout and use the best puppy eyes I can.

"Pretty please, Laney. It will be fun. We'll find a place that's not too crowded."

I move toward her and put my head on her shoulder, hoping that will win her over. She doesn't like big crowds or loud sounds, so I know her limits. I can cater to them as long as I can get out.

"I know a place down the street that has throwback nights on Fridays, and I saw a sign for a nineties night tonight. It would be so much fun. I know Becca would love to join. She's been moping since Shane left, and she has the night off."

I look up again at my sister, as she is taller than me. I can see her giving in the moment she gives me a little smile in return.

"Fine. Under one condition—I can invite Grant," she says.

Grant is Becca's younger brother, and he and my sister are best friends. Laney and Grant known one another since they were in diapers, and their friendship is one I know she cherishes. I always thought they'd end up together, but even entering their thirties, they're still claiming friendship is all they have between one another. I know there has to be something else there. The way they gravitate toward one another is pretty telling.

"Of course, Grant can come! Oh, I'm so excited!" I can't contain this burst of energy this has given me.

I walk toward the kitchen island, grab my phone, and text Becca. I can already feel my bad mood dissipating. It's early, but I know Becca's up getting her household in order before school, too. The moment I press send, I already see the little bubbles pop up, indicating she's responding.

She's my ride or die, and she is one of my favorite people. I hope she's up for a night out because I need this. It's been too long. We usually stay in and hang out at one another's homes, but this will be fun. Dressing up and hitting the town will definitely pull me out of this funk. Missing Beau, along with dealing with this annoying parent, I need this night to hang with my girls.

"Becca's in!" I shout a little too loudly.

Laney is looking at me funny, maybe feeling like I need to refrain from the caffeine, but I bound up the steps and start waking my kids up. Luckily, Tyler has a free night, and he's up for watching his sisters for me. Maybe I should have made sure I had a sitter before making plans, but it seems that aside from a student's grumpy parent, things are starting to perk up for me today.

* * *

Today was so fun with the kids. I think everyone was ready for the week break, and it showed in how excited all the kids were when they completed their turkey centerpieces. Each one shoved their masterpiece in the face of their parents who picked them up. Where I hold excitement, many of these parents look overwhelmed at the fact they have to entertain these kids for the next week.

I remember having only Thursday and Friday off for Thanksgiving week and always hating how quickly it passed by. It's nice to get the entire week now. For those who travel to visit loved ones, this is a great time to get out of town. In our case, we have stayed locally since moving to the city, and my parents come out to visit. This year, Beau's family will not come our way, as they claim to have some renovations occurring at their home. I wish they'd come this way every once in a while. The change of scenery could do them some good.

The holidays always bring up a lot of emotions for all of us due to Beau's absence. Even though we've done this a handful of times before, I feel that emptiness without him near me the same way I did the first holiday after he passed. Right now, it's hitting hard, seeing the kids growing up and knowing he's never going to be a part of these memories. My heart breaks each time I think too much about it.

I'm getting the mess cleaned up around my classroom, and I check my computer. No new emails from Mr. Christianson. I roll my eyes at how condescending he sounded in his last email to me. I always try to find the positive, but I'm having a hard time shaking this irritation he has caused me. I wish he understood how much I love each of my kids in the classroom, especially how much I adore his little girl.

Tessa has really captured my heart in a way I haven't experienced before with my other students, past and present. She has these beautiful eyes that seem to tug at my soul in ways I never thought possible. When she goes to the nurse at recess, she'll sometimes come in here after instead of heading off to the playground, and she helps me set up for the next activity the class will work on. She's so much fun to talk to, and I just see so much light in her.

It's hard to process how this beautiful creation came from what I've come to see as such a grump of a father. He doesn't exude much happiness in the correspondence we've shared. I keep reminding myself that it most likely comes from a place of pure love he has for his daughter. He simply fails to see how much love I hold for his child while she's in my care throughout the day.

I try to let my irritation for Xander Christianson go as I put the finishing touches throughout the classroom. I love decorating for the holidays, and now that Thanksgiving will be over by the time we return, the kids will come back to a room full of holiday cheer. I have all the holidays honored here, and I have weekly crafts we will focus on to work on the dexterity of their fingers, along with helping them understand there is more than just Christmas occurring in December.

I grab my belongings and head toward the door. My girls are waiting for me outside my classroom when I open the door to the hallway and seem to be anxious to head out.

"Mom, will Tyler let us stay up late tonight when he's watching us?" Hannah asks before even acknowledging me and how my day was.

"My day was wonderful, Han. Thanks so much for asking," I respond back, a little smirk marking my features.

"Sorry, Mom. I'm glad your day was good. Can Tyler let us stay up a little later? There's a YouTuber I want to see livestream some new holiday blind boxes, and they're supposed to be limited edition. I need to see them. Can I, Mom? Please?"

She's got her hands clasped in front of her, as if she's praying for me to give this one request to her. I wonder if that's how I looked this morning when I was begging my sister to come out with me tonight.

Also, what's up with kids these days and these damn blind boxes? What is the appeal? You shove so much money toward an unknown item, and then what? I think they're paying for the thrill and not the actual item, and I honestly can't wrap my head around it. But I relent because Hannah doesn't ask for much.

"As long as you help Tyler put the dirty dishes in the dishwasher like you're supposed to and get ready for bed without too much prompting, I will tell him you can watch this live event. What time does it end?" I ask as I walk down the hallway with them and out of the school.

The late fall chill is in full effect, and I cannot imagine how much colder it's going to get as the weeks progress.

I pull Mia closer to my side, as I see her shivering while we are walking. Hannah is rambling on and on about this YouTuber and this new collection that's being released. She has recently gotten into these little blind box items and she cannot stop talking about them. Her entire Christmas list revolves around getting these or asking for money for her to purchase said items.

Our house is close to the school, and we are soon home and ready to unwind for the holiday week ahead. Tyler was out early since he didn't have basketball practice after school and I find him in the family room with a large bowl of cereal and the television on to some Netflix Marvel show he loves to rewatch. He looks over at us as we walk through the house, pulling all our layers off and trying to warm up with the heat in the home.

"Hey, Mom. Han, Mia, how was the last day before break?"

The girls run over, but he's too quick and jumps up, bowl in hand, and starts a mad dash to the kitchen to avoid his little sisters from tickling him. The girls know how ticklish he is, and they never miss an opportunity to try and pin him down and make him laugh to the point of tears. Tyler is the most patient teen I've met, and I don't know what I'd do without him. He doesn't push me on matters I feel strongly about and always offers to help where needed.

I smile toward them, and that tightness returns in my chest. With all the laughter, a part of me constantly feels the pain of being a widower. I miss my partner. I miss having someone to share these moments with. I simply miss being loved in that way.

I make my way to the kitchen, making myself a coffee and grabbing a book to take to my room.

"Hey, kids, I'm going to unwind a bit before I head out tonight with Aunt Laney and Aunt Becca. Want me to order the pizza at five o'clock tonight?" I hear the kids yell back that it works for them, and I head up the stairs.

Once in my room, I set my drink and book down at my bedside table and sit on the edge of my bed. I look over to the family photo we took as a complete family before Beau's diagnosis. The smiles we share are something I never took for granted, but it's hard to see my happiness in that moment, so naive about what was soon to come.

It's been over five years since Beau passed away, and many of the painful moments still feel so fresh to me. But in many other ways, our lives look so different; it's hard not to feel like so much has happened since his death. I pull the frame into my hands, my fingers tracing Beau's face. His smile was always so vibrant, and it was one of my favorite things about him. He was not just a father to our children and my husband, but he was a good person. It's hard not to hold anger in my heart toward his fate.

Much like the day he died and my promise not to love another person, I have stayed true to that feeling. Since Beau's passing, I have not been with another man. I have not dated, nor have I looked at someone else in a romantic way. It feels like my heart was buried with him. I feel like a part of me will never return. It's as if a light went out that day when he took his last breath, and I feel nothing toward anyone else romantically.

Many people may rebel and go out and hook up with others to try to soothe the pain. That's not me. I want to feel the pain of losing Beau so I never forget how he impacted all our lives. He was my heart and my soul. And even though I live for my children now, I still feel like I belong to Beau in many ways. My vows from our marriage go beyond death because I don't feel like anything can part us. I have chosen to stay alone in that way since he left us. And I can't help but feel that's what I'm supposed to do.

A knock on my door interrupts my thoughts, and I hear Laney on the other end, asking if she can come in. I wipe the stray tear that has made its way down my cheek and put the framed photo back on the nightstand.

"Come in!" I say, and soon enough, the door is slowly being opened.

The moment I see my sister, I smile. I may have been through a lot in losing my spouse, but she lost so much before her life really even started. So, I will always show my sister light, even in my darker moments, because she needs that kind of strength by her side.

"Hey. How was your day?" she asks me as she moves to sit by my side.

She rests her head on my shoulder, and I can't help but bring my arm around her and run my fingers through her hair. She might be an adult, but she'll always be my little sister. I still remember how excited I was to have my very own baby to hold and play with when she was born. She's been such a blessing to us all, and to think she could have been taken from us still causes my heart to constrict.

"My day was good, aside from shitface Christianson emailing me this morning. I didn't let him bring me down though," I say with a little chuckle.

I feel her body shake, and I know I made her laugh, too. I was never one to cuss much, but since Beau's passing, I've let that side of me go a bit more, and I'm enjoying this new vocabulary I'm putting into the rotation.

"I'm glad you pushed past the negativity from him, sis," Laney says, looking down at me with those beautiful emerald eyes we all love.

"What time should we head over to Becca's house tonight? Are we eating here, or should we grab a bite there?"

"I think we can head out close to six, and we can eat there. I am ordering a pizza for the kids, and I have no energy to cook for just the two of us."

I hate dirtying dishes if I don't have to. Plus, a night with no need to cook before days of endless cooking to prepare for Thanksgiving sounds like the best idea yet.

Laney gets up and starts to walk toward my bedroom door.

"I think I'll go get ready then. I have no idea what to wear," she's fiddling with her hair, and I can see her anxiety coming out.

"Laney, are you sure you can handle going out tonight? I understand if you aren't up for it. I should have never made it sound like you couldn't say no to me."

I feel guilty. This morning, I wasn't thinking, and I made it sound like there was no other option but to go out with me.

"No, I want to go. I think it will be good. I haven't felt the best lately, so the distraction will help. Yoga isn't getting me out of this funk, and I napped earlier, so I should be energized," she says, another yawn pulling through after she finishes her sentence.

"You took a nap?" I stare at her, my eyes doubling in size.

My sister never naps, and here she is napping in the middle of the day? That's truly unlike her.

"Yeah, I was surprised too. I was reading one of my latest library picks and fell asleep in the middle of the second chapter. I woke up with drool on my face."

She's laughing at that thought, and I can't help but love the sound of her laughter. I don't get to hear it as much anymore, so it warms my heart to know she's finding some joy in life where she can.

It's in that moment I realize I need to let go and let my hair down tonight. I'm holding onto too much pain from my past and I need to simply live freely for the night. I know romance isn't in the cards for my heart, but I could let loose and enjoy these moments I have in front of me.

I grab my coffee, realizing it's now more cold than hot, and take a sip. I need the caffeine in whatever form I can get it. I let

Laney know I'm going to hop in the shower and start getting ready. She makes her way back to her room to do the same. I can't wait to hang out with my girls tonight. It's been long overdue.

***

We're dancing, and it's good to feel this free. I haven't danced in what feels like forever, and the fact I got Laney and Becca out with me tonight feels like a huge feat. I'm moving my hips to the beat, my sister by my side, with Becca on my other.

Grant joined us a few songs ago, and the smile on my sister's face doubled in size. Why she doesn't just admit her feelings for him is something I will never understand. If my story doesn't prove it, her past should teach her that life is too short to let things and people pass you by. I don't know who she's fooling; these two have definitely done the deed. However, I'm not going to push her to admit it until she's ready.

Soon, Laney is wrapping her arms around me and saying goodbye. She's tired, and Grant will walk her home. Although I've known him since he was in diapers, it's hard to wrap my head around him being a full-blown adult with a career he loves. He hugs me goodbye and kisses his sister on the cheek. I doubt he'll make it back to her place and will likely crash on my couch instead, much like he's done in the past. I look at Laney one last time and realize she is socially drained. I'm so proud of her for coming out, though. This isn't her scene, but I think the dancing and time together were good for her.

Becca and I throw our hands up in the air and continue dancing, continuing to sway our hips, and embracing our forties just like we've talked about before. I can't change how life has hurt me, but I can choose how I take each step forward. My heart will always miss him, but I don't have to constantly feel the pain of his loss in all my movements.

I push any sadness that feels like it's erupting to the surface and keep dancing my night away. I open my eyes to see someone I haven't laid eyes on in over twenty-five years. Shane Philips, looking as handsome as ever seems to focus only on my best friend, who is oblivious to his presence right now. He was out of town, and she had no inclination he would be surprising her. Neither did I. I let him wrap his arms around her from behind, and her eyes look like they're going to bulge out of her eye sockets. She quickly realizes who it is, and a smile overcomes her face.

As much as Shane's sudden departure from our lives really hurt all of us, it's hard not to love him all over again because he truly gives Becca the devotion she deserves now that he's back in her life. It doesn't mean I'm going to forgive him so easily, even if my friend seems to have done exactly that.

I eye him, giving him the meanest glare I can muster. When he looks up to meet my gaze, I can see he doesn't know what to say or how to react. He didn't only leave Becca behind; he left me, his friend from childhood, along with my husband, who was his best friend. He never reached out after Beau's passing, and I always held on to the hope that would bring Shane back to us. I can't help but want to bring that up with him and see how he'll answer for his shitty behavior.

"Look who decided to finally be a part of Becca's life again. How convenient, after all, she did it all without you, didn't she? Never mind the fact you never returned to be with Beau. He could have used a friend by his side when he was fighting for his life."

Holy crap. Did I just say that to Shane out loud? I can see I'm not the only one shocked by my words. I am not usually this feisty. But Shane hurt me so much, not just in his actions toward me and my family, but in leaving Becca behind to take care of everything he left in his departure.

Shit, I can feel the tears creeping up now. I do not want to cry. Ugh, I hate being an emotional mess. I shake my head, looking up toward the ceiling in hopes the tears will reverse.

Luckily, it seems I've kept them at bay, and I return my sights on Shane.

Shane begins to speak, his arms up as if shielding himself from my wrath.

"I know I've done a lot of things wrong, Ellie, and for that, I will always be sorry. But I'm here now, and my love for Becca never wavered. You have to understand I was young and dumb, and I had no idea what I was doing. I made the wrong choices, and I know each day I live will always hold that pain, but I hope that each step forward from now on will be ones we can smile and look back on as happier times for us all."

His words surprise me. I thought he'd put up a fight, but it seems all these years have left him feeling more sadness than anger, and for that, I'm appreciative. He needs to understand he didn't just hurt Becca. And he left behind a life I thought he would have run toward when Becca's path shifted gears. I feel the tension dissipate from my shoulders, and I look at him with less anger and more sadness. I know that no matter how much he apologizes, he's going to have to live with his decisions, and that might be punishment enough at this point.

"I suppose life is too short to hold grudges. But you better not fuck up this time, Shane. Losing Beau has shown me that life is precious and should be lived to the fullest. What you did in the past was wrong. But the way you show up now will hopefully soften the blow. Because what you did, in many ways, is unforgivable. But my love for Becca goes beyond myself, and I will try to remember that as we move forward as friends."

As I say this to him, I pat him on his cheek. I feel like they need some time together, and I need a minute to figure out where this woman within me emerged from. I am never verbal in that way, but I guess there's always room for growth in a person. I think Beau's passing really did cause a shift within myself. If you had asked me ten years ago how I'd react to Shane's return, I would have said I would have been seething but possibly not say a thing so I didn't upset Becca. Seeing that I let out my feelings but didn't ruin anything between Becca and me nor between Shane and Becca brings me comfort. It's okay to feel things, but it should be said so that resolution can be made.

I start walking off the dance floor, in the direction of the bar. I'm parched, so I continue until I reach my destination. The bartender gives me a megawatt smile, and I can't help but smile back. This is as far as my flirting will go. He's cute, definitely ten years younger, and I am no longer that girl.

My soulmate left me long ago, not by his choosing. He took my heart with him, and no matter how much life he wanted me to live in his absence, I don't see myself giving any piece of me to another man. I know my role as a wife and partner is in the past, and I am comforted to know I loved in that capacity to the fullest when my husband was still alive.

Waiting for my water, I'm people watching as the bartender is getting orders from everyone across the bar. I get my water and begin sipping it slowly. I am not used to being out this late. I'm usually curled up on the couch and reading a good book or watching some reality television with Laney and Becca. This isn't my scene, and I'm laughing at myself for suggesting a night out in this way. But I think nights like these are good for the soul every once in a while. My kids are home safe, and I can spend some extra time getting out every now and then.

My gaze cuts back to the dance floor, and I see my bestie cozying up with Shane, their movements slower than the beat of the song, but it seems they could care less. They only have eyes for one another, and they don't give a rat's ass what's going on around them. A small smile spreads across my lips as I see her getting pieces of the life she once dreamed of in the arms of the man I know she never stopped loving.

I keep moving my gaze across the bar, and soon, I lock in on a set of eyes that are looking back at me. He looks dangerous in many ways. I take in his dirty blond hair, stubble along his jaw and face, his blue eyes that look so clear even from this far away, and the tattoo he has on his left hand. The design looks to go further up his arm, but his long sleeves cover the rest of his upper body.

I have never found tattoos attractive. Beau was clean-cut in every way possible. His hair was styled with gel daily, and his facial hair meticulously shaved each morning. He had not one drop of ink on his body. And he was the small-town boy I fell in love with, just older with each year we shared together.

This guy across the bar though? He's the opposite of Beau in every single way. I can't take my eyes off him, and before I register what he's doing, he's standing from the stool and making his way over toward me. He's still scowling, but it doesn't seem menacing. It seems more alluring than anything, and I'm captivated. My heart rate picks up, and I feel like my hands are sweating, even with a cold cup of water in my hand. I watch as he makes his way toward me, people pulled into a trance by him, much like I am, staring at him as he takes a step closer to me.

Soon, he's right in front of me, and he's towering over me. This guy is big. His muscles bulge from his shirt, his beer bottle looks miniature in his large hand, and his gaze is even more intense when he's less than a foot in front of me.

Then he does something I least expect. He leans down, his lips mere inches from my skin, and he whispers in my ear, "I wonder if I were to reach into your panties if I would find them soaked for me."

Chapter Five

WYATT

I don't know how I find myself in this dive bar, but here I am. It seems the scowl I've sported all night is working because even with people recognizing me, they sense I do not want to be disturbed. I'm sipping my beer, looking around the crowded dance floor as people gyrate to the sounds of nineties music. I am more of a country song lover than this hip hop, but I also understand it's hard not to want to move when you're rubbing up against people.

Before becoming a father, I was always at scenes like these. I knew where to find puck bunnies, and I can't lie about how I enjoyed that part of my hockey life. But being the grumpy teammate was always part of my persona. The women ate that shit up too.

I won't even hide the fact that women love a man who has that permanent scowl on their face. I've been told it adds to my mysterious side, not that it was my intention to do so. I used that to my advantage until I had diaper duty most nights waiting for me at home. I always enjoyed my away games to meet my needs, but it never went further than that.

I know, I sound disgusting, but I was stressed and needed a release. I wasn't a saint and I never claimed to be. My life was always about hockey and hockey only. Although the perks of professional sports is the female attention and I didn't lack in that department. The only thing is, that changed drastically when Tessa came into my life.

I knew introducing Tessa to a woman was a step I was not ready for, and I am always extremely protective of my personal life and my daughter. That has resulted in me not dating around her, and I don't see that changing anytime soon.

My eyes scan the bar, and soon, I see a petite blond walking up to the bar to ask for a drink. I watch the bartender admire her. What is he, twenty? Fucking hell. Could his smile get any wider? Is he trying to show her his molars? I roll my eyes because I could give two fucks what anyone in this bar does, but I can't take my eyes off her. She is gorgeous, and I don't think she's even aware of it.

She's a tiny little thing, and she's smiling at absolutely no one in particular. There's something deeper though. I can see she's using that smile to hide her emotions. Something about the way she smiles and how it doesn't reach her eyes comes off as forced. I don't know who she's trying to convince about her happiness: herself or others. And something about her makes me want to take away whatever pain life has brought her. I feel compelled to continue looking at her because she's mesmerizing. Unlike many women, she's completely natural.

She looks like a woman who has lived life and hasn't tried to hide it. Her face seems to have laugh lines, and she's not overcompensating in her attire. She is dressed much like a woman who is comfortable in her body would. She isn't trying to be someone she's not, aside from that smile she is forcing on her face.

She looks around again and stops at the dance floor. Something in her gaze softens, and her smile now appears more genuine. It's evident she spots something that seems to bring her joy.

She continues moving her gaze, her eyes scoping out the

joint, much like I was doing prior to seeing her. Suddenly, her eyes move closer to my vicinity at the bar, and the minute they connect with mine, I feel like I can't breathe. She's one of the most beautiful women I have ever laid my eyes on, and her energy is pulling me to stand up and walk toward her. I don't even know what I'm going to say, but knowing me, I will say the first thing that comes to mind, which is likely sexual and inappropriate to see her react.

I move across the bar until I'm standing right in front of her. She could reach her hand out and touch me, and I can't even say I'd be mad about it. It's been too damn long since I've been touched in a sexual way, and my body is radiating with this need to be touched by her and her alone.

She's looking up at me, and her eyes look even more beautiful up close. The blue in them is much darker than I expected. Her eyes feel like I'm looking into a blue abyss, the layers telling me her story is much more complex than she lets on. Her blond hair is in waves down her back, and she's craning her neck to keep her gaze locked on mine.

Before I can think twice about it, I find myself bending down to say something in her ear. The moment I get closer, I see her body shiver at my proximity, her breaths accelerating. I bet if I put my hand on her throat, I'd feel the thumping of her pulse increasing.

"I wonder if I were to reach into your panties if I would find them soaked for me."

I pull my face away from her ear, enough to see her face, but stay in her personal space.

My words have the intended reaction. She gasps slightly at them, and I feel a smirk move across my face. She doesn't seem irritated by my words. I can tell by her hooded eyes and the blush that creeps up her cheeks that she likes what I said to her, and I can't help but feel a sense of satisfaction moving through my body. She exudes innocence, and I can bet my left nut no one ever speaks to her in this manner.

I'm loving the goosebumps I see popping up along her skin. I love the element of surprise when I speak to a woman, but for some reason, I need more from this one. Aside from the pain I saw in her smile earlier, she's a mystery I would love a closer look at. I look down at her hands, which are holding a cup of water as if it's her lifeline. I don't see a wedding ring on her finger, so I assume I'm not overstepping.

I sense with the way she's looking at me, she has no clue who I am. I keep my gaze on her, allowing the silence to stretch on. I have yet to hear her voice.

"I guess there's only one way to find out," she responds, taking me by surprise.

By the way her eyes widen, I think she just surprised herself. I see her blush deepen along her cheeks as she's just registering what she said out loud and not in her head. I feel my smile tug to one side. This girl is full of surprises already and we just started this interaction. I wonder what else I could say to get her to say.

"Well, Sunshine, I bet we can find a corner somewhere in this bar to find out."

I take a sip of my beer, and she watches my lips wrap around the bottle. She bites down on her bottom lip as I feel the coldness of my beer hit my tastebuds. I wonder what her lips would look like wrapped around my cock.

She's watching my Adam's apple bob as I swallow, and I can't help but feel immensely turned on by this girl. She must realize she's staring at my lips and neck and quickly moves her eyes back up to look straight at me.

She moves to put her water on the bar and says, "I need to use the restroom. Please excuse me."

Before I can even answer her, she's walking toward the restrooms in the back of the bar. She looks over her shoulder as she's moving, maybe checking to see if she did indeed just speak to me in that provocative way. I look right back at her, leaving a smirk across my face.

I put my beer down when she disappears toward the back, and I begin my walk to the same spot she disappeared to. I stand in the hallway, hidden from everyone else. The bass of the music causes the walls to thump along the beat, the lights from the dance floor giving some illumination to this section of the hallway. But for the most part, it's dark over in this corner, and someone would have to come looking to see me standing here.

Soon, the bathroom door swings open, and I see my mystery friend stop in her tracks when she notices me standing there. Her eyes widen, and she walks toward me, a little less composed than she had been a minute ago. She moves past me and proceeds to lean her back against the wall next to me.

Whatever this pull I'm feeling is for this woman, I can't put my finger on the why behind it. I move, and soon, I'm caging her in with my palms, holding steady on each side of her face. Instinctively, she brings her hands to my biceps and seems surprised by the muscles underneath my long-sleeve shirt. She bites her bottom lip again and moves her gaze from top to bottom, assessing my body as she does so. I feel like my skin is on fire where her fingers are touching my T-shirt. I need to touch this woman, or I feel like I might combust.

I move my head toward the side of her face, letting my nose trail along her jaw. She moves her head to give me easier access, and I see fresh goosebumps line her skin as I inhale her sweet coconut scent. She smells like summer, which I should expect as she seems to be a ray of sunshine, even if there's a storm hidden in those eyes.

I move my lips close to her ear, much like I did not too long ago, and I hear her whimper a bit with my lips near her body.

I whisper, "So, Sunshine, how wet are you for me?"

I hear her intake of breath, and I know she's feeling this attraction between us. I feel like sparks might go off if we don't put out this heat between us. Her hands move from my biceps to my chest, down toward my abdomen. I can't help but tense my muscles as she moves her fingers down this path. It feels like her touch is leaving a mark where she trails her fingertips.

I grab onto her earlobe with my lips, sucking and feeling her melt into me. She grabs onto my shirt, pulling me closer to her body. I take one of my hands off the wall and move it to her throat, putting a little pressure there. I feel her pulse throbbing erratically under my fingers. I like to be rough, and for some reason, I'm taking a huge leap with this one and showing her a side of me I feel almost certain she has never experienced with another person.

Her eyes are molten as I squeeze her a bit around her neck, and I feel the uptick of her pulse. Curiosity and heat are all I get back in her gaze, and it compels me to keep moving forward, pushing her limits in the way I like to feel with my partners.

I move my lips to kiss her, and she moves her face to the side, dodging my kiss. I almost pull back, but then I trail kisses down her jaw and her neck while her moans get swallowed by the loud music on the dance floor. My touch alone already initiates such a response from her, I am feeling all my resolve melt the longer my hands are on her. I need more, and I know she wants me to take her there.

I move my hands off her neck and begin to trail down her chest and her abdomen. Despite the cold, she's got a skirt on with dark tights covering her legs. I trail my hand down the outer portion of her thigh, only to ascend my fingers on the inner part of her leg, toward her center.

"Is this okay?" I ask, consent being at the forefront of my mind before I take this any further.

She nods.

"No, Sunshine. I need words. I need to hear you say you want me to fuck you with my hand," I whisper into her ear, hanging off of what she's about to say.

She moves her head back to meet my gaze, determination

evident in the way she is looking at me, and she finally speaks, "Yes, I want you to touch me and make me forget about the pain."

So, she is hiding behind that sunny disposition. I don't have time to focus on that just this second, so I table that for later.

Then I'm moving my hand to the seam, ripping a hole to get my hands where I want them. The moment I touch the outside of her underwear, I feel how wet she is.

"Fuck, Sunshine, you're soaking. Is this all for me?"

She nods her head, unable to form words. I get it, as I'm having a hard time firing on all cylinders, knowing this girl is so turned on by me, and we've only exchanged words up to this point.

I move her panties to the side, and I move my fingers through her folds. She is dripping for me, and my dick could not be more at attention than he is right now. He's seen my hand for far too long, and he's aching from me simply touching her pussy.

"Sunshine, you're making me so hard."

I move my hips to prove my point, my erection rubbing up on her belly, and she welcomes the friction in any way she can get it. I begin moving my fingers through her folds and take one finger and push it inside her. The moment I do, she moans, and her head falls back, arching her back away from the wall behind her. I quickly look around to make sure no one is around us. I want these moans all to myself. I could live for these sounds she's giving me, and I already crave more. What is going on with me? I am never this invested in a girl from just touching her like this.

I begin to move my fingers in and out. Before long, I'm adding another finger, and she's riding my hand. She still won't let me kiss her lips, so I continue to run my tongue down her neck and kiss her from her ear down to her collarbone.

She is not holding back with her sounds, and soon, I feel her walls constricting me. She's about to fall over the edge, and I'm here for it. She keeps moaning, unsure of what to say. She seems so consumed by her orgasm that she just keeps moaning, seemingly hard to form words. Her eyes are tightly shut, and she's moving her hips to the rhythm that gets her to climax, and I would be lying if I said I have seen something more beautiful. She's mesmerizing, and I haven't even fucked her yet.

"Fuck yeah, Sunshine. Fall off that cliff. Come for me."

That's all she needed to hear, and she tightens her grasp on my biceps and rides out her orgasm until she begins to slow her movements. Soon, I see a smile spread across her face, sated and fulfilled.

I pull my hand out, and I can't help but put those same fingers in my mouth to taste her. Fuck, she even tastes sweet. Her breathing still erratic, she slowly begins to open her eyes and catches me licking her arousal off my fingers.

Her eyes seem to register what I just did, and she straightens. She smooths her skirt down and starts to take in what just happened. I can see her putting all the pieces together, and at first, I think she feels regret. But the longer she looks at me and processes what just occurred, I think shame is a better term to use for what she's feeling.

"I'm so sorry. I should have never let that happen. I have to go. I don't even know your name. I don't know what I'm doing. This isn't me. I'm not this person."

She's frazzled, and I have no idea how to take in her behavior. She said she wanted me to do that, yet she seems to be regretting what just happened between us while I'm over here feeling like I had an out-of-body experience and I didn't even get my dick wet.

"Well, for starters, my name is Wyatt, and there's no need to apologize, Sunshine. I think that was the hottest thing I've ever seen."

I smile at her; truer words have never been spoken. I'm enthralled by this woman. She whips her head up and looks into my eyes at what I've just said.

"No, no, no, no, no. I shouldn't have done this. I'm a mother. I should have never come out. I can't believe I did this."

She's pushing me away.

"Sorry, Wyatt, to leave you hanging," she motions to my very noticeable bulge that I can't even care about because I'm starting to wonder if I've messed with a married woman.

"There's no ring on your finger. Are you married?"

I can't help but ask because that is a hard limit for me. I do not fuck around with anyone in a committed relationship. I have seen too many things happen to teammates who did that to their spouse or partner, and I do not want to be the wedge to drive families apart.

"Yes, I am married, and I just did something I promised myself I would never do."

With that, she turns and runs off to the dance floor. I can't even follow her because I feel sick. I've done something I judged people for doing, and here I am, doing exactly that. I should have asked before I touched her. She had no ring, and I simply assumed. People remove their rings for whatever reason these days. And here I am, touching a woman that is someone else's. And she just said she has kids. What have I done?

Chapter Six

ELODY

I shut the door behind me, and I feel all my sensations are on overdrive. I can't calm my speeding heartbeat, and I feel completely conflicted after what just happened in the bar. I rest my back against my front door, hearing the voices of Shane and Becca grow further away as they walk themselves home a few doors down. I kept my composure the entire walk back to the house, but now I can't help but close my eyes, allowing the tears to cascade down my cheeks.

I just came down from one of the most intense highs I've ever experienced, and it was all done by a man who isn't my husband. I'm trying to calm my breaths, but I can't seem to let go of the guilt I'm feeling. I just had an orgasm by someone else, and for those few minutes, I didn't think of Beau. In all honesty, I didn't think about anyone except myself.

When I looked into Wyatt's eyes, it was as if I was pulled into an alternate universe where all my past pain didn't exist. But the moment I fell off that cliff and experienced that euphoric state, my reality came crashing back to the forefront of my mind. I'm a mother. I'm a teacher. I *am* a wife. Yes, my husband is no longer here physically, but I do not feel disconnected from his soul. He lives in me, and tonight, I disrespected his memory. I let go so much that I forgot about him as I let another man touch me.

I slide down the door until my butt is on the ground, and I hug my knees together. Since Beau's death, I haven't even looked at another man romantically. I haven't been held or kissed by someone that wasn't my Beau. When we began dating in high school, we were each other's first, and from there, all our firsts were shared together. I planned on being his forever, and he mine. Little did I know his life would be cut short. But I still felt like, although he was no longer here physically, I would honor our vows beyond his life. And now I feel like I'm going to be sick from the guilt that is plaguing me.

I don't know how long I sit at the front door, letting the waves of guilt pass over me. The tears stop flowing, my eyes are puffy, and my body is beyond exhausted. I have to pull it together because tomorrow is the start of Thanksgiving break, and I know how busy the week ahead will be for all of us.

I pull myself off the ground and make sure the front door is locked. I turn off the lights as I move through my home, making my way to the kitchen. The layout of my house is similar to Becca's; however, our taste in furniture is vastly different. She's got more of a farmhouse vibe for her decor, whereas I have much more color and patterns throughout the walls and furniture. Nothing about the color I've splashed around my home is bringing light to my mood. The dark cloud of guilt is obscuring my vision now. Once I'm in the kitchen, I decide to make some tea to hopefully calm my nerves.

While the kettle is heating up the water, I sit with the empty mug in front of me. I close my eyes, and flashes of light blue eyes take over my vision. I rub my eyes in hopes I can erase what happened tonight. I still feel my heart beating erratically, and I try to use my breath to ease the panic taking over my body. I'm in my own world when I hear someone walk behind me, and I gasp.

I turn myself around to find Grant in my kitchen, looking at me with concern as he moves toward the refrigerator to grab some cold water. I completely forgot he was here and it's only now I realize he wasn't sleeping on the couch when I walked by. I put my hand over my heart, hoping I can keep it from bursting out of my chest.

"I'm sorry if I scared you, Ellie. My time zones are all out of whack, and I can't fall asleep. Laney is sleeping, so I thought I'd come down here instead of tossing and turning."

It's only now that I notice Grant is in nothing but basketball shorts. I must have a puzzled look on my face because he continues to explain himself.

"Please don't ask me any questions regarding your sister and me. I am as confused about everything as you are, so there's no use in trying to decode this thing between Laney and me."

A soft smile crosses my features. I know my sister has been through a lot, and I can tell she is pushing Grant away romantically. But it's hard to resist his charm. Grant has tan skin that looks like it's constantly warmed by the sun, a surfer's body with lean muscles throughout his features. However, the most captivating thing about Grant, much like his sister Becca, is his eyes. His eyes feel like they pull you in, in a way that you can't focus on anything or anyone else when he gives you his attention.

Growing up, even though he spent much of his childhood and teenage life here in the city once Becca was in college, I watched as girls stopped what they were doing to watch him when he entered the room. The thing is, he's always had a love for my sister, even after all these years. I know that whatever confusion he's feeling, it's my sister's doing because if Grant had any say, he'd be all in. I can tell from the way he looks at her whenever she enters the room that she holds his heart in her hands. The question is, what will she do with it?

"I won't pry, Grant. I understand it's complicated with

Laney," I say, hoping he doesn't ask why I look like a sad dog at the pound.

My electric kettle clicks, indicating the water is fully boiled, so I turn toward it and pour it into the mug.

"Do you want some tea? It can help you settle so you can hopefully get some sleep."

I look over my shoulder and see Grant shrug and nod. I reach up and grab an extra mug and begin the whole process for him.

"I put a little extra honey to make it sweeter than usual. It was a trick my grandmother used to do for us when we were having a hard time sleeping. No clue if it works, but it's a habit I can't seem to break."

I hand the mug to him, and he accepts with a smile stretched across his face. We both take a seat at the kitchen island, sipping our hot teas without saying much.

"Do you want to talk about it?" He is looking into his mug, as if he's asking this question of his hot beverage and not me.

I think everyone feels like they're walking on eggshells when dealing with a widower. There's no playbook for spouses in my shoes, let alone the family surrounding them. We all do the best we can, and we navigate struggles together in whatever way we see fit. Grant has always been like a little brother to me, even if he's over six feet tall and no longer talks with a lisp due to the missing teeth he had as a child.

"I just found myself in a position I promised I wouldn't be, and I am feeling guilty. Trying to process how I feel without having a meltdown," I say, feeling like if there's anyone I'd like to talk to, Grant feels like a good sounding board at this hour.

I take a few more sips, my gaze on my drink, and I can feel Grant's attention on the side of my face.

"You know, Ellie, I have no idea what it's like to be in your shoes. I can't imagine living a life without the person you expected to have all your moments with, suddenly taken from you too soon. But I do know what it's like to imagine a life without someone you love after watching your Laney's experience. I feel like my breath is only possible, knowing Laney is safe and healthy. I know you're my sister's best friend and the sister to the woman I love."

I can't help but look at him with shock at his declaration.

"What? You knew I had feelings for Laney, didn't you? But back to you."

He gives me a small smile I've seen thousands of times, and I feel like I can still see the little boy who used to run into the lake with my sister trailing behind him.

"Losing Beau must have left your world empty in so many ways. I got to know him so well. He was a big brother to me, and I remember some of our last conversations where he asked that I look out for you and the kids. He only wanted you to embrace life, even if he wasn't here to have those experiences with you."

I can't help the tears falling down my face as Grant talks about the only man I ever loved. I just nod because it feels like I have a rock lodged in my throat, impeding my ability to use my voice.

Grant keeps going, "I don't know what happened tonight, but from how you're looking at me, you look anguished. Like you've taken a bite of a cookie you knew was up for grabs, but you don't feel you deserve."

He takes another sip of his tea and leaves his words lingering in the air for me to fully absorb.

"Grant, you're much more perceptive than I ever gave you credit for. When Beau died, he asked that I live my life to the fullest, but I never agreed to do so beyond our children. I feel like I am living life to the fullest for them. That's what matters. I just had a moment of weakness tonight that made me feel guilty, and I'm having difficulty coming to terms with it."

I can't help but fiddle with the nail polish on my fingers, a habit I've had since I was a young girl.

Grant takes a deep breath, a pensive expression marring his features. He and Becca are thinkers regarding how they respond to the world around them. I've always admired that because I feel like I live with my heart on my sleeve, and my emotions are written on my face constantly. Plus, I talk a mile a minute when I'm uncomfortable, so I don't always use a filter. Beau always said he could tell when I had a bad day versus a great one just by how I walked into the house.

"The kids are thriving. I came home to three happy kids tonight when we got back from the bar. Do you know how hard that is to achieve, especially for a kid like Tyler who not only lives with the memories of his father but is the spitting image of the man when he looks in a mirror? They're going to be fine. They're going to live their lives and make memories with you in them, along with whomever they choose to meet along the way. I think it's about living a new normal without Beau. It doesn't mean you are disrespecting him if you begin living life in a different way. If you chose to never love another man again, I don't think anyone would say anything. But I'd hate to know you passed up the opportunity to smile and laugh with someone new. I think that would be a huge disservice, not only to you but to someone else. You're a gift in this life, El. I hope you know that," Grant gives me a small smile and grabs my hand, giving it a little squeeze.

Sometimes I forget we have a thirteen-year age gap because he's always been so wise. Becca said he has their father's sensitive side. Their father was a psychology professor and I think Grant somehow absorbed that side of Elliott before his passing.

"I don't think I'm doing a disservice to myself for not finding a new companion."

Grant gets up from his stool and walks over to the sink, washing the mug out and putting it on the drying rack. He's drying his hands when he walks back over to me, pulling me up from the stool and into a big bear hug. I soak it up because Grant truly gives some of the best hugs, aside from Beau's, which I miss each day that passes.

Grant pulls me away, putting his hands on my shoulders, bending down slightly so we are eye-to-eye, "Who said the disservice you're doing is to yourself? I was talking about the disservice you are doing to whomever that lucky guy could be. You are the sun, Ellie. You and your sister are. You're just letting the ugly clouds life brings cover up your sunshine. Take it from someone that has run away thinking it's better to give space; sometimes you need to take life into your own hands and live."

"Shouldn't you be taking your own advice? You just admitted to running away instead of facing my sister."

He didn't say exactly that, but I can read between the lines. Maybe a little nudge in the right direction could do both of us some good.

Grant drops his hands and gives me a sly look.

"Why do you think I'm here? I gotta win my girl, even if she's too stubborn to see I'm her destiny."

He winks and starts walking out of the kitchen. Cocky Grant. I haven't seen this version of him since Laney became this delicate flower he's been nursing back to health. I'm glad to see he's finally going to stand up to her, and hopefully, she'll pull her head out of her ass and realize he's it for her.

"I love you, Grant Stanley," I say, the small smile gracing my features after feeling overwhelmed by my actions tonight.

He looks over his shoulder, "I love you too, Ellie Belly."

Grant's nickname for me has stuck, and it's fun to hear this jovial side of him again. I hear his footsteps ascending the steps, and I finish my tea and wash my mug out. I guess there won't be any couch sleeping for Grant tonight. He must really be putting in the effort to win over my sister.

I repeat Grant's words in my mind as I move up the stairs

and hope I can find some solace in the fact that Beau wouldn't be mad at me for my carefree nature tonight. I'm walking into my room, removing my jewelry before going through my bedtime routine. I pull my jewelry box open, and the first thing I see staring back at me is my and Beau's wedding bands.

Then the guilt returns to the surface, and I hear myself whispering, "I'm so sorry, Beau. I will always love you beyond myself."

* * *

Thanksgiving comes and goes, and to say it was eventful is an understatement. Becca revealed that Shane was clueless about many things between the two of them in the past, and a lot had to be unearthed this past week. Instead of being upset at Shane for all his missed opportunities, I now feel sad for the way things have ended up for him.

He missed out on the lives of many people he loves, and although he has the opportunity to reconnect now, so many years have passed. Becca said she's excited she has this next chapter of her life to share with Shane, but I can see the pain in her eyes now that light has been shed on what really happened between her and Shane. It doesn't make it easier, but it allows for healing. I hope they're able to find answers as they travel back to California this week to confront Shane's mother.

I loved my week with my family, making new memories yet honoring old ones as we talked about some fun stories regarding Beau of Thanksgiving's past. I love having those stories to talk about how much fun we had together. Some brought me to tears, but it was food for my soul to remember him with such a love for life.

Now it's back to the grind, and my class was feeling it today. The students got yesterday off so we teachers could prepare for the week head. Although we are starting on a Tuesday this week and the children have a shortened week, it felt like the students were counting the minutes to quiet time this afternoon. They usually fight the time when we lay down in our nap sacks and try to get some rest in the middle of our day. While the kids lay quietly, I sit at my desk and get some tasks done that don't require much noisemaking from me.

I wish I could say the day flew by, but I have my meeting with Xander Christianson this afternoon, and I am semi-dreading it. I made sure I had some notes taken on the email he had written me from the first day of school. I also pulled out his laminated list and made some talking points regarding that as well. I feel like we can get on the same page when it comes to Tessa, but first and foremost, I want him to acknowledge that I have her best interest at heart.

Sure enough, the last child to be picked up is Tessa. Juliette usually arrives on time, but she had called the school earlier, stating she got pulled into a last-minute meeting and would be running about fifteen minutes behind. Kindergarten lets out at two forty-five in the afternoon, so even with her running late, I still have about an hour of dreaded preparation before Tessa's father comes strolling into my classroom. It's then I realize I better get an adult-sized chair in the room for him to sit in. If he played hockey, I assume he's larger than average. Sitting in a kindergarten chair is not a parent's dream, so I will remember to borrow one from my colleague next door.

Juliette comes running into the classroom, apologies flying out of her mouth the moment she sees Tessa and me putting papers away in cubbies. I love my little helper. She is still the sweetest student I've had, and I continue to love our one-on-one time together.

The moment Tessa spots her aunt, she asks if she can stop helping and get going. When I nod my okay, she puts her supplies down and starts running into Juliette's arms. They act like they haven't seen one another in weeks, instead of the full school day since drop off this morning. Juliette looks up after greeting Tessa, and she turns to her niece and asks her to gather her belongings. Tessa's off to her cubby as Juliette walks toward me.

"I'm so sorry for my tardiness. I hate being late, and I know my brother will ream me for the tardy pick up of Princess Tessa."

She chuckles and looks over her shoulder as her niece laughs at the nickname as well. There must be an inside joke I'm missing there, but I can only imagine these two take pride in driving Xander Christianson to his breaking point.

"It's not a problem. I love having Tessa in my class, and she's the best little helper," I smile, meaning everything I've said about the sweet six-year-old.

"Mrs. Lorrent says I'm the best stapler she's ever seen. Rights, Mrs. Lorrent?" Tessa says with her cute little voice. Her expression holds so much pride in the way she gets to help me around the classroom.

"Of course. I don't think I would have gotten even half of this sorting and stapling done if it weren't for you," I say back, my smile growing as I look at this sweet girl.

She comes running toward us, halting at her aunt's side. Juliette, I think without even realizing, automatically puts her hands on her niece's head and strokes her hair. Tessa has the most beautiful blond locks, which remind me of my own and my daughter's as well.

"I thought maybe Mr. Christianson was going to pick her up since he has a meeting with me in the next hour. This will be my first time meeting him face-to-face," I say, trying not to sound like I am going to vomit in my mouth at the thought of seeing this bane of my existence in the flesh.

"I don't know if I should say sorry or be excited for you," Juliette whispers, hopefully not loud enough that Tessa can hear her.

I can't help the laugh that escapes me at her comment. I think if I didn't have her niece in my class, I could see us being good friends, meeting up for drinks after a day with five and six-year-olds.

"It will be great. I think we can only go up from here," I say, trying to sound more confident than I feel.

I bring my hands together in front of me to avoid fidgeting with my nail polish. I just touched it up last night.

"Well, we better get going," she looks down at the sweet girl. "Tessa, don't forget, we have your endocrinologist this afternoon, and your dad is going to want a full report back once we finish there."

Juliette looks back at me, and I can't help but feel bad that her dad has a meeting with me instead of being able to attend the appointment with his child's doctor. Juliette must sense my apprehension and clarifies before I let the guilt consume me further.

"We try to keep my brother at arm's length with these appointments as he gets a bit, how should I say, jumpy when it comes to Tessa and her diabetic appointments. My mom and I have taken over, and we give him all the information condensed so he doesn't feel overwhelmed. He only comes with us when the doctor gives us a warning that it's an appointment he should attend."

"Oh well, that makes sense. I can tell he is very...passionate about Tessa's care," I say, hoping I'm coming off as light and caring. I know Tessa's condition is no walk in the park, but if Xander Christianson is as fierce in person as he seems to be via email, I feel for anyone in his path. It seems he only has eyes for his daughter, so it makes sense how he reacts. But he has to find a way to loosen up with those that know what they're doing. I imagine someone who specializes in diabetes, like her doctor, knows what he's doing.

"Thanks so much for entertaining Tessa while I was running behind. I want to say good luck with my brother, but I think you're going to need to find something bigger than that for this meeting. He's sort of crabby today." She begins to grab Tessa's backpack, "What am I saying? He's always crabby."

She laughs at her own joke, and I simply stand there, my demeanor stoic so I don't put off the impression I'm shaking with nerves.

They hurry off, and I'm left in my quiet room. I walk toward my desk and respond to a couple emails that have come through. It's about five minutes before my meeting with Xander Christianson when I realize I forgot to grab a chair from my coworker. I run over to Mr. Walder's room next door, and luckily, I haven't missed him. I am used to having my colleagues around later on days like these after a holiday. I hear a few people down the hall chatting, so I know I'm not the only one hanging around for a bit after school.

I'm wheeling the chair to my office, careful not to run over my own foot as I hold the door open for myself. I'm struggling, and Jerry, Mr. Walder to the kids, comes running over to help.

"Mrs. Lorrent, let me help you with that."

He gives me a warm smile, and I can't help but return the sentiment. I appreciate the help because this chair is so damn awkward to move through the doorway at this angle.

I finally get the chair in the room and turn to my helper, "Jerry, you can call me Ellie when the kids aren't around. Thanks for the help."

I plop myself down at my desk while Jerry and I exchange pleasantries about our breaks. He heads out not a minute later. I look up at the clock, and I have a minute to spare. I take the time to pull out my compact and assess the damage. After a whole day with little kids, you sometimes forget you can look slightly disheveled. Luckily, I seem to have my makeup on my side. I don't see any running mascara and no marker on my cheeks, so I put my mirror away and my purse back on the side of my desk.

I'm nervous to meet this man. I feel like my minimal interactions via email have been subpar so far, meaning a lot is being put on this face-to-face encounter. I keep waiting, each motion outside causing me to sit up a little taller, expecting him to waltz right into my classroom. But as the minutes tick by, it dawns on me that he isn't showing up. And I don't know if that leaves me fuming with rage or drowning in disappointment. Either way, it doesn't give me the best impression of Mr. Xander Christianson, former NHL hockey player and current pain in my ass.

Chapter Seven

WYATT

"Xander, do not be a complete douche to this woman. She is the sweetest thing since Tessa graced our family. Please be kind."

My sister tries to sound stern on the other end of my phone. Her annoyance really grates my nerves sometimes. I'm hustling to get my ass to this teacher's classroom, and my sister is wasting my time telling me praise after praise about this teacher while she's acting like I'm some evil villain in a Disney movie.

"Excuse me, Jules, but people find me charming, I'll have you know."

As I'm saying it, I sound like I'm grunting and gritting my teeth, the complete opposite of charming. Hopefully, Juliette doesn't pick up on my irritation and lets it go.

"Right, and I'm the professional hockey player in this family."

She nearly howls on the other side of my phone. Again, why did my parents not find me perfect enough to stop there and keep from breeding an annoying little sister to pester me my entire life?

I roll my eyes and try to keep my temper at bay. I know

Juliette is just fucking with my emotions, knowing I am wound too tight. In all honesty, she has no idea just how tight. Since that night at the bar, I'm losing my temper with everyone besides Tessa. I can't let go of that woman's face every single time I close my eyes at night.

Those deep blue eyes staring back at me, making those noises I want to hear on repeat when she came undone with my fingers inside her. I've been relieving my aching cock with my hand nightly since then, and I feel like a sick prick for doing so. That woman ended up being married, and I did something intimate with her behind her spouse's back. It makes me feel dirty, even though the act of what happened between us in the bar alone could possibly be viewed as such by some.

I feel my hands balling into fists as I hold my phone between my ear and my shoulder, listening to my sister ramble about some meeting that caused her to be late to pick up Tessa. She won't even let me interject to ask questions, probably a tactic to keep me from getting upset that she was, in fact, late picking up my daughter. I will have to let it go because I have more important things to focus on. I have this meeting with Tessa's teacher, and I want to make sure I don't rip off this woman's head the moment I see her.

I don't want my poor attitude to affect how this meeting goes between us. I realize that I need this relationship to be a positive one because we still have the rest of the school year to be in each other's lives. I need to be more kind with my interactions with her, and I don't need to bring my personal frustrations into the classroom this afternoon.

"Listen, Juliette, I have to go. I'm getting to the school now. I'll see you back home soon. Please keep me updated on Tessa's appointment with her doctor."

We say our goodbyes, and I proceed to give my love to my girl before hanging up. I walk up the steps with ease, taking each step two at a time, checking in with security, then walking through the doors with minutes to spare. I'm looking around the halls, acclimating myself to where everything is. I walked these halls in the summer when I was touring schools, but haven't been back since. My sister has been my savior when it comes to Tessa's care, and I need to tell her how appreciative I am for all she's been doing for us.

I hear someone huffing and puffing as I'm about to round the corner. The moment I turn down the hall, I see a blond woman pulling a chair through a doorway. At least she's struggling to do so. That chair looks ancient, so I can't imagine it's an easy task. I look up and see the room number matches the room I'm looking for. I look down at the woman again, about to speak up and rush to hold the door for her, when she turns her head slightly, giving me a view of her profile.

I stop in my tracks, and without realizing it, I'm retreating while taking in the person not that far in front of me. To confirm my fears, a gentleman comes running toward her, "Mrs. Lorrent, let me help you with that." He's an older man, dressed much like teachers of my past, holding the door for her to ease the chair into the room.

It's her, the woman from the bar. I am trying to put these puzzle pieces together while my brain feels like it's firing on all synapses at the same time. This can't be. The woman I finger fucked is my daughter's kindergarten teacher? To top it off, her married kindergarten teacher. Fucking hell. What have I done? I've really dug myself a hole now, haven't I?

I can't be here. I can't confront her right at this moment. I'll have to come up with an excuse while I figure out how to navigate this turn of events. I retreat toward the way I came in, luckily going undetected by the staff, aside from the security guards at the front that scanned my badge as I ran through just a moment ago. I feel my pulse racing as I am still putting these pieces together in my head. I cannot believe the woman I can't stop thinking about is the same one that watches my child on a daily basis. This is a clusterfuck if I have ever seen one.

* * *

Tessa is telling me all about her day, which feels like it includes her teacher's name in every sentence. Now that I know the correlation between my personal life and my daughter's education, I feel like an even shittier person. Who have I upset in such epic proportions to have this shitty luck?

I'm doing my best to listen to my little girl tell me how amazing her day was. One thing's for certain—she loves Mrs. Lorrent. Fuck, even thinking her name makes me grind my molars together. I don't know who I'm most upset at, myself or her two-timing teacher. I force a smile so Tessa has no idea I'm dealing with a really messed up situation right now. She seems unfazed by my demeanor because she has not stopped to even take a breath.

After being off from school for a week, I thought today would have been one of the worst to get her up and ready for school. I should have known my daughter would be the complete opposite. She was awake and full of energy before I even got to her room to get her up.

We started our day by making a quick breakfast and getting her ready to head out for school. I've become quite the braider, and I notice Tessa's fishtail braids remain intact, even after an entire day at school. I will take that as my biggest win today. She was so excited to return to her classroom, not only to see her friends but to hang out with her teacher. Per Tessa, Mrs. Lorrent is her best friend, and she thinks she walks on water.

"Are you done with your dinner, sweetie?" I ask as I gather my plate and utensils to take them back to the kitchen.

Without breaking the rhythm with her story, Tessa nods and keeps telling me how fun it was to help her teacher set up the arts and crafts project earlier today. Apparently, when Tessa is done at the nurse's office to check her blood sugar, she sometimes takes her recess in the classroom to help her teacher set up for the next activity. Tessa said that with the holidays coming up, Mrs. Lorrent has a lot of little projects for the kids to do to prepare for Hanukkah and Christmas.

Today, they started on a dreidel for Hanukkah, as that holiday is in a few days. At least she's learning something new because I don't know anything about the holiday except the eight nights of celebration. Turns out Tessa is a wealth of knowledge, and she has given me every little bit of newfound expertise she has learned about the holiday.

Mrs. Lorrent, per my daughter, has a menorah displayed in the class with LED candles she will eventually light each day of Hanukkah with her students. The classmates that celebrate have a parent visiting to explain different aspects of the holiday and give more personal accounts regarding their traditions.

Tessa continues her storytelling as we go through the motions of our dishwashing. She stops here and there to ask me a question about what I did as a kid for the holidays or something along those lines, but for the most part, I spend the remainder of the evening listening to everything that's planned for the weeks ahead, before winter break ensues the Friday before Christmas.

Once Tessa is tucked in, I grab a beer and sit on my couch. My house has all the holiday decorations displayed, something my girl insisted had to be done the Friday after Thanksgiving. I take in the homemade ornaments on the tree from years past, along with some new artwork Tessa has made recently to add to our new home. I personally love the Santa head she made, with his hat and all, made from a hand print in dough, where my sister drew in the eyes and other facial features. To think my little recently turned six years old causes my heart to constrict a bit. I feel like time is passing so quickly, and she's already taking hold of my heart in a way that causes me to lose my bearings sometimes when I think about how sick she was not so long ago. She's come a long way, and I appreciate that I can provide a comfortable life for her with top-of-the-line medication and resources.

The moment I was given the offer to coach in New York, I was quickly researching doctors in the city who could help make her life better while living with a chronic illness, which I'm well aware will take a toll on her body. I knew that getting this job in New York City opened many doors to research and physicians who are always at the forefront of the latest in diabetic care.

Turns out her checkup today was a good one, and he's happy to see the numbers that are being picked up with the Dexcom glucose monitor. When we were first learning about her condition, the strides medicine has taken to make the lives of type 1 diabetics more livable were really impressive. The fact that this little machine would get her blood sugar and send anyone connected on the app updates throughout the day and night was magnificent, to say the least. That her insulin pump will work with this monitor to ensure she gets the necessary dosing of insulin in a timely manner is another great stride forward in making life with this illness manageable for a lifetime.

While sitting here, my mind moves on to wonder about Tessa's teacher. I can't help but let my mind go back to her this afternoon in the school hallway. What are the chances the same person from that bar would be the person caring for my child? Of all the little bars I could have entered, it had to be the one where my daughter's teacher was looking for a hookup while her husband was likely home caring for their household and children. Just the thought makes me want to throw my beer bottle across the room.

My head falls back, and I let out a breath in frustration. I'm so fucking pissed, but I also don't want to come clean that I was on school grounds and ran away like a fucking prick instead of standing my ground and walking right up to her. I should have because then I could see the look of horror on her face when she realized I could out her to everyone at that school. I bet what I assume is her goody-goody personality would not like that piece of information being passed down to her spouse, colleagues, boss, or her students' parents.

I have to be smart on how I play my next move. She is still Tessa's teacher, so I need to find a way to reach out to her and delay our meeting at this moment. Unlike schools where I always see kids being shown off in a holiday performance, that isn't something this school does. Apparently, the parents from a few years back said it was too overwhelming with other commitments around the holidays to add yet another task to their already overflowing schedules. This means I don't have to confront Tessa's teacher in person for some time, maybe not until the next parent/teacher conference. So, I will hang back and continue my communications with her via email or through my sister.

As if my thoughts had the power, my email pings on my iPad, which is sitting on my coffee table in front of me. I grab it and see I have received an email from Tessa's teacher. I feel my shoulders tense, but decide to get this over with before attempting to get what I assume will be a restless night of sleep.

Dear Mr. Christianson,

I hope this email finds you well.

I wanted to reach out regarding our meeting that was scheduled for earlier this afternoon. Unfortunately, I should have reached out prior to confirm we were still set to meet. I know you are a very busy hockey coach with a schedule that can change spur-of-the-moment.

Please let me know another possible time to reschedule. I look forward to hearing from you.

Have a wonderful evening,
> Mrs. Elody Lorrent

As I sit there, I'm wondering how to move forward with this email. I feel like all I'd do right now is respond rudely, so I close my iPad, finish my beer, and head to bed. I don't want to burn down this bridge, especially out of respect for my daughter. The love she seems to have for her teacher surpasses any rage I might be feeling at the moment. Plus, admitting I know who this teacher is to my sister will only prompt her to ask more questions about how I know. Then I'd have to confess I showed up at the school and ran off like a coward.

When I enter my room, I begin stripping off my clothes and go straight to my bathroom to turn on the shower. As the water is warming up and the steam starts to take over the atmosphere of my bathroom, I begin to formulate how I should approach my next interaction with this woman.

I get under the stream of warmth and let the water hit my skin, hoping to wash off this irritation I feel coursing through my body. Unfortunately, all I feel is attraction toward the woman. Today intensified that feeling. Despite my anger at her actions, especially behind her husband's back, I feel a pull toward her in a way I can't describe. It's dangerous how much I want a repeat of what happened in that bar, and I need to find a way to let it go.

Shit, my emotions are everywhere because I'm livid and turned on all in the same breath. Unfortunately, my dick isn't getting the memo that we are supposed to be hating the woman, not feeling an intense attraction to her. He stands at attention, and I can't ignore how painful my balls are with my cock wanting its needed release. I do the one thing I shouldn't and stroke myself while closing my eyes and see her beauty staring back at me.

Chapter Eight

ELODY

It's been five weeks since my student's grumpy, flaky father has communicated with me. This asshole has been radio silent toward me, and he chooses today of all days to reach out. Well technically it wasn't today, but it's today that I saw it.

I knew I should have kept my email silent until right before we returned to school, but no, I had to be stubborn and check my email today. He did email me the Friday school got out for winter break, but I only saw his email today. And it has made my blood boil. Ugh, I could break something. I'm so mad.

I can hear myself mumbling as I make my way to the restaurant for the lunch I'm having with Becca and Shane. It's New Year's Eve today, and my mind is already dreaming of the Ellie in a few hours who will be ringing in the new year in pajamas with my girls and parents; no concern in sight other than what pajamas I am going to wear to see the ball drop.

Tyler usually stays up with me, but this is his first year he has a girlfriend, and he will be spending it with her and her family down at a rental they got in the Hamptons. He did promise a FaceTime with me to ease the blow that this is the first year since he was born that he won't be with me to ring in a new year. Now I'm sad and angry for two completely different reasons. Gosh, I hate feeling this way. It's not like me to be this uptight, but there's something about this hockey guy that just rubs me wrong. Add that to my son being away, and I can't help but fight the lump from forming in my throat.

I'm making my way through the crowds of people who are walking along the sidewalks of New York. This city is usually busy enough, but now it's ridiculous. This is my favorite time of year, but today is not my day. I feel like a grumpy jerk as I go through the streets, attempting to reach my destination. I'm already late, so I'm fighting the irritation that's rising inside me. I see the restaurant is right in front of me, and relief takes over. I need to eat something. I'm just hangry and seeing Becca will be a balm to my frayed nerves right now.

My daughters stayed home with my parents, who are visiting for the holidays, along with Laney. My sister has been feeling under the weather again, so I had to change plans on childcare, and luckily, my parents were willing to hang out in my home while I went to this lunch. They nearly kicked me out the door. They must have sensed I needed a break as much as I felt like I did.

I walk into the restaurant, and the warmth of the busy establishment instantly causes my body to thaw from the winter cold I just subjected myself to. I can feel the warmth on my cheeks, and I already feel the tension melting away, along with the ice I assume has formed around my nose. The winter cold has come in full force this year, and I will definitely not miss it when spring finally rolls around. I scan the restaurant, seeing my bestie and her boyfriend at a booth. I begin removing my scarf and what feels like a comforter of a jacket when I finally make it to them to sit down.

I begin to unload my frustrations on them so they can hopefully cheer me up and make me feel better. Too bad Shane doesn't understand girl code just yet, so I had to glare at him to make my point known.

After I unload how Xander is making me feel, Becca asks, "Have you met him in person yet?"

I get interrupted when I attempt to answer her to place our lunch orders with the server that comes up to our table. Once we get our food requests in, I word vomit everything, and I feel like I'm in a therapy session right now.

"That's the thing. The guy is constantly emailing me to intervene in some way, telling me how to do my job better. But does he come onto campus to talk to me? Of course not! When school started, my student's aunt came to the orientation and Back-to-School Night, explaining that her brother, said douchebag, was out of town for work. He's like those online trolls, constantly bothering me, but not coming out from behind the comfort of his computer to show his face. I bet he looks like a troll too. If he was a hockey player, doesn't that mean he has missing teeth and all?"

I'm worked up now, feeling like all the irritation from the first half of the school year is catching up to me. I try to calm myself down with controlled breathing, but my heart is still racing.

As I sit there, I see Shane typing into his phone. I really hope he isn't texting someone about my breakdown because I'll have to declare this friendship as once again on a break. Soon, he's looking up at me, pointing his phone in my face.

"Umm, it depends if you think this is what a troll would look like," he says while I pull my head back for my eyes to focus on the image in front of me.

I feel the blood drain from my face. This cannot be happening. Without thinking, I grab the phone and begin pinching my fingers on the screen to zoom in. I must be in some sort of surrealistic nightmare. This cannot be my life right now. But those majestic blue eyes stare back at me. Those aren't Xander's eyes; they're Wyatt's eyes. I keep staring at the phone, completely shocked by who is staring back at me.

I know this man, not as my student's father but as the man

whose hand I rode to seek out my pleasure. Holy shit! I think I'm going to be sick.

"What is it, Ellie?" Becca asks.

I forgot I was at this booth. I feel like I was transported to a different dimension as reality has hit me. I did this, and I just complicated my life in ways I never thought possible.

I shoot out of the booth and begin putting all my layers back on.

"I've gotta go!" I declare to both my friends as I rush out of the restaurant.

I hear Becca call out to me regarding the food that we ordered, but I'm too busy trying to figure out how I'm going to undo what I've done with my student's father.

Fuck, I'm going to be sick for real this time.

* * *

I rush home, and I honestly cannot remember anything about my walk from the restaurant to my front door. The only thought that plays on a loop is the one where I see Wyatt's hooded gaze as he watches me fall over the edge and orgasm all over his hand. Just the thought gets my pulse racing to the point that my heart might beat out of my chest.

I'm mortified on so many levels. First, I'm the teacher of this man's daughter. I should rephrase—I'm the teacher to this grumpy asshole's daughter, a student I absolutely adore, and a parent that makes me question my abilities as a teacher. Second, I feel a sense of absolute horror at the way I acted that night in the bar. I have never sought out another man's touch, and with one stare down with Wyatt, I was putty in his hands.

My heart belongs to my husband. Until that moment, I could say without a doubt I have never felt a pull toward someone other than Beau. And in one gaze, Wyatt had me in a trance of sorts that I still can't seem to comprehend all these weeks later.

I am not trying to find anything with anyone else, and in an instant, I seemed to have lost that concept. That ship has sailed; at least that's what I have been telling myself all these years. In all honesty, I never wavered. I never felt a pull toward someone else in all the years I was with Beau and since he passed.

My job now is to keep my kids happy and healthy. I have a job to care for my students and make sure they are introduced to school in the most positive way possible. Loving another man is not something I ever felt was in the cards for me again. I am utterly devoted to Beau. Those moments with my late husband were only meant for him. I feel like a cheater the way I acted with a complete stranger touching me and lighting my skin on fire like Wyatt Christianson did.

Third—wait, what kind of list was I compiling again? Oh, that's right, all the ways I want to dig a hole and bury myself right here in my backyard.

What the actual hell have I brought upon my life? I walk into my home, and I stand in the entryway, wondering what I should do. I hear my girls laughing at something my dad is probably doing. I remove my scarf and jacket, the cold from outside slowly dissipating as I allow the warmth to encircle me as I acclimate to the harsh changes from outside to my own shelter.

I begin to walk in and try to avoid my parents and girls from seeing me, with little success. Right as I am about to start up my stairs, my mother walks through, and her eyes take me in. She doesn't declare my arrival to everyone else, and her eyebrows furrow, trying to navigate how she wants to speak to me regarding however I'm looking back at her.

I can only imagine I have lost most of my coloring, even if the blistering winter cold usually paints my cheeks pink. If a facial expression could have a mix of anger, frustration, embarrassment, and anguish, I guess that's the look I'd expect across my features as well because I feel all those things at this moment.

My mom gets near me and wraps me in a hug. I know since Beau passed, she has a hard time talking to me for fear of hurting me further with her words. I know my mom has an immense amount of love for Laney and me, but I think having a widowed daughter is something she has a difficult time navigating. And right now, I am having a hard time navigating my feelings toward what I've done with a student's father. I guess we aren't too different in our feelings of inadequacy but in very mismatched ways.

I feel a tear fall down my cheek, my emotions feeling like they're overwhelming my entire soul. My heart and mind are being tugged in so many directions. I already felt guilt regarding my behavior at the bar. I had that weighing on me because I felt like I betrayed my husband in some fucked up way. Add in the realization that I messed around with a student's parent—I'm mortified.

My mom simply hugs me harder and gives me the space to let me pour my emotions onto her. I feel like I've failed my love for Beau, which seems ridiculous as he's no longer here physically. But my heart hurts just the same, as if I felt cared for by another man, and I have somehow gone against my vow to Beau all at the same time.

"Oh, sweet girl. What's hurting you?" my mom says quietly, so only I can hear her as the rest of the family is in the kitchen, most likely getting their snacks ready to ring in the new year.

My mom strokes my hair, and it feels like life has no pain when I'm in her arms.

"I feel like with each day and each movement, I am further away from my husband. I recently did some things, and I just don't recognize myself."

Could I sound more cryptic? My mom moves back slightly so her eyes are looking directly into mine. She and I share the same eye color, down to the dark storm mine seem to resemble lately. I can see my pain in her features because I know all too well how it feels to hold the sadness of our children in our own hearts.

"Beau will always feel your love, even though he isn't here to surround himself with it physically." My mom moves her hand over my cheek, catching my tears.

I nod in agreement, but I don't feel it deep down the way I wish I did. My life is moving forward, while my life with Beau is further in the past and nowhere in my future. The guilt I feel with that alone is crippling. Add in the fact that I have experienced something so intimate with a complete stranger, my student's father, to top it off, is something I can't quite wrap my mind around at the moment.

I give my mom another hug, and when I pull away, I add, "I'm going to take a quick shower so I'm ready for tonight's festivities. I promise I'll be downstairs shortly. Tyler won't be here tonight, so Dad will once again be surrounded by a lot of estrogen."

I smile and hope my joke gives my mom the comfort I know she needs when she sees me in pain. I have to try to pull out the sunshine people expect of me. I think my mom sees right through my bullshit, but she allows a small smile across her features.

My mom gives me a slight nod and keeps her eyes on me as I move up the stairs. I know she is trying to be supportive in whatever capacity she can provide for me, but she also has stated she has no idea how it feels to live without her life partner at such a young age. Her honesty wasn't something others understood, but I always appreciated it because she wasn't trying to be pushy regarding how she cared for me. She left that honesty on the table, so I was aware she was simply there for me in the best way she understood how.

I think any support either of my parents can provide is something I cling to because I love having their help as I navigate this new normal of my life. Each milestone I have with my kids feels like a whole slew of emotions come over me. Apparently, milestones of my own are having the same effect, although mine feel like they're destroying me from the inside out.

I reach my room upstairs at the end of the hallway, and start to devise a plan of what I need to do to confront Wyatt. I need to find a way to apologize, but I also need him to stop being a complete dick to me. I'm going to confront this right now because I doubt sleep will come easy with this looming over me now that I know Xander is Wyatt, the man from the bar.

Come to think of it, did he know who I was in that bar? Did he think I knew what he looked like, and he sought me out once he saw me staring at him? That kickstarts another swell of anger from deep in my bones if this jackass thinks he can play with people's minds like this. The behavior, if I'm assuming correctly, is another level of fucked up.

I rush through a shower and allow my mind to come up with my next step. Once I'm in my comfy pajamas, the required attire per my girls, I log in to my work site and look up information on Tessa's address through the parent portal. Is this a violation of some school rule? Probably. But I doubt the school has a policy about hooking up with a parent in a dark corner of a bar, too.

Before heading downstairs, I stare at my reflection in my bedroom mirror. I still see the bright version of who I always was most of my life. But deeper, I see the pain that I hope I mask well for others as I move forward. I want to be as happy as I once was, but it seems the more I try to find it, the harder it seems to attain. It feels that with all my effort to shove my sadness down, it's starting to pile up, and the weight of my loss is sitting on my shoulders, front and center, more than ever before.

I decide to head down the stairs and go straight to the

kitchen. I try to interject in their tasks, hoping to busy my mind with some cooking with my family, but my dad hands me a sparkling beverage with more than just juice. With a wink, my dad makes a spot at the island for me to sit, and I watch my family move around my kitchen.

As I watch them with food splayed on every portion of the counter in front of me, I can't help but see the lightness in my kids as they move through their afternoon. They seem so carefree. Growing up without a father figure is a tough one for most children, but aside from Tyler, my girls don't really remember their father. Just the thought of that breaks my heart further. I sip on my drink and listen to the level of excitement in my daughters' voices as they are incredibly thrilled to try some new spices from a YouTube cooking channel they found recently to experiment with new recipes.

* * *

My body is protesting every movement this morning. It's New Year's Day, and all I am thinking about is a new, younger body. I am absolutely spent, and I did not party like I was in my twenties. I had told my parents last night I had some early morning errands to run today, and they agreed to watch the girls for me. The moment I walk out my front door, careful not to wake my parents or the girls, I feel the blistering cold hit my cheeks. I think that's all I've exposed of my skin because I'm covered, head to toe, in my snow gear.

As cold as Nebraska is in the winter, I feel like this cold just hits me differently than it ever did back home. I think it's because this city is where I mostly find myself walking or using public transportation. Back home in Saddle Ridge, it was rare to see us walking through the cold weather in the winter. Since moving to New York, I've had to become comfortable being exposed to this wretched weather, even if I'm cursing myself with each step I take out of my house.

I decide to drive to my destination, as my poor car needs some attention after sitting on the street for far too long. This car isn't always utilized the way it once was in my hometown. I bring the car to life and begin my drive. I soak up this time in my car, with the heat blasting me, along with my favorite songs from home blaring through the speakers. I always found that alone time in the car was a blessing for me with a hectic schedule and busy children at home.

The closer I get to Wyatt's address, the more my heart begins to race. I pull up to the building, and I can't help but crouch a bit to get a full view through my windshield of the massive structure. It is beyond tall. To top it off, a doorman is standing and looking into my car. I assume Wyatt isn't the only celebrity type calling this place home, so the concern across this man's face is obvious. I take a deep breath and make my way out of my car.

I go straight to the gentleman and explain who I am here to see. He takes a moment to call up to Wyatt, I assume, and then I realize there's no backing out now. I look like a complete lunatic coming directly here, but I need to start the new year with a clean slate and hopefully better terms with this grump of a man.

He doesn't need to know he brought me to the most powerful orgasm of my entire life. Even with the thought of his skillful fingers moving across my most intimate parts, I can't help the pang of sadness I have sweeping across my heart. Having this memory with Wyatt comes with the harsh reality that I didn't quite have the same physical connection with Beau. And for that, my heart shatters a tiny bit more.

Chapter Nine

WYATT

I get off my phone, and the sly look on my sister's face tells me she heard the conversation on the other end of the call that just came through. Her smile looks a lot like mine, probably one of the only physical attributes we share. She has so much innocence in her features that no one thinks she can be sneaky. She got away with a lot when we were kids because she knew she was the baby of the family and used that to her advantage.

"Don't give me that look, Jules. I have no idea what's going on." I got a call from my bellman, stating Mrs. Lorrent was here and asking if she could come up.

I can't help the increase in my pulse at just the thought of her being in my home. I look around and make sure I don't have my underwear hanging across the couch. The next thought is the need to roll my eyes at myself because I have a child. I don't live like a bachelor, so I have no clue what I'm expecting to see in my home aside from scattered pieces of Tessa's toys throughout it.

"Why is the cute teacher headed over? Huh Xan?" She seems to be holding in more questions because she knows if she pushes too far, I won't speak at all.

I can't look over at her, so I decide to get what she came up to my apartment for, delaying answering her question for a moment longer. I open the fridge to retrieve the eggs she needs to make this epic breakfast for my girl—her words, not mine.

"I have no clue. Isn't this sort of creepy? The teacher is here at my home during a school break? Not just that, but on a holiday of all days. Seems a bit needy, especially if her husband and kids are sitting at home wondering where she is."

I can't help but spit the last part out. I guess I'm letting my irritation show through my tone. I feel so much anger that she's living this lie with a man who probably looks at her like she's the sunshine of his day. I know I would look at her like that if she were mine.

Where did that thought come from?

My sister gives me a weird expression, taking a beat to answer my questions.

"What do you mean, 'her husband?'" My sister uses air quotes for the last part and seems annoyed by my comment. I have no idea what is ruffling her feathers.

"It's New Year's Day, and it's a holiday break. She has her kids at home with a husband who is probably waiting for her so they can relax the day away." I throw one more item into the bag, knowing Tessa loves to cook alongside my sister with her own apron.

Tessa is downstairs with my parents, at my sister's place, waiting for Jules to start her year off with a huge breakfast that must include French toast. Too bad for Juliette, in all her planning, she didn't account for the right number of eggs and ran out mid-recipe. My sister had Tessa stay the night last night, and they had a party that involved sleeping on the floor of her living room and decorating her apartment like they were in the chaos of Times Square.

I stopped by to ring in the new year with my favorite little girl, but I'm too old to wing it on a couch or the floor of my sister's apartment. I did not need my body reminding me I'm no longer in my twenties with the sore neck and locked back I would most definitely wake up with today. Plus, I was up earlier than usual this morning, not only to work out in my home gym but to get some work done before meeting with my coaching staff tomorrow.

We took today off to unwind with our families. We don't have a game for two more days, and it's an away game. So, I will need to make sure everything is in order so we can jump right in with the drills I'm envisioning for my guys.

"Xander, sometimes I think you're the most clueless guy I've ever met," my sister interrupts my thoughts. "Mrs. Lorrent is a widower. I don't know the details, but I know her husband passed away a few years ago, and she's a mother of three. I don't know much else. She keeps the the majority of her personal life close to her chest, but she did explain these little bits of information at back-to-school night. She is the sweetest person. I don't think she has a mean bone in her body." My sister talks about this woman as if they've been friends for years. I can't help but feel stunned by this revelation about my daughter's teacher.

Now I feel like the biggest douche for judging her actions and not having all the information. I let my mind wander, and I came up with assumptions that did not paint her in a positive light. That's on me, and I guess I'm once again going to be apologizing for my actions. Actually, now that I think about it, I have never apologized to her for my poor behavior and attitude when communicating with her via email.

If she's the nicest person, as my sister claims, she won't hold my poor attitude against me. Right? I mean, I'm lovable after people get over my grumpy predisposition. I scratch my chin, the stubble peppering my jaw a reminder I need to shave before my meeting tomorrow. I'm once again lost in thought when my sister snaps her fingers in front of me.

"Xander, where did you just go?" Jules is waving her hands in front of my face. "I have to head back to my place before my niece calls up here and says I'm taking too long. I can't anger my guest," she says while walking through my front door. As she usually does, my sister takes the stairs, claiming she needs to get in as many steps as possible.

I know Mrs. Lorrent, Elody from what I gathered from the website from the school, is headed up that elevator any minute now, so I wait at the door for her arrival. The moment the elevator dings, I see the doors open, and she's standing there, looking quite pissed, if I were to guess.

I lean against the doorframe and cross my arms over my chest. I wait for her to say something, since she's the one visiting me. But she just stares back at me like a pot that's on the verge of boiling and spilling over. I can't help feeling the uptick at the corners of my mouth. As grumpy as I usually am, something about this one just makes me melt a bit on the inside. I won't admit that to anyone, but I'll keep this information to myself and enjoy the lightness she seems to add to my grumpiness when I see her.

I've only been around her three times, counting this moment, and I feel a pull toward her, unlike anyone I've ever been around. Like something about her was made to be around me. In a way, she feels like a magnet, an opposite pull that is attracted to me in some way. I can't ignore the electricity in the air when we've been around each other. At least I remember feeling that intensity in that dark corner of the bar, and I feel it right now.

She finally steps forward when the elevator sounds like the doors are closing. She walks into the hallway right outside my apartment; however, she doesn't budge from there. She's left at least six feet between us, and I don't think it's due to social distancing practices. I can tell no matter how angry she is, she's now realized the extent of her tantrum and doesn't know how to react to me right now.

"Hey, Sunshine. Happy New Year," I say to her as she still seems absolutely petrified standing in front of me. "Do you want to come in?"

She doesn't even nod. I hold the door open as she moves past me with her head held high, as if trying to either convince me or herself that she's got a hold of whatever she came here to do or say. As she passes me and enters my home, I think I see fumes coming out of her ears. I can't help but laugh to myself because she's cute when she's pissed.

She comes to a stop in the middle of my living room, turns around, and points a finger in my face.

"What is this? Some sort of game to you? Were you just trying to mess with your daughter's teacher in some demented game you're playing?" Oh, she's really pissed, and the puzzle pieces are coming together now that she's had her outburst.

I put my hands up as if I'm surrendering. I'm opening my mouth to say something, but she continues, her rant not quite at its end.

"So what, *Wyatt*? You just saw me at the bar and felt the compulsion to push a little further? You just wanted to see how far you could take this little game? What is it? You just needed to see me having the best orgasm ever and add that to your spank bank? Are your rude responses to our emails not enough to get yourself off? Ugh!"

Her hands are balled into fists at her side, and she stomps her feet. Then she finally snaps out of whatever trance we're in and takes in her surroundings. Soon, she's turning around and looking over the expanse of my living room. I, on the other hand, can't let go of the fact that I gave her the best orgasm she's ever had. Why is that the most important little tidbit she gave me in that entire little verbal explosion? Of course, that's what I decide to lead with.

"Best orgasm ever, huh?"

She seems starstruck by my apartment and keeps walking further into the living room, stopping at the large windows that give me the most amazing views of Central Park and the rest of New York City.

She looks exasperated when her gaze snaps back to mine,

noticeably annoyed that she let that little fact out, which I assume she didn't do on purpose.

"That's all you got out of all I said?" She rolls her eyes, annoyed by my comment, while I feel like I'm floating on cloud nine with her little slip-up. Turning her head toward the window again, she says, "This view is breathtaking."

It isn't the clearest day, but it's clear enough to envision how epic the sights would be if there were no clouds in the sky and we could see miles ahead of us.

Elody Lorrent is one hell of a firecracker if I've ever seen one. She's beyond pissed at me, that I'm sure of, but she's also completely mesmerized by the views in the distance.

"It absolutely is," I say, but when I respond, I'm not looking at the view outside. I am taking this woman in. I know it's wrong of me to be drooling over my daughter's teacher, but for me, things have changed slightly. I was under the impression she was currently married, so I let my anger take hold of the wheel. But now that I know she's not deceiving anyone, I feel like a part of me wants to know what makes her tick.

She turns her head to face me again and looks right into my eyes. She is gorgeous. She has a small-town look, so she stands out even more to me in this busy city. Her eyes are large and doe-like, making her look younger and probably more innocent than she actually is. I know that the sounds I heard coming out of her mouth that night in the bar were not ones from a woman who wasn't turned on by things that pushed the envelope a bit. Just the thought has my dick straining against my zipper. Fuck. I need to have this conversation and then have her leave my apartment. Only then can I take a cold shower. I'm not a pubescent teen who acts like he's never seen an attractive woman, so I have no idea what has gotten over me. But I need these feelings to stop.

Her reaction at the bar that night after I saw her climax in that way were not the emotions of someone who was comfortable with her actions. She could not get away from me fast enough. At first, I thought it was from guilt regarding her marriage, but it seems her guilt runs deeper, toward a man who is no longer here.

She takes a deep inhale, and when she lets go of that breath, she keeps her attention on me.

"Listen, Wyatt," she puts her hand up for a moment, as if stopping me from interjecting, "I mean, Mr. Christianson," her spine straightening, somehow believing that will give her the resolve to get through this conversation professionally. "I don't know what you think of me from my actions, but I want you to know I had no idea who you were that night in the bar. It wasn't until yesterday that I found out what you looked like, and all the pieces started coming together. On top of that, I don't usually fool around with the parents of my students. This behavior just isn't me, and I wanted to come over here and clear the air."

She's trying to act like this chemistry crackling in the air between us is just a coincidence and will pass. I make sure I think about my response properly because I don't want to fuck this up. As much as I thought we'd get through this conversation and she'd go on her merry way, I'm starting to think there's no way I can let this woman walk out my door without even trying to explore what's going on between us. It's as if I'm addicted to her, and I've only touched her once.

"First of all, you didn't know who I was before yesterday? I'm not trying to sound arrogant, but I'm sort of a big deal," I say with a sly smile directed at her. Something about this woman is pushing me to show off a bit, puffing out my chest in the proverbial sense. I don't know why her opinion of me matters so much, but her not knowing who I am in any capacity sort of hurts more than it should. "Second of all, I think you can call me Wyatt because you came on my fingers, *Elody*."

Yeah, the way she's looking back at me, I'm pushing her buttons, and I'm living for it right now.

She tries to give off a zero-fucks-given vibe, but I know what I just said to her is making her hot and bothered. "I don't follow hockey. My husband was more of a basketball fan. I know you used to play hockey, and you're now a coach. But in basketball, I saw a lot of great coaches that sucked at basketball. I assumed you were one of those."

Is her nose slightly up toward the sky like she's stuck up with her preferred sport? Also, what's the dig for? Does she think she's going to hurt my feelings with her little comment? She said all that, not at all embarrassed that she found a way to insult me with her assumptions.

I can't help the laugh that escapes. I cannot believe this. I found the one woman in this country that is so far from a puck bunny that she not only had no idea who I was but made the assumption I was terrible at the sport. I am not usually attracted to a woman past sleeping with her, yet this one I touch once, and I want her to look at me like I'm the only man who exists. My laugh seems to startle her, and I realize I've inched up closer to her; we're now toe to toe.

I rub the scruff on my face, trying to figure out what to say next. "Yeah, Sunshine, I'm a big deal. I used to be one of the best. Some say the GOAT of hockey. Coaching wasn't my first choice after retirement. Apparently, I was a bit much to handle not having an outlet like hockey, so my family said I had to go back to work. Playing the game was my everything before Tess, but I'm also in my forties, so going back on the rink to get beat up didn't have the same draw as it did when I was drafted to the NHL years ago. So, the coaching job came up, and I took it. Gives Tessa more stability while keeping my family from going crazy with my micromanaging skills."

"You micromanage? That's impossible," she snorts, letting out a laugh and rolling her eyes. Her attention is back on the view outside my window. I use this as an opportunity to look her up and down. She is perfect. That long, wavy blond hair, petite figure, and full lips that I wouldn't mind seeing wrapped around my dick. Shit. There I go again. Letting my mind wander. Although today she looks to be wrapped in a duvet, the jacket is so puffy. But I know from what I felt against my palms at the bar, she's got the perfect figure with hips and an ass that my hands itch to touch again.

I can't take my eyes off her, and she must sense my gaze on her still because she whips her head back so her deep blue eyes are looking right into my own. When her eyes are on me, I feel like she can see right through me. Her gaze is penetrating, and I feel it to my core.

"We can't let what happened at the bar happen again." I don't know if her words are for me or more of a reminder for herself. She doesn't say them with much conviction.

But then I sense a shift as we return to looking at one another. I don't miss the quick glances she makes at my mouth. It's what she does next that throws me for the biggest loop.

One second, we are looking at one another, and the next, she is leaping onto me, our mouths coming together as if our next breath depends on our touch. I kiss her hard and hear a moan come from her throat. That pushes me further, backing her against the glass and moving my hips so she can feel how much I want her.

She grabs onto my waist, keeping my movements on her center, seeming to need the friction against her core. I begin moving my kisses down her jaw, back toward her ear, nibbling on her flesh, enjoying the goosebumps that line her skin at my touch.

"You're such an asshole, yet all I want to do is consume you."

I smile at her words. She feels this attraction between us, and I'm glad I'm not alone in these feelings. I have no idea what her purpose was to come over, aside from confirming that I am indeed the man from the bar and the father of one of her students, but I can't complain at this point. I love feeling her skin under my palms. She ignites a fire in me that I didn't know I possessed.

She's got so many layers on, but I find it my new favorite game to try and remove each article of clothing from her as I continue to kiss each piece of skin I expose. Soon, she's in her leggings, but she's only wearing a bra on her upper half. Her tits are fucking fantastic. She's had three kids, and all I can say is that her fucking body is a temple. Each little stretch mark I see only spearheads me to want more. So I kiss the skin where her bra is holding her breasts. Now that I've gotten this opportunity to touch her again, I need to unwrap this gift in front of me.

I pull down the cup of her bra, and her left breast pops out. Fuck, if I stare long enough, I could sit and drool at it; so marvelous and fits perfectly in my hand. She's got this beautiful milky skin, and her breast is absolute perfection. She's even more beautiful than I could imagine. I grab hold of her breast, my calloused hand squeezing her tit, and it spears me forward to do more. It's like her peeked nipple is calling to be sucked, and I do just that. I'm not gentle, either. That's not my style. I don't do slow-moving type of sex. I will worship her body and have her screaming my name as I watch her jump off that orgasmic cliff.

The moment I suck on her nipple, I feel the bite of her nails in my hair, her moan is louder this time, and she moves her hips to meet mine. She wants this, and I need to relieve this ache for both of us. I begin removing her leggings, pulling them down, along with her underwear, and throwing them over my shoulder. Her bra is next, and soon I'm staring at a completely naked goddess that I will possess.

"This is only happening once. Let's scratch this itch," she's got a stronger voice than I expected, but I still can't help but smile cockily toward her.

She thinks this is a one-time thing? Fuck that. I'm not letting this thing between us last just once. We're too mature for this cat-and-mouse game.

She doesn't seem to like my cocky smirk as an answer to her words, so she asks, "What's with that smile? You think I'm kidding?"

"I sure do, Sunshine. You're kidding yourself if you think this will end after this one time. I don't think so. I already know you'll be coming back for more."

I can't help my arrogance from coming through the surface even more. But there's something about her I know I won't be able to keep from returning to once we have this experience together.

"So fucking cocky," she throws back at me. I can tell she's not one to curse often; something about how the words don't fall naturally from her lips because each time she does, she seems surprised by them.

She's breathing heavily, looking at me with hooded eyes and a fire within her glare that I know she is simply taking in what we're about to do. She doesn't seem scared or nervous. She definitely doesn't come off as embarrassed, so I move toward her like a lion about to pounce on its prey. The moment I'm close enough, she pulls on my shirt and gets me to eye level with her.

"You better take your clothes off, or I'm ripping them off. NOW!" I don't know her well, but I think bossy Elody might be my favorite. She has no playfulness in her tone. She doesn't just want this, she needs it. So, I don't waste time removing every piece of clothing before I stand stark naked in front of her, stroking my cock as I take in the sight in front of me.

As it's January first, if this is telling of how my year will go, I think I'm a very lucky man. She's watching my arms as I stroke myself, her gaze taking in the massive amount of tattoos I have on my left arm and hand. I've got some ink scattered across my chest and down my right upper arm. I'm not shy that I have ink on a lot of my upper body, but it's hard to imagine just how much until I remove my clothing for people to take it all in. The more she stares at me, the more I feel my cock grow in my grip. Fuck, this woman might actually be the end of me.

I move toward her, my left hand letting go of my dick and grabbing her hands and pinning them above her head. She's completely naked against my glass window. No one can see in, but she doesn't seem to question it either way. My right hand moves around her neck, not forcefully, but in a way that shows I'm about to fuck her until she sees stars. She seems to get the message, and her eyes are lit with fire regarding the possibilities ahead for us together physically.

"I need you to tell me what you want, Sunshine," I may see the desire swimming in her gaze, but I still need to hear her words.

"I'm not standing here naked for nothing. Show me what you got, Wyatt." She uses my name in a way that signifies she knows many people don't call me by my birth name. I'm used to Xander, but the way she says Wyatt makes it feel like she knows me in a way others don't, when in reality, we barely know each other.

"Fuck, I need to grab a condom. Shit." I hate the fact I will be walking away, possibly spoiling the moment between us.

She shakes her head. "No. Don't leave me."

For a moment, I sense she is afraid she will walk away from this if I leave the room. I keep looking at her, waiting for her to elaborate. Maybe she doesn't want this as much as I do, and I was misreading this entire situation.

"I'm clean. I can't get pregnant. My tubes are tied." I've never gone bare with a woman besides Tessa's mother. Tessa was conceived from a drunk night with her mother, and we forgot to use protection. I was a different person then, constantly partying like the hockey legend I was known to be. Little did I realize in our drunken state, no birth control was used, and, soon enough, I found out I would be a father.

"I get tested regularly. I promise I'm clean."

She nods as if she's trying to convince herself this is a good idea. I push her back against the window and get myself to her level.

"Are you sure you want me, Sunshine?" I say with more conviction than I'm feeling. For some reason, it's not even that I don't want this. I love sex. But if she says no, I fear that the disappointment will be for more than the pleasure. It's as if this ability to connect in this way is something I'm longing for beyond the release we'll both have. She nods and kisses me, pulling me out of my thoughts and bringing that fire back between us.

Our kisses are sloppier, like we can't get enough of one another. I turn her around and place her hands on the window. I make sure she's bent over enough to give me a perfect view of her ass. I move my left hand up her spine, my lips trailing along her skin. I can't get enough of her reactions to my touch. She shivers as I move to touch her along her upper body. My dick has started to feel neglected, and I can't help but move my hips, slipping through her wet folds. She's got longer legs than I realized, and she aligns perfectly with me. I stand straight and start to separate her cheeks and see how soaked she is.

"Fuck, Sunshine. You're dripping for me again. How much do you want me?" I ask, and I slap her ass. She yelps and wiggles her ass, making me harder, if that's even possible. "I'm doing everything possible to keep from kneeling and tasting this fucking pussy. Maybe next time."

"There you go being cocky again, thinking there will be a next time, coach," she says teasingly. I can't help but laugh at her new sense of self-esteem. She turns her head, and nothing about how she's looking at me says she's even convinced herself that this will be it between us.

"Oh, once you get a piece of me, I promise you'll be begging me to fuck you again." It feels good to have this type of banter with her. For so long, I've felt like I've been wound tight because so much lies on my shoulders to keep everyone around me safe. But with her, I feel like I'm lighter. Like I can let go of all my resentment and anger and simply be my old self again.

"Enough talking and more doing. Get inside me," she demands, not knowing how those words are fuel to my soul.

I line myself up, looking at her ass and hoping I can try that little puckered hole one day. She turns her head back to look at me, but soon enough, I'm pushing into her, no slowness to my movements. The moment I feel the warmth of her pussy, I feel like the universe brought this person into my life. She was made for me, and everything else rights itself in my world. Fuck. I have never felt like this before, and I haven't even started moving yet. I have to breathe through my nose to ensure I can last longer than a minute.

What the fuck is going on with me?

I begin to pump in and out of her, my eyes closing and my head falling back. Both of us are moaning, and soon she's screaming with each thrust, the slapping of skin the only other sound in the room. She's just as entranced as I am. I look down where we are joined, and I see myself moving in and out of her, and it only spears me on even more. I see her move one hand off the window, and it disappears between her legs. If that isn't the biggest turn-on, I don't know what is. I feel her walls constrict, and I know she's close.

"Fuck, Sunshine. You better fucking come soon because I can't do this much longer."

No sooner is she strangling my dick as she falls off the cliff. She's yelling my name, and it pushes me to move faster. I feel the orgasm build down my spine, and soon, my balls are tightening, and I'm coming inside her. Shit, this is the longest orgasm of my life. I can't stop moving my hips, feeling myself shooting into her what feels like endless ropes of my cum.

Our movements slow, and we fall to the ground, dripping in sweat and satisfied smirks across our faces. I don't know what comes next, but I am certain we will be doing that again. In no way am I letting her walk away from something as earth-shattering as what we just experienced together.

Chapter Ten

ELODY

My heart is racing as I lay on this man's floor, coming down off the high of that orgasm. That was one of the most intense experiences of my life. Add to the fact I came over here with a plan to clear the air around us and move forward without awkwardness. But what did I do instead? I let him take my clothes off and show me all the stars in the universe.

I'm going to take a moment to praise this man's body. The moment he took his clothes off, I couldn't stop staring at him. I mean, the man has enough muscle to be a model on a GQ cover. Each part of him looked to be perfectly sculpted into the masterpiece he is. He's all muscle and ridges. Now add in that dick of his, and I have no idea what the powers above were doing when they made this man. His body is absolutely flawless in ways I didn't know were real in a human being. When I saw athletes in photos, I thought Photoshop must have been utilized to a degree because I never thought it could be natural. I was completely wrong, though. Looking at a naked Wyatt was like staring at magnificence.

I obviously feel a pull when I'm around him, and I don't know how to describe it outside of that. All the strength and anger I had mustered up at what had previously happened between us simply disintegrated when I saw him. Even feeling upset and telling him we couldn't let what happened at the bar repeat itself, I took it in the complete opposite direction. Did I have amnesia regarding all the cons I had mentally listed as to why this was a bad idea?

He feels like the comfort of coming home, which makes no sense to me because he's practically a stranger. Aside from the fact that he knows every button to make me detonate, I don't know much about this man. He does know how to make my body convulse in a way I never thought possible, so that's something, at least.

And what the hell was I thinking about not using a condom? The moment I felt him pulling away to grab one, I held on tighter, fear taking over my thoughts that once he'd leave, I'd lose my nerve. I needed this connection, more than I ever thought. But now I realize how irresponsible I am around him.

I'm still panting and feeling like my heart is going to beat out of my chest, and I see Wyatt having the same reaction from my periphery. For someone with his athletic build, it's comforting to see him have the same post-sex reaction as me.

While I am coming off this high, my mind begins to wander, which is a dangerous thing. I can't help but look at Wyatt and compare him to the person I married. Beau was everything Wyatt isn't when it comes to physical appearance. Beau was darker in his features. He had olive skin, along with darker brown hair and brown eyes. He was tall, maybe just an inch shorter than Wyatt; however, his body never had the muscle mass that Wyatt Christianson has worked for. Beau was tall and lean, whereas Wyatt is tall and bulky. I think he has muscles on top of his muscles.

Add in that Wyatt looks like a sinful treat with his tattoos, and I can't think of two people who are more opposite. Plus, that dirty-talking mouth is not something I ever had with Beau. My late husband was incredibly sweet when we were intimate. I have never been spoken to in the manner Wyatt has done with me in such a short amount of time.

I glance over to my left to look at Wyatt lying by my side. He must feel my eyes on him, and he turns his head so we are staring at one another, a satisfied smirk taking over his features. He's full of sex appeal, which I have never really been drawn to. But something about Wyatt brings me to my knees. I don't know if it's that bad boy persona I feel when I'm with him, the feeling like I can be someone completely different than what people have come to expect of me, or if there truly is some commonality in our foundation that attracts me to him.

The longer I look at him, the more what I've done sinks in. If I felt guilty after the bar, I feel like the worst person on the planet as reality truly starts to hit me. Is this how it feels to betray a person you love? Is betrayal even the right word if that person you feel guilty moving on without isn't even here in your physical world? If Beau saw me right now, would he be disappointed in me and my actions?

Who am I kidding? If Beau were here, my life would still be in Saddle Ridge. I feel my eyes pool with emotion, and I turn toward my right, hiding my reaction with so much shame, I feel it consuming me.

"Hey, where's your mind at?" I feel Wyatt pulling my upper shoulder over so he can see me better.

I keep my head turned toward the windows, hoping whatever I'm feeling will pass, and I can compose myself enough to get the hell out of here. I just need to say my piece and leave his apartment. I wasn't kidding when I said this was the only time we'd do this. But sitting here, letting what we did sink in, it's hard to ignore this desire I have deep down to have so many more of these moments with a man I barely know.

Now that I've gotten a taste of the connection I've felt with another man, it's like my body longs for it again, even if my heart is feeling torn and confused. I feel like being far away from one another might be the only way we can move forward and conduct ourselves in a more appropriate way, where our clothes stay on at least. I don't know what he does to my walls, but he's making these emotional barriers I've worked years to build crumble to the ground.

"Elody, what is it?" This time, he uses my name, and it makes the whole thing feel even more personal. "Please don't shut me out. Don't do that. When you ran off in the bar, I honestly thought it was for other reasons, but I can't let you do it again. Please. Talk to me. What's wrong?" he sounds genuinely concerned. "Did I hurt you?"

A single tear escapes, and I brush it away in hopes it will tame the rest from falling. No such luck, and I'm vigorously wiping to try and control this waterfall that's happening on my face right now.

"I have never done that before."

I feel Wyatt chuckle behind me, and I move my head to get a look at him. Is he laughing at me while I cry? What kind of jerk does that?

"I'm glad my heartbreak is so amusing to you," I spit back.

That shuts down whatever amusement he was feeling.

"I'm not laughing at you, Sunshine. I just think it's funny that you say this was your first time when I know for a fact you have children."

He throws one of those sly smirks my way, kissing my shoulder, and then he's back to lying on the ground, covering his face with his masculine, beautiful arm. When did arms become a beautiful feature on a man? Apparently today.

"I didn't mean this was my first time having sex, jackass," I use my elbow to jab him in his side.

He really does find ways to bring out a sassy side to me that I've never unleashed. In all honesty, I had no idea I was capable of saying such things to another person.

"I meant that it was my first time having sex in five years."

That shuts him up quite fast, and he throws his arm off his

face, and his eyes are bulging. Even now, he looks spectacular. I'm fucked.

"Hold up, you haven't had sex in five years? Why? How? Why?" He is stumbling over his words, and I can't help but find that endearing.

"You said why twice. And for your information, I wasn't running to hook up with people after my husband died. I'm not sure your sister told you, but I lost my husband."

I look up at him and moves his head in a slight nod, giving me his undivided attention. "I lost Beau, and since then, my sole focus has been my kids. You are the first man to touch me, including that night in the bar, since I buried my late husband. That's why I ran off that night. I was embarrassed and also upset at myself. This isn't typical behavior for me. Add the fact that I found out you are Tessa's father while at lunch with my friends yesterday, I'm beyond mortified. I swear I had no idea who you were. I have never even looked twice at a parent of any of my students in the twenty years I've been teaching."

I probably said all that way too fast. It's something I do when I'm upset or nervous. I regurgitated all that while looking at my hands, my fingers twisting together, another tell that I'm uncomfortable right now. I finally bring my gaze up to meet his, and I'm lost in a trance.

Wyatt's eyes are much like the sky. They feel endless, and I can't help but feel comfort when I look at him, even now as I panic over what I've just done. When he saw me at that bar, his eyes were the first feature I noticed. His penetrating gaze is the same as that night, but there's a kindness to his expression as he unpacks everything I just confessed.

He pulls his large hand to the side of my face, and it feels like my skin is on fire where we connect. I close my eyes and lean into his touch because he's not only comforting to feel against me, but he also brings me a sense of stability I haven't felt in so long.

Again, comparing him to Beau is wrong, but feeling this

support from someone after feeling so lonely for this long is something I didn't realize I missed so much. His thumb strokes my cheek, and that's when I realize I'm once again experiencing a leaking from my eyes. Fucking emotional wreck, Ellie! The tears seem to just happen on their own, and it's uncontrollable. I keep my eyes closed and savor the feel of his hand on my face.

"Sunshine, I am a grumpy bastard, and I'm sorry. I'm sorry I've been treating you poorly when we've been communicating since school started. But most of all, I'm fucking sorry I misjudged. That night at the bar, I thought your reaction came from the fact you were married and had cheated on your spouse."

That causes my eyes to open. It's when he utters those words that I return to the realization that I am doing exactly what I said I wouldn't do with another man. My mind is in a forever loop between reaching for whatever this is with Wyatt, while pulling back toward my memory of Beau.

My heart can't belong to anyone else. I cannot go through that kind of loss again because I promised forever to someone else. And forever is what I had planned on giving Beau. He might not be here to receive my love, but I never thought I'd find anything after him. I came here with an intention to set ground rules. One look at Wyatt and everything I've sought to be since Beau's death, I've let it fall to my feet.

I feel my resolve grow, and my purpose of this encounter rises as I shift to get myself up off the floor.

"Hey, what are you doing? What did I say that upset you?" He's moving along with me, trying to grab things out of my hand while I'm trying to gather my belongings to make my way out of here.

"I can't do this, Wyatt. This is the one thing I promised myself I wouldn't do. My heart isn't mine to do with what I want. I already gave it to another man. My husband might not be with me anymore, but I vowed to walk this life for the two of us since his death. It's best we just try to be courteous to one another and realize that Tessa's well-being is number one."

I'm still gathering my items. My words seem to have stunned Wyatt because he's given up efforts to remove my clothing from my grasp and is now standing there in silence. Little by little, I see the tension take over his body, and his stance is getting more rigid. It's hard not to see the grumpy man I know come back, and the well-sated and relaxed version of him quickly vanish.

"You're fucking kidding me? So that's it? I just had the best sex of my life, and you're just going to walk off? You don't think this warrants a conversation? Fuck, Elody. Or shall I go back to calling you Mrs. Lorrent? Because we are back to formalities now, right? I thought we were adults and would talk it through. I know we have just had physical encounters, and that's really all we know about one another, but I'm more mature than a twenty-year-old here. I think I know how complicated things are. But I also know that the older we get, the more baggage we carry. Don't, for one second, put this on my daughter's well-being because if anything is first and foremost in this life of mine, it's Tessa. And I guess...I don't fucking know!" he throws his arms in the air, frustration radiating off of him.

"I'll admit, I saw you after Thanksgiving, the day we were supposed to meet at the school. I saw you from far away, and I panicked." I can't help my intake of breath at his confession.

"At that point, I thought you were married, and the moment I saw you, I fled. I kept telling myself it was because I didn't want to complicate things for Tessa. But now here you are, and I feel like we have this chance. Now that I know how you're processing this after not being intimate with anyone after your husband, I just thought you'd talk this through with me. Get to know me. Not treat me like a piece of meat and walk away."

He's pacing now, moving his hands through is hair. Then

he stops and looks right at me, his blue irises sucking me into this vortex we seem for form together.

"You're treating this entire situation one-sided. Like it's about your needs but ignoring mine. You are forgetting I have feelings. I have a heart too, damn it. I guess this feeling is on me, and we don't share this weird cosmic connection. What the actual fuck am I saying? I don't speak like this. This isn't me! You put some voodoo shit on me, and I'm all gaga over you while you're thinking of the quickest exit route." Shit, now he looks even more worked up. He's pacing again after putting his boxers back on while giving his little speech.

Am I being selfish here? Should I explore this?

"I have not dated or been with another man ever. Not once, aside from Beau. He was my first everything. Try growing up with someone who is your friend. Then, that person completes you in every way. Then, build a life with that person and then have them taken away. Try to imagine that. Don't stand there and act like I'm walking away from this incredible life we have built for one another. We had sex, Wyatt. I assume you've had a lot of that if my knowledge of athletes and their little fan clubs has any truth to it. I doubt I'm that amazing. I think it's just been a while for you. Maybe this is a kink you have—sleeping with a widower."

The moment I say it, I regret it. That was below the belt, and this isn't who I am. But something about Wyatt just pushes me over the edge. Top that with me feeling incredibly confused and pitying myself for my poor choices, and I say the wrong thing. In this case, something very hurtful and something I feel deep down is incredibly false.

His words earlier made it sound like I lacked a heart with how I was reacting. And what I just said confirmed that. But we aren't in a committed relationship. He's made a lot of assumptions, but I can't say I'm good with starting something with him. I have kids to consider. So does he. No matter what explanation I justify my words with, I come up short. I was wrong with my outburst, and by the way he's looking at me right now, I've pushed too far.

He moves his fingers through his hair. "You're right. I'll just cross this new fetish off my list. That's all I am, some dumb jock who has no feelings. I guess I'll let you get out of here so I can hit the town and find my next widower to fuck!"

He stalks off. He goes down a hallway that I assume leads to his bedroom. I hear the slam of a door, and I can't help but jump from the sound.

I stand there, and now the tears are back and flowing freely down my face again. What have I done? I look up toward the sky and let the emotions pass over me. Is this normal, Beau? Is it weird that I'm looking up toward the heavens in hopes you'll give me a little sign after what I've just done with another man? A sign never comes. What comes over me is immense guilt. Wyatt isn't wrong in what he's saying. I'm not being mature in handling this. I'm acting juvenile. But I honestly don't know what he expects of me. What I do know is that I never gave him a chance to speak. I just made assumptions and let it act as truth. I never let him tell me his feelings, as he's probably swimming with feelings over what this attraction between us is. Plus, I made him feel used, which is heartbreaking.

Without putting on the multitude of layers I came here with, I simply slip on one of his shirts that I find on the ground, and walk off in the direction Wyatt went, the rest of my clothes forgotten. I have no clue where this maze of an apartment leads, but who knew so much could fit in a penthouse? I didn't grow up with apartments that posed as full-blown homes. I bet this place is bigger than my detached home in Nebraska.

I see a light on down the hall and walk toward it. Once I open the door to what looks like a primary bedroom, I hear the water running, and I walk closer to what must be the attached restroom. I slowly open the door and see the steam taking over the space. This bathroom alone is larger than my room, I think.

I walk toward the shower, the glass fogging up, but I see Wyatt under the water, rinsing his hair. I don't know what this is between us. It might be two times that I've seen him in person, but I feel like he's been a part of me for far longer. I take off his shirt and walk into the shower.

Wyatt's back is to me, and I bring my arms around him, letting my hands move across the ridges of his abdomen. I kiss his back, peppering his spine with my lips. He grabs hold of my hands and turns in my arms. He lets my back hit the tile wall behind me, and he kisses me hard. Our tongues meet and all I feel is this kiss overtake all my senses. I feel my body turn on again, itching for a release. I can feel his excitement poking me in the stomach. I guess the whole hockey stamina thing is real, even for a retired player in his forties.

As the dirty thoughts begin to swirl in my mind, Wyatt pulls away, his body detangling from mine, and he takes a few steps back, as if our close proximity puts him in a trance. The distance is his only savior at the moment.

"No, Elody. I can't do this. I need to have you, all of you, with me if we allow this physical thing to move forward. I want to explore what this is. I wish I understood this pull I feel with you, but right now, I don't. What I do know is I deserve more than a brushoff. If you aren't capable of giving me something, anything more, than don't do this. I don't want to just let us fall into a pattern of sex, and then you end each encounter with a freakout. I can already tell that's the direction we're headed if we allow this to continue. I want to see where this goes because I have honestly never felt this before."

Something about his expression tells me he's surprised by his own confession. As much as I've always been a monogamous lover, I don't know if that's something Wyatt is used to. So, for him to confess his feelings in such a manner must surprise him on many levels.

He looks so vulnerable when he says this to me. Thank goodness water is surrounding us and splashing all over, or he'd see the tears falling down my face again. I nod and look down at my feet.

"I can't promise you much, Wyatt. I meant what I said. My heart isn't really up for grabs. I have rules for a reason. But I feel something toward you that I've never felt, even after being married most of my adult life. And that scares me. I feel this connection to you in a way I have never even dreamed of having again with another man. But I have a past that will always be with me. He lives on in my children, and he lives on in me."

"I'm not trying to replace a feeling or a life you once had. I just feel like most of my life, I have only chased one thing: hockey. Then Tessa came into my life, and my whole world shifted to her and her needs. For a moment there, I had both the loves of my life—hockey and my little girl. But now, my sole focus is Tess. And all I'm asking is for you to give whatever this attraction is a chance. You're coming out of left field for me, too, Elody.

"Hell, I'm not even asking for much except the ability to get to know you. I don't want to just have sex with you and walk away. I need to explore this between us because I haven't stopped thinking of you since that night in November. Your sounds have haunted me because all I wanted was to feel you squirm under my touch. But I can't do that if you're going to be closed off from the get-go. I need honesty if we are going to share intimacy together. I've done the faking it to see where things lead with Tessa's mother, and that blew up in not only my face but in my daughter's. I don't need that again. That's what's changed for me since Tessa. Her mother already left her and left me to figure out parenthood alone. I don't need that type of abandonment either. But I also don't want to feel used without being given a chance to have a say in how I'm treated. What you said out there was wrong, and I need to know you don't think that of me."

I hear the vulnerability in his words. I know what it's like to be left behind, but for Wyatt, someone chose that route, versus my path was chosen for Beau and I. Abandonment issues are seeping under both Wyatt and myself, however, we both feel those things for completely different reasons.

I am alone, with no male comfort for years, and the one time I think this will be just physical, I find a man that needs more. What are the chances? But he's right. We aren't kids goofing off. We have a lot that we bring to the table, some good and some bad. It's naive to think that we won't have our lives to live without intermixing those together. Plus, I don't know who I think I'm fooling if I believed I could walk out of this apartment and not feel a piece of my mind returning to the what-ifs of this situation. I think it's safe to say I would not have let this go.

I think we'd be back here in a number of days, fighting whatever this attraction is. He drives me mad and that's something I became aware of quite early on with how we email one another and argue in the few interactions we've had. I can tell Wyatt likes to be an alpha male, which I think was something I thought I'd love maybe twenty years ago. Beau and I didn't fight much because our personalities were very similar. But now, I think I like the fightback that I have experienced with Wyatt. I am not really one to push back with people because I love pleasing others. It feels like he sees past that and wants to see me show a fight, and a part of me respects him for that push into the unknown for me.

"Fine, we can try whatever this is. But we keep it casual. This isn't love, Wyatt. This is just us scratching an itch and seeing how it evolves. No promises."

I can see he wants to push me on this. His features are thinking what I've said over and soon I see a sense of calm wash over his expression. When his eyes meet mine, I can see a playful side of him emerging, that tension dissipating from earlier.

"Oh, Sunshine, I knew you'd cave to my charms," he says with a little smirk that tells me he's used to getting his way.

I must admit I love seeing him be a little lighter, compared to the grumpy hockey player he seems to be ninety-eight percent of the time. I bite my bottom lip and give him whatever sexy smolder I can, which he seems to like, and he pulls me to him. The cockiness in his tone is back, and all I see is the sex god he is.

I feel him growing against my belly again, and I can't help the excitement I feel. This is so not me. I'm the put-together Ellie who has her classroom in order, and all the meals prepped the weekend before the school week. I am not the woman that drives over to a student's home to confront their hot as fuck parent. Also, I'm not the woman who says words like shit and fuck all the time, and my mind seems to be throwing those out there like it's nobody's business. Something about Wyatt sets a part of me free, and I'm starting to embrace that instead of running from it.

My hands begin their descent, wrapping one hand around his cock. I start stroking him and love the reaction I'm getting from him with just this type of movement. I was never one to feel empowered during sex, but I feel like unleashing that side of me with Wyatt. I want to explore this side and see where it takes me if I'm taking this newfound leap. I keep up my movements along his shaft, and Wyatt rewards me with a moan that pushes me further.

"Fuck, El, that feels incredible. Don't stop." The moment he says that, I feel a little confident with control. I let my hands fall to my side. The stare down Wyatt gives me is one with so much sexual frustration, I have to bite my bottom lip to keep myself from letting out a laugh.

"I said don't stop, not the opposite," he says into my ear right before he nibbles on my neck.

I tilt my head to the side, letting him move his lips along the column of my neck, relishing in the heat building within me. Before I can talk myself out of it, I drop to my knees. If I'm going to embrace this side of me, I may as well rip off the band-aid and go all in.

The moment my movements register for Wyatt, he says, "I'd say you don't have to do that, but I am not going to stop you. Seeing your lips around my cock is something I've fantasized about since the bar."

I lick along his shaft and back up toward the mushroom head, then taking his dick into my mouth and closing my eyes while hearing Wyatt's moans echo in the shower. That spears me on, and I bob up and down, feeling that power take over. I open my eyes and bring my gaze up to look into his eyes, which seems to give me even more confidence.

Knowing I'm the cause of his sounds brings me more energy to keep going. He's so big; it doesn't take much to feel him at the back of my throat. I've taken on the whole spicy romance book genre by storm these last few years, so I decide to see how far I can push Wyatt while I've got this control.

I bring my hand that was resting on his thighs to cup his balls, and the sound Wyatt makes in approval makes me want to pump my fist into the air. I keep it going, sucking him off while playing with his balls. Soon, I feel Wyatt put one hand in my hair while the other arm is resting on the tiled wall, his forehead now against the wall as well. He's moving his hips in rhythm to my movements, and I can tell he's close.

"Fuck, El, I'm going to cum. Shit, fuck, yes."

His movements are erratic, and I begin sucking harder and quicker. To say my jaw is tired is an understatement. How do women do this and not have some sort of jaw disorder? But while those thoughts start to pierce my mind, I also feel completely in control here. And feeling like I'm in control of a man like Wyatt is beyond empowering. So I keep at it, and soon I feel the warmth of his release in my mouth, making its way down my throat. Shit, that's hot. I get it now. The jaw pain will be worth it because the way I've rendered him speechless is priceless.

I pull his dick out of my mouth and then move to kiss up along his abdomen, needing to feel his tight muscles under my lips. The moment I touch him there, he squirms. I guess it's not just his dick that's sensitive. I smile at his reaction and come off the ground to stand in front of him again. The moment I'm upright, he grabs my face and kisses me hard. I feel my body ignite all over again and feel like a bit of a teen again. I can't keep my hands or lips off this man.

"Shit, Elody, you are incredible. That mouth of yours can be quite sassy, but you sucked me off to the point of seeing stars. Fuck."

He begins peppering kisses down my neck, soon going to my breasts, giving them equal attention. I feel like I'm sensitive all over, little zings of electricity being left behind each kiss Wyatt places on my body. I can't help the sounds I make as I feel his tongue swirl around each nipple. Soon, he's moving further south, and I can't help but feel excited about what's to come. He's at the apex of my thighs, and he's just staring at me.

"I love your pussy. From the little taste I got at that bar, it's a piece of heaven."

I try not to focus on heaven and angels because my thoughts will veer toward Beau at the worst time. I choose to look down and focus my attention on the man between my legs, getting ready to devour me. The first swipe of his tongue through my folds has me nearly buckling. I feel my spine coming off the tile wall and my head rearing back, closing my eyes at the intensity of his tongue on my most sensitive spot.

"Oh my gosh. Right there, yes," I moan, and Wyatt takes over. He works my clit, while he moves two fingers into me. The feeling of his fingers has nothing on his cock, but I also can't seem to focus much on that because soon he's curving those fingers and rubbing that special spot within that sets me off. Soon, I'm moving my hips in an uncontrollable manner. What the hell? How is this so intense when I just had sex within the last hour?

What seems like seconds later, I feel the build of my orgasm starting. It's moving through my body, and I feel like parts of me are lighting on fire as I start to fall off the edge of that cliff.

"Don't stop. Right there. Yes, Wyatt."

I feel my hips moving involuntarily, the water hitting both of us and doing nothing to cool down this fire inside me. Wyatt slows his movements but continues to ride this wave with me as I come down from that high. I feel him pull his fingers out and bring my leg down. I wish I could say I remember him draping one of my legs over his shoulder, but the orgasm was so intense that I may have blacked out as he licked and sucked my core.

From the moan he lets out right now, I assume he's licking his fingers. I keep my eyes closed but smile, thinking about how my arousal tastes good to him. He begins peppering me with kisses along the inside of my thighs, and I laugh from the sensitivity. Everything on me feels like it's heightened. I open my eyes to find him looking right at me.

"Sunshine, hearing you climax might be my favorite new thing."

He makes his way back up toward my face and kisses me slowly, and I taste myself on his lips. I never thought that would be hot, but damn, is it ever. I move my arms to wrap around his neck, and he pulls me directly under the stream of water. We use the rest of our time in the shower to wash one another off. It feels good to be connected like this again to someone. I didn't realize how much I missed it, always believing I simply missed Beau and our time together. But I never put much weight on the fact that companionship, even if just in a physical way, was possible with anyone else.

Chapter Eleven

WYATT

Elody and I finished showering, and we quickly got dried off and dressed. Once we were done in the restroom, I saw the time and panicked, as I am supposed to be down at my sister's in fifteen minutes. We had a day in the city planned out. As cold as it was, Tessa wanted to go down to the tree at Rockefeller Center and get hot cocoa. I know we'll be in the mix of every tourist today, but this is our first holiday season in New York, and I couldn't keep from giving my girl one last look at the tree for the season.

We press the button and while we wait for the elevator, I bring Elody toward my body and give her a kiss that's not at all PG in nature. I can feel her body melt into mine, and I wish I could have her come along with us this afternoon. The moment I pull away, I see a calm smile wash over her features. It seems she's finally embracing this magnetic charge between us, even if just a bit of time has passed since we decided to give this a shot. I think this will be an up-road battle with her, but I'll be patient and take it one step at a time.

This is new for both of us in very different ways, so I need to respect how she wants to handle it while also respecting my own feelings toward the matter. As a successful athlete, I've grown accustomed to people using me, and I honestly couldn't deal with that rejection from Elody earlier. We do agree on one thing, though: we will keep this between us for a few weeks to see how things progress forward.

"So I'll call you later?" I ask, as I know our time being this close together is seconds from ending.

"Sure, if I had your number," she says, again with the sass. I smile and look down at her.

"Such a little spitfire, Sunshine. Also, you looked up my address but not my phone number in the school directory?" I smile at her while she rolls her eyes and realize I haven't smiled this much without my daughter present since—-well, maybe ever. I like how light I feel around Elody.

"I put my number in your phone when you left it open on my kitchen table. You were looking for your socks in the living room." I kiss her nose, and then we come apart when the elevator dings and the doors open.

I put my hand out and ensure the doors don't close on us as we move into the elevator. I press the buttons for both my sister's floor and the lobby.

"I'll be out all afternoon with Tessa and my family, but I can call once she's in bed." I sound like a desperate teen who needs to know the girl he likes will answer his call. I haven't been like this since freshman year of high school, when I played hockey but hadn't quite grown into the confident man I later became in college.

"My son should be home soon, and he stays up late each night. I will text you when I have some time to myself to chat a bit before bed. Luckily, the break started later this year so I still have a few days to get myself mentally prepared for my students, who will likely be on a holiday hangover when they all return," she says, and I can see the small smile spread across her face. I can sense that being a teacher is such a huge part of her, and I can feel the love she has for her profession.

Soon enough, the elevator dings, and the doors open on

my sister's floor. Without realizing what's happening, I hear a loud sound from the hallway, and then I hear my daughter screaming, "Mrs. Lorrent! Hi, Mrs. Lorrent!"

My daughter comes barreling into the elevator, and my sister is following behind, embarrassment written all over her face.

"I'm so sorry. She opened the door, waiting for you, Xan, and before I knew it, she was running toward you both. Sorry about that."

At this point, we hop off the elevator because this will take longer than a second. I can see the concern etched all over Elody's face, but she's doing a good job of giving my daughter attention and asking about her holiday break.

"Hi, sweet girl. I ran into your dad in the elevator. This is such a coincidence," Ellie explains as Tessa smiles back. I can feel my daughter's excitement radiating off her as she talks to her favorite teacher, although Ellie's the only teacher Tess has ever had.

"Are you coming to see the tree too?" Tessa asks, hopping on her feet with anticipation that Elody will be joining us.

"Oh no, sweetie. I have to get home. I was just running an errand, and I have to go see my kids now. I've been gone longer than expected already."

At that, Elody's eyes find mine, and we share a little smile with one another. My thoughts automatically go to what we were doing not too long before now, and I can't help the excitement that passes over me as I wonder when we'll have some time together again.

Elody gives Tessa a hug, and right as she's about to turn around to click the button for the elevator, my parents come out of my sister's apartment. Holy hell, what in the world? Talk about jumping feet first into this whole thing. Shit, if Elody wasn't concerned before, she's going to flee after this encounter.

I can see the smile on my mother's face is more than happiness. This is utterly delightful for her. She always envisioned me being married off at this point, and after everything with Tessa's mother went sideways, I could tell her heart hurt for many reasons besides the abandonment of a mother toward her infant child.

"Who do we have here, son?" That's my father, putting a hand on my shoulder and looking at Ellie. His mischievous smile matches my mother's; however, he can sense how uncomfortable I am and is feeding off that to make fun of me later.

I get my height and stature from my father, but my hair color and eyes from my mother. My sister falls in line with my dad's darker features of hair and eyes. Her fair skin is a toss-up as neither of my parents shares that with Juliette. I look at Dad, pleading with my gaze to let this go and we can talk about it later.

"Hi. I'm Robin, Wyatt's mother. And this is my husband, Wyatt's father, Jeremy. It seems you've met the rest of my family." She is so sweet, it's hard not to appreciate this incredible person in my life.

My parents are both softies, but my mom can make anyone feel welcome. No one understands where my broody personality comes from because my parents are equally kind in a way I seem to lack.

Elody must sense the genuine sweetness in my mother's tone and reaches her hand out to shake my mother's.

"I'm Elody, Mrs. Lorrent as the kids know me. I'm Tessa's kindergarten teacher and just happened to run into Mr. Christianson in the building." Ellie hopes my mom will catch on that we cannot expand on this matter with little ears listening.

"Oh yes, what a happen-chance meet-up, if I do say so myself." My mom swings her gaze between me and Elody, and I can see Ellie's cheeks flame with the realization my mother is not blind to the fact that this isn't a coincidence of an encounter.

And if my mother is really paying attention, she will put two and two together because I know my sister returned to her apartment earlier this morning with news that Tessa's teacher was headed upstairs for a visit with me. Looking down at my watch, I realize Elody has been with me for some time now. With the sneaky smile across both my parent's faces, they are definitely connecting the dots on how our meeting went. Fuck my life. I will not hear the end of it. I don't even try to look at Juliette right now because I know she'll have all her thoughts written across her face.

"Well, I should get going. Have a lovely afternoon looking at the tree," she looks down at Tessa for the last part. I can't take my eyes off Ellie. She is purely that magical, and I can't wait to get to know her even more. From the little bit we got to talk while getting ourselves cleaned up just now, she's pretty involved with her kids and has spent a great deal of her life making sure those around her are taken care of.

"Thanks for everything," I say, giving her a nod that I hope comes off more business-like than anything. Right then, my sister snorts, likely loving this awkward encounter. I can't help but cut her a look to shut the fuck up, and my sister does a shit job of hiding her amusement.

This time, the clown car that is my sister's apartment does not hold any more surprises, and Elody successfully clicks the button for the elevator and rushes through the doors once it arrives. She waves and smiles, and my family does the same back; everyone entranced with her beauty in the same way I feel I am already. I simply stare at her, hoping she can sense the heat in my gaze as I watch the doors close. Her cheeks flame again, and I know my watchful glare had the intended desire.

The moment the doors close, Tessa is jumping up and down, talking about how excited she is to have seen Mrs. Lorrent outside of the classroom. I instruct her to grab her jacket and beanie from Auntie Julie's apartment, and my daughter dashes inside to get everything she needs for our afternoon adventure.

The moment Tessa is gone from the hallway, I have three pairs of eyes staring at me, hoping for some clarification.

"Thanks so much for watching Tessa for me. I know she had a blast." I move to click on the elevator door, hoping to avoid any verbal onslaught from my family, but of course, I'm not so lucky. They all speak at once.

"Well, she's pretty," I hear my mother say, as my sister chimes in, "You better not wreck this, Xander." My father follows with, "I like her," and I feel overwhelmed by everyone's two cents being thrown at me all at once.

I sigh, and the grumpiness I usually exhibit is back, which I assume is what they expected.

"Listen, we are not talking about this right now. Maybe ever. Got me? I'm trying something new with her, and I do not need to get Tessa's hopes up. Elody and I have this like/hate thing going, and I'm sort of okay with it right now. Let me see where it goes. Please don't make a big deal out of it." I keep clicking the elevator button in hopes the urgency I'm presenting will be answered by the universe at this exact moment.

"I know, Wyatt, but remember, we just want what's best for you. Seeing you put your heart out there is all we can ask for. We know how much Sabrina imploded your dating life," my father says, and I know he's right. They just want what's best for me.

"Speak for yourself. I want what's best for Elody, if you ask me." My parents glare at my sister when she says this, and I smirk, knowing I love this game we play where I'm the favorite child.

My sister rolls her eyes, "Fine! I guess Xander's happiness means something, too," she relents, and I can tell it probably felt like a mouthful of glass for as painful that must have been for her to admit.

My daughter comes bounding out right then, and she looks set for our adventure. We all get into the elevator when it arrives and start to head downstairs. I let go of all I'm feeling toward whatever is brewing with Elody. I can't let that get in the way of my time with Tessa. But throughout the entire afternoon, I can't help but think of her pretty teacher and how she would fit in perfectly with my family.

I'm royally fucked, aren't I?

Chapter Twelve

ELODY

After returning from Wyatt's earlier today, I went right into mom mode. I had a late lunch with my girls while I waited for Tyler to return home. You'd think he was gone a month with how we greeted him at the door. I really do enjoy his company, even when everyone said I should dread the teenage years.

I think with Beau's passing, Tyler took on the role of the man of the house. As outdated as that term might be, I really appreciated the supportive role he brought to our family dynamic after his father passed. Tyler had every reason to be angry and resentful that his life had changed so drastically. It doesn't mean Tyler didn't have outbursts, but he has been much more mature than I thought I'd get during these difficult and hormonal years.

We've had our moments where we were trying to figure out how life would look without Beau around, but with many nights of us laying out our fears on the table, I think we have come to a great understanding of how we should work together instead of against one another to ensure things flow smoothly within the home.

I am well aware that Tyler needs a life of his own, and I try my hardest not to impose my sorrow and difficulties onto him.

But he still sees me as a grieving mother. That's just proof my sunny disposition isn't working as much as I had hoped. He offers to watch the girls more often than I take him up on because I feel like he is still a teen. Now he's a teenager with a girlfriend, and I remember how fun those times were hanging out and watching love bloom. But it also brings to the forefront that we'll be having a few more talks about safety soon. I do not need to become a grandmother at this point in my life. I'm way too young for that.

Now we're on the couch, relaxing after we finished cleaning up the kitchen. I took stock of my fridge and the pantry earlier to see what we needed from the market. Much like years prior, Becca and I will be running to the store tomorrow together to grab food for the upcoming week. She has cut back at work quite a bit, so I'm happy Shane is now in her life to bring an added element to her day-to-day. But we've kept our shopping trips; however, we modified it due to the holiday and will be taking a trip for restocking on Tuesday instead of Sunday. I can almost bet money that Shane will likely be added to our shopping trips in the months to come because that man is head over heels in love with my best friend.

As if I conjured her up, there's a knock on my door, and when I check the doorbell app, I see her standing there, making faces at the camera. I roll my eyes at her goofiness, but it makes my heart happy to see this side of her that I felt had disappeared years ago when Shane left after high school.

I rush to open the door, and soon I'm embracing one of my favorite people. Despite marriages, kids, divorce, and death, I still feel like she and I are one another's person. I feel lucky in that way, that life has definitely thrown curveballs, but she's been there through it all. Her twins come rushing in behind her, hoping to play with my kids while Becca and I catch up.

I look behind her again and can't help my question, "No Shane?"

Becca shakes her head. "No. When Olive and my parents dropped the twins off from their little New Year's getaway, Shane decided to go back with Liv to hang out a bit with her." Olive and Shane just reconnected, and I can tell he is itching to get to know his daughter better.

"Come in. Let's grab some tea. Are we still good to go shopping tomorrow?" Becca nods at my question, and I feel a sense of relief.

With the way things went with Wyatt earlier, I feel like I need some of my normal routines to keep me grounded. I am still feeling antsy with the fact that I'm doing this thing with Wyatt and continue to feel guilt sweep over me that I'm somehow betraying Beau at the same time. Maybe a call to my therapist is warranted.

I push my thoughts aside and walk to my kitchen, filling the electric kettle up and moving toward the pantry for my little tray of tea sachets that we can choose from. Becca always makes fun of me, saying I'm like Monica from *Friends* because I'm always so organized. This tray is no different; all teas organized by color and whether they are caffeinated or not. I guess I am a little neurotic, but at this point, she's stuck with me, so she'll live with it.

Becca chuckles when she sees the assortment, although she's seen it before. Each time, she laughs because it's a reminder of how I ease my stress by cleaning and organizing. She's not so far off from my cleaning habits, but I definitely take it to a whole new level. She picks chamomile, and I do the same, hoping this tea will hold the magic potion to calm my racing heart rate that hasn't eased since I left Wyatt's house earlier.

I'm grabbing mugs when Becca pulls the stool out, making an awful sound as it scrapes along my floor. I'm not expecting it, and I jump.

"Woah, what has you so jumpy? What's up with you, Ellie?"

Of course, she can tell that I'm a little off, and I can't lie to her. I finish preparing our teas and sit on the stool beside her. The kids are now upstairs; Tyler in his room, likely starting a load of laundry because the apple does fall far from the tree, and my girls and Becca's twins playing on their Switches. My place is like an extended home for Mallory and Jackson, so they fit into our routine no matter what time of day they come over.

The moment I sit down, I feel Becca's eyes on me. I won't get out of this without laying it all out there, so I do. I let out everything from what happened at the bar, to after I left her and Shane at the restaurant up to the point where I got on the elevator with Wyatt's gaze undressing me as the doors closed. The moment I'm done rehashing all that happened, I finally look up from my tea to find Becca hasn't touched her mug and is just sitting there, mouth agape, with eyes wide. She's looking at me like I've grown an extra head. I feel uncomfortable under her gaze and start to squirm in my seat.

"What?" I finally ask because I can't stand the silence and the possibility she stroked out while I told my story.

I feel the guilt creep in the longer she doesn't say anything. Maybe this isn't the right thing to do. Here I was saying I was going to keep this between Wyatt and me, but since we talked about it in his home, his parents, sister, and now my bestie have been looped in. We are terrible secret keepers, that I know for certain. From this point on, I have to be careful because I do not want the kids to find out just yet. I don't want to start commotion over something that most likely won't make it past a month.

Becca finally blinks and takes a sip of her tea, which I assume is now lukewarm at best. "You fucked an NHL star, and you're still walking straight?"

A Cheshire cat's smile crosses her face, and I can't help the laughter that bubbles out of me. It feels good to laugh. Only Becca would say something like that after everything I just confessed.

"I can't believe it. You have no sex for years, and the first guy you sleep with is the GOAT of the NHL? Wow. You really aim high, huh, Ellie?"

Now she's laughing so hard she has tears falling down her face. I can't help it, I'm laughing, too, because it all seems a bit surreal and so out of my norm that I just let all the emotions out as we both grab our bellies and laugh even harder, having trouble catching our breath. We both are so lost in laughter that we don't hear Laney and Grant walk into the kitchen.

"What's so funny?" Laney asks while Grant has a concerned look on his face. They both probably think we're losing it.

"Is this a perimenopausal thing or something?" Grant opens his dumb mouth, and in seconds, Becca stops laughing, shoots daggers at her brother, and throws a decorative apple at him. He dodges the apple while Laney keeps her gaze locked on us. She has always been perceptive when it comes to those she loves, and tonight is no different.

"Seriously, what's going on here? What's so funny?" Now my sister is looking directly at me while Becca has gotten up to hug her brother, then tries to pinch him as payback for the menopause comment.

"Nothing. Becca is just cracking jokes at my expense. How was the show?"

Grant gifted Laney Broadway tickets to Aladdin, her favorite Disney movie growing up, for Christmas. Laney was hesitant to be in an auditorium with that many people, but Grant really wanted her to take this step with him and somehow convinced her to try it out. The gift was one with an out clause: if she wanted to leave mid-show, he would. Seems she was able to endure the entire thing.

"It was really nice," Laney looks back at Grant, and his smile speaks volumes.

He loves doing things like this for her. I know how much he loves my sister and how patient he has been with her since her incident. Hopefully, with little steps forward like this, she can embrace life to the fullest, much like she once did.

Grant and Becca begin chatting, and I start to clear the mugs from the table. I'm loading the dishwasher, and Laney comes up next to me and whispers, "I know there's more to that giggle-fest between you and Becca. Don't think for a minute you're getting off that easy." I roll my eyes like a teenager and keep my mouth shut. I will give Laney the details, but after this long day, I'm ready to call it a night.

The moment that thought passes through, my phone chimes, and I quickly run toward it, but Laney is faster and closer to it.

"Who's 'GOAT in Bed,' and why is he texting right now?" Damn it, Wyatt. Such a jackass. He programmed himself with that name?

"It's an inside joke from a friend," I say as I try to grab the phone from my sister.

Becca is once again laughing, knowing I'm mortified. At least we are laughing and not crying, which is something we've done a lot throughout the years. So, I'll take this as a win. I take the time to quickly explain an abbreviated version to Grant and Laney while the kids are still upstairs. I am exhausted by this storytelling for a second time in thirty minutes, and I hope no one else walks in who needs a recap.

Grant is stunned; apparently, he's a huge NHL fan and watches their games a lot when time allows. The way he talks about Wyatt as an athlete, I'm starting to understand where the muscles come from. He's apparently very rigid with his workout regime to the point Sports Illustrated did an entire article on what his nutritionist came up with for his dietary needs during the hockey season. He has also been featured multiple times, talking about his rigorous exercise routine on sports programs throughout his career. And he continues his regimented workouts even now in retirement.

The kids come barreling downstairs, and I quickly reiterate that this stays between us and will not go any further than the four of us. Becca pleads for permission to tell Shane, and I give in because she can be quite persistent. She was married to a lawyer prior, so she's picked up some skills along the way. I also point a finger toward my sister, then make a gesture to zip her lips and pretend to throw away an imaginary key when talking around Mom and Dad. I do not need them going gaga over this whole situation, especially because I am confident it will be short-lived.

After she rolls her eyes at me, she gives me her promise by crossing her fingers over her heart, and we all disperse. I get my girls ready for bed, and Tyler says goodnight. He said he's wiped after all the festivities with his girlfriend over the holiday weekend.

I head to my room and get ready for bed. I look down at my phone and remember I have a text to read from Wyatt:

> **GOAT IN BED**
>
> Hey. I got Tessa down and am winding down. Give me a call if you can. I'll wait to hear from you.

There's a softness to Wyatt now that we've cleared the air. He didn't text much, but hearing him say he's waiting to hear from me gives me butterflies.

What the hell is wrong with me now? I go from hating the guy to having butterflies?

I finish getting ready and head toward my bed. I decide to FaceTime him instead of calling or texting. It rings for what feels like a second, and a sleepy Wyatt picks up. His voice is groggy, and I know I just woke him.

"Hey, Sunshine," he says, his eyes still trying to adjust to the light in his room.

"I'm so sorry. I didn't mean to wake you. It's not too late, so I thought I'd call you." I feel awful. I'm a parent. I know many go to bed quite early. I'm a night owl, which is something Becca loved when she was up late caring for Olive or studying for a test.

"No. It's not a problem at all. I fell asleep reading a really boring book. Sorry about that. It was a long afternoon. Tessa was adamant about going ice skating, and I bet you can envision how crowded it was today of all days. We had to wait forever for skates, and then the rink was packed. But she had such a huge smile on her face, it was worth it. I'll send you some pictures once we hang up."

A sweet smile crosses his features, and I can't help the smile I return. He has so much love for that little girl, and I can tell he moves through life to make her happy. There's nothing sexier than a dad who has his daughter wrapped around his finger.

"That sounds precious. I can't wait to hear her version of events when we return to school. How have her sugars been throughout the holidays? Is it tough to manage?"

Wyatt rubs his hand down his face, attempting to wake up a little more.

"Yeah, it's still a learning process for all of us. This was our second holiday season since she was diagnosed, so I think each year, we'll figure things out more and more. Luckily, she's got that positive disposition, so she seems to let it all roll off her back. But I know that this illness will have its ups and downs. I just hope it doesn't take her positive spirit with it."

I can see the anguish across his face as he thinks about how she'll have to live with her diagnosis for the rest of her life.

"Medicine has come a long way. I've been talking to Becca about the advances in type 1 diabetes, and she gives me updates."

This seems to bring joy to his features as he points his bright blue eyes my way. I feel his eyes to my core, and I can't help the uptick it does to my pulse.

"You learned more about it for the sake of my kid?"

"Becca is an OB-GYN, and she has to care for a lot of pregnant women with the disease. I knew about Tessa's condition before her grumpy, demanding father gave me a laminated list of her needs," I say teasingly, and he chuckles. "I wanted to make sure that no big changes had come up since my last student that had it was a few years back, right before the pandemic."

"You're one of a kind, Sunshine. I appreciate you looking out for her. And I'm sorry I ever made you feel less than with the way I was demanding things of you regarding Tessa's care. You are the first person, aside from my family, to care for her. So I was a bit protective," he says, and I can hear how genuine he is through his words.

"A bit? I would say immensely. But I will chalk it up to you being a good dad and not being a total douche canoe to me," I laugh.

"Douche canoe? What in the world is that?" he asks, his features showing distaste toward the terminology.

"I read it all the time in my romance novels, and it sort of stuck. I find the phrase hilarious, and I like using it in a sentence whenever I can," I explain, feeling proud of my hip terminology, if I do say so myself.

"Well, as long as I'm the only douche canoe in your life, I'm okay with it," he replies, trying to be all sly, but I catch on to what he's saying.

"Wyatt, you're the only man I'm seeing right now. Remember, first in five years? Yeah, I don't have the bandwidth for more," I say, trying to sound playful with this banter, even though I feel a part of my anxiety rise, knowing all this is a lot to take on after years of pushing anything remotely romantic away from my life.

"You're the only Sunshine in my life. So I guess we're going to see where this goes then," he says, and the smile he throws at me makes my panties melt.

He might be the most beautiful man walking this earth right now, and I could look at him smile all day. He doesn't give out his playful side much from what I could tell in our interactions so far, and I'm feeling lucky I'm seeing so much of it right now.

"I know you're tired, and I have a feeling my kids will be up early tomorrow. They soak in any moment of break they can muster, then complain every morning I wake them up to go to school. The vicious cycle of parenting, I guess. My parents are leaving tomorrow night, so I'll be busy with them all day," I tell him, wishing I could see him at some point but having no idea when we will be able to squeeze some time in together. Luckily, he must read my mind because his response is one that makes me anticipate our next meet-up.

"I have meetings and scrimmages with my guys tomorrow. I have a string of away games coming up, but I'd love to take you out on a date when we get back. Would that be okay?" I can tell he's nervous as he asks me out, and I can't help the butterflies multiplying in my belly.

"I'd love that." We get our schedules mapped out, and it sounds like I'm going on a date with Wyatt Christianson in ten days, and I'm already counting down.

Chapter Thirteen

WYATT

"This game is taking years off my life."

The days are inching closer to playoffs, and our record is promising enough that we will reach the coveted spot to play on that level if we keep it up. The team is playing well together, and that's always the hardest part if you ask me. Even if they don't make the playoffs, they've put in a lot of effort that will work as a great stepping stone for next season. This game, however, is getting the best of the guys on the ice. Tonight has been more physical than most of the games we've played this season. The hits have been brutal, and I'm counting the seconds on the clock for this to be over.

We are up by one goal, and that's adding fuel to the fire for the other team. I can see my guys are wiped, and they are counting down that clock just as much as me. The captain is on the bench taking a breather, but he's amped to get back in. The moment I tap him back to return to the ice, I see that fire ignite under his ass. His energy carries over to his teammates.

As the seconds wind down, I look to my left and see Tessa sitting in the stands. She's got headphones on to drown out the sound of the crowd. My sister and parents sit with her, looking excited as the players zip by with the same tenacity I had when I was playing. My daughter is fully engrossed in the movements of the players. I love having her at the games I coach.

This job is one I'm still getting used to, but this is a perk for me when it comes to being a part of a sport I love. Having my daughter here to see what I do brings pride to my heart. I also don't have to worry about her seeing me get injured, so that has been a pleasant shift in all of this.

The buzzer finally sounds, indicating the game is over, and the players and I start heading toward the locker room. Each of my players spots Tessa and give her a high five or fist bump, and her smile growing with the attention. She's come to a few of my coaching sessions when Juliette has brought her, and the players love having her cheer them along as they run drills.

"I'll be right out, Tess. Wait with Auntie Julie and your grandparents."

I nod toward my parents and sister as I make my way through the hall toward the locker room. The commotion is loud as I enter the locker room and see the players sitting on the bench, giving their bodies a moment to recover from the chaos that was that game.

The moment I walk in, they grow quiet, waiting to hear what I have to say. This part of my job is one I'm still growing into, but knowing these guys look up to me, not just as a former athlete, but as their coach, is something I take pride in.

"Alright. That was brutal, but you played a solid game. I know this opponent was quite exhausting, but we only have one option: to look ahead. I want you guys to take tonight to rest, and we'll be back on that ice tomorrow to condition. Keep in mind that games like these are going to become more common as we get closer to the playoffs. All the teams are gunning for that coveted playoff spot, but remember, the end result is about strength and perseverance.

"Your hard work is paying off, and I can see that in your efforts out there. Continue to push forward with the same determination, and you will be rewarded with wins like these. For the sake of my blood pressure, try to score a few more instead of making it such a nail-biter."

The guys laugh at that and I continue, "Now get your asses up and go shower. I can smell you from here. If you need to see the team doc, go right ahead. Good game, guys."

With that, the captain of the team gets up and gives a little speech of his own, trying to show his appreciation to his teammates as they put this game behind them and move forward to the next.

I'm walking back toward my office when I feel someone tap on my shoulder. I turn around and see one of my players behind me. Rodriguez is one of our younger players, still quite green, but a hell of a player.

"Hey, coach, do you have a moment?" he asks, and I immediately feel the hairs on the back of my neck stand at attention.

I motion for him to follow me and open my door for him to walk through. Once inside, I close my door and stay quiet. He can lead this discussion, but I hope what he's about to say doesn't throw us all for a loop.

"So Sammie has been feeling sick lately. She's been really tired and not eating much. I found out before today's game that she's been diagnosed with type 1 diabetes."

He looks anguished as he says these words, and I'm taken back in time to the moment I heard the same diagnosis for my own little girl. Rodriguez may be young, but he is the father of a little girl who's turning four years old at the end of the month.

His high school girlfriend got pregnant while they were both freshman in college. They've gone through a lot of adjustments throughout the years, but when he was drafted to the NHL, that was something he always made clear to his teammates: his daughter always came first. My heart aches for him because I know the road ahead is one full of uncertainty.

It takes time to get used to all the dynamics related to this disease, and with no idea how to care for people with this chronic condition, it can feel quite cumbersome.

"I'm sorry to hear that."

I move toward the front of my desk and sit at the edge, crossing my legs in front of me as Rodriguez sits in one of the seats in front of the desk.

"I remember, all too well, how it feels to be in your shoes. I know it feels like something you'll never understand, but with time, you'll get used to how the disease works and how to mitigate her sugars to manageable parameters."

"I just thought you should know after my outburst on the ice with Campbell."

Rodriguez is usually pretty even-tempered, and he got into a fight on the ice after one of our opponents, Eric Campbell, got in Rodriguez's face and talked shit. Both ended up in the penalty box, and at the time, I wondered if there was more to the argument than Rodriguez was letting on.

"I didn't want to unload all this during the game, so I thought I'd come talk to you now. I'm sorry for that, but Campbell was being a dick, pushed my buttons, and I just lost it. I promise I won't lose my cool and cost my team precious time. I could be on the ice being an asset to my team instead of sitting in the sin bin."

He looks down at his hands, fidgeting with his fingers, showing me he's definitely processing what's going on now that his life has taken a turn.

"Listen, I know what you're feeling. I don't mind you bringing some fire to the game, but moments like you had can have a drastic effect on the team's behavior. Make sure you tame whatever anger you're dealing with. And I'm here for a reason. Next time something is going on, just come to me prior. I can at least offer to help you navigate things like this. I get the anger. I felt it too.

"I remember feeling like I was in the penalty box more

than I wasn't. And you're no use to the team if you're spending most of the game in the bender. If you'd like, we can get together, maybe even have the girls spend some time together, and that way, Sammie can see another child with the same equipment she will likely have. I know it helps Tessa when she hangs out with kids that have the same or similar device she has on her arm."

I remember feeling helpless during that time at the very beginning. I wish someone had offered to bring me under their wing to show me the diabetic ropes, per se.

A smile stretches across his face, and I can see him relax slightly.

"That would be great, coach. Just let me know when, and we'll make it happen." He brings his hand out in front of me, and I take it, letting him know he isn't tackling this on his own.

I smile back, "Now go take a shower. You seriously stink." He chuckles and heads toward his teammates.

"Oh, and Rodriguez, if you need the name of a good doctor in the city, I've got one," Rodriguez nods as he heads out.

Once Rodriguez leaves my office, I sit down and pull out my phone. I have a text from Ellie, and my features soften as I open my phone to see what she's written to me.

> SUNSHINE
> Hey. I'm looking forward to our date tomorrow night. What should I wear?

I can't help how quickly my fingers glide across the little keyboard, trying to hold back from saying all the naughty things I want to say.

> I wish I could say nothing, but I think you'd see my jealous side come out if people gawked at you at the restaurant. So, I guess something casual works.

> **SUNSHINE**
> I mean, is this place fancy or can I wear jeans?

> Maybe something a step up from jeans. Maybe no underwear. ;)

I guess I failed at containing the dirty thoughts, but it was tame compared to the images in my head. The thought of being around Ellie again gets my heart pumping. I have thought of her endlessly these last nine days. I have been counting each day as a step closer to seeing her. I've had a string of away games that took all my attention.

I did, however, get a few FaceTime calls in, along with keeping our lines of communication open with texts throughout the day. In that time, I've gotten to know Ellie a little more. I feel like technology has not given the younger generation the ability to sit on the phone and talk, like I did with girls I wanted to date back in high school. I feel like Ellie and I were transported back in ways, forced to get to know one another the old fashioned way.

I made reservations at a spot in the city with some privacy in the back room. I doubt us going out will get the attention of any paparazzi, but I'm still playing it safe. If we are truly keeping this between us, I'd like to keep it that way with no interruption. Paparazzi was a norm I had to deal with back when I was a rookie up to the point of retirement. I haven't seen too much attention on me when I leave the arena, so I'm hoping we are in the clear for a while. I really want to explore where this goes with Ellie without outside interference.

> **SUNSHINE**
> I see where your mind is at. I'll see what I can do about no underwear. I'm feeling pretty free without it now, so I guess I could work something out tomorrow night. ;)

I groan. What the fuck is she trying to do to me? I need to throw a bucket of cold water on me before I head over to see my family. I send her a burning-up emoji and flames so she knows she's wrecking me over here. I move around my office to grab items to work from home later tonight and early tomorrow.

The moment I walk out of the locker room and into the corridor where families wait, Tessa sees me and starts running my way. I put my bag down, crouch, and pick her up. I swing her in a circle, and she giggles. Hearing that sound never gets old, and I hold it dear, as I know I'll blink and she'll be off with her friends and not wanting to hang out with her dad. At least for now, I hang the moon in her eyes.

I put her down and grab her hand, putting my bag on the opposite shoulder. Soon enough, my family catches up to us, and we start to make our way out of the arena.

"Want us to order some food on the way home?" my mother asks.

I nod, and Tessa is quick to chime in on what we should get. Everyone piles in my car, and we make our way toward our building. Luckily, the arena isn't far from the apartment, and we make it home before the food is delivered.

I'll admit, this is an aspect of New York City I love: mostly everything can be delivered. The moment the food arrives, the entire apartment starts to smell like Chinese cuisine. My sister is doling out the food onto plates. I had already given Tessa her insulin to prepare for the meal, and I'm making sure she gets her food in time to not bottom her out.

That's the thing about type 1 diabetics: you have to account for everything their pancreas does, so it's a learning process figuring out how to manage blood sugar when the body should be doing it naturally. I feel like I've gained a medical degree with all the studying I did to ensure I was well-versed in caring for a diabetic child. Luckily, Tessa's easygoing nature has made it a process I can manage, even with a hectic work life.

Once we finish dinner, I ask if my parents and sister can help put the food away, as I wanted to take Tessa for a bath myself. I needed some one-on-one time with my girl, especially if she's going to be out with my family tomorrow night while I go on a date with Elody.

"How was school today, bug? Did you learn anything fun?" I ask her while pulling her hair up so she doesn't get it wet. I then move toward her en-suite bathroom, turn on the water, and begin to fill her tub for her bath.

"Extra bubbles, Daddy," she says as she runs around the room, pulling her clothes off as I get her bath the exact way she likes it. She catches the look I give her and she yells, "Please!" Soon enough, she's hopping in the water and picking up bubbles and smearing them on the tile walls.

"So, Tess, tell me about your day." Kids get distracted with everything, and bringing bubbles into the mix will only cause her to deviate her thoughts even more.

"It was fun. Mrs. Lorrent did a puppet show today, and then she said we get to make puppets out of socks and do a puppet show of our own! Isn't that funny, Daddy? But she said no dirty socks allowed; only clean ones." Now she's putting the bubbles along her face and jawline to make it look like she's got a beard.

This has been my favorite age so far. As much as I prepare the bath for her, she's pretty independent, so I get to simply sit outside the tub and interact with her. I love getting her side of how her day was. Now that I'm being less of a jerk to her teacher since the holidays, it's been fun to watch her grow and learn this year while she's in school.

"Oh, so you don't want my fun socks that I'm wearing now?" I lift my foot to show her the socks I chose.

"Ew, Daddy, no. Your socks stink," she scrunches her nose and I can't help the laugh that escapes me.

Since I started coaching, Tessa chooses my socks before each game. It started as a coping mechanism for me mostly. When I first started this position as a coach, I felt a lot of guilt for leaving Tess with my family to go back to work. I didn't need the money, so I regretted my agreement of coaching a team. I felt like I was being forced to do this new thing that I didn't think I'd excel at, on top of the fact I was spending less time with Tessa.

To soften the blow, I thought it would be fun to have Tessa pick my socks for game days, and now it's our new tradition. Today, she chose a navy blue sock with dog faces all over. Most of the socks I have now are hideous, especially since Christmas when my sister went wild with our little tradition and splurged to ensure I had enough hideous socks to last me the rest of the season.

"I know which ones I'll pick next time, Daddy," she says and starts giggling. I can see how excited she is about whatever pair she grabs next time, and I'm happy this little routine brings her a smile. She even picks my socks for my away games. It's a fun little thing we can do together, and she seems to get a kick out of it.

The rest of her bath is uneventful, and soon enough, she's ready for bed, and I'm tucking her in. My family comes in to say goodnight, and I leave her room to sit back at the table and chat with my parents. My sister ran down to her apartment to get some work done, so it's just the three of us.

"Is she sleeping already?" my dad asks, and I nod, and he sits across from me with a cup of water. My mom is already seated and looking at me like she has a million questions. Here we go.

"Out with it, Mom," I say, but my tone is playful.

"Oh, I'm waiting for you to tell me about your plans for tomorrow with the pretty teacher," my mother says, acting all innocent in her inquisition. She looks at her nails as if they weren't just manicured. She inspects them knowing there is nothing wrong with them. She feigns nonchalance, but I know her too well.

"We're going on a date. Not much else to say about it."

I try to pass it off as nothing, but my mom has some sort of superpower and sees right through me. She always has. Most of the time in the past, she could sense if something was bothering me or if I had a dilemma I needed help resolving. It's rarely been something relating to the opposite sex.

Even with Tessa's mother, I didn't put much weight on the fact that I would be a single father. Once Tessa's mom decided not to be a part of our lives, I held on to the abandonment, but I also saw I couldn't ponder it much as I had a baby to care for.

"Well, she's quite pretty. I heard she has three kids. Have you met them?" I can tell my mom is simply excited about the prospect of me dating again.

"Mom, we haven't even gone out together yet. And we are taking it slow regarding introductions to her kids and incorporating Tessa. She's a widower, and I'm the first person she's given a shot to date," I say, hoping this conversation is nearing its end.

"Poor thing. Your sister mentioned something about her husband passing away a few years back. I can't imagine being a young mother and also grieving a spouse at the same time."

She looks over at my dad and pats his hand. He takes a hold of it and squeezes. I want what they have together. I think that's why I have never really dated much in the last few years. It also explains why I tried so hard with Tessa's mom because I longed to have that kind of connection with someone as I got older.

I wanted to enjoy my twenties and didn't want to settle down. Then as the years passed, my ability to trust someone wanted to be with me for who I am and not my bank account, a lot of time had flown by. I went far into my thirties before I became a father, so once I accepted that Sabrina was carrying our child, I was excited for this next chapter of my life.

When Tessa was born, and her mother left, I knew I wanted to find stability in a different way outside of the NHL. I had achieved so many achievements as a player in the game, but I had wanted to be a partner with someone for quite some time after I became a father, and I felt robbed of that opportunity with Sabrina gone. Looking back at everything Tessa's mom said throughout the pregnancy, I see she and I were a terrible fit together, so I think everything worked out.

It doesn't mean I didn't hold a grudge and long for something I couldn't seem to find. I felt used in so many ways, and the way women tossed themselves at me like I was a prize and a story for them to tell felt really abusive, especially the older I got. Since I felt that pull toward Elody at that bar, something told me she might be my chance to have more in my life. Just the idea of being with her in any capacity lit something inside me.

My mother continues, "But I know how you might be feeling as well. You haven't dated much since Tessa was born, so I wasn't sure how you've navigated this."

My mom is right; I haven't dated much since becoming a father, but I did see women when I had a night to myself. That night at the bar, I'm not going to act like I was only there to grab a drink.

I had lost hope in finding a stronger connection with a woman as the recent years have passed, so that night, I was planning on releasing some tension. I'll be the first to admit, I'm no boy scout. Little did I know I would be releasing someone else's tension and then feeling like I imprinted myself onto said person. Since meeting Elody, it's her blue eyes that pop into my thoughts when I think of being around anyone in a sexual way.

"I haven't dated much, but I think I remember how to do it," I say, getting up to retrieve a drink of my own but mostly trying to veer this conversation in a different direction. My dad must sense my discomfort and throws me a bone.

"How are you feeling about the team making it to the play-offs?" he asks; his love for hockey the reason I ever picked up a puck and threw on a pair of skates.

"If the guys can play the way they have and work together, I think our shot is a good one. I don't want to put pressure on the guys as most of them are so new to the professional circuit, but this would be a great way to feel out how they handle themselves in a platform like the playoffs. Being in a championship series is an added pressure, and that alone can make or break a good streak for a team. I'm excited to see how the guys react if we get that far."

And I mean that. I think we can really grow if we continue like we are now. That's something I didn't expect: this feeling of accomplishment through the hands of others on the ice. I always felt it toward my teammates, but we all played a role physically to get further in a season. But a coach has no playing time, yet the pride I've felt watching these guys thrive on that ice has been something beyond what I ever felt before.

I called my old coach up a few weeks back to tell him just that; I wanted to tell him I finally understood why he was always so invested in how we were off the ice, just as much as he wanted our dedication in the rink. Sports go beyond the physical part itself. It is something personal and mental, in addition to being about character development and trust. Seeing that flourish and grow is something I have gotten to be a part of on a different level now, and I have a new appreciation for the coaching staff that followed me throughout my career.

"This is a special team. I've been trying to tell them that the best way I can, but Juliette says I'm still too intimidating, and I have to soften up a bit more. I guess she says I grunt a lot when people address me."

Juliette, for not having a sporty bone in her body, has a lot to say about my persona and how I handle my team.

"Well, for what it's worth, I think you're doing a fine job with those boys."

I roll my eyes because my mother refers to all my previous teammates, and now my players, as "boys," although they're mostly in their twenties, with some in their thirties. We only have one guy who is nineteen, and the longer I train with him, the more I see his potential only growing from here. My team is young, but I still don't see them as "boys" as my mother does. It's laughable that these huge, burley guys skate around and cause fights, and she still acts like this is a pee-wee team with eight and nine-year-old children.

"I appreciate the support. I'm going to call it a night. Are you staying here tonight?" My parents will sometimes stay the night instead of going home if it's too late.

They both tell me they're staying at my sister's house, as they will not be getting up early to take Tessa to school. They live a few buildings over, but with the cold of winter, sometimes staying with one of their kids is easier for them. I have an early start tomorrow with my coaches to go over some plays and discuss some game tape, so Juliette is meeting me here early in the morning to take Tessa for me. I still haven't gotten a chance to get my girl to school in the mornings, but I'll find my rhythm and begin taking her when time allows.

I say my goodbyes and head toward my room to get myself ready for bed. Once I'm in bed and staring at the ceiling, sleep escaping me, I can't help but grab my phone. I decide to send one sweet text to Elody just to make sure she knows I'm excited. Maybe the more I tell her how excited I am, the more she will see that she should shoot this shot with me without hesitation. I know she's skeptical this will work out, but I have this feeling, something deep down, that's telling me that there's something more between us that she's just not seeing.

> I hope you sleep well, Sunshine. Can't wait to see you tomorrow night. Don't think about me too much as you count the hours until our date. ;)

SUNSHINE

Always so humble (*eye roll emoji)

I chuckle at her response. I don't know what's come over me, but I can't let go of this lightness that's consuming me. I feel like I have something new to look forward to, and I never thought that would come in the form of a woman who emits so much lightness around her it's hard not to react to it. But here I am, counting the hours myself because I cannot wait to take her out tomorrow.

Chapter Fourteen

ELODY

What's more intense than butterflies in my belly? Because right now, whatever is a step above that, that's where I'm at. Maybe a swarm of bees? Yeah, it feels like an entire hive of bees has been released in my torso, and I feel the buzz of anxiety in every fiber of my body. Why did I agree to this? I'm nearly forty-four years old, mother of three, mind you, who happens to be a widow, who's going on a first date with an Adonis of a man.

When Beau passed away, it was said a good resource was a grief counseling group. I didn't join one until I moved to the city because, being from a small town, I didn't find it helpful to sit in a group setting where I pretty much knew everyone. This past week, I went to one of the weekly group sessions, and I spoke up about my apprehensions with this date and how guilty I was feeling. I don't always attend anymore, as I was feeling comfortable in my day-to-day routine.

That being said, it was hard to shake the nerves that felt like they multiplied by the day as this date approached. Many in my group were kind with their words and helped me see that it's just that, a first date. No big expectations have to be tied to the dinner, and I should enjoy it as a way to get to know someone new. I didn't tell them who it was I was seeing, nor did I confess I had already seen this man naked.

I'm staring at my reflection now, my best friend cackling while she watches me have a mini freak out in my bedroom. I take a moment to look at Becca, who is typing into her phone with a smile spread across her face. Who is she texting right now?

"Who are you talking to Becca?" I ask, my nerves tapered down now that I am focusing on the fact that Becca is sending texts to someone, and I can bet it's either Shane or my sister. And by the guilty expression on her face, it's most likely about me.

"Texting? Who's texting?" Becca responds, throwing her phone to the side and giving me her undivided attention.

I squint my eyes, knowing she's up to something.

"Becca, who were you texting?" I stomp my foot, like one of my students, because I know she has been up to something while texting someone we both know.

"Okay, okay. Geez. I was texting Shane. I told him you were nervous, and he reminded me of that time when we were in high school, and you went to our freshman dance wearing a Looney Tunes-inspired dress. Remember? It was plaid with Looney Tunes characters embroidered on it, like peeking out of the seam where the buttons were on the top?"

This has her rolling, and I can't help but laugh with her because, thinking back, my style was questionable in my early teens.

"He said, however nervous you are right now, it won't be as bad as that outfit." She's barely able to finish relaying what Shane said because she is now crying from her laughter. At my expense, mind you.

"Looney Tunes was really popular in 1995, Becca!" I stomp my foot again, yet Shane's little stroll through memory lane dissipates the anxiety I feel coursing through my veins. I take one last look at myself in the mirror and decide this is as good as it's going to get.

"Are you sure you're good with my kids tonight? Tyler is with his basketball team for an away game, but he's spending the night with a teammate once he's back in the city. I told him to call me if he needs anything, but I also said you'd be home tonight."

Becca has settled herself down and waves her hands at me, a gesture indicating it's not a problem.

"You know I love your kids as if they were my own. And if Tyler needs anything, even if he calls you, tell him to text or call me as well. I'm around. Your girls are always so sweet. Jackson is at the neighbor's house playing video games, so it's just the girls and me."

"I loved seeing Olive when I dropped my girls off earlier. You did good with that one," I wink at Becca.

My best friend has been through a lot, raising her oldest on her own for the most part. But it's amazing to see Liv thriving right now. Beau and I would always come to visit, or they'd come to us, on summer breaks. Olive was always such a great kid, and seeing her be a strong, confident woman is an even bigger gift. I think Beau would be so proud to see the woman she is growing into.

"Yeah, I love when she's in the city. She said she needed some time away from all the studying. She said she craved the honking horns and irritated people of the city."

She laughs, knowing exactly how much her oldest daughter loves city life and has been doing everything possible to adjust to the small-town life she's surrounded by as she finishes her graduate program.

"Listen, lady, I'm off. I can't wait to hear how this date goes. Don't you worry about a thing with the girls. We've got manis and pedis lined up, with some Disney movies, along with my favorite part—popcorn!"

I roll my eyes. Becca and her popcorn is always a sacred

snack for her. I saw her smack Shane's hand away recently when we were all watching a movie. She's pretty patient of a person, but sharing popcorn is like Joey from *Friends* sharing food. Becca doesn't share popcorn!

"Well, you know you can call me if something comes up. But I'm glad this worked out. The girls don't really pry too much, but Tyler is at the age he'd ask a lot of questions if he knew I was going on a date, and me being dressed up to go out while you're home would raise all the questions possible. I just need time to see where this goes. If it goes anywhere, that is." I move my hands down my top for the millionth time, hoping with each movement, I can bring my heart rate down.

"I completely get it, Ellie. But try to relax and have fun tonight. That's what this is about. Don't think about any stressors you might have going on. And get out of your own head. Please!"

She is now right in front of me, looking up into my eyes, holding my shoulders to keep me steady. She slaps my ass as I begin to walk out the door of my room, "Now get out there and score!" she yells as someone rings the doorbell.

I look at my watch and realize he's early. I feel the panic begin to rise again, and I look at Becca, my eyes the size of saucers.

"I can't do this, Becca. Oh my gosh. He's early. What am I doing? I can't do this."

Becca once again grabs my shoulders, pep talk in full effect, this time with more of a stern tone to her speech, "You, Elody Lorrent, are a strong, confident woman. You are brave, you are bold, and you are absolutely capable of going on a date with the guy that made you scream his name on New Year's Day. Stand up straight..." I do as she says, "...pull your shoulders back," I follow her command, "...and show that hot hockey player who's boss."

I nod with more confidence than I feel and begin

descending the stairs. Becca is hot on my tail, probably chomping at the bit to see Wyatt for herself.

I open the door, and there he is, with what I can only describe as a confident smile spreading across his face. I look down and see him holding a bouquet of flowers. Not just any flowers, but sunflowers, my favorite.

He speaks, and I can't help but notice he sounds nervous, "Hey, Sunshine. I brought you these."

He hands me the bouquet, and right then, Becca pulls the door open all the way, making her way through so she's standing between us, staring up at Wyatt.

"Wow, you are tall," she lets her gaze roam his entire body, not letting her features change.

She looks back at me, and I can tell she wants to say more than whatever she's about to let out.

"I'm Becca, her favorite person. You two have fun. Remember to be careful out there."

She winks at me, and I can tell she's going to give me a full review of the beautiful man next time I talk to her.

She turns her full attention to Wyatt and pokes his chest, "The flowers are a nice touch. But fuck with my friend, and I promise I'll fuck with you."

She pats him on the shoulder, a big smile taking over her face, acting as if her words weren't a threat. Wyatt goes to laugh because Becca is so small he could probably carry her in his back pocket. He must see the no-nonsense look she's giving him and quickly clears his throat.

"Of course. Only the best for Sun—Elody."

Yeah, Becca is small, but she is fierce. She can pack a punch with her words, and I know not to mess with her when it comes to those she loves. She will fight tooth and nail to ensure those around her are loved.

She seems to like that answer and says, "I expect nothing less for my Ellie."

She turns back to me and gives me a hug and a kiss on the

cheek. She quickly whispers, "I think Sunshine is going to see stars tonight," and chuckles as she walks down the steps. My cheeks pink, and the nerves I had earlier are back but not overwhelming me to the point of canceling my plans.

I gesture for him to come in, and I walk through my house to put the flowers in a vase.

"These are beautiful, Wyatt. Thank you," I put my nose to them. "I didn't think it was the right time of year for sunflowers. Where did you find them in this cold?" I look back and see him looking around my house, taking in all the photos and furniture.

"I, um, may have put in a special request. I know a florist that makes the impossible happen."

He seems shy with his confession, and I feel a tug in my heart for this sweetness he's showing me. I recognize that Wyatt is quite a grumpy soul, but something about this side of him makes me want to let go of my walls and go all in. If I didn't have the past I have, I could see myself falling for someone like Wyatt. I feel this connection to him, but I know my heart will never open like that again.

I find a vase and fill it with water. While doing so, he asks, "Where are your kids?" He seems a bit hesitant to keep walking around the house.

"Oh, my girls are with Becca and her daughters, and Tyler is at an away game with his basketball team. Tessa told me she was having a girl's night with your sister. She was really excited when she told me about it."

Wyatt nods, "Yeah, Tessa and Jules are quite close. I think Juliette is the closest thing to a mother figure that Tessa has, so whenever they have girl days or nights together, she talks about it nonstop."

He looks off in my backyard, taking everything about my home in while his smile spreads, and I know he's picturing Tessa. I'm familiar with the feeling.

"So your son plays basketball, huh?"

"Yeah, my husband played most of his life until we graduated from college. He was tall, and Tyler, luckily, got that gene from Beau, so he's taken a liking to the sport. Beau used to coach his teams when Ty was younger. I'm glad he's found some good teammates here since we moved." I finish getting the flowers in the vase and put them on the kitchen island. I love the joy sunflowers seem to add to a room.

"How did you know I loved sunflowers?" I can't take my eyes off them. They're absolutely beautiful. "Hold on." I put my hand up, my mind wandering back to a conversation earlier this week when Tessa brought up flowers and asked me what my favorite was. "Did you make your daughter a spy?"

The look that passes his face makes me picture a younger version of Wyatt, getting away with so much trouble with that face of his. He has this boyish charm sometimes if you discount the massive tattoo peeking through his sleeve and the large one on his left hand.

As much as we have been well acquainted with one another in the naked fashion, I still don't know all these sides of him. I think we are both trying to figure out where we go from where we left off. I go to grab my purse off the kitchen table, and I feel strong hands grab me and turn me around.

"Ellie, I need to—" but instead of finishing his sentence, his lips crash on mine with a kiss that takes my breath away. It's filled with passion and rawness, too. His tongue slides into my mouth, and I can't help the moan that comes from deep in my throat. It seems to spear him on, and he kisses me even harder if that's possible. I feel him grow against my belly, and I grab onto his ass and realize what an ass he has. It is so firm and round, and I am adding this to my favorites list.

We begin to come down from the frenzy of our kiss, and he slows his movements, his hands now holding my cheeks. I'm starting to realize I love when a man takes control of a kiss, and Wyatt is pretty skilled at that. I blink my eyes open and move my gaze up toward his icy blue eyes. A soft smile cascades across his features, and he seems so content at this moment.

"I've been needing to do that since I saw you last. These last ten days have been brutal, and that commando comment you texted me nearly did me in. I felt like a teen again, getting a hard-on thinking about your pussy and all the things I want to do to it."

I feel the heat creep up my cheeks, and I try to move my face away. I've never really been spoken to like this, even after years of marriage. Beau was romantic and kind, but he was never bold in this way. His love felt like those small-town romances that everyone dreams about. He kissed me softly, loved me kindly, and was always gentle, especially in the bedroom. And until I met Wyatt, I would say that was the best kind of touch. But now I see a new side to me that I long for the rough nature of Wyatt's touch. I feel like that's how I can keep things different between Wyatt and myself. I don't share the softness I shared with Beau, and that helps my mind separate the two forms of intimacy.

Wyatt moves my chin back to center, forcing my gaze back to him.

"Sunshine, none of that. No shyness with me. You know I want to see that side of you come out. I can already tell those panties are soaked from my dirty words."

I grab his wrists and remove his hands from my face. I begin to move away from him and look back, "What panties?"

I chuckle and start walking toward the front door, hearing him grunt his approval as we make our way out into the town for my first, first date since I was sixteen.

* * *

"This is fancy," I say as the waiter walks away after we ordered. I look around, and I take in the atmosphere of this place. Elegant lighting lines the ceiling, while the atmosphere has a darker feel with the furniture that was chosen. It's crowded tonight, and I can see Wyatt pulled all the stops when making reservations tonight. We were seated in a private section of the restaurant, away from other patrons.

"I thought you'd enjoy a nice night out. I know how much work goes into taking care of kids, and I think adult interaction is something you might crave more than the average person." He takes a sip of his wine, his eyes never leaving mine.

"I appreciate it. I get my fair share of adult interaction on the weekends and some weeknights, but yes, most of my time is spent with five and six-year-olds. This is a nice change of pace," I say, still trying to rid the butterflies that seem to be multiplying with each minute that passes, and he keeps that ice-blue stare intended for me and me alone.

"Tessa is really enjoying kindergarten this year. She said you're her favorite teacher." He smiles, and I can see the love he has for his daughter in just that little bit he's confessed to me. "She said she wants you to teach first grade next year."

I chuckle. It's a hard concept for kids to understand the importance of changing teachers each year.

"I appreciate hearing that. I'll admit that I have tried first grade, and it's not for me. When I taught back home, I tried different grades before settling for this age range. I love my kinder students because everything is a discovery. But older than this, it doesn't fit my personality. I guess it's like a parent who loves certain phases compared to others. We all find our spot, and we try to hold on to that as much as possible. Luckily, this school isn't one to move us teachers around unless we request a change. I know the first-grade staff well, and you can't go wrong with any of them. They're all lovely."

"Agree to disagree." He lets that smirk move across his face, and I can't help but feel like I'm putty in his hands.

Is it hot in here? He moves his glass back to the table, and I look at his forearms. The moment we arrived at our table, Wyatt was quick to remove his suit jacket and roll up his sleeves. I could tell he preferred to be comfortable than to keep up the fancy act with his attire. The folded-up shirt shows his forearms, exposing the skin and the ink. The flexing of just that small portion of his arm is making me hot and bothered. Who knew arms could be considered sexy?

"So tell me why you moved to New York if you were already established in your hometown." It's a simple question, but my answer feels so complex. It's never easy to talk about a deceased spouse, and it always feels like a downer topic if I'm being completely transparent.

"Um..." I look around, trying to let the lump that has formed in my throat dissolve so I can speak, "I'm from Saddle Ridge. It's in Nebraska."

His head is tilted to the side, as if he's trying to figure me out without an explanation. "I've never been. Is it a pretty small town?"

"Oh yes. The small-town feel of the place will probably never change. I grew up there and raised my kids there until about five years ago. I moved not long after my husband passed away."

"I'd love to hear about him. I believe you mentioned his name is Beau. I know he coached your son's basketball team and a few other details you sprinkled out in conversation, but I'd love to learn more about the person you married. If you feel comfortable sharing, of course."

He doesn't seem at all put off by the fact that he's asking me about the only man I've ever loved. Really, the only other man I've been with. I imagined most men would find this a difficult topic, possibly intimidating because most of those who pass are put on a pedestal of sorts, and many would shy away from the topic. Of course, Wyatt Christianson is the exact opposite. And a part of my heart melts that Wyatt isn't scared to ask the tough questions, even on a first date. So I don't hold back.

"Yeah, Beau. Um, let's see, I'll start at the beginning. I

grew up with Beau. We were friends, mostly because we were in the same grade and always in the same class. Like I said, my town is small, and there's only one grade per year, so the kids are stuck with one another until middle school, where we move around. I did hear this year, they had to add one more kindergarten class to accommodate all the kids. So that might be the direction they're headed, but even then, the class sizes are small." I grab my wine and take a little sip, hoping for some liquid courage to help me through my conversation about my late husband.

I'm looking at the table, avoiding eye contact, but then Wyatt speaks up.

"Listen, Ellie, I get that speaking about Beau is hard. I don't know what it's like to lose someone so special, but I can imagine talking about them feels good in some way. I want you to be able to talk about him with me. I know we didn't start on the right foot with my communication skills being subpar, but I want you to feel comfortable opening up to me, even if it's not the common topic most expect." I can tell he's genuine in what he says, and that gives me the conviction I need to continue.

"Beau and I were always in each other's lives. We went through all our big milestones together, even if we didn't choose to. Our good friends started dating, so we ultimately began seeing one another. Until he passed, I was under the impression I liked him a lot longer than he liked me. But it seems we were both attracted to one another much earlier than we ever admitted.

"From there, we went to college together and got married young. We did all the things that were expected of us: bought the home, expanded our family, white picket fence and all. It was a fairytale until it wasn't. Beau passed away over five years ago from cancer, and I just couldn't stay surrounded by everything we shared together. I mean, my entire life had a piece of him in it, and by leaving Nebraska, I feel like I've preserved that time in my life, and this is a new chapter."

I take a breath, knowing I've just thrown a lot out there for him to digest, and I can guarantee I said it all at lightning speed, something Becca always hounds me about because I've done it to her since I met her. What can I say? I'm nervous!

"And your kids? You have your oldest, a son. Tell me about the younger ones." Wyatt must sense I'm uncomfortable with speaking more about Beau, so he lets that topic go for a bit and asks me about something hard for me not to feel pure joy over.

"Yeah, I have Tyler, my oldest, then my girls, Hannah and Mia. Hannah is nine, and Mia is seven. Tyler just turned sixteen and has his first girlfriend, so that's been an adjustment. Hannah and Mia are little besties, and all three bring my day the light it needs to flourish. Of course, that doesn't reflect in the way they pick up their toys in their rooms, but some battles will continue, I guess."

I laugh, thinking of the last time I went into the girls' room that they share and saw what looked like a war zone of stuffed animals and dolls scattered across their floor.

Wyatt has a smile across his face, as if he understands exactly what I mean. "I completely get that feeling. My sister and I shared a room for a few years when we were young, but my mom had to separate us because of the fighting. Let's just say my grumpy disposition didn't happen overnight. I've always been a bit grumpier than Jules."

"You don't say," I can't help but laugh. Although he's given me a lot of his attitude, I can't help but appreciate this new side I've gotten from him as well. "Tell me more about you."

"Sadly, a lot of information about me is out there for all to read online."

The waiter comes by at that exact moment and drops off our food. It looks amazing, and my mouth is watering. I was so nervous about tonight I failed to eat much of my lunch earlier. Then I panicked and didn't have a snack either.

"Okay, let me rephrase. Give me the information that I can't find on the internet about you," I say as I get myself ready to devour my meal. I'm so glad I went with the vegetable ravioli; it smells divine.

He smiles at me as he takes a bite of his steak. "Let's see. Well, people speculate that I retired from hockey because I was too pissed about Tessa's mom dating her newest moneymaker, when in actuality, it was Tessa's diagnosis that caused me to take a step back. I was one of the oldest players in the league at that point, and I should have retired a few years prior, but I think I used the sport as a crutch to get through my feelings of being a single parent those last few years in the league. What else is not out there for the world?" He looks up at the sky and taps his chin, "I'm a bit obsessive with things because I love control, which I know is news to you," he chuckles, and I gasp, acting as if this information is mind-blowing.

I put my hand to my chest, "Wow! That's probably the most surprising thing you've said tonight," I wink and smile at him. I could be hallucinating, but I think a little blush moves across his cheeks.

"Yeah, well, I feel like I got to where I am because of the discipline I carry out in my daily routines. That has bled into my day-to-day life, especially since Tessa got diagnosed with diabetes. She is my reason for everything I do, and anything I can do to make things better for her, I will."

And I have no doubt he will because he seems to devote each movement toward the well-being of his daughter. It's commendable, especially after seeing so many families come through my door. I've seen many professional athletes and their personal lives suffer. Sadly, the children are the ones who suffer the most. Their little minds just can't understand the extent of such adult interactions and why it's not working out for them. Seeing Wyatt's passion for not only his sport but his daughter really is a breath of fresh air.

"I think you're doing an amazing job with her. She is always gushing about you as her hero. You must be doing something right. She's a well-adjusted kid, and you should feel proud. She really is a ray of light in our classroom. She is always happy, and she includes as many friends as she can in whatever she's doing, be it on the playground or in class doing a project. It's cute to see."

Wyatt's smile grows, and my heart does this fluttery thing I didn't know it was capable of. The rest of the night keeps going, and as nervous as I was, I can't help but feel a weight lift off my back. I feel like a piece of myself is returning to my life. I didn't realize I had let go of a big part of myself when I said my goodbyes to my husband. I feel like the more I let go of the tension I was harboring for this first date, the more I don't want this night to end.

Chapter Fifteen

WYATT

I know Ellie said her heart wasn't up for grabs, but man, do I feel like she has mine in a vice after just one date with her. The way she looks at me with those big blue eyes feels like a trance. I feel her energy connect as we sit at the table, and all I want to do is be closer to her.

The moment we finish our meals, I reach across the table and put her hand in mine. I feel something significant forming between us, and I think with time, Ellie will let go of this wall she has built and let me in. I'll tire her out enough to grab hold of her heart because I honestly feel like I'm all in. It's only been one meal with her and I already see things I never thought possible with a potential partner. I won't tell her that for fear of scaring her off, but I do think there's more here than she's willing to see.

I pay the bill, and we begin our walk through the private exit the staff provided me with. We have children, and she has a job to be careful with. If anything, we need to keep this bubble we are forming as just the two of us. I heard what Ellie said before, and I think the slower we take this when it comes to our kids knowing about this relationship, the better it will be for us to move forward.

Once we are back in the car, I only start the car to get the heat going. This winter has been brutal; then again, I haven't been in the city a full year to experience all the seasons yet. I got used to Nashville temperatures, and New York definitely wins the award for cold winters between the two states. We are allowing the interior of the car to warm, and I turn my attention to the beauty by my side.

"So, I don't want to be too forward, but I'd love to bring you back to my place. I understand if you want to take a step back and go slower, and I have no expectations about where this is headed tonight." I sound nervous as I say all this. I don't want tonight to end, and I'm hoping she feels the same.

She nods and chews her bottom lip as if she's contemplating everything I just said. "Well, I didn't go commando for nothing," she says, tipping her head back and letting out a loud laugh as she takes in my stunned expression.

"Oh, Wyatt, your face is priceless. Yes, I would like to go back to your place. I have the night to myself for a reason." She gives me a wink and a little smile, and I just want to bottle up her sweet and sassy moments because they add so much warmth to my heart.

I drive us back to my place; the underground parking is a godsend, so we don't need to walk outside in the blistering weather. Our walk toward the elevators is quiet, but I feel Ellie's pinkie grab hold of my own, and I feel the warmth of that simple touch radiate up my arm.

When we get into the elevator, I press my penthouse, and we begin the ascent toward my place. The moment the doors close, I can't take it any longer, and I push her against the wall of the metal box we're traveling in and shove my hand into her hair, tilting her head up toward me. I kiss her hard, putting all this pent-up emotion into this single kiss. She moans, and I can't help but swallow her sounds as if they're my fuel.

"Fuck, Ellie, I've thought about this body for all these days we've been apart, and I'd be lying if I said I haven't been counting the moments until you let me feel you again."

She pulls at my button-up and brings my lips to hers again. She moves her hips forward, the pressure exactly what I wanted and still not enough, putting me at the precipice to relieve this ache in my cock. I move my hips against her, this time making sure she feels just how much I want her as my dick strains against my pants.

The elevator dings far too soon, and I grab her hand and pull her toward my front door. I open it, and the moment I close the door, I push her against it, and begin ravaging her with my mouth again. I will kiss every piece of skin on her body tonight. I will show her with my mouth and the rest of my body what she does to me. She leaves me hungry for another touch, and I can't take the addiction I feel toward her already.

We continue to kiss one another, yet we are on the move, leaving pieces of our clothing along the way. We enter my room, and the moment the back of her legs hits the edge of my bed, I pick her up and throw her on my mattress. Her small body bounces, and she giggles from the movement. She's naked, and the moment she looks back at me, fire in her eyes, she opens her legs wider so I can see exactly what I'm doing to her.

Fuck, I can see her pussy glistening, and without thinking twice, I grab behind her knees and pull her to the edge of the bed.

I look up at her, "Ellie, you are the most beautiful sight I've ever seen, and this pussy is mine." I move my face between her legs and swipe my tongue along her folds.

Ellie arches her back, her head falling back as she yells, "Yours, Wyatt."

That spears me on to continue sucking and licking her. Soon, I'm pushing one, then two fingers into her, curving my fingers to that spot where I know will have her seeing stars and screaming my name even more. My fingers are pumping into her while I'm sucking on her clit, and I feel Ellie put her hands into my hair and move her hips erratically, chasing her release. Her legs begin to squeeze my head, and I know she's falling off that cliff as she orgasms against my tongue. Fuck, there's nothing sweeter.

I continue to stroke her folds as she calms her movements down. She grabs onto the sheets, melting into them further as a blissful smile passes across her face.

"That was amazing," she says, and I think she's the happiest I've ever seen her since I've met her. I start kissing up her body, along her abdomen, moving upward toward her breasts, where I give each one a little attention, tugging on her nipples and hearing her yelp. She starts to move as if she's trying to climb off the bed, and I can tell where she's going from here.

"Ellie, I wish for nothing more than to see your lips around my cock, but there's only one place I'm coming tonight, and it's in that pussy."

A smile creeps over her, and I can tell she likes how I command the bedroom. "Now grab the headboard. I'm going to fuck the ever loving shit out of you."

She crawls up toward the top of my bed on her hands and knees, and the movement nearly has me coming without even feeling her wrapped around me. I grab my cock and start stroking, pre-cum on the tip of the head.

She grabs onto the headboard, and I spread her ass cheeks and let my dick move along her wetness. I slap her ass once, and she yelps.

"Whose fucking pussy does this belong to?" I ask, and she immediately answers, "You." I smile at her response.

"That's right. And soon, I'll claim this ass. Has this ass been fucked before, Sunshine?" My lips are kissing along her back, my hands reaching and playing with her nipples, something I already know she loves.

She shakes her head.

"Well, soon, this ass will be mine. Is that virgin ass ready for my cock, baby?"

She nods, and she's panting, wanting this more than I anticipated.

"Oh, Ellie, the things I have planned for you. I can't wait." I bite her shoulder, then bring my upper body back upright to align myself. I enjoy the feel of my cock moving in her wet folds for another stroke or two then I can't take it anymore. I line up and thrust into her without warning.

Ellie screams, and I see her knuckles whiten with her grip on my headboard. I waste no time fucking her. I pump into her hard, my balls slapping against her with my force. I look down and watch myself get lost in her pussy, and the sight urges me on. I know I won't last long because being inside Ellie makes me wild.

I move positions, bending forward a bit to slow my movements, and whisper into her ear, "You like the way my cock fills you up, baby?"

I move my fingers forward to touch that little magic nub that will cause her to detonate around my dick. The moment she feels me playing with her clit, she starts to moan a little more, and soon she's orgasming, and I feel those walls constrict around me. This urges me on, and I start fucking her hard again, my hands back to her hips, my movements more impulsive, my dick pumping in and out of her like a piston.

Soon enough, I feel that tingle down my spine, my balls tightening, and I let go, falling over, calling her name and filling her up. I throw my head back, and I practically see stars. I let her pussy milk me to my last drop, and then we are both falling into a pile of bliss and sweat, panting like we just ran a marathon.

Once we catch our breath, we both head to the restroom to clean ourselves up. We take a shower where we share a moment of washing one another off, and something about it feels more intimate than what we just did.

I hand her one of my shirts, and I can't help but soak up the sight. Seeing Ellie dressed up tonight at dinner was a vision I had trouble looking away from, but seeing her now, in my clothes, does something to me. The moment we head under the sheets, I pull her toward me, her back to my front, and I take a big whiff of her hair. Still that coconut smell I'm growing addicted to smelling on her.

"I don't cuddle much, so don't be surprised if you find me on the other side of this bed by morning," she yawns, and I kiss her cheek.

"I have a feeling I'll wake up with a pile of your hair in my face come morning. Sleep well, baby." She makes a little sound like I'm tickling her with the scruff of my facial hair, but I can tell she's exhausted and already falling asleep before I close my eyes and drift off.

Sure enough, the next morning, I wake up with a blond mess of hair in my face as she's nestled in the crook of my arm and drooling on my chest. The smile that it brings me lasts for days because I'm starting to realize that I cannot get enough of this beautiful woman.

* * *

One Month Later

"So let me get this straight. Shane went twenty-five years without any contact with Becca, then came to find out she had his child after high school, and raised the child on her own without his knowledge?"

My head is spinning as we make our way up the steps to Becca's brownstone. We were invited over because Becca stated that we can't keep seeing each other without her full approval.

At first, I thought Ellie was kidding, but she didn't laugh after she stated these facts, going off on a tangent that Becca is her person and telling me something regarding that show, *Grey's Anatomy*, and going on and on about being Christina's Meredith. I was so lost that I just nodded my agreement, and here I am, standing by the girl I know I'm starting to fall for more than I intended.

"Yes, it was a slew of misunderstandings that led to that outcome. They're together now, taking it slow when it comes to Becca's kids, but I doubt this steady pace will last long. Shane isn't a very patient person when it comes to his love for Becca. I wouldn't be surprised if she has a ring on her finger by the time the clock strikes midnight for the New Year." Ellie looks at all the items in our hands, probably making sure we didn't forget anything for our potluck.

The door swings open, and a man is standing there, greeting me with a huge smile. I can already tell he knows who I am, not just from me dating Elody, but in the sports world.

"Xander Christianson, as I live and breathe."

I nod and smile. Before I have too much time to move from my spot outside this home, I hear someone running toward the door.

"I told you to wait for me, Shane. I wanted to open the door first."

The petite woman that I recognize as Becca from that first date I took Ellie on, comes running toward the front door, fixing her hair and glaring at Shane, although her gaze holds little strength, especially when he chuckles back in response. Becca pushes herself in front of her boyfriend, her aqua eyes finding mine, her gaze jumping to Ellie's, then back to me.

A small smile crosses her features, and I'm immediately at ease. Something about her is comforting, even if she threatened me that first night. I can see why she's a doctor. She probably has an amazing bedside manner if this is the calmness she exudes with others.

"Hi, I'm Wyatt," I say to Shane, as I already met Becca briefly when I picked Ellie up for our first date. I turn my eyes toward his girlfriend, "And it's nice to see you again, Becca."

We begin to shuffle into the house, Becca helping Ellie with the items she's holding. We make our way through the house, and right as we make it to the kitchen, a little dog comes waltzing over. Ellie immediately crouches down and starts talking to it.

"Well, hello, pretty Betty. How's my favorite little fur bestie?"

She scratches behind Betty's ears, and the dog doesn't seem to reciprocate the love Ellie seems to dose out. Soon Betty is headed toward me, I assume because I'm a new person to smell.

I'm putting my items on the kitchen island when I hear Ellie huff behind me, "Damn it, Becca, your dog still doesn't care for me."

She's watching Betty sniff my leg, and soon the dog is rubbing her head against my calf. It's hard to resist such cuteness, so I bend down and show the dog some love with some ear scratches too. Betty is lapping this attention up as if no one gives her the time of day.

Shane laughs in the corner, and Becca points at him and says, "Don't you start, Shane. You already stole my dog by making her fall in love with you. Now she doesn't even sit with me on the couch. You hog all her attention."

He puts his arms around Becca, kissing her cheek. "Oh Becs, don't fool yourself. That dog never loved you the way she loves me."

That earns him a smack in the chest, and she's trying to pull out of his grip while he laughs at his own joke. I can see the love they both have for one another because it's palpable. I see what Ellie means. Shane looks at her with so much passion and love it's hard to ignore it.

I stand back up and start to remove things from the bag.

"You have a lovely home. Thanks so much for having us over."

The timing was perfect. We don't have a game today, and Tessa is with my parents for the day to visit a museum. Ellie's girls are out with friends, while Tyler took his girlfriend out on a date. We still haven't told any of our kids about our relationship, but I have a feeling we will soon. I want to be out with this secret because it's eating me alive. I want to invite Ellie and her family to games. I want to see her after I get home because I miss her even if we've only been doing this for just over a month.

My heart longs to be around her, and it hurts to hide this, especially from my favorite little girl. Tessa deserves to know. I feel like this is more than just a fling that will go away after a while. The more doses I get of Ellie, the more addicted I become. Her laugh, her smile, her lips touching any part of my body—it's becoming a need I can't live without.

"Are you kidding me? We're happy to have you over. I'm glad it worked out with all of our schedules." Becca says as she continues putting the finishing touches on her charcuterie board. Soon, she pulls out the wine carafe, and I stop my actions and stare at her with this apparatus in her hands.

"Is that..." I can't even form words. The moment I go silent, it prompts Shane to look back to see what has the room silenced. He sees what's in his girlfriend's hand and rolls his eyes. His hands are against the counter, and he hangs his head down.

"Becs, please tell me you did not pull out a penis-shaped wine dispenser for our guests?" He is fighting a laugh, and I am still stunned at what I'm looking at. I had no idea something like that even existed.

"What? I thought it would break the tension. Wine, anyone?" Becca motions with the dildo-inspired wine dispenser in her hand.

Ellie finally breaks and starts laughing, tears falling down her face. I laugh, and it seems to give Shane the permission he needed to break out in a laugh at how ridiculous Becca is with her hosting skills.

Ellie grabs a glass, looking like she's right at home here, and puts it out for Becca to serve her. Becca seems proud of herself for this added joke and starts pouring wine for all of us. We cheers and sit down on the stools lining the kitchen island. Shane is preparing something to put in the oven, and Becca is finishing the salad. While the food is cooking in the oven, they join us at the counter.

"So Wyatt, how's the season going? Are you getting used to coaching now that you're nearing the playoffs?" Shane starts the conversation, and I can't help but appreciate his interest in what I'm doing now versus dwelling on how I am no longer playing in the league.

I don't want to get lost in my own shadow as a retired player in the NHL and have my coaching abilities thrown to the side. Playing the game was something I treasured, but now that I've walked away in that capacity, I see how beat up my body was after every hit. Coaching has really checked all the boxes without adding injuries to the post-game routine.

The conversation is easy, and every so often, I catch Becca looking at Ellie. I can't decipher if it's awe or sadness. But she looks at my girl with so much care in her expression. I can see Becca truly wants what's best for her, no matter what. Shane mindlessly has his fingers playing with Becca's hair while his arm is slung across the back of her chair as if it's the most normal thing.

The afternoon carries on, and I feel like I'm part of this group. I wasn't sure how it would go, knowing that all three of them pretty much grew up together. I was afraid to feel left out of their inside jokes, but not a moment passed where some jab was brought up, and a story was hard to follow. Each one told memories, and I can see that despite the few decades Shane missed out on, neither one of these women held it against him now that their differences have been sorted. They simply jump over that time and continue their friendship as if they've been around one another, uninterrupted, since they were kids.

When we start heading toward the door, I feel like I've made a friend in both of them, but most of all in Shane. He's a cool dude, and I wouldn't mind grabbing a beer with him. I haven't made many friends since moving to the city, and a connection would be nice.

"Maybe we can grab some beers when I'm back from my next slew of games. I have a stretch of away games with the team, but once I'm back, I'll give you a call." Shane smiles wide, and I can see he's holding back.

Becca pats his chest, chuckling. "I think that would be great, Wyatt. I think you stunned Shane speechless. He's a big fan."

I smile back; my grumpy demeanor seems to be melting off me little by little since Ellie entered my life.

"Of course. I can also arrange for you to join us at the arena, and you can watch a game there. I would love to offer that to everyone. We've got a family box there, and I never get to fill it. It's just my parents, Tessa, and my sister. So we'd love to get everyone together when possible."

I feel Ellie tense by my side. We need to have this conversation because talking to our kids needs to happen before a paparazzi photo springs, and Tyler sees that instead of hearing it from his mother. I look down at her and give her a reassuring smile, rubbing her back where my hand seems to be permanently planted for the day.

We walk out, saying our goodbyes, and start to walk toward Ellie's home, a few doors down. It's a nice neighborhood, and it's hard to ignore all the movies I've watched in the past that depict this part of New York as quaint in the mix of a busy city surrounding it. It feels like I'm on a movie set.

The cold, however, feels less exciting. Luckily, we are at

Ellie's door sooner rather than later, and we walk in. I don't plan to stay long as I need to get home to hang out with Tessa before my away games take over my schedule these next few days.

"Listen, I think we need to get things in order to tell the kids what's going on. I noticed you seemed to clam up when I mentioned having you guys at one of the games. But I think sooner or later, this is going to come up, and I'd hate for our kids to find out from someone else instead of from us."

Ellie is looking down at the kitchen counter, playing with the label of a bottled water she grabbed right after entering the kitchen.

"Ellie, look at me."

Her eyes find mine, and I see the turmoil in them. This is hard for her, and I won't discount how much pain she holds in her heart. If I wasn't a famous hockey player turned coach, I think we could keep this up a little longer. But my publicist called a few days back, telling me a photo was circulating of me and a woman walking out of a restaurant. I had covered her face, and you couldn't decipher who I was with, but it will soon become common knowledge. I'm amazed they haven't focused more on this mystery woman as they describe her.

"I know, I know. It's hard though. Bringing kids into the mix is a whole other level, and I worry, that's all. Tyler remembers his dad, and I worry he'll react negatively. Then, my girls don't remember their dad very well, which is heartbreaking alone. Add in a man I'm dating and the feelings that will stem from that, and it consumes me with dread.

"What if everything falls apart? What if they hate me? Not to mention, I'm your kid's teacher. Top that with the fact that although there aren't rules against dating a parent, I feel awkward telling the principal what's going on. I like this bubble we've created, but I know it will pop, and we should stay ahead of it."

Tears have pooled in her eyes, and it breaks my heart. I

wish I could ease her fears, but the truth is, many of those things are realities we, as parents, have to face. She also has a teenager who can react poorly to this news. So, we need to be mindful of his feelings.

"Listen, I won't act like I know exactly what you're going through. I'm not in your shoes as a person that has lost a spouse. But I know for a fact you are an amazing mother. Hating you isn't an option. Preparing yourself for your kids, especially Tyler, to react poorly to this news is important. But expecting it? I don't think that's necessarily the way, either. Regarding the school, I think we should focus on one milestone at a time. We jump over these hurdles and navigate them, and then we move forward to the next thing. Let's get this right and move from there."

I caress her cheek, and a lone tear falls, and my thumb swipes it away. It's at the tip of my tongue to tell her I love her. But if this is already causing distress, professing my love for her might throw her off the deep end.

She nods her head and finally speaks, "I know you're right. I know it's the right step forward, but it feels like a huge step, Wyatt. My heart is soaring, and it's also hurting. Does that make sense?"

I nod. It does make sense, but it doesn't mean it doesn't sting. I want to be her everything, but I know her heart doesn't fully belong to me, and that's a reality I am still getting used to.

"I will talk to the kids tonight. I think it's time." She looks at me, and she sounds more determined than she appears.

I nod my head in agreement and give her a soft kiss against her lips. Our touch sparks more intensity in our embrace, and soon, I'm pulling away, knowing that if I don't walk away now, I never will. Her kids are due home any moment, and I do not need to be here to have us out ourselves from acting like horny teens in her kitchen.

I say my goodbyes to her, determined to talk to Tessa this

week. I get home, and the moment I walk through my door, my purpose for living comes barreling toward me, full of smiles and laughter. I decide to wait until I return from my away games to tell Tessa about Ellie. I want to be here for her to process the information and come to me with questions she may have.

I also want to hear how things go with Ellie's kids before I start down my path with my own child. It's almost like I need to hear Ellie's conversation happen before I dive into the deep end with my own daughter. I guess a part of me feels like I'm all in while I'm begging for the woman I know I'm falling in love with to jump in with me.

Chapter Sixteen

ELODY

My heart feels like it's going to beat out of my chest. I think my palms are sweating, and I can't let go of the nerves taking over my body. I think I'm going to be sick.

"Maybe this is too soon. Maybe I should wait just a bit longer before I let this cat out of the bag." Becca is sitting in the corner, watching me. She came over as my moral support as I worked through the anxiety coursing through my veins.

"Stop it, El! You're working yourself up!"

She stands up and sits by my side, her arm going over my shoulder. I rest my head on her, or at least I attempt to. She's so tiny and even a few inches shorter than me; it feels like I tower over her when we sit like this. Doesn't help that where she's sitting, the couch has an indent that is making her sink into the cushions.

"I just feel like they're going to hate me."

That causes her to pull away and look at me. I see the concern in her gaze, and I know she understands the place I'm coming from.

"Listen, I won't act like what you're doing is no big deal. This is a huge step for you. And I know it's not the step you ever saw yourself taking. But don't you think, despite the initial shock the kids might feel, they'll be happy for you? I know it doesn't feel that way, but don't you think they'll start to see how happy you are and simply focus on that?"

"I'm worried the most about Tyler. He's put so much on his shoulders, and I feel like he's going to be so upset with me. Like I'm disrespecting his father's memory."

I put my hands through my hair and look up toward my ceiling.

"I think you aren't giving Tyler enough credit. The kid needs to be just that, a kid. He's acting like an adult when he still has years of terrible decisions ahead of him." She smiles at me, hoping to bring a little humor to release the tension I'm feeling. "He may not react the way you would like, but he may also surprise you with the love he will show this relationship that obviously means a lot to you."

I nod at my best friend and feel the courage to go through with this incredibly difficult step for me until I hear the shuffle of the kids at the door, and all that strength seems to have melted off of me again. I take a few calming breaths as I hear Tyler helping the girls remove their coats.

Great, they're all home at the exact same time, so I'll have to confront this at once. The moment the kids walk in, they stop in their tracks. I stand up, smoothing my outfit in front of me, hoping the gesture shows a calm mother in front of them versus the mess I'm feeling inside.

"Who died?" Tyler says, taking in the scene in front of him.

My poor boy, always jumping to the worst since losing his father. I don't blame him. Plus, my behavior warrants a death announcement instead of the happy thought of me finding someone to spend my time with.

"No one, honey. Why don't you three come sit down."

The girls bounce into the room, first greeting Becca before making their way to the couch. Tyler is more hesitant with his steps, giving Becca a nod in her direction but feeling apprehensive nonetheless.

"If no one died, why is Aunt Becca here? And why do you look so upset, Mom?" He sits down with his sisters, their only concern surfacing due to their brother's questions. I think if he had not noticed I was acting strange, they wouldn't question me standing in front of them.

"I wanted to talk to you about something important to me. But I promise no one is sick, and everyone in the family is fine."

My words don't seem to bring Ty the comfort I was hoping for, and he looks over at Becca, waiting for her to give some sort of sign to confirm my words. Once he feels appeased by her simple nod, I continue.

"I hope you know that I love you all very much, and I always will. I will put you ahead of anyone and anything in this world, even my own needs." I look at each one as I speak, hoping they feel my love as I lean over and grab each of their hands, fidgeting because I am truly feeling more nervous as the words spill out. "That being said, I wanted to tell you I've met someone I really like spending time with." I let that sink in before I continue.

I begin to speak again, but I'm interrupted by Mia, "Like a boy?"

I nod at her innocence and smile at her.

"Yes, sweetie. A boy. And I've grown to enjoy his company. He is fun, and he makes me smile."

The girls look at one another and then to Tyler. I think they look up to their brother for most things, and this is no different. Tyler's expression is like a mask, not giving way to any feelings just yet. I bet he's taking it all in, much like his father did when he was given new information. Beau was never one to overreact or have outbursts. He always digested information before giving his opinion. Tyler is growing to be much like his father in that respect.

"I didn't want you to find out any other way, and I thought it was best to be honest with you before I keep seeing him. I like spending time with him, and I hope I can bring him over to meet you when you feel comfortable."

The girls are already giggling, and they can't seem to sit still. Although they were looking at Tyler for some sign on how to move forward, they seemed to have ditched his feelings and look excited by the prospect of meeting someone new.

"Does he have kids?" Hannah asks.

"Yes, he has a daughter who is six. She's in my class."

That causes Tyler's eyes to widen, and the girls simply smile at me.

"I'm excited to make a new friend. Thanks for telling me, Mommy. Can we go up and play now?" That's from Mia, while her older sister nods in agreement. I would say two out of the three are fine with my big announcement, but the jury's still out on my oldest. I give both of them hugs, and they wave goodbye to Becca and head upstairs.

I watch them disappear up the stairs and take a deep breath, wiping my hands on my thighs, before I bring my attention back to Tyler, who is looking down now, seemingly processing what he has just learned.

"Okay, so let me get this straight. You've been seeing someone for..." he waits for me to answer.

"A little over a month," I respond but wait to see where he goes with his thoughts.

"A little over a month," he repeats softly, almost as if he's letting the pieces fall into place one tidbit at a time. "And you like him. And you want to introduce him to us?"

I nod, nervous about what direction this conversation is going. Tyler is hard to read when he's processing things because he never wants to be rude, much like his dad. He's always careful with his words, and I realize that's more a hereditary trait than anything.

I let him go through the motions, repeating the facts to

himself. Once he seems to want me to engage with me, he asks, "And he's a parent at the school? Is that even legal?"

I chuckle but stop when I see he's being serious.

"Yes, sweetie, it's legal. There is no rule against it, but of course, it's up to us teachers to keep our relationship outside the school and not let it interfere with how we care for the students. No one student is more important than the other, and that is not changing the dynamic of my classroom."

I grab his hand, and he accepts the gesture. While I'm sitting there, Becca must feel like it's safe for her to get up and busy herself in the kitchen. Shane is back at her place while her ex-husband has the twins for a few more hours. So she's not in a rush to leave, something I appreciate more than I can put into words. I'll need a glass of wine and a full bestie session to dissect this entire experience tonight.

"Is this a parent of someone I know? Oh gosh, is it a friend's father? Ew, gross. Please tell me it isn't."

"No, it's not. You don't have to worry about that. But he is someone you might know."

I give it a second because I feel like this is another part of this whole thing that makes my relationship with Wyatt completely different.

"He's a coach for an NHL team. Here in New York. Do you know who the New York Brawlers are?" I never see Tyler watching hockey, so I honestly don't know if he'll even recognize the name.

Tyler immediately stands up and begins pacing. "Hold on, Mom. You're dating Xander Christianson?" He looks at me, and I don't know if it's horror or excitement. But now I know he is well-versed in hockey, at least enough to know the coaches and the teams.

I nod, not sure if this will push him down a road of anger or envy, so I let this play out in front of me.

"My mom hasn't dated anyone since my dad, and she goes

off and starts by dating Wyatt Xander Christianson? What in the world, Mom!"

Shoot, I've pissed him off. I'm bracing for him to get mad, but the opposite happens.

"Holy fucking shit!" he says while I respond, "Watch your mouth, Tyler!"

He's laughing now, and the sound is a balm to my nerves.

"Sorry, Mom. But what the fu—fudge is happening? I cannot believe this. Can I meet him? Wait until my friends find out. I cannot believe this."

In a trance, he gives me a kiss on the cheek. He yells over his shoulder, "You should have started with his name first, Mom. Unbelievable!" He's repeating this as he walks up the steps.

I guess that went well?

Once Tyler is upstairs, I hear him walk into his room, and his door closes. I look over at Becca, who's in the kitchen, peeking at me. I head over and sit down at my kitchen table.

"I think that went well," she says when I walk in.

Like the bestie she is, she's got some wine waiting for me and joins me at the table. She even pulled out some popcorn from a ready-made bag, which I will admit is more for her than it is for me. Becca will, hands down, choose popcorn over wine any day of the week.

I nod and take a sip of my wine.

"I agree. But I'm still waiting for that other shoe to drop. I think this is all so new to me, it's hard to imagine this being such a smooth process. I appreciate how all the kids reacted, but it doesn't mean I'm not holding on to any anxiety."

Right then, my phone vibrates, and I look down to see Wyatt has sent a message.

> GOAT IN BED
> Hey, Sunshine. How did the talk go?

> Apparently, my son likes hockey. I can't guarantee he won't drool the first time he sees you. The girls were fine with it. I think they are just excited to have a new person to meet. Did you tell Tessa?

GOAT IN BED

> That sounds uneventful in the best way possible. I decided not to just yet because I would drop this on her then leave, and it didn't sit right with me. I'd rather do it when I'm home for a few days straight, then she can ask me questions.

> Makes sense. Let me know when you do so I can be prepared at school. Once she knows, the whole school will know. Kindergartners are the worst secret keepers, let me tell you.

We message back and forth, and I forget my surroundings until I hear a throat clear. I look up to find Becca showcasing her biggest smile.

"What?" I say, looking around to see if I missed something important.

"Oh, nothing. I just haven't seen you smile at your phone like that in quite some time."

I blush at her comment because my texts with Wyatt have gone from PG to X-rated at this point. Something about him brings out a side of me I didn't even know I had. I send a quick goodnight text to him, and I put my phone down.

Becca and I spend the rest of the evening chatting about some plans we have once the weather improves and about incorporating Shane into their dynamic. Hudson is warming up to the idea of weaving Shane into the lives of their twins a little more, and Becca seems relieved.

I see my old friend from high school emerging from the ashes of her divorce and the pain she held living a life without

Shane in it for so long. By the time she leaves, I'm emotionally spent and feel like my bed is not just calling to me, but it's screaming my name.

As I go through the house and turn off the lights downstairs, I walk up the steps, stopping at each room to say goodnight. I save Tyler's for last, and he's looking at his phone, probably texting his girlfriend. Nothing about the way kids communicate replicates what we did as kids. I am in that strange generation that is old enough to remember life without all this technology but still dependent on how we use it today.

"Hey, may I come in?" Ty looks up at me, nods, and gives me a smile. I continue, "How are you doing? Ready for school this week?" I ask, knowing I, for one, still have stuff to do tomorrow to prepare for Monday.

I sit at the edge of his bed and wait because I feel like now that a bit of time has passed, he might have more questions for me.

"Yeah. Just trying to picture you with someone else. Sort of strange, but at the same time, I get it. I'm not mad, Mom. Just figuring it out. Plus, of all people, the GOAT himself. I mean, that's pretty cool."

He puts his phone down and gives me his undivided attention, something I don't get much of these days simply because, as great as my son is, he's still a teenager with a social life that trumps everything else going on.

"I guess I just don't see him that way because I never really watched hockey. I know him as someone I met, independently from his role as a parent of one of my students nor knowing he was a hockey player—a good one at that." I shrug, trying to be honest but definitely trying to keep the details of my first official encounter with Wyatt at the bar to myself.

"You definitely aim high, Mom," he laughs, and I can't help but join him. "So, does this mean you're going to be famous?"

Shit. I hadn't even thought of how this might go with my face splattered across the pages of entertainment news. I think Tyler sees the panic across my face and gives me a side hug.

"Don't worry, Mom. It will all work out. I can't wait to meet him. I wish I could say because I want to see how he is around you, but selfishly, I want to simply meet him. I mean, the guy is iconic."

Tyler pulls his phone out and starts showing me some highlights of Wyatt's career, and I feel like I'm watching another person. His grumpy persona is the same, but the way he carries himself on that ice, it's like it was built for him. He really is remarkable out on that rink.

I say goodnight to Tyler and head to my room. I feel like I've gotten a second wind, and I know I'll pay for this tomorrow when I'm dragging. I pull my phone out and Google Wyatt, and I am immediately bombarded by photos of him with different women on his arm. I can tell the photos are a mix of his early years in the league to more recent, probably right before Tessa came into his life. But it's hard not to look at these women he was photographed with and compare them to me.

They're supermodels with gorgeous, flawless makeup, long legs, and designer outfits. I'm a mother of three, a widow who likes her knockoff lulus. I'm not part of this world of his, and because Wyatt is no longer playing in the NHL, it doesn't mean he's still not accustomed to a different world of sports and celebrity. I know how sporting events go. There's a lot of glitz and glamor associated with that lifestyle, and I am certain I will not live up to this expectation.

I feel the doubt creep in. Feeling like I'm not good enough isn't something I ever felt with Beau because we grew up together. There were no paparazzi in our lives, nor was there ever friction. In all honesty, there was never a bump in our road. We just meshed seamlessly. We didn't ever have to work for our love for one another, aside from having crushes on one another before we acted on them. My love with Beau was a fairytale with a nightmare of an ending. With Wyatt, though, I can see us crashing and burning in so many crazy scenarios.

I try to push those feelings aside, but as I close my eyes, I just see myself not living up to that expectation. I toss and turn, dreaming I'm watching from the other side of the velvet rope as Wyatt walks down the red carpet with a leggy brunette by his side. His hand, which is usually splayed across my back, embraces this other woman. At that moment, in this dream, I realize how different we are and how I have to make sure I keep my heart where it has been this whole time: buried with my husband.

Chapter Seventeen

WYATT

As each day passed this week, my mood just got more sour. I was yelling plays to my guys with so much force, I'm amazed I wasn't kicked out of the game by my own players. Somehow, my team played well, and they're playing like they deserve to be in the playoffs. We are inching closer to our goal, but personally I can't help this feeling that Elody is distant from me. She's been pushing me away this week for reasons I can't explain.

She told her kids about us, so I can't be too far off that we are moving forward the way we had planned. Maybe I pushed things too far by asking her to come clean with her kids? I know it's been less than two months, but we're not in our twenties with no responsibilities. It's harder to keep this charade going of dating and keeping our kids on the sidelines. It's Friday now, and I will return home late tonight. Cummings is eyeing me, and by the fifth time his gaze moves to mine, I snap.

"Spit it out, Phil. I can feel your eyes on me every few seconds." Again, I'm a dick. My friend is nothing but kind and patient, and I snap his head off.

"Hey, I'm the good guy here. We played well this week, so I

know your piss-poor attitude isn't from this team. What's going on?"

We're getting our stuff loaded on the private plane the team uses for away games, and we are situated next to one another while the players finish loading their things. The plane is loud inside because the guys are full of energy after their wins this week, and they're itching to get back home to their families.

"I've started seeing someone."

I let that sink in for Phil because he's well aware I barely see women anymore since becoming a father. And even before that, dating usually consisted of getting laid and never getting attached. I look over to see a stunned expression on his face, so I continue.

"She's Tessa's teacher, and before you say anything, I met her outside of that context; it just turns out the coincidence existed there. We've been together for nearly two months now. It's not a long time, but it just feels right, you know?"

Phil nods, but he's waiting for me to continue.

"Last weekend, we decided it was time for her to tell her kids and for me to tell Tessa. I have yet to sit my daughter down to explain what's going on, but Elody told her kids last week. It seemed to have gone well, but since Sunday, our text exchanges have felt a little off. I can't figure out what changed, especially because I've been gone this entire week. I tried calling her last night, but she didn't answer. It just makes me uneasy."

I look over to find Phil smiling like a lunatic.

"What?" I can't help but want to wipe that smile right off his fucking face. What did I say to warrant an excited sentiment?

"You're seeing someone, man. That's great. I'm proud of you." He grabs my shoulder and starts shaking me, and I can't help but smile in response.

"Yeah, it is great, and I really like her. But like I said, something feels off with her this week, and I feel like I'm running through everything that was said leading up to this moment, and I can't think of a thing to justify the silent treatment."

Phil is quiet, and he's looking at some of the airline staff making their rounds before starting their emergency instruction.

"I get it. I understand where you're coming from. I'm no expert, believe me, but I will say that I would not fall down that path of wondering what you did wrong. She might have gotten in her head, and I think it's best to clarify when you return. Maybe it's nothing, and you're reading into it. I can guarantee you're making it bigger in your head than it actually is. Or if you truly haven't done anything, then maybe she's making whatever is going on in her mind bigger than it is. In actuality, she could simply be busy with work and her kids. But wait to see what it could be. Don't freak out before you even speak to her properly."

I nod, agreeing with what he says. It's so much easier said than done though. I rest my head back and close my eyes. It's been an exhausting leg of the season with all this travel. I just want to get back to my girls, one of whom feels like she holds my heart in her hands in a way I never thought possible.

* * *

We land a few hours later, and my legs carry me off the plane as quickly as possible. By the time I see my car, I'm yelling my goodbyes to whoever is trying to wish me a good night. The moment I'm in the car, I call Ellie, and she finally picks up my call.

"Hello?" She sounds groggy, and I realize it's after eleven at night. I know how exhausting her week is with all the little kids, but I ignore my guilt and go right into it.

"Why have you been avoiding me all week?" I sound grumpier than I had intended, but I don't apologize for it. I'm annoyed and frustrated, and I don't understand what I did wrong.

"Well, hello to you too, Wyatt. And what do you mean avoiding you? We've texted all week." Now she sounds awake, and from the tone she's throwing back to me, she sounds pissed.

"Don't act like you don't know what I'm talking about. You only texted short answers and did not take the bait for my dirty messages. You're usually playful, and you had no part of it this past week. What's going on, Ellie?"

I hear her breathe on the other end, and it confirms I wasn't wrong and my instinct was correct. Something is on her mind.

I push again, "Ellie, come on. What could I have possibly done?"

She finally speaks, "After I spoke to Tyler again last weekend, he showed me some of your best plays, a compilation of sorts. It was really cool; you were an exceptional player. But when I left his room, I couldn't help it. I looked you up on my own phone, and I fell down the rabbit hole of images. I think you are allergic to regular-looking people because all the women on your arm looked like supermodels, Wyatt. I guess I let that get to me. I don't think I'll ever be able to be that for you. I have never had a relationship like this, where my boyfriend has fucked models before."

I can't help but smile about what she's saying because it's sort of sweet, she's jeal— "Hold up, did you just refer to me as your boyfriend?"

"Of all the stuff I said, that's what you're focusing on?" If it's possible, I can hear her rolling her eyes, but I'm not letting this go.

"Just answer the question." I know what she said, but I have to hear it again.

"Yes, you heard me correctly. I mean, that's what you are, right? I know I haven't been in the dating game for much time, even when I was younger, but you're so possessive over my parts, I assume that's what we are to one another. I mean, I can't refer to you as my fuck buddy to my kids because that's absolutely inappropriate, and I think Tyler might vomit on the spot if I use the term hooking up."

"Okay, *girlfriend*, so are you jealous?" I hear her make some noise on her end as if she's getting out of bed and moving around her room. "Ellie?"

"No. Yes. Maybe! Ugh, you're infuriating, you know that?" she says, exasperation dripping off her tone.

"Oh, Ellie. It's okay to admit you like me more than you imagined."

She goes off on a tangent and doesn't stop. She's rambling, that one hundred-mile-an-hour non-stop word vomit she does when she's nervous, and I just let her go. I don't interrupt, and I just smile to myself that I've flustered her about this.

My speed picks up, and I get to her house in record time while we are speaking to one another. I park the car and make my way up her steps. I wait at the door in hopes she'll take a breath between sentences. I finally have my break, and I take it.

"Hey, can you stop your rambling and come downstairs to your front door?"

"What in the world are you talking about Wy—" and she opens the door, but her phone remains on her ear.

She seems stunned to see me standing in front of her at this hour.

I drop my phone and hang up, and she does the same. I pull her closer, making her step out into the cold night, and grab her cheeks, feeling her warmth against my palms.

"It's okay to be jealous. I know if the tables were turned, I'd be seeing red if I saw a man touching what's mine. But here's the thing, baby, with all those women you saw in those photos, none of those ever had what you have."

She's looking at me, and I can see her melting right in front of me. "And what do I have that they don't?" she asks.

I let a smile creep over my face. "The biggest fucking heart I've ever seen. You are the sun, the moon, and all the stars, Sunshine." I give her a soft kiss, the feeling of her against me reminding me why my world felt like it wasn't right this entire week.

I pull my lips away, but I don't let go of her. While we're lost in one another's gaze, something makes a sound behind her, and we both look toward it. I see a young man standing at the bottom of the stairs, looking stunned at the sight. I feel Ellie's face fall a bit, and I let go of her. I also hear her whisper, "Shit."

"Hey, Tyler. I thought you were asleep," she says, a little more delicate than I expect for a mother of a teen.

"Yeah, I, um, ran out of water." But he stays rooted in place, staring between his mother and myself.

I can't help but take in his features. If Ellie could have birthed her opposite, it would be him. He's pretty tall, almost my height, with brown hair and brown eyes. His skin tone is a little darker than his mother's, even in the dead of winter. I have gotten quick glances at Ellie's family photos where her late husband was in them, and I will say that Tyler is on his way to looking like an exact replica of his father. But when he smiles, I see Elody. Just from that smile, I can tell he's got a heart like his mama.

Ellie looks up at me, "This isn't how I pictured this going, but why don't you come in just for a few to meet my son."

She seems to be giving me more with her gaze than her words. I can see that this is a test, and she hopes Tyler approves of me. His opinion matters to her, maybe more than either of her other kids, because she's mentioned that Tyler remembers Beau the most.

I nod and place my hand on her lower back to guide her in front of me as we make our way inside. The moment I'm in the foyer of the house, we close the door behind me, and the silence is deafening.

I put my hand out. "It's nice to meet you, Tyler."

He grabs onto my hand, and I notice he has a firm grip. He stands a little taller, hoping to intimidate me, and it's admirable. I think if Beau were to see his son right now, he'd be proud. I can feel the love Tyler has for his mother in just this interaction alone, and he's assessing me to see if I will hurt her in any way.

"So you're dating my mother?" So formal, and I suppress my laugh. I know Ellie, and I doubt he calls her by such formalities usually, but he's trying to show he's the man of the house, and I respect that.

"Yes, sir, I am." I nod and smile, hoping he can sense I really do care for her.

"And what are your intentions with her? Why her all of the people you can date?" That throws me off because I wasn't expecting that as his second and third questions.

"Well, um, Tyler, your mother is one of the most amazing people I've ever met. She captivates me, and I want to see where this goes."

Tyler takes in what I'm saying, tilting his head and assessing me a little more. His face goes to stone, and he nods slowly, and I have no idea where he's going next.

"I see. And in that last play in the third period, what were you thinking putting in Dranko instead of keeping Lemo in the game? It seems to have been a shit call on your part."

This kid has balls, and I can't hold in the laughter that bubbles out of me. The moment I laugh, Tyler joins in, and we are soon laughing together as Ellie looks between us, completely confused. Knowing I coach a professional hockey team does not mean Ellie understands the sport and the way she's looking at us, it's telling that she has some more lessons needed to comprehend the plays, the players, and what in the world I do out there with my guys.

"Yeah, that was a poor choice on our part. Maybe I can go

over some plays with you sometime, and you can keep me in check so I can get these guys through the playoffs."

That earns me a smile from both Ellie and Tyler.

"What? That would be awesome!" I've won him over, and my heart feels lighter with that knowledge.

I know what it is to be a parent and how it feels to have something weighing on you. It's not that Ellie and I are doing anything wrong, but I know having Tyler's approval is a huge hurdle for Elody, and we've conquered it, at least for now.

I have to say my goodbyes fairly quickly, and I move to give Ellie a quick peck on the lips.

"Dude, don't push your luck just yet. That's my mom."

I change course and kiss her cheek instead. Ellie mouths a quick, "Thank you," as I walk myself out and make my way back to my house, now counting the hours until I have to have a very similar conversation with my little girl because I think I just left a huge piece of my heart with Ellie.

Chapter Eighteen

WYATT

I'm slicing apples in my kitchen as Ellie's grabbing peanut butter from a cabinet by my side. We're getting a snack ready for Tessa, and something about all these day-to-day movements feels right between us. I look over and allow myself to imagine this scenario down the road, where we are simply working around one another. It feels so easy, and I can't help but want to hold on to that feeling as much as possible.

I woke up to a very excited Tessa in my room, asking for pancakes and fruit. I used that time to explain to her my relationship with Ellie, and I don't think I've ever seen the smile on my daughter's face as big as it was at that moment. Of course, being the six-year-old that she is, I was hit with every question possible. The one she hasn't let go of relates to Elody's children and when she'll get to meet them.

We've decided to have dinner tonight to have the kids meet one another. I'm a little nervous myself, even though I feel like meeting Tyler was a huge step last night. But now I have two little girls to introduce myself to, and I fear they won't be charmed by my hockey stats. Luckily, I have a few more hours before heading over to dinner. Elody came over to spend a few hours with us after I texted her about Tessa finding out. She wanted to take some time to sit with Tessa herself and see if there were any questions Tess had for her, girl to girl. Her words, not mine.

As I grab a slab of peanut butter to throw it on the plate with some sliced apples, I decide to whisper some dirty words to the woman who has taken over my thoughts.

"You know, I could think of other things I could slather this peanut butter on, baby. I wouldn't mind you licking it off me while you're on your knees, showing me how much you missed me. Maybe you could call me Daddy after I cum in your mouth." I can see my words affect her, and her breathing picks up.

She licks her lips and turns her attention to me. "I wouldn't mind showing you my skills. But calling you Daddy? Not going to happen."

I drop the knife and look at her in mock horror, "And why not?"

"Daddy, Ms. Ellie, look at this drawing I made for Tyler, Hannah, and Mia." She comes running into the kitchen.

Ellie moves closer to me and pulls herself up so she can whisper in my ear, "That's why I'm not calling you Daddy." I can't help the laugh that escapes my lips when she crouches down to see the drawing my daughter made.

"Here you go, little miss." I hand Tessa the plate. "Please make sure you eat the apple and the peanut butter, alright? No skipping meals like you tried to do the other day. Remember what the doctor told you about having all the food in your tummy for the insulin?"

She nods, her eyes wide as she remembers how the doctor explained that she needs to be careful with the food she leaves behind after getting a dose of insulin.

Tessa takes the plate, and I hear her say, "Yes, Daddy. I'll eat all of it. I promise." She settles in front of the television, where her favorite movie, Beauty and the Beast, is playing. I get things put together in my kitchen and lean against the counter, giving Ellie my attention.

"So, when can we have a playdate of our own?" I keep my voice quiet so little ears don't hear me.

Ellie is looking over toward Tessa but brings her attention back to me when she hears my question. I can see the fire in her eyes that she's missing our physical connection as much as I am.

"Well, *'Daddy'*, maybe next weekend?" She uses air quotes like the brat she is. "I think the schedule you gave me, as long as it's not different, would work. Tyler has a family thing he's going to with his girlfriend, and the girls are going to a birthday party that's a sleepover. They're friends with siblings at the school, so it works out that they're at the same house on the same night."

The smile grows on my face, and I start to think of all the naughty things I want to do to her.

"Well, do you mind meeting me here in the morning, then we can head over to your place if you need to greet the kids the next morning?" I look down at my calendar on my phone, which I share with my family, and note a bit of a conflict. "My sister has a work thing Saturday morning, most likely remote, and I don't want Tessa interrupting her. That way, she can have her night to herself and grab Tess after her meeting for a few hours."

"Wyatt, I can see you after you drop Tess off. You can have that time with your daughter." I don't think she understands where my mind is, and I think it's best if I remind her.

"I think you're forgetting that you're kid-free mid-morning, and I want to see you as much as I can. Hanging out with both my favorite girls isn't a huge ask for me, Ellie."

I put my finger through her belt loop and tug her toward me. I take a quick glance over toward the couch, and Tessa is engrossed in the movie, so I take this opportunity to kiss Elody. I bring my hand up and hold her cheek, kissing her softly. I feel her hands grip my shirt and pull me a little closer.

This feels intimate, and I wish I could throw her over my shoulder, drag her to bed, and kiss her all over. I can feel the intensity of this kiss mounting, and I have to pull away. I open my eyes and see her looking back at me, her cheeks tinged pink.

She grabs hold of that lower lip, and I can't help myself from saying, "You drive me fucking crazy." I smack her ass, and she gathers her things, says her goodbyes to Tessa, and heads home.

* * *

This past week has flown by, and I was able to take both Ellie, her daughters, and Tessa out on a little pizza date earlier this week. Tyler couldn't make it because he had basketball practice.

Last weekend, things couldn't have gone smoother, incorporating both our families. Tyler had many more questions about the team dynamics, and he told me a little bit about his time playing basketball. He seems to really love the sport, and not because his father played it. He seems to enjoy the competition and the camaraderie between his teammates.

I will say that I feel a connection to the kid, and I look forward to getting to know him more. Ellie's girls, though—talk about replicas. I see so much of Elody in her girls; it's hard not to compare. They already have me wrapped around their fingers, and I only saw them for an afternoon. Seeing the ease of blending our families together is something I am loving.

Now I'm at my doorway, saying goodbye to Tessa while my little girl is attached to my girlfriend. Apparently, I'm chopped liver now that Ellie is in the picture. Tessa whispers something in Ellie's ear, and they both giggle. My sister is looking at me, and I can tell she has more she'd like to say. I brush it off because I know I'll hear an earful when my sister corners me sometime this coming week.

Tessa blows a kiss our way, and I pretend to catch it mid-air. I am quickly told the kiss was meant for Elody, and I had to mush the air kiss against Ellie's face to satisfy Tessa. After the elevator doors close, I look over at Ellie.

"So you've taken the coveted number one spot, huh?" I can't help but tickle her because hearing her laugh is one of my favorite things.

When I first saw Elody in that bar, I saw a lot of pain behind her eyes. But as the weeks have passed and we've gotten to be together, especially without the weight of hiding this relationship from our children, I've seen her come alive. She's so free with her smiles and happiness, it's infectious. I guess it's carrying over to me because Cummings and even some of the players said I'm smiling during practice. Phil thought I was having a stroke during one of the drills because I couldn't hide how happy I was feeling.

I close my front door with my foot and carry Ellie toward my room, quickly going from playful to serious. I have missed her so fucking much, and I am going to use every free moment to show her. She wraps her legs around me, and I push her against the hallway wall and devour her lips against mine. Our movements are frantic, something I've grown accustomed to because we both can't seem to keep our hands off one another when we're alone.

Once we get to my room, and I put her down, only to have her drop to her knees and take me between her swollen lips. Fuck me, she's perfect. I look down, pulling my fingers through her hair to get a better look at the sight before me. She's taking me in, all the way to where I can feel the back of her throat, and the movement causes me to moan and drop my head back. I will not last with her doing this to me because it's been too long since I've been with her in this way.

I pull my dick out of her mouth abruptly, so much so a big pop sounds from the tight suction she had on me. I know that decision might become a regret later, but I have plans for the two of us, and I do not want to waste it spilling down her throat. I grab her face between my palms and kiss her hard, pulling a moan out of her. Shit, her sounds alone make me want to lose it. I pull away, and I can see the dazed expression across her face.

"Do you trust me?" I ask her while I walk us toward my bed. She nods, and a smirk moves across my lips.

I grab two handfuls of her perfectly round ass and say, "Trust me enough to take this?" I squeeze her ass a little harder, and I feel her move her hips involuntarily toward my cock.

"Mmmhmm," she answers, still in this trance between us.

"Good, because I have been wanting to fuck you in that tight hole for some time now. Get on that bed, on your hands and knees, and show me that perfect ass in the air," I command with a whack across her ass cheek. I see my palm print form immediately, and I feel myself grow harder.

I spread her cheeks, passing my tongue through her pussy and up toward that puckered hole. I bite her ass, and she yelps. I love that I can be unexpected for her in the bedroom. I can tell she likes exploring new things, and I feel like I'm walking on water that she trusts me to go through these motions with.

I open my bedside table and find the bottle of lube and the butt plug I've been saving for this very moment. I bought both in hopes of using them with her today. I drip the lube down her backside and use my fingers to start massaging that hole. I start to coax a finger into her slowly and watch her reaction. She tenses at my touch, and I whisper for her to relax.

Once she gets more used to my movements, she moans, looking back toward me, curiosity etching her features. I see my finger disappear inside her, and the moans that come out of my girl's mouth make me want to cum on the spot. Fuck, that's hot.

I keep massaging, then I remove my finger and replace it with the toy to stretch her further. She feels the difference immediately, and from her expression, I can tell she's feeling more curious than concerned. She takes it perfectly, and I keep talking to her, telling her what a good girl she's being for me.

Leaving the butt plug where it is, I reach around and cup her breasts, kissing her along her shoulders, down her spine, until I reach her ass again and take a bite. She yelps again, and I know all these sensations are turning her on even more. I decide to let the butt plug stay where it's at while I get her to climax for me with my lips on her clit first.

I flip her body over and begin my descent towards the junction of her legs and her hands move toward her breasts, kneading them and pinching her nipples, only causing me to be more turned on. I lick her center and she nearly jumps off the bed. She's sensitive all over, that I know, so I take my time to kiss the inside of her thighs and move my lips to her center again. My tongue flicks her clit and her moans gets louder.

She's riding my face and calling my name, quicker than I expect. She's coming and I'm in awe of her beauty. She's completely drenched when I'm done with her and I know she's ready for what's next.

Soon I'm lubing up my dick and telling her to flip back onto her stomach. I see her gaze watching my movements as she moves herself into position. She seems to be getting more turned on with each stroke of my cock, which spurs me on.

I rub the mushroom head along her folds, and then I stop as I inch up toward her ass, removing the toy and tossing it aside.

"I'll go real slow for you, baby. Just remember to breathe."

She nods, and that's all she's capable of. I bring my cock to her entrance, and I take a moment to admire this beauty in front of me. I begin to inch in slowly, and I watch the head of my cock slowly disappear in this sacred hole no one has been before me.

Shit, she's so goddamn tight.

Once I get the tip in, I ask, "Are you okay, baby?" She nods again. "You're doing so good taking me like this. You look so fucking hot, Ellie."

I keep sliding in little by little until I'm completely seated inside her. I don't move because I know she needs a minute to adjust to the fullness.

I begin to move slowly, pulling out and then pushing back in, while simultaneously I want to make her feel good, so I insert a finger, then another, in her pussy. I keep my dick moving in and out of her. She's writhing beneath me, telling me how good it feels and how full she feels. She starts to move her hips to meet mine, the feeling intensifying with each stroke. We're moving at a steady rhythm, and I have to breathe through my nose to keep from losing control and coming at the sight of my dick in this forbidden hole.

I feel her pussy begin to constrict my fingers, and I know she is incredibly close.

Our pace picks up, and she can't control her sounds now, "Fuck, Wyatt, I'm going to...oh my God. Yes, yes, yes."

She unravels around me, and I follow suit. I see stars, that's how far gone I am. I collapse beside her, and we are both panting, trying to control our breathing and catch our breaths.

We're both looking up at my ceiling, daylight still shining through the windows, when she finally breaks her silence, "That was...intense."

She giggles, and I can't help the happiness that's floating over us right now. I've met my match in this life, and I don't know how to handle whatever comes next.

I turn my head to look at Ellie, and that's when it hits me: I'm absolutely, head over heels, in love with this woman. Not because of what we just did. The love has been there, growing each time we've connected, and she's done something to this grumpy soul of mine. She's brought me light when I thought my world was lit enough. She's made each day better when I thought I was living at maximum capacity.

The only issue now is, how do I tell her? Because if there's one thing I know for sure, Elody's heart is not up for grabs.

Chapter Nineteen

ELODY

The weeks are passing, and so much has happened around me. My kids are thriving as we head into spring. The school year has flown, and I see so much growth as my students show signs they're picking up the lesson plans with more ease. I've got a good rhythm with Wyatt and Tessa; incorporating his life with mine seems seamless when I never imagined that was possible.

As I've been acclimating to having Wyatt and Tessa in my personal life, my sister has had quite a start to this year these last few months. Laney's life has shifted and seeing her make some changes for her future are bringing me a piece of comfort I didn't realize I was lacking. She and Grant are figuring things out, even if the road to get there has been unconventional, to say the least.

Wyatt is preparing for the playoffs, so a lot of his life away from the arena is spent studying plays and figuring out new strategies to keep his team above the rest. If he ever doubted his ability as a coach, I hope he now recognizes that he was made for this outside of being a player of the sport. It's incredible to watch. We've been to a few games this season, and watching him navigate everything is incredible.

I've started watching old games of his throughout his

career, and I appreciate the strides he's made after seeing the gruesome sport he has been a part of most of his life. I especially appreciate that he has all his teeth. Those injuries are gruesome.

I'm saying my goodbyes to the students as they leave for the day, putting things in their rightful spot, the minutes winding down for spring break to commence. As we are headed for a week off from school, the kids leave hyped up on candy from the party we threw in the class. I make sure no food is left behind where a disgusting smell might be discovered upon our return from the break.

I'm throwing out some trash at my desk when I look up to find Tessa sitting at her desk. She's got her head down, and I realize she's gotten quieter as the day has progressed. She went to see the nurse at lunch, like she always does, but something about her demeanor since then is making the hairs at the back of my neck stand at attention. This isn't the girl I know and love. She's usually the first to offer to help and the last to sit down, even after a full day of fun.

I walk over, calling her name as I do. My concern heightens when she mumbles, but she's not coherent when doing so.

"Tessa, sweetie, can you lift your head for me."

She shakes her head slowly, her forehead never leaving her desk, showing me she can't lift it, then moves her head to the side. I crouch down beside her and move her hair to the side. The moment I do, my heart stops. She's cold and clammy, paleness taking over her tiny features, and she's barely able to open her eyes.

I check my phone and click into the glucose monitor app. Her numbers look like they're within range. What's going on?

I make a call to 9-1-1, then proceed to call up to the nurse's office while I'm stroking Tessa's hair. Soon, my classroom is surrounded by staff, and I can hear the ambulance making its way outside. I call Wyatt, and it goes to voicemail.

As a parent, I would not like to get a frantic message on a voicemail, so I send a quick text explaining Tessa's symptoms just as EMTs make their way into the room.

The emergency personnel quickly check vitals, and she's placed on a stretcher. As she is getting wheeled out of the room, there are parents surrounding us in the corridor. My girls come rushing up, concern etched across their faces. They follow me out, and once we hit the cool spring air, I see Juliette rushing toward me. She was planning on getting Tessa from school and taking her home before Wyatt got home.

She grabs hold of Tessa, telling her she's going to be okay and that she'll ride with her in the ambulance. I tell Juliette I'll meet her at the hospital, and soon they're off, growing distant down the street. With shaky fingers, I send another text to Wyatt letting him know what hospital to meet us at. It's in that moment I feel a rush of emotion consume me, and I let the tears fall. I have never been so scared before with one of my students.

My girls stay with me as we make our way to the hospital. It's the same one Becca works at, and she's at the emergency room doors the moment I pass through them. Luckily, she had just finished a delivery when she got my text.

She rushes me to the waiting room, and then Becca leaves to get information for me, as she has badge access to pass through the personnel doors. She comes back and explains that they're still assessing Tessa. In the meantime, Wyatt's parents have arrived to be with both Tess and Juliette, rushing through the waiting area in the emergency room. I keep calling Wyatt, but it's going to voicemail.

In the rush of everything, I forgot I had his offensive coach's number saved in my phone for situations just like this. I call him, my foot bouncing with nerves, and Phil picks up, probably unsure who is calling him. The moment I tell him who I am and he hears the distress in my voice, he must hand the phone over to Wyatt without much explanation. I hear the panic in Wyatt's voice as I explain what happened, and he quickly hangs up the call after I tell him what hospital we are at.

I slump in my seat as Becca grabs my girls and takes them to the vending machine for a snack. My hands are shaking, and I feel like I've just finished running a marathon.

I hate hospitals. Why do they all smell the same and have the same damn flooring? Being here brings back memories that are all too familiar and reminds me of an all-too-draining time in my life.

I close my eyes and let my head fall back. The emotional toll of the last sixty minutes catches up to me, and I start to do some breathing exercises, hoping it will calm the anxiety I feel throughout my body. I keep pleading to Beau to watch out for Tessa, begging that I discovered her symptoms in time for them to help her. Dating Wyatt, I've tried hard to have a better grasp on insulin-dependent diabetics, and the symptoms she exhibited came out of nowhere, fast.

I hear him before I see him, and I can tell he's losing his mind. Wyatt runs through the double doors of the emergency room, flustered and looking for a way to get to his daughter. He locks eyes with me, but I can tell he can't react to my presence right now. I nod so he knows I'm good, and Becca grabs his arm and takes him through the large metal doors, taking him straight to Tessa.

My girls take a seat on each side of me and start asking me questions. I'm consumed with fear, along with memories of the last time I had to sit in a waiting room at a hospital, and my heart is breaking. But I throw on my brave face and explain in the simplest terms I know, what's going on. I try to hide my heartache and the pain I'm feeling about how hospitals are the last place I want to be.

I get a hold of Tyler, and he happens to have a night off, as it's spring break for him as well. He meets us at the emergency room and, after spending some time with me, takes his sisters home. I hand him my car keys, and he asks me to keep them updated on Tessa's condition.

I feel numb at this point. The sun is starting to set through the windows of the waiting room, and I feel like time is moving so slowly while I have no update on Tessa's condition. Becca texted, saying they were still working on her and trying to understand what happened, but then she got called into another delivery and couldn't come back out to sit with me. I close my eyes, letting the tears trickle down my cheeks.

I must doze off because I'm woken up by a simple stroke of a thumb across my face. I blink my eyes open, and I see my favorite set of clear blue eyes staring back at me. I smile, forgetting where I am, but then reality hits me, and I sit up and take in my surroundings. He looks pained looking at me, but then he speaks and puts my heart at ease.

"She's going to be okay. She has to stay overnight, but she's going to be fine."

The dam breaks, and I jump into his arms. My shoulders quake as the tears take over. The relief I feel is instant, and I take a moment to thank my guardian angel above for watching out for this precious little girl.

Once I calm down, Wyatt helps me back in my seat, and he sits by my side.

"They're getting her ready to move to the children's wing of the hospital. She's acting like herself, just a little tired from all the chaos."

He's moving the hair from my face, taking me in. I don't even know if he realizes he's consoling me when I should be the one consoling him.

"I don't get it, Wyatt. She was fine most of the day. All of a sudden, I looked, and she was completely lethargic. And her blood sugar on the monitor was completely within range." I had no idea I had more to shed, but the tears don't stop coming.

"Shhh. You could never have predicted this. Her glucose

monitor failed, which can happen with these devices sometimes. The numbers we saw on the app were not consistent with her actual blood sugar. She got a dose of insulin before eating lunch, but apparently, with all the running around, she burned off more than her monitor was reading after she ate, and the insulin was too much for her body."

He looks exhausted from this one incident, and I bet today shed a few years off him. I know it did me.

"I can't believe I didn't realize it sooner. I'm so sorry, Wyatt. I should have seen the signs before she got so sick."

I feel awful for what this poor girl has gone through after such a fun day with her friends. I could never have imagined.

"What do you mean, Ellie? You saved my little girl's life. Thank you."

He grabs my face and kisses me. Then our lips disconnect, but our foreheads stay together, and he keeps thanking me and telling me that I'm the one who got her the help she needed even though the monitor seemed to show everything was normal. I latch onto his wrists and keep him close as I take in his words.

Before I left the hospital and Tessa was situated in her room, I was able to go in and say a quick goodbye before leaving. She looked so fragile in that hospital bed, hooked up to so many machines. It broke my heart. But she was all smiles, and her hug felt like the best gift. I said my goodbyes and told her we would do lots of crafts during spring break.

Wyatt stays the night with Tessa, and I make my way home. I can't help but hug my kids a little tighter tonight.

I'm lying in bed later that night when a text comes through. I almost don't pick my phone up, the exhaustion nearly consuming me at this hour, but I know it could be an update about Tess, so I quickly swipe it off my bedside table. I see it's from Wyatt, and I open it:

GOAT IN BED

I didn't even ask, how are you holding up after coming into the hospital? I doubt it's easy for you to be around hospitals after all you've been through.

> Don't even worry about me. I am fine. How's Tessa?

GOAT IN BED

She's good. She's got all these nurses wrapped around her little finger. It's funny to see I'm not the only one who falls for her charms. <wink emoji>

> I'm so relieved she's okay. I was so scared, Wyatt. I'm so sorry this happened.

GOAT IN BED

El, it could have happened to anyone. Thank you for taking care of my girl.

> I'll have my phone on if you need me throughout the night. Can I get anything ready for you before you two head home tomorrow?

GOAT IN BED

Juliette is getting all of Tessa's favorites. She doesn't do well when Tessa's in the hospital, so I can bet money she's cleaning her apartment and making her way through mine. Thanks for offering, though.

> I get the same way. If anything changes, just let me know. Go get some sleep if you can. I know all the nurses will be coming in to check on her throughout the night and check on Coach Xander <winky emoji> <blushing emoji>

> **GOAT IN BED**
> Very funny. Sleep tight. I'll talk to you tomorrow. <kissy emoji>

I put my phone down next to me and turn off my light. Today wiped me, and I am mentally exhausted. Sleep doesn't come easy, with thoughts of Beau and Tessa in their hospital beds floating through my restless mind.

Chapter Twenty

WYATT

We've made it to the playoffs, and life is hectic, to say the least. The playoff games haven't started yet, but I know the moment they begin, we will be in a full-on hockey mindset. Finding time for my team is the top priority right now, but I would be lying if I said my heart didn't ache to be with Tessa, Ellie, and her family. They've all become a part of my routine, and not seeing them regularly puts me in a mood. I miss everyone like crazy, so any chance I get, I spend it at Ellie's. Tessa has fun with her daughters, and it also gives Juliette a break.

Tonight, I'm at Elody's house, using her office while the girls have a sleepover together. Tessa loves the bunk beds in the girls' room, so they're playing upstairs, and we'll soon go and say our goodnights. This will be the first time I sleep over here, and Ellie's quite nervous.

Turns out my girlfriend is a lot like my sister—-she cleans when she's stressed. She is currently removing all contents from her fridge to wipe it all down inside. I can hear her clanking things around, talking to herself as she *Beautiful Minds* the shit out of the fridge configuration. I tried to offer help, but she glared at me, and I decided it was best to walk away. As nervous as she is, I'm not feeling any anxiety about it at all. I think this is the only logical next step for us. But Ellie is in her head about it, so I'll let her work through it.

Tessa recovered well from her low blood sugar episode before spring break. Ellie is a little more neurotic about the device malfunctioning, but the doctor said it happens, and the way Elody handled the situation was exactly what he would have done. Each day that passes, she seems to let it go a little more, and she's not hovering over Tess after each meal like she was when she first got released from the hospital.

I'm starting to see double on these plays in front of me, so I close my laptop and head toward the kitchen. I find Ellie partially in the refrigerator, and I decide to reach my arms around her and kiss her neck. She yelps, bumping her head in the process.

"What the hell, Wyatt! You could have given me a heart attack!"

She tries to elbow me, but I just squeeze her tighter. I bury my face into her neck and kiss her, and I feel her melt a bit into my grasp.

"Elody, why don't we call the cleaning-fest a night for now, huh? It looks good to me." I keep trailing kisses down her neck, and I see goosebumps pop up along her arms.

She was about to protest, but she relents and nods, telling me she's tired anyway. I help her get the items back into the fridge, and the moment she closes the door, we hear the front door slam shut. We look over to find Tyler storming through the house. He's making his way into the kitchen.

"Hey, Ty, sweetie, what's wrong?"

Elody immediately looks concerned, and she quickly glances at me. I keep my eye on him, and he's fuming. He won't look at us, but I can tell he has tears in his eyes.

"It's nothing. I'm grabbing some water and going to bed."

He heads into the pantry and grabs a room-temperature bottled water, rushing out of the kitchen as fast as he came through it.

Ellie watches her eldest, and she's about to follow him when I put my hand on her arm to stop her.

"Let me go check on him. Why don't you check on the girls, and I'll be right in to say goodnight."

She nods, and I give her a quick peck on the cheek and make my way upstairs. I have a feeling I know what's going on, and I think he'll be more inclined to talk to me than his mom.

I walk down the hall, soaking in the giggles from the girls as I pass their room. The minute I get to Tyler's door, it's closed, but I hear him moving around behind it.

I knock gently, "Hey, Tyler, can I come in?"

I hear a faint, "Yes," and I turn the knob and swing the door open.

I see him slumped on his bed, sitting at the edge, head down, while his shoulders are shaking a bit. I take a seat next to him and let the silence consume us.

"I never knew it could hurt this bad." Tyler finally speaks up, and my heart breaks that I was right in my intuition. Heartbreak is consuming him.

"Why don't you tell me what happened?"

He looks up at me then, and I see the pain in his eyes.

"Emma broke up with me. She said she thinks I spend too much time playing basketball and not enough time with her."

My heart breaks for the kid because I know how everything is magnified when we're his age. It feels like the worst thing at that moment, and we have no idea how we'll crawl out of this hole.

"I'm sorry, man. I know the feeling. It's hard to lose a first love like that," he nods but stays silent.

"I mean, I gave her everything."

The way he says *everything*, I read between the lines and know he probably lost his virginity to this girl. That shit hurts, to be left behind by your first. I can't say I had the same experience, but I saw buddies of mine have that happen. Being in sports, it's hard to date. Sometimes, we don't care, and we like the attention. But I can see that Tyler isn't that kid.

He loves with his whole heart, and he doesn't get involved with someone unless he truly feels a connection. I admire him for that, and I hope this doesn't sway him toward being heartless in future relationships. I have seen that happen, too, and it doesn't make it any easier.

"How did you handle it?"

His question throws me off. I don't think this is the time to tell him that I never loved anyone before. Until becoming a father, I never really gave myself to anyone in any way. But then my mind veers to his mother, and I know how I would feel now if Elody walked away from me. I can't help but feel the pain in my chest grow just thinking about it. Instead of giving him a scenario where his mother is involved, I decide to make my answer relatable without lying.

"Honestly, I never fell in love at your age. My love was hockey, and I can tell you that it brought along a fair share of pain for those I dated. Usually, girls were mad at me that I didn't care about them as much as the sport. But you, Tyler, love big, man, and that's okay. I think girls dig that because it's so rare."

"Then why did she leave me?" he asks, and I can see him pleading for a definitive answer.

"I can't speak for Emma, and it's hard to say for sure. She could feel neglected, and this was the best way to let go before things got more serious. Or she felt like it was an unfair situation between the two of you, and she was upset and made this huge decision without thinking it through. Or she just isn't the girl for you."

I see him nodding, taking in what I just said.

"But the most important thing to remember is to stay true to who you are because one day, you'll find someone who lifts you up and won't want to bring you down. I promise that person is out there, just waiting to give you so much love that it hurts to live without it."

He looks at me, giving me an expression I don't quite recognize.

"You love her, don't you?"

His question is so far from what I was expecting that I clam up, coughing because my mouth is suddenly parched. Is it hot in here?

Tyler keeps his eyes on me, and I feel like my skin is on fire.

"Um, we, um, let's stay focused on you." I shrug, and hopefully, he takes the bait.

He chuckles, wiping tears from his face, and gives me a look like he can see right through me, and I'm suddenly unable to stop my mind from wandering. His words hold truth, and I haven't taken the time to verbally express my feelings for his mother but realize they have evolved and are probably pretty evident in my actions toward her.

I stay with Tyler a little longer, and by the time I say goodnight, he seems a little lighter regarding his heartbreak, and hopefully, he can see that there's so much more life to be lived beyond Emma. I also hope I handled that the way his father would have. I don't know why that comparison has popped into my head, but feeling the blessing from a man I will never meet is the avenue my mind decides to go down.

I leave Tyler's room and head over to say goodnight to the girls. By the time everyone is tucked in bed, I see the bedroom light is on. I open the door, and Ellie is reading a book while lying under the covers. The routine seems so easy, something you'd assume we've done countless times before.

She looks up, pulling her reading glasses off, and a small smile crosses her face.

"I heard what you said to Tyler when I walked by. You seemed to have calmed him down. My heart hurts knowing my baby is hurting." She sticks out her lower lip, and the adorable expression makes my heart burst.

The only thing I can think of when I stare back at her is that I am utterly in love with this woman, and I don't know what to do about it. I know what she said when we first started seeing each other, but I thought by now, we would have broached the subject and moved forward. I didn't think I'd feel so blind walking forward with her by my side.

I nod at her words and move toward the restroom to get ready for bed. My things are in a drawer she emptied for me. I feel like I belong here, within her things, walking life with her. Doesn't she see it? Doesn't she sense we are good together and we can make this work?

Once I'm ready for bed, I go to my side of the bed and get under the sheets. Unlike Ellie, who is currently in a pajama set when she usually sleeps in the nude with me, I'm going to bed in my boxers. There is no way in hell I can sleep with anything more than these boxers because I feel like I'm on fire most of the time at night.

The moment I get under the sheets, she scoots closer. She's not close enough for me, so I grab her hips and pull her closer, pulling her leg to rest above my hip. She can probably feel me growing under her right now.

Her eyes widen, and she whispers, "You can tell your little friend we are not doing that tonight."

I give her a horrified look.

"Please don't call my gigantic hockey stick little. He's offended. And, I think a little fun might be on the agenda."

I waggle my eyebrows and move my hips so my dick rubs up against her center, the way I know she likes it.

She grabs her bottom lip with her top teeth and lets the friction continue as she starts moving her hips at a rhythm that suits her. I can't help myself, and I kiss her, letting my tongue slide inside her mouth, colliding with her own. I let out a groan, and she immediately breaks free.

"If we're doing this, you best keep it down," she scolds me, and I mimic zipping my lips and throwing away the key.

We go back to kissing, and I start to slowly unbutton her pajama top. I'm sliding it off her arms while she shimmies out of her pants, taking her panties along with them. I get rid of my boxers as quickly as I can, and my cock springs free.

Trying to be as quiet as possible, I push her to lay on her back while I hover over her. I'm still kissing her, moving my hips to let my dick slide between her folds. She's writhing beneath me, and I decide to take her out of her misery.

I gently begin sliding in, ever so fucking slowly, until I'm fully inside her. I bury my face in her neck and take some deep breaths, making sure I don't moan my pleasure for the entire house to hear. Fuck, this feels different for some reason. I pull my face away from her and look into her eyes. I'm caging her in with my forearms and I simply look into her eyes, feeling this love crackle around us. She owns me, and this connection is just one of the ways I have fallen in love with her.

I begin moving slowly, in and out of her, keeping my eyes connected with hers. We aren't intimate like this usually. We're rough. We have had sex in every position possible. I've taken her in every hole, and I've claimed her in all the ways I know how. But this—this feels like a different level. Before we fucked, but tonight we're making love. I feel warmth carry through my chest, and I feel the build-up of my orgasm creep up on me. We keep our movements slow and steady, enjoying the pace.

My release is waiting for me to let go, but I'm trying to cherish each stroke until I finally whisper to her, "Ellie, please let go, baby. I can't last much longer."

With that, she wraps her legs around me tighter, her clit rubbing against my pelvis, while using her heels to dig into my ass, her hands moving along my back, and her nails digging into my skin.

The movements pull my orgasm to the brink. But the friction hits her in all the right spots, and she detonates around me. I begin pumping into her, trying to keep our noises to a minimum. I chase my release, and soon I'm burying my face into her neck, telling her how good she feels and how her pussy was made for me.

By the time I pull out, I'm wiped. I feel like that wasn't about a release. It was about giving her my entire heart because that's what has happened. I'm lost without this woman. The worst part is I have no idea if she can move through life with me.

I close my eyes and inhale her scent, and I whisper words I've never told anyone outside of my family, "I love you, Elody."

With that confession, I feel light, but I also realize that the silence I get in exchange breaks my heart.

Chapter Twenty-One

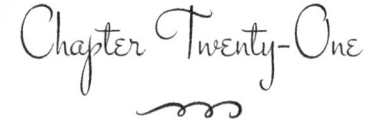

ELODY

"I love you, Elody."

I hate myself the moment I hear his words because instead of melting into him, I stiffen. All the reasons I laid out before about not being able to love this man come to the forefront of my thoughts. And after all those barriers I put in front of us, which he found ways to crack, he still found room to fall in love.

Wyatt lays next to me after his confession, my back to his front, and I slowly hear his breathing even, sleep finally taking over him. I, however, watch the morning light shine in, sleep never finding me.

Last night was different when we were intimate. The way Wyatt moved inside me, slow and comforting, was not our usual routine. And in feeling this change in his behavior, I already knew I saw something different in his eyes.

He usually throws me on the bed and has his way with me. He'd find a way to get me on my hands and knees and drive into me until we both got what we wanted out of the connection. But last night, he was intentional and slow. I know we were limited due to our surroundings regarding our children down the hall and them overhearing us, but the way he looked at me, I saw love staring back. Before he uttered those words, I already knew where his heart was.

I can't lie and say I'm uncomfortable with the idea of laying in Wyatt's arms night after night and sleeping with him while we are all under one roof. Something about it feels comforting. But this can't be something we do together beyond dating.

Nothing we are doing can lead to anything more serious. I promised, vowed, that I would always be Beau's. But I can't help the way my mind wanders to scenarios that just aren't our reality. If only I weren't a widow. If only I could be open to connecting to someone in that way again. If only I weren't broken inside.

I have nothing more than this to offer Wyatt. I don't have myself put together enough to be there for someone else in that capacity. I've lost someone I've loved before, and I can't do something that resembles that kind of love again. I think if I dig deep, I will come to terms that I am capable of loving Wyatt. But I can't love him the way he deserves. My heart will never be his when it already belongs to Beau. No matter how I look at this, I'm not a whole person to give myself to another. I slip out of bed while Wyatt is still in a deep sleep. I make my way downstairs to get my day started.

The hours pass and it's late morning when I'm in the kitchen, sipping my coffee, zoned out, and reflecting on what transpired when Wyatt walks in. I can tell he's a little more closed off this morning. I have a pang of sadness pass through me that I'm the reason for his coldness, and it's on the tip of my tongue to return his words and say that I love him too. I simply cannot do that to him. Even if I feel whole with him by my side, I can't do this again with someone else. It feels like a betrayal on some level that's hard to explain.

Whatever we are doing has to be pulled back because I

cannot be what he needs. Wyatt grabs a to-go cup of coffee and gives me a soft kiss on the lips, staring at me and taking me in with his gaze. He puts his hand on my cheek, and I feel the movement of his thumb under my eye. It's a simple gesture that speaks volumes. He's telling me with his gaze that he loves me, but I cannot feel as confident with my physical behavior back.

I'm lost in his eyes, pulling me in much like he did the first time I saw him. He tells me he'll call me later, and then he takes Tessa along with him. She waves from the entryway of the kitchen, and they're both off. I know Wyatt has a full day of meetings, and I'm sitting here figuring out what occurred in the last few months that led me to be in the exact spot I was trying to avoid.

When did he veer into the love category? Did I miss the signs? I know we blended our families recently, but I never felt like we were already falling in love with one another. I thought dating Wyatt was a safe bet because he wasn't one to get attached so easily. And yet, here we are, and I'm feeling my walls closing me off once again.

I'm going about the rest of my morning, my mind focused on anything but the task in front of me. I'm getting breakfast made for Tyler, so he has something ready when he's up in a bit. Maybe we can head out to a movie, the four of us, so I can connect with my kids for a little bit. I'm waiting near the toaster oven for my bread, and I hear my phone buzzing on the counter behind me.

"Hey, Becca. How are you?" I say, less enthusiasm than my usual greeting, while taking a bite of my toast.

"Hi. I wanted to see how you're doing. I know we didn't talk much leading up to this weekend, and you had a lot going on, but I know yesterday was probably hard on you."

I know she can't see me, but I scrunch my face in confusion. What is she talking about? I know I was anxious about having Wyatt spend the night, but the way she's talking to me, you'd think I was preparing for my upcoming wedding. Wyatt's comment from last night is being put behind my thoughts as I try to figure out what Becca is referring to.

"I'm sorry...what?" Did I freak out yesterday with Becca and blackout about it this morning?

"The anniversary of Beau's passing. I know each year it's hard on you. I usually come and spend it with you and a side of ice cream, and you have a good cry, but I know things shift when we are in a relationship. I hope Wyatt was a comfort for you on such a hard day. Did he handle it properly, or do I need to tell him what ice cream to purchase on emotionally heavy days like that for you?"

Becca is talking, but as she's speaking on the other end of this call, it feels like her words are getting muffled, being drowned out by the intensity of my heart pounding through my ears. I drop the butter knife and rush over to the calendar I have hung up in my office. There, in black and white, is the date, circled like it usually is.

Every single year, I dread this date. Each year prior, since Beau passed away, I spent it with a gallon-sized ice cream and looking through photos and home movies where Beau was still by my side, healthy and strong. The kids would usually be out with friends, something I made sure of each time this dreaded anniversary came around so that I could grieve in my own sadness without taking them down with me. If school were in session, I'd get a substitute to take over that day because I always reserved that day for Beau.

The anniversary of his death has always been one I wanted to remember because I never wanted to forget the hole he left in my life. It's a way I have chosen to honor him because our time together was robbed. I used this one day out of the entire year to sit in my grief and let it consume me. I had all three-hundred and sixty-four days of the year to push my grief aside, but this one day was something reserved to remember him.

I feel a lump forming in my throat as Becca tries to get my

attention on the phone. I have gone mute because I feel like my world is caving in on me.

"Ellie, are you okay? Was it that bad? Was Wyatt not understanding?" She huffs, "No, he doesn't seem like the type to disregard your feelings. Not with the way he looks at you. I saw it when we hung out last time. He doesn't come off as someone that could be that insecure." She scoffs this time.

I finally find my voice and speak, "No, it wasn't anything Wyatt did because he had no idea. I, um, I…" I feel like an awful person. "He didn't react because I forgot to tell him. I forgot, Becca. What kind of wife am I? To forget the day my world crumbled and all it took was a new relationship with a famous hockey player."

I cover my mouth with my hand as a sob breaks free. I don't want my kids hearing me cry. I am not this person. I leave my emotions at the door in all areas of my life. I may hold the sadness within, but I can't let it out and let it bleed into my life with my kids. I have to keep up this appearance that I'm going to be okay because my kids have gone through enough. I don't need to add this to their plates as they figure out how to navigate life.

Becca speaks, but there's an incoming call. I pull the phone away from my ear and see it's my mother-in-law.

"Becca, it's Candace. I have to take this. I'll call you back." I rush off and hop on the incoming call.

"Hey, Candy. How are you?" I barely get the words out as I know I'm about to be hit with an onslaught of her emotional dialogue.

On top of forgetting my late husband's passing, I forgot to call my in-laws. I always call to check in on them because I know that if my pain is all-encompassing, theirs is devastating. To bury a child is something no one ever thinks they'll have to live through, and they continue to live this nightmare daily since his passing.

"It's nice to know you still remember us."

Her passive-aggressive nature shines through more than ever. This woman was made of sugar when Beau was still alive. But as my husband withered away, so did the woman I once knew. She was always so welcoming and kind toward me. Much like my heart died with Beau, her kindness was buried alongside her son. My father-in-law, Luke, is still the sweetest, but his wife doesn't let him speak to chime in if he agrees with her behavior toward me. The longer Candace lives without her son, the angrier she gets. My forgetting the anniversary of his death is probably the fuel she's looking for to pack on the guilt trip.

"I'm so sorry I didn't reach out yesterday, Candy." I have nothing else I can add, and I am truly sorry for my lack of memory. I don't expand further because I don't need to open that can of worms, as I'm already feeling guilty enough. The less she knows about Wyatt, the better at this point.

"Oh, so you forgetting to call us has nothing to do with the famous hockey coach you're hitting the town with these days? Word around town is that you've moved on to someone who can pay to make your sadness disappear. What a way to honor my son's life, to move on without him in this way, with your photos plastered in magazines and online articles."

This causes me to pause. How did she know I was seeing Wyatt? Candace was never one to follow gossip magazines; then again, I haven't lived around her in years. I shouldn't make assumptions about someone who is now unrecognizable to me.

My spine straightens for a moment. "Candace, my relationship with Wyatt is not something I'm going to discuss with you. I've apologized for not calling, and I feel guilty enough for letting yesterday pass without realizing the date."

Shit. Until that slipped, Candy probably assumed I got busy with life and forgot to call her. She didn't know I forgot as a whole. I brace myself for the wreckage headed my way.

"Not only do you move on from my son's memory, but

you forget about him altogether. What kind of widow are you? What kind of memory are you keeping of my son for his children?"

She goes on, the verbal beating continuing as I simply sit and listen to it. I'm sinking deeper into this hole of guilt that I deserve. I do not have the mental energy to respond to her berating words. She's coming from a place of hurt, and I don't think it's my place to sit here and have a temper tantrum at her.

Now, my thoughts are going everywhere, but the blame is pointing straight toward me and only me on all accounts. From the feelings I had circling my mind after Wyatt's love confession last night to the realization I forgot my husband's death anniversary, I feel overwhelmed with guilt. I thought this was fine, that Wyatt and I starting this thing would be okay between the two of us. I didn't think anything more would come of it. Yet, I didn't stop it from moving forward.

If I dig deep, I contributed to him falling in love with me. I let him love me even when I said I am unlovable. I mean, I didn't say those words per se, but I told him my heart wasn't up for grabs. Then I let him into my life anyway, into my children's life, allowing him to counsel Tyler through heartbreak, allowing my kids to fall in love with him right back. I incorporated him into our routine, and last night, I allowed him to stay the night. And of all nights, I let him sleep in my bed when, six years ago, I was saying goodbye to my dying husband. What kind of person am I? I'm selfish, and all I saw was my happiness, but I ignored the grief I should live with.

Candy goes on for another thirty minutes, barely letting me get a word in. I allow her anger because I feel like I deserve it the more I process how I've royally screwed up. A day I thought I'd never let pass is one that I fully forgot about the moment I found a replacement.

That's exactly what my actions feel like—I've found a

replacement for Beau in Wyatt. I focused so much on how different the two of them are from one another I didn't really take into account how much Wyatt was infiltrating my surroundings. I just let it happen. I never experienced life beyond Beau. Wyatt opened up my world and showed me a side of myself I never expected, but I also didn't put much weight on the fact that even with the differences, I was letting go of who I was with Beau to fit with this new life I was building with Wyatt.

Once Candy hangs up with me, I slump into the chair in my kitchen. I bury my face in my hands and allow tears to flow. I should be careful. My girls are up, and Tyler could come out of his room at any moment.

I finally get myself composed and finish the breakfast I was preparing for Ty. I leave the food on a plate under the warmer and head upstairs. I hear my girls playing with dolls, and I let myself get lost in their little voices. They sound so happy and carefree. I remember going through life without thinking about how the next minute would be.

I always pictured myself growing old with Beau. Once that life was figured out, it was perfect. But then he died, and I was left to take each day picking up the pieces. I felt like I was just getting through each day, and the next morning would come, and I would do it all again. No plan in place. The only thing I knew was that my love for my kids would continue and grow. But aside from that, nothing I did moving forward was for me.

When Wyatt entered the picture, I felt like all those fallen pieces I was trying to pick up were finally manageable. All I was doing was covering the pieces up with this momentary happiness. Now I'm here, pieces thrown all in front of me, and I have no idea if I have the strength to pick them all up and arrange my life the way it could be with a new man. I'm lost in such a profound way, I don't know how to maneuver all these feelings overwhelming me now.

I decide to wash my face again and cover up my puffy eyes with some makeup. I need to put these jumbled feelings back in order and get myself together again. This thing with Wyatt is just not sitting right with me. This morning has been the wake-up call I needed. I can't lead him on like this. I saw his expression last night. I saw love, not lust, in his eyes, and I can't navigate those feelings right now.

I'm not a single mom looking for a partner. My partner died, and I have to remember that as I continue to live my life to see my kids thrive. I'm not looking for a replacement. This isn't about me finding a fairytale ending. It hasn't been since I touched Beau's casket and promised him I was his forever.

* * *

Becca didn't even need me to ask. The moment I called her back, she answered with an order to meet at her house in an hour. I did exactly that, leaving Tyler to watch his sisters while I was out. Before leaving, I took some time to compose myself and talk to Tyler about what happened between him and Emma. It broke my heart that he was hurting, but he did say that Wyatt helped him see that he wasn't necessarily in the wrong and that time had its way of healing what felt broken.

I don't last long as a calm and collected adult when I knock on Becca's door an hour later. The moment her door opens, I break down and fall into her arms, tears streaming down my face. She guides me to her living room, and we sit on her couch, where she caresses my back, moving her fingers through my blond hair and telling me how much she loves me and that it will all be okay. I feel like I'm the furthest thing from okay, but I let her words soothe me as I feel the guilt settle further into my soul.

Once I settle down, I relax into the cushions and let my gaze move toward the ceiling. I feel so many different emotions, guilt being at the forefront. I'm still holding Becca's hand, and she squeezes mine to remind me I'm not alone. We've been through a lot together, and I know that no matter what, she'll have my back. I'm still trying to process everything I'm feeling, but I begin to speak, hoping with my words will come clarity.

"Wyatt loves me, Becca." I can tell she's about to ask questions, and I beat her to it and continue explaining, "He said it last night when I was laying in his arms, but even before he uttered those words, I felt like things with him were different all of a sudden. Feeling the weight of his emotions on my shoulders is making me realize just how confused I truly am. Top that with forgetting about Beau's anniversary of his passing, I'm feeling like the worst human. I can't give a man my heart when it's been promised to someone else."

The tears are falling, but I'm unable to control the sobs.

"Oh, Ellie. I won't act like I've experienced your type of heartbreak, losing your life partner like that. Add to the fact that your children were so young when he died."

She rearranges herself to kneel in front of me, her knees on the floor. She squeezes my legs to get me to look down at her.

Becca takes a few breaths before she continues. "When Beau died, I was really sad." She looks down at the ground, and I can tell she's wiping a tear that escaped.

"I was sad for the life you had mentally built being gone; I was devastated for your kids, my own children who looked up to him and myself. Most of all, I was just sad that the love of your life was no longer by your side. It took me some time to recover from feeling like our lives were never going to be the same. And when you moved here, I thought I'd see this immense change in your demeanor."

She smiles, laughing to herself. "It was silly and naive on my part. I thought moving here would change everything for you in some strange way. Don't get me wrong, you were and continue to be an exceptional mother, giving off this feeling of happiness that you share with everyone around you. But I could tell you were missing something, much like missing a limb. As if a part of you had stayed in Nebraska, buried with Beau.

"Days became months, and those months turned into years, and I saw you begin a new routine and build new memories. But even when you had these new moments to treasure, it felt like they never really brought life back to your movements."

She gives me this sad smile because what she's saying isn't just hard to hear, but it makes me realize that I wasn't hiding my sadness as well as I thought I was.

"Then, when you met Wyatt, this spark returned to your eyes, Ellie. It's not that you started to live life as if Beau's passing never broke your heart, but you lived life without holding his death on your shoulders. You started to simply live again without the hesitation that I saw so much of before. It was a beautiful yet devastating realization for me as your friend. It was devastating because it took your relationship with Wyatt for me to fully wrap my head around what you were lacking since Beau died. Then again, it was beautiful because I got to witness you rise from the ashes in a way you didn't do prior to Wyatt's presence."

I'm a blubbering mess again, but find the strength to stand up, pulling my best friend up with me. Becca pulls me in a hug, and I feel her love wrap around me with this embrace.

"I'm so proud of you," she says, and I can't help but feel her words deep down. "I know how hard life has been, going through the motions without Beau for six years now, but you're finding a way to try new things, and I am just so proud of you," she says and sits down on the coffee table behind her.

I keep standing there, in a bit of shock, if I'm being honest, because this morning, I've been viewing my actions as selfish. I did not want to upset Beau, which sounds stupid, but it's how I've felt as I let myself get lost in this relationship with Wyatt.

To hear her say she's proud of me pulls me out of this weird sense of guilt I have been holding onto. I've felt like I cannot love another person as much as I love Beau. But I never put any weight on the fact that love isn't a linear feeling. It has so many avenues and dimensions, so many sides, that my love for Wyatt doesn't have to mirror or replace the love I have for my late husband. And the love I have for both of them can exist together.

By choosing to fall and truly embrace love with Wyatt, I'm not closing my heart off to the love I have for my Beau. But in many ways, by choosing to love Wyatt, I'm choosing to love myself as well. What I've been letting myself see as selfish isn't that at all. And the words Candy hurtfully said on the phone today were her way of reflecting her own anger about herself onto me.

I've just been stubborn, looking at this whole thing with the wrong set of eyes this entire time.

Becca keeps looking at me, taking me in as I have this mental conversation with myself. I've treated Wyatt like he needs to compete with a deceased soul when, in reality, I'm the one competing with a form of myself that doesn't exist anymore. Instead of feeling angry, I now feel deserving of the possibility of this life I could build with another person.

This amazing man who has shown me a side of himself that he barely lets others see, let alone love. This man who has shown me a side of myself that's more take-charge and stands confidently in asking what she wants. But most of all, a man that sees me, sees my pain, and doesn't ask me to mask it.

Since I've been with Wyatt, I haven't tried to put Beau's death at the precipice of our relationship. What I realize now is that Wyatt is allowing Beau to have a place at the table. He recognizes that Beau will always be a part of my puzzle pieces, and he isn't trying to replace my husband's memories with new ones of himself. He's adding to my life story instead of trying to put his own story on top of something I've already made a part of my foundation. Wyatt might be grumpy and personifying this cold exterior, but all he's shown me is love and devotion to those he loves.

Becca gives me this space to let the thoughts come and go. I speak freely about how I'm feeling and how foolish I think I've been when dealing with my feelings regarding Beau and Wyatt. I think it's fair to say I've been putting both these men against each other when I should have been looking at them separately. Beau is part of my past, and he will always be a part of my future. But in having him be a piece of my past, he isn't the only piece I'll sew into the fabric of this life I am still putting together.

Wyatt is part of the new version of my life. He is the one that will help me keep growing and wanting to strive for more when I thought my heart was forever stuck behind me. I know Wyatt would never push me to give up the pieces of myself I built with Beau. On the contrary, he would help me foster a better understanding toward my thoughts of how Beau enriched my life, not focusing on how Beau left it.

Now that I've taken some time to reflect, I realize that I can openly admit that I love Wyatt. But most of all, I realize that it's okay for me to love him. I think that's what held me back last night when I heard his confession. I need to talk to him and clarify that I was confused and I was scared. I can't let him think that I don't love him.

The truth of the matter is that I was a coward, not just with Wyatt but in my inability to defend myself and defend my relationship with Wyatt to Candace. I let her belittle me and make me feel like I was at fault for living my life. How I grieve is mine to embrace. If she doesn't know me well enough to realize that my heart will always have a piece of her son woven into the fabric of it, then that is something I can't spend my time convincing her of.

I made a beautiful life with her son, that is not up for debate. Beau died, and my heart has been forever altered. But my heart is not to be forever suffering. I thought it was, and I had accepted that for so long. In reality, it's healing and, with that, brings the ability to open up to new people who enrich my path to new experiences and new relationships.

Chapter Twenty-Two

WYATT

I watch the guys scrimmage while I speak to Cummings regarding a player's injury from the last game. The team doctor gave us his opinion on how the ankle should heal. Phil and I have to come up with some new plays to showcase the strengths of the guys on the ice right now because this injury won't be resolved by our next game.

Our game is tomorrow night, and it's at home. Our spot is guaranteed for the playoffs, and I can't have the distraction of Ellie and how she reacted to my confession at the forefront of my thoughts right now. What I need is to focus; since I can't play this game to let go of the tension I'm feeling in my shoulders, I've learned that coaching is second-best. I've found my place as a retired player, and seeing this team thrive is something I've become addicted to.

However, I'm human, and my mind keeps returning to last night. It's like I'm replaying her rigid body reacting to my words on a loop in my thoughts. I can't help but feel it take over my mind because it stings. I get what she said when we first started, that her heart isn't mine to win over. I am trying to put myself in her shoes, but there's a part of me that questions how much of me is enough then?

I've had a woman walk away from me the moment our child was put in her arms. I know I can handle heartache, but with Elody, it feels different. I feel a connection to her beyond anything I felt with Sabrina. Shit, Sabrina birthed our child, and I did not have half the connection with her that I do with Ellie.

I want to be upset at Elody, but I also need to consider where she's coming from. I know she feels something more than attraction toward me. I'm not imagining the way she touches me when we lay together after connecting in the most intimate way. I'm not overanalyzing how she thinks of my needs when we are out together. I'm not on this ship alone. I know she feels something more, even if she doesn't want to recognize it.

The thing is, I can't be the one to show her how she feels. She needs to figure this out. And it's not too far off to feel like she needs to figure herself out. I cannot drag my heart through all this and hope for the best. I have a daughter to think of in this scenario, too. If I am being completely honest, I could see forever with Ellie. I could see us walking this life together, but the problem is she feels like she's stuck in a life with a partner who isn't here anymore.

I deserve better than to be left behind. I made the time, and I put in the effort. I think if I've learned anything in the past, it's that I deserve to be loved. For so long, I thought my role was to be the brooding type that played hockey and had my fun with puck bunnies. When Tessa came along, I made sure that my decisions were not reckless anymore. I ensured I would give her the life she deserved with the one parent that she had to carry her into a more solid future.

With that decision came growth for me. When I met Elody, I only wanted to enhance the life I had cultivated by adding this incredible person to our dynamic. If Elody doesn't see that she deserves love after loss, that's not something I can show her. She needs to want that for herself.

Phil pulls my attention to some other plays that could use some work, and we follow through with practice as planned. Once the guys are back in the locker room, I'm rounding some things out, putting some finishing touches on the playbook that I feel would help us for the next game.

I'm grabbing my things when I turn around to find Ellie standing right at the opening of the tunnel. Just the sight of her stops me. If I hadn't already come to the realization I loved this woman, I would right now. Just looking at her, this beautiful person who makes my day shine even when I feel down, I see how my life cannot move forward without her in it. I need her to feel that way about me. That's the journey she needs to pursue and figure out.

Pulling my bag further up my shoulder, I reach her. "Hey, Sunshine." She smiles softly at that, and my heart bursts. *I love you*. It's at the tip of my tongue, but with the way she reacted in my arms last night, telling her is the furthest thing from where my actions should be right now.

"Hey." She looks nervous while she fiddles with her hands. "I wanted to talk to you, but I wasn't sure if coming here was okay."

"Of course it is. Do you want to go to my office?"

She shakes her head. "No, I think it's okay if we stay here."

I motion for us to move toward the stands, and we sit down next to one another. I put my bag down and look toward her, hoping what she has to say is something to make my day versus ruining it.

"Um, I..." She looks around the arena, delaying whatever is on her mind. "I messed up yesterday. I forgot something important to me." I keep looking at her, worried that if I interject, she won't continue her thought. "I forgot yesterday was the anniversary of Beau's death."

Now that was not something I was expecting. I had never asked her when he passed away, so I didn't even know when to look out for it. It was never something I wanted to bring up because Ellie and I had made this little bubble for ourselves, and I think we were both on pins and needles with fear that something would eventually interrupt the easy flow of this relationship we had made. I personally wanted to shield us from the pain of any outside troubles.

"Oh, I'm sorry about that." I honestly have no idea what else I should say right now. I put my hand on her knee, and she places her hand on top of my own. Even after a million little touches, I feel the electricity move along my flesh where we are connected.

"Yeah, it sort of threw me for a loop when reality hit me this morning."

I nod, but I don't know what to say to that. Luckily, she continues.

"And some things were said to me, and it only made me feel worse about us." When she says that, I can't help my shoulders from tensing up.

Her comment causes me to pull my hand away.

"Worse about us? What does that even mean?" It's hard for me not to feel offended by her words.

I get not being ready for what we are building together, but to feel bad about us together is something that makes no sense to me. She makes what we have sound wrong and dirty, and that doesn't sit well with me.

"That's not what I mean." She takes a deep breath, agitated by whatever she's working through in her head. "I mean, I am trying to process what we are doing. I know I didn't say it back, but I didn't miss what you said to me last night."

I nod, "I wasn't sure if you had dozed off when I said it with your back up against me, but once the words were out, your body reacted in my arms, and I knew you heard me."

She pauses and locks her gaze on mine.

"I didn't want to push you to reciprocate something you were trying to figure out. But I can't say it didn't hurt to say something so deep and not hear the words repeated back to me," I confess.

"Well, this morning, I was playing your words on repeat in my mind, and then Becca called and reminded me what yesterday was. She thought I had remembered, and it was then I realized I had completely forgotten. Then my mother-in-law added fuel to the fire, making me feel guilty for living a life and moving on with ease."

I clench my jaw, feeling my molars grind in the back. I don't know her mother-in-law, but just the thought of someone insinuating that Ellie isn't considerate enough to care about her late husband makes me furious. Elody won't move forward with me because of this love she feels for Beau.

"I was sort of stunned silent by Candy—my mother-in-law. She said some awful things, and I just felt really upset. It took me going to Becca to process my feelings. I let go of a lot of things I was feeling, and I've come to this big realization that I should have had before."

I can't say that hearing her run to Becca instead of coming to me doesn't sting. It fucking does. I want to be her person; where she runs to me and tells me how she feels, and we work it out together. But I think what's becoming more evident with what she's saying is that I'm not as high on her list as she is on mine.

"Okay." That's all I can say without being an asshole. The moment I say it, I can tell my tone is a little more clipped than I intended.

"You sort of came out of left field, Wyatt. You are this bigger-than-life person with a past that is full of experiences. I'm a small-town girl who married the first boy she ever kissed and built a family that didn't go past Saddle Ridge's main road. I come from a different life, one where I made a promise to my husband after he took his last breath. I promised him I would never give my heart to someone else."

"But I think you can agree that promise was something

you can't hold on to, especially seeing as you have built a life beyond Saddle Ridge, right?" I hold my breath and hope that what she says is that her life leads to me. I want that so badly because loving her is something I know will only add to my life.

"I see that now. But it doesn't mean it's easy to let go of my promise to Beau and walk forward." She clears her throat, fighting the lump that's probably forming. "But what I realized is that I love you."

My gaze had shifted down to our joined hands, but the moment she says the words I've longed to hear, I look up at her, and I feel my heart soaring through my chest. You'd think I would be jumping up and down and running on the ice and screaming it through the arena so it can echo off all the walls.

But instead, my stupid mouth opens, and the last thing I expect to say comes out, "My love for you, Ellie, is something that I never expected. You were unexpected and completely what I needed for my life. My love for you goes beyond anything I could have predicted. And when I see you look at me, I feel your love, even if you didn't realize it was love when you did it. But is that enough for you? Am I enough for you?"

Where the fuck did that come from? Worst thing is I don't stop there.

"What happens the next time you forget something you shared with Beau? Or better yet, when you and I do something that you had wished to share with Beau. How will you react then? Will the love you have for me be enough to carry you through that guilt?"

I'm a fucking moron. What am I saying? She said she loves me, and this is the moment I decide to become philosophical?

What I say seems to throw Elody off as well. She looks stumped by my questions. I can't blame her. I said all that shit, and I'm feeling confused by my own words. However, now I'm starting to see where my questioning is coming from. I love her, and now I know she loves me as well.

The thing is, she needs to understand what our love means. She has to realize that our love goes further than this moment. I don't want her to have to talk herself off a ledge if she forgets something she shared with Beau, convincing her mind that her love for me is permitted, that she deserves this love between us. I want her to feel what we have so deep to her core that guilt has no room to bleed through.

She nods, seeming to take in what I'm saying to her. Loving her isn't hard. Love should never feel hard to give. If it does, then it shouldn't be labeled as love. Love is free. Love is boundless. Love is ever-changing. Love should feel comfortable, even if confessing it is uncomfortable. Love should not need reminders attached to it. Love should feel all-encompassing. It should feel like a hug when you need the embrace. It should feel like, without it, you're unable to breathe.

However, the way I think Ellie is seeing love seems to hold guilt. Her love for me right now feels like it needs to be justified. That's not the love I want from her. I haven't ever loved another woman, and I think if I'm going to give my heart to her, I deserve for it to feel cared for in the same way I would care for hers.

I want our love to feel limitless. I want her love to feel like it's being given without an asterisk explaining the boundaries attached. I deserve that just as much as she deserves to feel loved after losing it in the past. I have no choice but to stand tall with what I'm saying because I think Ellie has some work that needs to be done.

"Listen, Ellie, I'm not going to lie. I'm all in with you. I know we started this, and you had set boundaries with me. Maybe I ignored them and made my own rules. I don't know. What I do know is that my life is fulfilled with you living in it with me. You add to my life. You give it meaning beyond what it already has. But I think what you need to figure out is if I bring meaning to your life or if I bring a weight to your heart. I think that's something you need to decipher. Because I think we are just too old to play games with one another.

"I want to have your heart. I can't compete with someone who will never be here to fight for it. I think that no matter what you go through in this life from now on, you will always love Beau. But losing him, I think you hold a lot of that loss on your shoulders still. I think today is a huge sign that moving forward feels like you're moving on without him. You need to understand that loving me does not take away from loving him."

She tries to speak up, but I keep going. "Maybe you believe you're showing me a love that stands on its own. But from where I see it, it feels like you are saying words you don't believe yet. You want to move forward so badly, but you still have too much pulling you back. You need to find your two feet steady on the ground so you can move those steps forward with me. That's only fair for both of us. Do you understand that, baby?"

I move my hand to cup her cheek, memorizing her face and her beautiful eyes that are pleading with me to wait for her to figure it out.

"I'm not walking away from us. I'm actually doing the opposite. I'm asking you to give this some thought and work on this journey for yourself so we can come together and be a team. I love you so much, Ellie." A tear falls down her face ,and I catch it with my thumb.

"That's not changing for me. I just want to know you love us enough to fight those moments that I know will arise in the future when you feel the guilt begin to rise. You deserve that kind of love, and so do I. I don't want to replace Beau, but I also don't want Beau at my side while I try to love you. I want to love you on my own. Does that make sense?" She nods, and I can't hold back any longer.

I lean forward and bring her lips to mine. Feeling her against me nearly breaks me, but I feel strong enough to say this isn't it for us. I'm not breaking up with her. I'm simply making her take a moment and pause. I need her to figure out how her past is holding her back from loving with her whole heart.

Our lips part and I rest my forehead on hers, both my hands now cupping her face.

"I'll be here. Find me when you feel like you're standing on a solid two feet, Sunshine. I love you, Ellie. I know you love me. I just want you to believe it with your whole being, not just with a part of your heart."

I stand up, pull my bag on my shoulder, and walk out of the arena, hoping that I did the right thing and didn't just ruin everything with the only woman I have ever loved.

Chapter Twenty-Three

ELODY

I get off the plane, and I feel a rush of emotions. My kids came along with me, an opportunity to see their grandparents while visiting Saddle Ridge. The kids have come back here a few times since we moved away, but as the years passed, I felt the distance between my in-laws only increased.

The calls became more sporadic, and then the effort became one-sided, partly by me being the only one reaching out. After my call with Candace and my talk with Wyatt, I decided to face some issues I've had back in a place I once thought I'd spend the rest of my life living with Beau.

Hearing what Wyatt had to say was devastating to me. I felt completely lost inside when he walked away from me in that cold arena. But the more I pondered his words, the more I realized he was right.

I need to love him with no boundaries conflicting with my thoughts. I need to figure out my grief and how to move forward before I could commit to him and love him the way he deserved. I focused all these years after losing Beau on how to live with my grief, however, if I'm being honest, I didn't put much weight on learning how to love with my grief. The amount of love I have for Wyatt and Tessa is beyond anything

I expected, but the way I hold on to the guilt of moving on without Beau at the center of everything is a significant area that needs to be addressed.

Once I got home from seeing Wyatt, I took the time to pull back and focus on what needed to be done to move forward in a healthy manner. I couldn't ignore how I was feeling and hope for the best anymore. I had to face my fears, and returning to Nebraska was where I'd start. I spoke to the kids, and they were all for seeing their grandparents.

We quickly packed up and hopped on a flight early this morning, and now that we've returned, it feels like I never left. I know the moment I start to drive into my hometown, I'll be flooded with emotions. A huge part of the place I once called home is filled with memories I can't simply ignore. Being in New York, I don't see Beau at every corner. I don't expect him in my life because he has never lived there with me.

We grab our rental, as my in-laws do not know of our arrival, and we begin our drive. Saddle Ridge is nestled about two hours away from the airport. I feel the uptick of my pulse with each mile we drive. As we get closer to where my life began, I start pointing things out to the kids. Tyler seems to remember the most, telling the girls stories about when we lived here almost six years ago. My daughters have their faces glued to their windows, taking in the scenery, as being in a small town is very different from the city we have grown to call home now. Even though they have returned since we moved away, there's a lot of the past that slips through the cracks for them.

We take our last turn before reaching Candace and Luke's house, and the moment we start down their driveway, I see their sprawling home on acres of land. Their house is exactly what anyone would expect from a small town. It's light blue, with white shutters, and they have a wrap-around porch, similar to the one I had in the house I built with Beau.

There's a swing that they've had since I was first dating

their son. With the breeze, I see the swing swaying, and I almost expect Beau to come walking out the front door. This is why I left. These emotional expectations that creep up nearly cripple me, even after so much time.

The car slows down, and soon I'm turning off the car, and the kids are running out, excited to surprise their grandparents. Luke must hear the commotion and opens the front screen. At first, he's processing what he's seeing, then he's opening his arms, and the girls run right into him. His smile doubles in size, and I see him close his eyes and relish the feel of his granddaughters in his embrace.

Before you know it, Candy is walking out, shock written all over her face. She takes Tyler in, and I can see she's stunned by the resemblance to Beau. It jolts people if they're not expecting it. Ty looks like a replica of their son, and I find it a gift to see my late husband in our oldest child. Some might find it hard, but it's a piece of my life that brings me comfort. I feel like it's Beau's way of reminding me that he's always with me.

I take my time to get out of the car and walk to the house. "I hope you don't mind the surprise visit. The kids wanted to see you."

Luke nods his head, speechless with our company. Candy is still taking in each of the kids, looking them over and repeating how grown they all are. She looks over at me, and a sad smile crosses her features. If I weren't watching, I'd miss it because the next second, she's ushering the kids inside, telling them that she's got some banana bread baking. Luke hangs back and waits for me on the porch.

"It's good to see you, Ellie girl."

I smile and feel his words like a balm to my aching heart. He's always called me that, and I didn't realize until right now how much I missed his voice.

"It's good to see you, Luke. It's been too long."

We haven't seen my in-laws in some time. They used to

put in so much effort, and it hurts to know that they didn't take the time to visit us much once we left, when we were also grieving. I always let it go prior and tried to give excuses for their behavior, but I'm done trying to placate their behavior. What they did hurt, and if I really dig deep, I know Luke had little say in how we were treated.

"The house looks good. Are these planks new?"

He shakes his head and moves his foot along the panels.

"No, ma'am. I sanded them down and re-stained them. They were weathered from the rain this past winter but still usable. Had a break in the cold front and used that time to get it done to enjoy this summer." He smiles up at me, and I see his pride all over his features.

"You did good. I love how it looks. Actually, everything looks lovely. I love that you still have the sunflowers throughout the perimeter."

Beau had planted the flowers for me years prior, and Luke had kept it up since Beau and I moved into our own home. Each time we came to visit, and the flowers bloomed, Beau would comment how he has my happiness sprinkled throughout all aspects of his life.

I keep the lump in my throat down so I don't get emotional with the memory. I knew coming back would be hard, but now that I'm here, I realize it could ruin me if I didn't have my mind focused on why I came back. I need to figure this out so I can live my life with Wyatt and Tessa. My love for them is something worth growing stronger for.

"Come in. Let's get some of Cay's lemonade." He puts his arm around me and kisses the top of his head.

Beau got his height from his father, and the man towers over me. He's got Beau's features, although his hair is now almost completely gray. Beau had warm brown eyes, and looking at Luke, it feels like I'm looking at an older version of Beau had he lived years beyond his time. I thought seeing Luke after so long would hurt, but there's something comforting in his presence.

We walk into the house, and I hear the kids asking all sorts of questions. They're firing a mile a minute, and from the enthusiasm in Candy's voice, I know she's enjoying this time with her grandkids. Entering the kitchen, her smile is big, but when her gaze lands on me, I see her smile falter a little.

I hate this wedge we've built between us. When Beau was still alive, I saw myself as the lucky one, having a mother-in-law whom I longed to spend time with. Maybe I'm being unfair in all this, and I'm not recognizing the shift in me when Beau died as well. I think it's fair to say we both caused this turmoil in our relationship, and it's not one-sided.

I sit at the kitchen table, and Luke brings me lemonade. I sit back and watch my kids get their fill. Every once in a while, I see Tyler look over at me, his eyebrows scrunching, like he's trying to piece together the tension he's sensing between his grandmother and myself. I give him a small nod, and it seems to appease him enough that his worry lines lessen.

Once the kids exhaust their grandmother with all the questions possible, they move on to Luke. Their grandfather can't sit still for long, so he ushers the kids to follow him outside, where he still has some gardening to do before supper. My children laugh at his word for dinner, but they all trickle out, leaving Candace and me alone for the first time in years.

I feel awkward for a moment, but I realize that this is why I came out here. I need to face my fears and discuss how she made me feel on that phone call. Honestly, there's a lot about the cold shoulder she's given me that needs addressing.

I can tell from the way Candy makes herself busy in the kitchen that she's nervous to bring it up, so I decide to spearhead the conversation.

"So Candy, a few days ago, when you called, you said a few hurtful things to me," I begin, my heart pounding so hard in my chest I'm surprised she doesn't hear it.

She's wiping her kitchen counter, and the moment I finish what I say, she stops and closes her eyes. I can't tell what direction she's going in with her thoughts, so I wait to see how she responds to my words.

"I'm aware of what I said. I mean, I said it after all."

She has her walls up, and I know that this version of Candy doesn't have the sweetness she once did. Twisted being that her nickname is essentially that in and of itself. It made sense why we shortened her name that way years ago, but now the nickname seems more ironic than fitting.

"I think it's time we talk about how things have unfolded since Beau passed away. Can you see how your words might have hurt me the other day? Better yet, can you understand why your behavior toward me doesn't really push me to want to be around you?"

I let it all go because what do I have to lose? My kids rarely see their grandparents as it is, and it's not from a lack of trying. They know how hard coming back here is for me, as the first few times I returned, I felt like my heart was being ripped out again and again. I had begged them to visit so many times, and it became useless as time moved on.

"My behavior? You think my behavior hurt you on that call? Let's talk about your actions, young lady." Ugh. She's talking to me like I'm back in high school and got caught fooling around with her son in their home. "Let's really dissect why I might feel angry with you."

She moves toward me and pulls out a chair. I can see the fire behind her eyes. I thought I'd cower, but I find this fueling me to push further. I want this feud over between us because it's not helping either of us to move forward in a healthy way.

"Tell me, Candace. What have I done to you that you need to address? I'm here for that reason, so let it out."

I straighten my spine. I can tell this response is the opposite of what she expected, and she softens a bit, realizing that fighting with me will bring only emotional harm. It offers no good toward anyone if we are rifting.

She looks down at the table, her fingers fidgeting with the doily I have no doubt she made. It's yellow, much like the sunflowers lining her home. It brings a brightness to the kitchen, and I hope it will bring some luck because right now, I feel a dark cloud looming over us.

"Did you know that getting pregnant with Beau was an accident? Have I ever told you that?"

I shake my head, stunned by her admission.

The way she looked at Beau, it was as if he was her everything, her reason for living.

"Yeah, I wasn't sure I wanted children. But the moment I found out I was going to be a mama, something in me changed. From that moment, I vowed to give my child the world. Little did I realize that he would give me mine. He gave me all the reasons I needed to live."

I see the struggle pass along her face, her pain palpable as she speaks. I remain silent because I have no idea what she's going to say.

"When Beau died, I felt like my reason on this earth was taken from me. Some describe feeling like a part of them was buried with their loved one who died. The thing is, I didn't feel a piece of me missing. I died with him, you see. Ellie, my soul went with my son."

Two lone tears fall down her cheeks, and I can't help the emotion that takes over me. I grab her hand that's fiddling with the doily and grasp it within mine. My gesture urging her to keep going.

"It took me a few months after the funeral to sort of snap out of it. I was consumed by grief and heartache, and I had to dig deep to find a reason to wake up and live each day. Luke said I wasn't even living; I was just existing. That man really is my rock. He got me up, sometimes having to pull me out of bed and dress me, just to get me to feel like I was doing something. Eventually, his gestures weren't needed, and I started getting up by myself. I started moving through my home. Finally, I got myself out of this house and into town again, just for a little bit at a time each day.

"I knew you were grieving, and you had such tiny babies to care for. I was selfish in my grief, and a part of me thought you were young and were preoccupied with your children, so you'd get out of the pain you were feeling easier than I would. Your entire reason for existing wasn't gone. You still had your babies."

She scoffs and rolls her eyes, "Just saying it out loud makes me realize what a horrible person I was then. I knew your parents were there to help you. And sweet Becca was there each chance she got."

She wipes the tears, but it's useless because they're falling freely now.

"Eventually, I went to your house. Luke was so happy to see me putting in some effort. Do you remember that day?"

I nod, recalling the day she came over because I was wracked with nerves at my news for them.

"You sat us down and told us you were leaving Saddle Ridge. Not only that, you were leaving Nebraska as a whole."

She looks away from me, and I can feel the resentment she is still holding on to from my decision.

"I was so mad at you. I finally pulled myself out of my hole, only to find out you were leaving. My baby's kids were leaving. And instead of realizing how good this move would be for all of you, I held on to the fact that you just left Beau and all the memories you had built behind. I was furious at you. I guess I should say I held on to that anger throughout the years."

I'm stunned by her words. Here, I thought, she'd understand the pain I was experiencing and my reasoning for leaving. I left Nebraska thinking I had their support.

"I thought you understood my reasons for leaving." I say it

almost as a whisper, my voice lost in memories from that day. She seemed indifferent when I told them, and I perceived that as understanding my side.

"I honestly didn't know how to act. It was your life. I had no hold on you four, and I didn't want to throw a tantrum that day," she says as if it makes perfect sense.

"So instead, you decide to draw out your tantrum and throw one each chance you had when we reunited or when we spoke on the phone?" I can't help the irritation from boiling over at her confession.

She nods, not even fighting the truth behind my words.

"Yes, it wasn't my finest moment. I wish I could say I would have seen my wrongs at some point on my own, but I didn't. It had to be thrown in my face after I hung up the phone with you a few days ago when I finished talking to you." My mouth hangs open, still stunned by her behavior and for the length of time she was carrying this with her.

"Luke got pretty upset at me this past weekend after I said all those things to you. He's usually so calm and collected, so to hear him raise his voice at me, telling me how inappropriate I was toward you, really caused me to take a step back."

She closes her eyes and shakes her head from side to side.

"I reacted poorly, not just on the phone but with all my interactions with you since you decided to leave Saddle Ridge. I focused on this resentment toward you instead of focusing on the pain I was feeling about Beau's passing. I decided to put my grief to the side and focused all my energy on my anger instead. And you got all of it, unfortunately. For that, I'm sorry." She sounds sincere, but I can't help but feel anger coursing through my body.

"I appreciate the apology, Candace, I really do. But now that I know where you were coming from, it's best I tell you how your actions affected me. My love for Beau was soul-binding. He was my everything, and losing him felt like I lost a limb. I made this promise to him when he died that I would never love someone with my whole heart the way I loved him. I kept that promise all these years. I don't know if your behavior spearheaded that because the way you made me feel just pioneered my mission to uphold my love for your son. But somewhere along the way, I started to believe that I wasn't supposed to love anyone else.

"But then I met Wyatt and Tessa. His daughter is my student, and I fell in love with this little girl. And I just happened to feel a connection to her father. This man welcomed me and my broken heart with open arms. This man gives me moments of laughter and light; he comforts me with his patience as I navigate my feelings. Not once did he try to convince me to love him more and to love Beau less. He honored my heart and never asked for more. And with all that, I fell in love with him."

Candy flinches at my words. I can't imagine it's easy to hear me say those words that were long reserved for her son now being said about another man.

"Beau died, Candace. I don't say that to be crass and inconsiderate. I say that for you to understand that our Beau is no longer here with us in that capacity anymore. And for so long, I've been honoring a version of myself that no longer exists as well. I was honoring him because of this promise I made, which he never asked of me. I built these walls around my heart, and when I met Wyatt, I honored my late husband instead of allowing love to shine through.

"Even then, I found room to fall in love with this incredible man without really comprehending it was happening. He fell for me, Candace. He loves me. And you know what I was able to give him in return for his confession? Nothing. Because I was pulled down by my own guilt. Top that off with endless moments of feeling like I wasn't enough to love another person, which you only contributed to by making me feel like I was dishonoring your son. You didn't accept the way I chose to grieve because it didn't line up with your way of grieving."

My hands are balled up in front of me, and the tension in my shoulders is mounting.

"I am going to love Wyatt. I want him to look at me and see someone who is choosing him. I want to love again, Candy. I am choosing to feel loved again by another man. My love for Beau will always be there. It's not going anywhere. But I also recognize that it's in my past, and Wyatt is a part of my future. I deserve that new start, much like Wyatt deserves a woman who can give him a heart that isn't broken.

"He deserves a fresh start with me, with no cracks in my soul to give him. I might hurt at times because of losing my husband, your son, but it doesn't mean that I cannot find joy in new moments with Wyatt. You should feel honored that I am still here, with the children who share your son's blood, growing and thriving in this world. That's the legacy Beau left for us to witness. I am not Beau's legacy. I am his widow."

I close my eyes, take a breath, and feel the sadness consume me because as much as I believe in what I'm saying, it doesn't make it less difficult to hear my words said out loud.

I stand up and move toward my mother-in-law, and she stands so we are eye-to-eye.

"Candace, I think you have a choice to make. You can choose to be bitter. You can carry this anger in your heart, and you'll be left with only that as you live out your life. Or you can embrace the changes happening that are out of your control. You can watch my children, your son's children, live their lives for the rest of your years with laughter, happiness, and growth, or you can sit in your displeasure and bitterness. The latter sounds pretty awful, so I hope you choose wisely."

I stand there for an extra beat and then turn and move toward the back door to see the kids and Luke, but a hand stops me from moving forward. I turn back toward Candace to find her eyes softening. She pulls me in a hug, her arms wrapping around my neck.

Then she says, "I don't need to think about my decision,

Ellie. I choose you. I choose those kids. And by doing that, I choose to watch Beau's legacy grow. You're right. I was selfish, mean, and cruel. And that behavior served no one, including me. I'm so sorry. I hope with time you can forgive me for my actions and my negativity."

I squeeze her tighter, and in that moment, I vow to let go of the anger and the pain that had grown with this woman's spiteful ways. Beau would want peace. He would want us to live with harmony and not this hate that seems to have been festering between us. We pull away from one another, and she grabs my cheeks.

"Thank you for coming here and making me see what really matters. But most of all, thank you for the chance to win back your forgiveness."

I smile. "Candy, you're forgiven. It doesn't mean we won't have some work to do, but I love you. You are the mother of the man I married, the man that made me a mama. My heart doesn't have room for hate or anger. It has room for love. That's something we are both worthy of, don't you think?" Candace nods in agreement, and we embrace again.

Soon, we hear the back screen door open, "Finally, you made up. Now, what's for supper?" Luke says, and we look over to see a goofy smile across his face.

Chapter Twenty-Four

ELODY

The next day, I'm sitting on the porch, swinging and taking in the scenery before me. I can hear the laughter of my children in the house as they bake cookies with their grandmother. I smile to myself, enjoying this break from the city and soaking in this small town that holds so many precious memories for me.

I have to admit that this chapter of my life is behind me. I thought coming here, I'd feel the pull to come back, to return to the simplicity of this lifestyle. The problem now lies in the fact that Wyatt isn't here. Tessa's infectious laugh isn't trailing the halls of the house while I watch her dad chase her around. The pieces of my life I have added recently feel like pieces of the puzzle that I have left back in New York.

I hear the creaking of the screen door open and close, and I look over my right to see Luke walking toward me.

"Hey, Luke. Are you all done in the garden?" He's covered in dirt, and he seems happiest when he's getting his hands dirty, working on this home he's kept standing all these years.

"Oh, you know me. One project done only means another one is waiting around the corner." He beams his brilliant smile my way, and I feel Beau with Luke's grin.

I move my gaze toward the land in front of me, and I close my eyes, hoping for a breeze to carry through so I can feel my late husband engulf me with a reminder from beyond that he's watching over me. The weather is uncharacteristically muggy right now, so the air is stagnant. Spring is usually much more pleasant, but for some reason, the sun is shining, and the warmth is seeping in like summer instead of the late April spring our state usually feels right now.

"May I have a seat here with you?" Luke asks, walking in front of me and gesturing to the space by my side on the swing.

"Luke, it's your home and your swing. Of course, you can." I chuckle, moving myself over so there's a little more space for him to sit.

"I'm glad you and Candy are working out your differences. I know my girl can be difficult, but please know it comes from a place of love. I hope you know how much you and the kids mean to us."

His sincerity pours out of him, and I smile at this man who doesn't have a mean bone in his body.

I nod, "Of course I do, Luke. I love you both very much."

He reaches in his back pocket and retrieves an envelope. I see the edges are worn, like this letter has been carried around throughout the years, and I can't help the confusion that passes over my face.

"My Beau loved you very much. I hope you know that. I hope you feel it, even now, as he's not here to tell you."

I nod, the lump in my throat reappearing, and I truly hope I can contain the emotion I feel swelling on the inside.

"When he was sick, he and I had a lot of long talks. We got to talk about the kids and even shared his hopes and dreams for the children as they got older. He asked that I watch over them. But he seemed most concerned about you."

I scrunch my nose, wondering why Beau would be more concerned about me versus our children.

"I think I've done alright." I offer the best smile I can as I try to understand where this conversation is going.

"Yes, you have, my dear. Better than anyone expected, in all honesty. I think your move to New York was probably the best course of action, even if Cay didn't want to hear my opinion on the matter. That being said, Ellie girl, I think you should know I spoke to Beau about you. He spoke to me tirelessly about how he wanted you to be happy, even though he wouldn't be by your side. He told me how he wanted me to ensure you'd be okay.

"I guess all that time we spoke about the future, he decided putting his thoughts in writing was best for you. He asked that I not share it with you until the time was right. I felt this letter weighing on me. I spent countless hours looking at it throughout the years. My wife didn't even know of its existence. Beau told me to give it to you when I thought you'd need it most. That's the only instruction he gave me. I am using my better judgment here, so I'm sorry if I waited too long. But something about this visit is pulling me toward giving you the letter."

He hands the letter to me, Beau's writing sprawled across the front, messy as always. I let my fingers pass over it, trying to feel a piece of my husband as I look at this paper, thinking that he once touched this, and now it's in my hands.

"I know you love my Beau. I know how much he owns your heart, even if you are trying to give your heart to someone else. Something about this letter makes me think that Beau wanted to tell you himself how he felt. He just didn't want to spend his last few months talking about this part of your life because he knew the pain he'd cause. You don't have to read this now. But I have a feeling when you do, you'll feel more free than you thought possible."

He gives me a kiss on my cheek, but I feel numb at this point.

When Beau died, he didn't leave notes for any of us. I had

come to terms with that, realizing he was probably too weak to write. I let the thought go, losing myself to grief in those early months when I felt like life was caving in on me.

Luke stands up, and I keep my gaze on the note. I can feel Luke's presence up to the moment he opens the front screen door and closes it behind him. His footsteps start to fade, and I turn the envelope over and open it at the seam where Beau had likely licked it shut at the adhesive.

The moment I pull the folded paper out, I feel the heaviness of seeing his writing in front of me. All the memories of previous notes he had written to me come barreling back to the forefront of my mind, and I already feel the first tear fall from my eye.

My Dearest Ellie,

Does it ever feel to you like just yesterday we were two kids, walking the halls of our school, hand in hand. I have been reflecting a lot on that. It's hard not to think back after the news we just got.

You just left me in the kitchen, saying you needed to take a shower. But I can hear your sobs from here. My sweet Ellie, always full of joy and hiding your pain so you don't bring down those around you. I'm sorry you'll have to live life without me at some point. So, as I sit at our kitchen table and write these words, I can hear you upstairs, letting your emotions get the best of you. Also, you're a terrible liar. ;) I knew you were going upstairs to cry, but you gave me some big excuse about feeling gross after a long day.

This is really hard for me because since I was young, you've been my sole focus, Ellie. Even after having our beautiful children, I've looked to you for guidance on a dark day. You have been my guiding light in all passages of life, and now I will be leaving you behind. I know you're going to put your best foot forward and live life to the fullest for the sake of our kids. I know that you will love them and give them the best this life has to offer. But I can't help but wonder what you will do for yourself as you move on in life.

You've made me so proud to call you my wife. You've made me happier beyond anything I ever imagined. Through our highs, you've shown me the highest peak of a mountain. And when life got hard, you held my hand and gave me strength to move forward without fear. And now I fear you will not do that for yourself when your world is about to change forever.

The kids will be fine. Something inside tells me that with you as their mother, they will see the beauty of life instead of focusing on how hard things can get. You do a good job of that already with Ty, and I don't think you will allow resentment and anger to feed your soul. It's just not in you, my sweet Ellie.

The question still lies, though—will you allow yourself to love wholeheartedly? Will you give your life love when you're deserving of it all? I want you to open yourself up to love again. I know it will be hard, and you might take your time to find that in your life. Something tells me, though, you'll captivate everyone you meet as the years pass. And one day, that person will come that your heart will need in order for it to beat properly again. That person is such a lucky one because I've gotten your heart for all these years, and I still think it's the best feeling in the world to be loved by you.

With all the tears you shed, remember that I love you. But don't cry over a love lost. Smile for the foundation we built. And open your arms to someone who will hold you and protect you. You are my everything and even from above, I will love you eternally. My soul is yours. My heart is yours. But now I give you permission to give your heart to someone else. I've had it for so long, and I'm not selfish enough to keep it all to myself, even when I'm gone.

Give my love to those beautiful children we

made together. They are our everything. We did that, and I know this Earth will have light because you will be on it with them.

I love you, Ellie.
Beau xoxo

My tears are transferring to the paper, and it doesn't matter how much I wipe them away, they're constant. The tears are unstoppable, and the beating of my heart relentless. I feel like my breath has been taken away as I feel my husband's words engulf me. Even from beyond, he knows exactly what to say.

I fold up the letter and replace it in the envelope. I bring the papers to my chest, and I close my eyes. I'm thinking of the last time I held his hand. I'm seeing his face and his big, brown eyes looking at me with so much love; I feel it coat my skin even now as a memory.

Before I have time to react, I feel a breeze come over the porch, blowing through my hair and causing my eyes to flutter open. I smile, knowing my heart has been set free by the first boy I ever loved.

I say into the breeze, "*Thank you, Beau.*"

I wipe the tears and stand from the swing. I think of all the moments, this time is as good as any to make a necessary a special visit with my kids.

* * *

We park the car, and the sun is shining across the mountaintop. Beau's grave is farther ahead, but we have to park a bit further from the site due to a service taking place nearby. My kids and I grab the sunflowers we picked from Luke's garden and make our way out of the car. The kids are quiet, knowing how heavy this place is for us.

The girls, even though they have no recollection of the man they call Dad, are taking in the sights around them. Mia is holding my hand, and I feel her squeeze as we begin to step onto the grassy hill. Tyler's head is down, probably feeling a flood of emotions, and it's all to be expected.

"It shouldn't be much further. We'll make a right at the path ahead, and his headstone will be a little way down that direction." I motion ahead, even though we aren't quite there yet.

We keep walking, Hannah asking if Beau liked sunflowers. I explain how his face lit up each time he found them at the florist or in the market. She smiles at my story, and it soothes my heart that she holds no anger or pain but welcomes stories about her father because she feels like he is her guardian angel. That's always what I told her—that her dad was her biggest fan and would always look out for her.

We get to the end of the path, turning right, and that's when I see two figures standing where Beau is buried. At first, I can't make out who they are, the sun shining right into my eyes, but as we approach, I see the hulking figure of one belonging to only one man I know...Wyatt.

Chapter Twenty-Five

WYATT

"You think it's possible to love the same way twice?" Shane asks while looking out the window of the plane.

"What do you mean?" I look over at him, curious about where this line of questioning is going.

"Well, I heard this once, and I have no idea where, that we don't ever love the same way as we did before."

"Do you love Becca the same as you did years ago?"

Shane chuckles, "Well, yes and no, but that's different."

I stare at him, perplexed by his answer.

He continues. "You see, Becs is someone I never stopped loving. Yes, our circumstances kept us apart, but my love for her never wavered. And I never loved another woman after Becca. But if I had tried at some point to connect someone on a deeper level, I can say with utmost certainty it wouldn't be the same kind of love. I think with each heartbreak and moments where we move on, our heart morphs into a new version of itself. Like it's shedding skin."

"Dude, are you trying to inspire me or make me doubt myself?"

"Just hear me out." He adjusts himself so his body is facing mine, his back to the window now. "I just thought it was an interesting thought for you dealing with Ellie." I stare at him, hoping my expression pushes him to elaborate.

"Stay with me, 'kay?"

I nod, and he continues, "With Beau, Ellie loved like she's never loved before. Her firsts were all taken by Beau, and his were taken by Ellie. They had all the same experiences together. Each milestone was shared. Their hearts were fused in this way, not just by attraction but also by these moments in life that solidify us as human beings. Does that make sense?"

"Oddly enough, it does."

I scratch at my chin that now houses the beard I'm growing as traditions with hockey and playoffs seem to be something I can't let go of. I never shaved my facial hair during playoffs, and now that the team is headed in that direction, I keep the good luck going as a coach.

"What I'm trying to say is that the love Ellie has for Beau, even now, is going to be different than any other love she has from this point on. But that love doesn't mean it's less than or not at the same level. It's simply different. I just wanted to say that because you deserve to know that this love you're hoping to see grow with Ellie is no less than what she had with Beau. It's simply different."

Shane turns his attention back out the window of the private plane we're on. I called in a favor from an old teammate. Shane almost shit a brick when he saw our accommodations for the flight. I wish I had filmed it because Becca would have bottled up that reaction for the rest of her life. It was priceless. Of course, he FaceTimed her the moment he got on the plane and gave her a grand tour.

It was cute to see—when did I become the guy to gush over someone's relationship and call them cute? Apparently, falling in love has made me a lovesick fool.

"What was Beau like?" I have been itching to ask this question, but I also fear what Shane will say about him. It's hard to live in the shadow of someone who's put on a pedestal, even if he's in the afterlife.

"Oh, Beau, he had the biggest heart." I can see Shane's mind takes him to years before, and a smile moves across his face. I don't even know if he's aware of this reaction he's having.

"He personified happiness. He was probably the kindest person I've ever met." I give him a look to say Becca better not hear that.

"Believe me, Becs would agree. He was just an amazing person, even as a kid. He always had my back. Granted, I missed all of his adult life, but if he carried through in his twenties and thirties the way he was in his younger years, he was absolutely incredible."

I'm starting to regret this conversation already, but I don't let my jealousy shine through. I love Ellie enough to recognize she deserved that kind of partner.

"That being said, he wasn't perfect. None of us are. Hell, I'm still finding ways I can grow, and I bet you are, too. Anyway, he and Ellie were quite similar overall. They were both radiated happiness and always took over a room with their excitement. But if I really dig deep, especially with all the stories Becs has filled me in on, they didn't quite challenge one another. Don't get me wrong, they were great together, but it was all so easy between them. And although that sounds like a dream, there's something about lighting that fire to see the other shine. You get what I mean?"

I nod but don't know what to say.

"When I see El with you, I can see you push her out of her comfort zone, and I think that's really great to witness. I've known Ellie pretty much since we were born. The moms went from mommy-and-me type classes to putting us in school together. I know her pretty well, even with the twenty-five-year gap."

I need to keep reminding myself that Shane was absent for

quite some time. He, too, is using this trip as a form of closure, whereas I'm using it to say my piece to an important person I feel I should meet—if that's the right word.

"Love is about comfort, but it's also about passion and pushing your partner to uncomfortable places so they can see how far they can stretch themselves. Feeling too comfortable can lead to some uncomfortable feelings as well. But most don't want to lean into that spot in their minds. So we see a lot of people lose that drive when they're with a partner sometimes."

"Ellie has told me a lot about how important Becca is in her life. Have they always been that close? I mean, the other night, I found Ellie crying from laughter on the phone with Becca, and it was all from something that happened in high school. I guess something online sparked the memory, and they both couldn't stop laughing about it."

"Yeah, those two have been close since Becs stepped foot in our high school. My girl tells me that Ellie is her ride or die, and I can't really argue that. Their relationship is so intense; one can't live without the other. I don't think they ever have. Even being far apart when Ellie and Beau lived in Nebraska, Becs said she and Elody always sent letters, emailed, or called one another. Plus, Becs had a lot of help from them when she had Olive. I'll always have a special place in my heart for Ellie, and Beau for that matter, because they took care of my Becs." Shane chuckles, and if a man could have hearts in his eyes, he would right now.

Shane gives me food for thought with everything he has told me. We chat a little more and decide to get some sleep. Things have been nonstop for the team and me as we prepare to move forward into the playoff games. I have two days off, so I decided to use this small break to fly out to Nebraska.

Luckily, I could lean on Shane to ask for help because I know I'll need it. The moment I asked, Becca was the first to respond for him on the call. She started screaming, her excitement palpable on the receiving end of the phone. Once she managed to catch her breath, I explained my entire plan to both of them. He mentioned that he hadn't returned to Saddle Ridge since his high school graduation, and this was a great opportunity for him to close up some loose ends. He was quick to get himself ready, and we hopped on the plane with a red-eye to Nebraska.

I had my teammates who have become good friends throughout the years, but retirement put all of us in different parts of the country. We're scattered about, and when I took the coaching position, I have a similar schedule to the players, so it doesn't leave me with much time to step out of the city unless I'm working. Building a close circle around me makes my life easier to manage.

Add to the fact that Ellie has taken up most of my time outside of my family members, I rarely see my friends from the league. Having a friendship with Shane feels easy, and he's always down to hang out with me. As starstruck as he was when we first met, he seems to have settled down. I look over and find my new friend sleeping, and I decide I should do the same.

* * *

We arrive in Saddle Ridge by morning, and it's unreasonably hot here for a spring day. Even Shane mentioned this is unusual for his hometown. We drive through their main street, and Shane points out spots where he holds memories with Becca, Ellie, and Beau. Hearing about this time in their lives doesn't make me sad for missing out. Each memory is a window into her past, and I enjoy learning about these facets of her life that have made her into the woman I love today.

Becca gave Shane all the information he needed to make our visit to the cemetery. We keep driving, the scenery breathtaking at every turn. Once we enter the cemetery grounds, I notice Shane's demeanor change. I know this must be hard for him, feeling like he is opening up an old wound. The fact that he never got to reconnect to his best friend, and how all that came about, feels like he was robbed in many ways.

Apparently, his mother is a heartless and miserable person, making him believe he had nothing left to return to in Saddle Ridge. But I think what eats at him is that he didn't push back and didn't try to find his friend until it was too late. He told me he has many regrets, but that is one of the things that sits at the top. That and the fact that he missed out on seeing his daughter grow up.

We make a few more turns and park at the bottom of a hill. We walk through the grass and finally find Beau's headstone. It's well-kept, no overgrowth around the headstone, and the property surrounding it looks well-kept. Shane explains that Beau's parents still live in the area, and he thinks they've kept his resting place clean throughout the years. I don't walk all the way forward just yet, letting Shane have a moment. He kneels down, pulling out a small basketball keychain from his back pocket.

"Hey there, buddy." He places the keychain on the headstone and glides his fingers along the stone.

I can tell the grief Shane carries sits on his chest, and this is something that will take the weight off him but will also feel like one of his hardest moments.

"I brought your keychain back for you. I had your house key on it all these years. The day I left, I forgot to give it back. I guess a part of me always thought I'd get to give it back to you in person. I'm sorry, though, that I didn't return."

He inhales, and I hear him choke out his words, the sadness taking a front seat as he continues to speak, "Thank you, Beau, for taking care of my girls. I should have been there, but if I couldn't be, I'm glad they had you. I will never be able to repay you, but if you're watching from above, I hope that you see what an impact you've made. I love you, man. Until we meet again."

He wipes the tears that have escaped his eyes and stands back up, not hiding the emotion he's feeling when he turns his gaze toward me.

"Um, Beau, this is my new friend, Wyatt. Well, more like Elody's friend, but I think you probably knew that."

He smiles at me, and I try to return the gesture, my heart still hurting from the words he just released into the air for his friend to hear.

"He's a good guy, Beau. One of the best, and he's been the one to bring your Ellie back to life." He pats me on the shoulder and walks away, giving me the space to speak to Beau myself.

Some people might think this is silly. Some might see me and wonder what I'm thinking, coming here, introducing myself to a gravesite. I've felt compelled to do this since I told Ellie to figure out how to be whole without Beau's memory weighing her down. And I think a part of me felt like I needed to face her late husband, even if in spirit.

"Hi, Beau. I'm Wyatt." I stand there, not sure why I pause because a response isn't coming my way. I decide to let go and talk.

"I met Ellie a few months back. She stole my breath the moment I saw her at a crowded bar. I see why you felt drawn to her throughout the years because, in one instant, my life changed when I saw her in front of me. She brings so much light into my life. But most of all, she brings me happiness. I know you can understand what I mean. Listen, I know you aren't here anymore. But I think your spirit, your memory, will always be woven into our lives. And I just feel like I should come here and introduce myself. I promise to watch out for our girl. I also promise to look out for your kids.

"By the way, Tyler just suffered his first heartbreak, and I think you'd be proud of how he handled it. Hannah and Mia are little Ellies moving along in the house, and they have so much love to share in this world. My Tessa, that's my daughter, fits in perfectly with your kids. You and Ellie have done an amazing job creating these three beautiful children. I hope you'll see that your family is cared for. I guess I should say our family is cared for. I will never try to replace you or let anyone forget how you fit into our lives moving forward."

I pull out a sunflower and place it on the headstone. I know it's Ellie's favorite, but Shane mentioned Beau planted a ton around his parent's property, so I have a feeling her favorites became his throughout the years.

I look back and find Shane wiping his hands across his face.

"Damn it, Wyatt. My eyes are sweating now!"

We both laugh, and he walks up to stand next to me. We look down and take in our surroundings.

"Beau would have liked this spot. He loved nature and being outside. He loved big trees on a hot summer day. This spot is so close to that tree," he points to our right to a tree nestled along the hill, "and he would have loved that this place feels open like a field."

I look around me and see how calming this place is. I see why people fall in love with the quiet that a small town brings with it.

While standing there, I hear movement behind us and quickly turn to find those deep blue eyes looking at me, wide and surprised, taking us in. This is why Becca seemed to be holding back when she heard about my plan to come to Nebraska. She knew Ellie was already here.

"Hey, Sunshine." I smile and move closer to her. The pull I feel toward her is still so strong. She smiles as I get closer, and my heart soars.

"Hey, Shane." She looks at her childhood friend and then shifts her gaze back to me. "Wyatt."

Tyler moves toward us, giving both Shane and I a fist

bump. His sisters come up next, smiles as bright as the morning sun.

"What are you doing here?" Elody is still taking us in at her late husband's gravesite.

"I thought I'd come by and introduce myself to Beau. Thought it was time we met, formally and all." I feel lighter now that I've gotten a chance to sit here and talk to Beau, even if it was one-sided.

"Oh, and did you pass the test?" Her smile widens, and Shane chuckles.

"I think the hockey star conceded that basketball is the better sport." Shane laughs, and Tyler does the same.

We might be standing at Beau's grave, but it seems everyone feels comfortable because Beau instilled this ability to calm everyone surrounding him. I guess he continues to do that, even without physically standing with us.

"Um, can you give us a minute to talk to Beau? Is that alright?" Ellie asks, and I nod. I don't feel the need to listen in on this private conversation. I know I wanted the same done without her present, or I would have asked her to come along.

For the next forty-five minutes, I watch as the woman I love talks to the man she loved before me. In all honesty, it's the man she will always love. I watch her wipe a few spots of the fallen leaves that have nestled along the grass where he lies. I see her put her arms around her kids, and I see her body shake as she cries and laughs while her kids do the same; telling stories, filling him in on all the things happening in their lives. Shane and I stay back the entire time, taking in the sight of a family saying all they need to say but also promising his legacy will live on.

They begin to head back, and once they're closer, Shane offers to take the kids with him in the car. They decide ice cream is in order. As they walk away, Shane throws a wink our way, and I stay standing with Ellie by my side.

"Why are you here, Wyatt?" she asks, no malice or anger in her tone.

"I wanted to tell Beau I love you and that I'd care for you. I know he's not someone you will ever let go of in that way, but I told him how you made me feel. I told him how proud he would be to see you four thriving. I needed to talk to him, man to man, about the woman we both love."

Tears start to fall, and I can't help but reach for her and wipe her cheeks. She leans into my hand, and that gesture alone makes me want to soar.

We begin walking to her car, and she tells me, "I stood up to my mother-in-law yesterday. I told her how she made me feel."

I look down at her, knowing my interruption will break her thoughts. I decide to stay quiet.

"I think it went well, and I hope that from this point on, our relationship will be less volatile and more comforting."

I nod, really hoping for the same. Life is too short, this family should know, to keep holding on to something that will result in heartache.

"I'm glad, Sunshine. And how are you feeling overall?" I want to hear her say she wants to continue growing with me. I don't see a moment in the future when she isn't by my side.

"I got a letter from Beau that he wrote when we found out his illness was terminal. It was like he knew what I needed, even without being present to actually know. Does that make sense?"

I nod, my heart racing for whatever else she's going to say.

"The letter was hard to read. But it was also necessary. And I feel like it was the last piece of the puzzle for our life together —mine and Beau's."

We stop at the car, and she leans against it, while I stand in front of her, waiting for more crumbs to fall so I can pick them up.

"I want forever with you, Wyatt. I want you to own my heart just as much as I own yours."

That's all I hear before I kiss her, pulling her toward me, her body embraced in mine. It's all I wanted, and it feels like nothing else matters because I'm the luckiest man alive. All I need are my girls with me, and now I get to incorporate three more kids into the mix. I want everything with Ellie. Building our future together feels right, and it makes me feel like anything is possible.

Our lips come apart, and I let my forehead rest on hers, my palms holding her face, "Thank you, Ellie. Thank you for being my sunshine and my stars. I love you so much. I promise to love you, every piece of you, your past, your present, and our future. I want it all with you, Sunshine."

She nods and smiles. "That better be the case because I can't see tomorrow without you and Tessa in it. I love you, and I love that little girl."

My heart is bursting, and we kiss again before getting in the car and driving away.

Chapter Twenty-Six

WYATT

"I was made for this life. I mean, don't I look good in this lap of luxury lifestyle, Mom?" Tyler says as he nestles into the seat on the private jet. I can't help but laugh while Ellie looks at her son with a horrified expression.

"Tyler Anthony, don't you dare speak as if you don't remember where you came from!" she scolds, which is the first time I've seen her do so since we've met.

I turn to her and whisper so only she can hear, "It is pretty nice."

She whispers back, "Oh, this is the life, but I'm not letting this kid think this is the norm at the age of sixteen. He needs to understand this lifestyle isn't given to him, it's earned."

I kiss her cheek and hand her champagne. The adults are already with a glass in their hands, while the kids have sparkling apple cider.

Shane puts his glass in the air, "To finding forever." We all raise our glasses and clink them with one another.

Once we are up in the air and Ellie is playing a card game with her girls, I head over to sit next to Tyler, who looks lost in thought. Sitting down, I nudge him with my knee, and he looks over.

"How are you doing?" I ask him, as I haven't gotten to speak much with him since that night he and Emma had broken up.

"I'm okay. This trip was hard for me, but it's ending on a high. I'm really happy for you and my mom. I think you're good for her," he says, and I don't take for granted anything between this kid and me because he is not a typical teenager.

"I know you've been a rock for your mom, and your strength hasn't gone unnoticed. Thank you for being there for her while she needed you. And for your sisters."

"Of course. They're my people and I love them." He looks over and smiles. "Even if my sisters listen to my conversations when I'm talking to my friends."

I smile, remembering my sister doing the same to me and hating it at the time.

"Yeah, I think that's in the sister rulebook or something. Are you sure you're okay with everything going on with your mom and me? Do you have any questions for me? I want you to know you can talk to me."

"Yeah, I know. You're not as intimidating as you act on TV," he says, smiling as he takes a sip of his drink.

"Excuse me, I'm very intimidating." I try to look serious but fail miserably.

"Ha. Sorry, Wyatt, but you are a sucker. My mom, your daughter, and my sisters all have you wrapped around their fingers. It's kind of funny to watch."

This guy. I roll my eyes, but I can't argue with him. All four of those girls have a piece of me, and I'd move through fire to make sure they're cared for. I guess all of them are *my* people now.

The remainder of the flight is uneventful, and when we land in the city, I'm itching to see Tessa. My sister was kind enough to meet us at Elody's place, so the minute we pull up, Becca, her twins, Tessa, and my sister are waiting for us.

Shane practically pushes us out of the way, running

toward Becca. They embrace, and her kids immediately gag with the affection he's giving his girlfriend. Tessa comes running toward me, and I pull her up and twirl her around. Our reunion is short-lived as she spots Ellie and wiggles to be put down and runs into her arms, telling her how much she missed her. I'm definitely in the second spot now.

I turn, and my sister is there, so I pull her in for a tight hug. "Everything worked out?" she asks, her volume low so only I can hear her.

I nod, and her smile doubles. I think Ellie has been a part of this family since before I recognized I loved her. Knowing she'll fit right in makes me feel like pieces of my life are falling into place. I'm excited to see where our love will take us next.

Epilogue

ELODY

Seven Months Later

Summer flew by, and hockey season is back. I'm so excited to be a part of this from the start of the season this year and to cheer on the sexy coach who is currently yelling plays to his team. Watching him in action, even if not on the ice, does something to me.

"Mom, stop staring, it's creepy." Tyler and his teenage attitude are not welcome here today.

I'm ignoring him, but he still smiles, so I think somewhere deep down, where his teenage hormones aren't seeping in, he finds my love for Wyatt endearing instead of repulsing.

"One day, sweet boy, you'll find a love that's grand, and you'll be smitten," I say as I keep my eyes on Wyatt and all his movements. He commands the arena, if you ask me.

Last season, they made it to the Eastern Conference championship but lost in game seven. The Brawlers kept it a nail-biter, but in that last game, the opposing team scored with seconds left. It was a huge loss, but Wyatt was a big advocate for how strong the team became last season and how much they learned to go into this year's games. But by the looks of it, he's not letting his guys sulk. He is making sure they look ahead, and not behind, when playing this season.

I've been soaking up the season since it started two months ago. Fall is almost over, Thanksgiving only a few days away, and being at a home game on a Friday night is the perfect end to a crazy week with more than a dozen kindergarteners.

Apparently, I am a huge fan of hockey, and it took dating the coach of a professional team to realize this. Becca and Shane watch the away games with me at my house, and they said that I have a tendency to yell too loud, and they're scared of a little throwing of food.

Right as I'm thinking of that last part, Shane grabs my hotdog and says, "Please don't throw that at the glass, El. I do not need security coming by here and kicking us out. These seats are too good to pass up."

I smack his hand away before he takes my food. I hear Becca laugh next to him, and I take a moment to look around, taking in the seats around me. We opted out of the box seats tonight because we wanted to be part of the crowd, and I wanted to be closer to Wyatt as he coached.

Since we got back from Nebraska last spring, Wyatt and I jumped right into life together, blending our families. We are a beautiful mix of two separate lives that have come together to support one another. Shortly after the season ended, my kids took the initiative, without me prompting, inquiring about Wyatt and Tessa moving in. They didn't understand prolonging something that was bound to happen.

Wyatt and I were hesitant at first, but since he and Tessa have joined us at the brownstone home, we've found it an easy transition. I will admit that after long stretches of away games, it's nice to have him return and love on us after feeling so far from him while he was traveling with the team.

* * *

Once the game ends, we wait outside the locker room until Wyatt emerges with the rest of the coaching staff. The moment he sees his family, his face lights up. Tessa is always the first to run toward him, and he pulls her into his arms and tells her how much he loves her. From there, he has a whole fanbase ready to give him love after a job well done.

Wyatt has a date night planned for us, and he said we have to dress up. The kids head home with Becca for a big sleepover while Wyatt and I slowly make our way out of the arena to get ready for this secret date he has planned.

Once back at the house, we get all dolled up, and the moment I step outside the front door, I feel the chill of winter trying to creep through the last of fall. We run to the car and head into the city, the lights enchanting as the holiday season is in full swing. To think a year ago, I was complaining about the grumpy father of a student, and now I'm sitting next to him, living a life alongside him and his daughter, which brings a smile to my face.

We pull up to Rockefeller Center and I'm instantly giddy. I feel like a child on Christmas morning, and I bounce in my seat as Wyatt makes his way over to open my door.

The moment I get out, I reach up on my toes to give him a kiss. "I love you, and I already love whatever plan you have."

"I know you do, Sunshine. Let's head in. I'm freezing." I laugh because he's stuck on the ice in an arena more often than not. This can't be that bad to him.

We make the climb up the elevator, and the moment the elevator dings, the doors open, and a path of candles is lining the walkway. We step out, and I'm taken aback by the illumination created by all the candles throughout the room. I follow the trail, and I gasp.

At the end of the path are my children: Tyler, Hannah, Mia, and Tessa. Yes, my littlest student has asked me to become her mother, and we've started the proceedings for me to adopt her. This girl holds a piece of my heart already, and I don't see any other way to move forward without calling her mine as well.

Tears begin to stream down my cheeks. As we move through the room, I notice sunflowers on the floor scattered throughout. I smile because that flower holds so much meaning in it, and Wyatt has always given them to me, knowing they brighten my day.

We get to the end, and it's only then I look over Tyler's shoulder and notice a framed photo. I see Beau, his smile lighting the room, and I know he's here with us as I embark on a new journey with my family.

I turn to comment on the photo, and that's when I see Wyatt down on one knee, holding open a box with a beautiful princess cut ring. It's glowing as it sits on the little cushion, but the most beautiful sight is the man in front of me, about to formally ask me to be his forever.

"Ellie, Sunshine, the moment I saw you in that bar a year ago, I felt a pull toward you. Before I could think about it, I was walking over because I couldn't go another second not knowing who you were. Little did I know you were already a part of my life as Tessa's teacher. Your smile, your heart, your kids—*our* kids—have made me a better man. And I don't think I can go another day without making it official. Will you be my wife to share in all the beauty this life will offer us?"

I had started nodding before he even spoke, but I finally yell out, "YES!" and the kids begin shouting and jumping.

I hold Wyatt's cheeks in my hands and pull him up to kiss me. I'm smiling and kissing the man I love and feeling so much love around me. He slips the ring on my finger, and soon enough, I hear more cheering as the room fills. I gasp as I look around, taking in all those who mean the world to me, clapping and wiping tears from their faces. Each one has played a role in the person I am today, and I couldn't have gotten here without them.

Becca comes running toward me and congratulates me.

Shane is close behind her, along with Olive and the twins. My parents, Wyatt's parents, his sister, and even Beau's parents are here, smiles stretched across all their faces.

Becca's mom and her husband appear, and I am simply in shock so many people chose to be here with us. I look over to see Grant and my sister, two people who have had a rough go of it in the recent months, standing proudly as they smile at everything that's happening in front of me. Those two have tried hard to fight that pull between them, but love has a way of winning each time.

My heart is full at this moment, and I try to bottle up the feeling while I look around at everyone celebrating this union. We all toast, and once we are filling plates with food and finding a spot to sit, a long table stretched out so we can all sit together, I pull away to find a moment to say hello to someone special to me.

I stand in front of Beau's picture, and I feel another tear fall. I pick up the frame and touch the photo, my fingertips feeling the cold from the glass.

I whisper to him, "Thank you, Beau, for bringing me sunshine after the storm. I love you, always and forever." I put the frame down and feel arms wrap around my middle.

Wyatt nestles his face in my neck. "I didn't ask your dad's permission to marry you."

"Oh, I bet he loved that," I laugh.

"I actually made a quick trip back to see Beau in Nebraska and asked him for permission. I let the breeze be the answer I needed. I then went to each of our kids and asked their permission. Of course, they all said yes."

He pulls his face away to wink at me.

"Then I went to your dad, and I told him Beau and the kids were okay with it. That's all he needed to hear."

"I love you, Wyatt Alexander Christianson."

I give him a kiss and let my palm rest on his cheek.

"I love you, Sunshine."

✵ *The End* ✵

Also by Stefanie

Want to know how Laney and Grant's story unfolds? Stay tuned for *If Only You Hurt*, coming June 3, 2024. Preorder online.

Need to catch up with book one of the *If Only* Series? Discover Becca and Shane's love story in *If Only You Knew*, available online.

Acknowledgments

The idea of Elody and Wyatt was a storyline I wasn't quite sure about as I began typing. I knew key elements that would take place, but overall, I wasn't sure how life revolved around them. With each page written, new ideas began coming to me and that's how their love was built in this book.

As an avid reader myself, I felt like Elody to be the one on the fence. I wanted her grief to cripple her emotionally so she wouldn't allow Wyatt in completely. That being said, I knew as I wrote Wyatt's personality more and more, he needed to be the one with two solid feet on the ground.

Elody's loss of Beau is something not all of us can relate to, but it's really the idea that what we expected of our lives doesn't always fall into place. I felt her life was so picturesque, but with Beau's passing, she was thrown for a loop. I wanted to highlight the struggles she is faced with and really highlight how that can keep her from experiencing life to the fullest.

If you can't tell already, I love a good emotional read. I am a mood reader for the most part, and I've grown to love writing my characters with depth and layers. I feel that each book of this series takes the reader down a different emotional path and I hope their stories have given insight into different experiences and perspectives. That's something I love about reading—the ability to give me a new lens to look through.

I wanted her to be someone that felt uneasy with love because it's not often portrayed that way in stories. I wanted to reverse the storyline with Elody and Wyatt for that exact reason. I know that her hesitation felt frustrating for some reading, but please know that was intentional.

I can't really do an acknowledgements section without telling Joanna thank you for keeping me going on this series. Imposter syndrome is real and all I can say is she talks me off the ledge of doubt more often than not. To say I sit at the edge of my seat waiting to hear her thoughts on my books is an understatement. Thank you, Jo, for the continued support and love, always.

There were portions of this book I know wouldn't have worked out without the help of Allie and Jeff. You were both lifesavers and were so sweet to sit on a call with me to get me some support on portions of this storyline.

When I write a book, I pretty much feel like I'm irritated until the story is fully written. Patience, space and love are necessary to make a story come forward, not simply from the author, but from those that support said writer. Brandon, you are patient and kind when I'm brainstorming, holing myself in my office to write at night, and even help me figure out portions of the storyline that don't seem to come together smoothly. Thank you for being my sounding board, along with my cheerleader from the sidelines.

Carlie, you were quick to offer help when I came to you with questions about Type I Diabetes. Your guidance and knowledge helped me ensure I was representing those with this chronic illness properly and kindly. I know you are an advocate for this group and I hope that the representation in this book helps give some knowledge to others out there. You are a warrior mama and I appreciate you so very much!

Ashley, thank you for being a shoulder to lean on as I learned how this chronic illness has impacted your life since you were young. You have always been an open-book about how this illness has impacted you throughout the years. You've made me aware of stigmas I didn't know existed and I hope that my words have given those without the knowledge a better understanding of how people live with this on a daily basis.

To my Beta readers: Joanna, Allie, and Noelle—thank you for taking the time to read my work and give me feedback. Your words encourage me to keep going and I truly am blessed with people like you in my life.

To those out there with a chronic illness of any kind: your strength on a daily basis is something I wish more people understood and cheered on. This book is not just a love story between two characters, but a way of highlighting the shift illness has not only on the person who has it, but also to those around the chronically ill. Lives get rearranged and outlooks change. I wanted a book that showed how all-consuming chronic illness can be for people who live with it. But I also wanted to highlight how the effect ripples through those surrounding it as well.

There are a lot of moving parts to becoming an author. Many of those parts feel overwhelming, to say the least. I started a virtual bookclub years ago and Jennifer became a member while we were still primarily homebound due to the Covid-19 Pandemic. Jennifer, you are incredibly skilled with websites, newsletters, and graphics. I envy your quick turn-around and your ability to tell me it will all work out. You have been a support and a joy. I can't wait to hang out in August and have some fun, this time on the author side of things. Here's to many more laughs in the future years!

Now that I have gotten a chance to work with Kat's Literary Services for a year now and edited all three of my books with them, I can, without a doubt, say my relationship with you has only blossomed since my memoir. You're so quick to offer help, share my work on social media, and applaud me when I feel doubtful about what I'm doing. You encourage me more than you even know.

Without Kat's Literary Services, I wouldn't have been linked to Steph White. My *editor extraordinaire* is what you're now going to be known as because you are a boost to my ego when I feel apprehensive with the stories I'm writing. You don't just edit, you guide me when I feel like I can't find a path. You give me strength and motivation to keep up the work and you help me smile when I may have been nervously awaiting your feedback.

To Kristin, at K.B.Barrett Designs, you are such a talented artist with an eye for beauty. The covers for this series have been incredible and I love that we've gotten to work together. I can't wait for all the projects to come because it's always fun to see my ideas come to life. Not only that, you are a wizard with the chapter headings in the paperbacks and I can't thank you enough for making this process so much easier on me.

To my ARC readers—THANK YOU! Your reviews, questions, excitement and support go further than you will ever understand for an indie reader like me. I appreciate your time in reading my work and I hope you will continue on this journey with me as more of my books are released into the wild.

Now to my readers, there are not enough words to express my appreciation for taking the leap of faith and reading my words. I recently met a bookstore employee that had read my first romance book, *If Only You Knew*. The moment she told me this, I couldn't help the smile that broke out across my face. To say I was stunned is an understatement.

Writing is a humbling journey and there are times I wonder who is ever going to read my work. Then this encounter happened and I must say, I felt like my day, no my year, was made! I left that store with tears welled up in my eyes because it was the realization that my words are read by others outside of my inner circle.

Right now, you're holding my novel in your hands and it is because of you that I do this. You make this journey one that grips at my heart and pushes me to move forward. I thank you, from the bottom of my heart, for taking a chance on someone new like me. There are so many authors and books out there and I appreciate you taking the time to read what I have to share. I hope my stories take you out of your norm and give you a little reprieve from whatever is happening in your world.

Thank you so much, to all of you, for making this dream a reality and for pushing me to continue on this journey. If you find it in you, I'd appreciate a review wherever you can to spread the word about my work. Each review pushes my book further in this digital world and helps other readers find new authors.

Here's to many more books to come!
-Stefanie xoxo

About the Author

Stefanie Castro is a Registered Nurse, certified doula and yoga instructor. She specialized in the field of obstetrics and loves everything about her career. She is a first-generation Brazilian American and is fluent in English, Portuguese and Spanish. Stefanie is a wife of nearly 18 years and mother to her son and daughter, along with her very rambunctious Cavalier King Charles dog. She has grown in her love of reading throughout the years and now it's hard to find her without her kindle by her side. Her favorite foods are popcorn and sushi. She is also very excited about Christmas and begins plotting her next year's decor on December 26th. Stefanie has started two bookclubs and is avidly reading whenever she has a free moment in her day. She loves to cuddle on the couch with her dog, along with a great book and a cup of tea. This is Stefanie's third published novel, second of the *If Only* series.

Copyright

If Only You Fell

Stefanie Castro

Copyright © 2024 by Stefanie Castro

Visit the author's Instagram on @stefaniecastro.author and website authorstefaniecastro.com

ISBN: 979–8-9889847-2-6 (eBook)

ISBN: 979-8-9889847-3-3 (paperback)

All rights reserved.

If Only You Fell is a work of fiction. Names, characters, places, and incidents are all a product of the author's imagination. Any resemblance to actual events, locations, or individuals that are living or dead, is coincidental.

Except as permitted under the U.S. Copyright Act of 1976, no product of this publication may be reproduced, distributed, or transmitted in any form or by any means, stored in or introduced into a retrieval system, or transmitted, in any form, including photocopying, recording, or other electronic or mechanical methods, without the prior written permission of the above author of this book.

Proofread by Steph White (Kat's Literary Services)

Interior Formatting & Design by Kristin Barrett (K.B. Barrett Designs) and Stefanie Castro

Cover design by Kristin Barrett (K.B. Barrett Designs)

Paperback Cover Photography by Kristin Barrett (K.B. Barrett Designs)

Links and Social Media:

Email: stefanie.castro.writes@gmail.com

Instagram: @stefaniecastro.author — https://www.instagram.com/stefaniecastro.author/

TikTok: booklovingnurse — https://www.tiktok.com/@booklovingnurse

Goodreads: Stefanie Castro — https://www.goodreads.com/user/show/108038362-stefanie-castro

Facebook: Author Stefanie Castro – https://www.facebook.com/profile.php?id=61551400180728

Created with Vellum

Made in the USA
Las Vegas, NV
13 March 2024

87121208R00194